NEAR YOU

D0026951

ALSO BY MARY BURTON

Never Look Back

I See You

Hide and Seek

Cut and Run

Her Last Word

The Last Move

Burn You Twice

The Forgotten Files

The Shark

The Dollmaker

The Hangman

Morgans of Nashville

Cover Your Eyes

Be Afraid

I'll Never Let You Go

Vulnerable

Texas Rangers

The Seventh Victim

No Escape

You're Not Safe

Alexandria Series

Senseless

Merciless

Before She Dies

Richmond Series

I'm Watching You

Dead Ringer

Dying Scream

Praise for Mary Burton

THE SHARK

"This romantic thriller is tense, sexy, and pleasingly complex."

—*Publishers Weekly*

"Precise storytelling complete with strong conflict and heightened tension are the highlights of Burton's latest. With a tough, vulnerable heroine in Riley at the story's center, Burton's novel is a well-crafted, suspenseful mystery with a ruthless villain who would put any reader on edge. A thrilling read."

—*RT Book Reviews*, four stars

BEFORE SHE DIES

"Will keep readers sleeping with the lights on."

—*Publishers Weekly* (starred review)

MERCILESS

"Burton keeps getting better!"

—*RT Book Reviews*

YOU'RE NOT SAFE

"Burton once again demonstrates her romantic suspense chops with this taut novel. Burton plays cat and mouse with the reader through a tight plot, credible suspects, and romantic spice keeping it real."

—*Publishers Weekly*

BE AFRAID

"Mary Burton [is] the modern-day queen of romantic suspense."

—Bookreporter

NEAR YOU

MARY BURTON

This is a work of fiction. Names, characters, organizations, places, events, and incidents are either products of the author's imagination or are used fictitiously.

Text copyright © 2021 by Mary Burton
All rights reserved.

No part of this book may be reproduced, or stored in a retrieval system, or transmitted in any form or by any means, electronic, mechanical, photocopying, recording, or otherwise, without express written permission of the publisher.

Published by Montlake, Seattle

www.apub.com

Amazon, the Amazon logo, and Montlake are trademarks of Amazon.com, Inc., or its affiliates.

ISBN-13: 9781542021371
ISBN-10: 1542021375

Cover design by Amanda Kain

Printed in the United States of America

NEAR YOU

PAUL THOMPSON'S CRIME FILES

Eleven years ago, Elijah James Weston was convicted of arson two days after his nineteenth birthday. He had not only finished his freshman year at the University of Montana on full academic scholarship but had proven to be a brilliant student. After the house fire nearly claimed the lives of two senior coeds, Ann Bailey and Joan Mason, rumors quickly circulated that Elijah had been acquainted with both women. Stories of his troubled childhood, a juvenile history of arson, and an obsession with Ann dominated all conversations in Missoula that summer. After his DNA was found on one of the surviving incendiary devices, he was arrested.

The media quickly swirled around him, like moths to a flame. A physically beautiful man, his blond hair and gray eyes summoned comparisons to Paul Walker, Brad Pitt, or a young Robert Redford. Anyone who attended high school or college with Elijah was interviewed. Local vigilantes threatened trouble if he were released. Women from all over the country, soon to be known as the Fireflies, began to write him.

During his weeklong trial, he showed no emotion. Reporters hired body language experts to decode his every move, whether he turned his head, rested his fingers on the defense table, or shifted in his seat. Each expert had an opinion, but no one really knew what he was thinking.

The prosecution made its case, and the public defender made hers. The jury deliberated for five hours and sentenced Elijah Weston to ten years in the Montana State Prison.

For many, this verdict was an ending, but for Elijah and the Fireflies, it was just the beginning.

PROLOGUE

Anaconda, Montana
Tuesday, August 17
8:40 p.m.
Present Day

Point and shoot.

A cool, moist breeze ruffles my jacket as I raise the Polaroid camera and center the lens on the woman standing at the mountain's edge. The sun hovers above the horizon, backlighting the range in a soft, buttery auburn light.

The woman's smile is bright. Blond bangs brush over lively eyes sparkling with excitement as she holds her arms up and juts out her chest like a world champion who has crossed the finish line. Behind her, the city's boxy low-rise structures, twinkling like gems, are cushioned in the rolling mossy-green foothills of the Anaconda Range.

She is addicted to the attention. But all women like her love it. And in this moment, she has mine.

I should be restless and worried about a random passerby on the trail below. Sunset is a popular time for hikers and mountain bikers. They are attracted to the view as much as the exercise. But I am not worried. In fact, I am oddly calm. This is not my first time, after all, and I have learned from my mistakes. I would not say I am cocky, but I know what I am doing.

"Why don't you use a cell phone?" She nervously shoves the fringe of hair from her eyes. Her cheeks are an attractive rosy red, though too round for my tastes, and her teeth could use whitening. But she has sex appeal that is hard to ignore.

"I'm old school," I say. "You know that. I've never been a fan of cells." If anyone is going to be tracked by GPS in these mountains, it will be her, not me.

"But you can't post those pictures." She shifts her feet. She is already restless. "Where do you keep all the printed pictures?"

"I have a box."

"Do you have a lot of pictures?" Hints of jealousy pepper the words.

"Not enough of you." I snap the first picture as her grin returns, and the machine grinds out an image.

"Can you take an extra one for me, too?" she asks. "Might be fun to tape it to the dashboard of my car. Retro, you know?"

I snap the button again, and the small machine gushes another blank picture. I set it beside the first on rain-soaked soil, watching until I am satisfied my images will work before I reach for her phone.

"Say *cheese*," I say, raising it to my face.

"Cheese!" Her grin broadens.

I snap ten digital pictures in one hundredth of the time it will take the two Polaroid images to develop.

"Can I see?" she asks.

"Of course."

The woman climbs off the rock and nervously burrows her fingers into her pockets. She leans close, and the breeze catches her lavender scent. She reaches for the first Polaroid.

I push her hand away. "All good things come to those who wait."

Her pout is neither cute nor attractive. "I hate to wait."

"It won't be much longer."

Humoring her vanity suddenly irritates me, but this is going to be her last glimpse of her face, so it seems fair to give her a peek. She leans close but is quickly disappointed the picture has not materialized. She retrieves her phone and scrutinizes the crisp images. The Polaroid slowly reveals a more subdued image of her and the sweeping vista.

She selects her picture and tries to post it. "There's no service up here."

"Wait until we get down the mountain."

She holds up her cell phone and nestles close to me. "Let's do a selfie."

"I don't do selfies."

Narrow shoulders shrug as she tucks a strand of hair behind her ear. "Why not?"

"I just don't."

"Weird."

Her face finally appears on the thick ZINK paper, and I trace the outline of her brow.

She shoves her phone in her back pocket and studies the picture. "Very old school."

"That's what I like about it."

"I think you were born in the wrong time," she says.

"Why do you say that?"

"You don't have a cell, and you don't let me post anything about you."

"You're far more interesting than me."

Air sweeps up the mountainside, ruffling the fluted edges of her shirt. It catches one of the print pictures and carries it over the side of the mountain. I am tempted to chase after it, but I do not have time, and in the growing darkness, I know I will never find it. Frustrated, I quickly pocket the first.

"Let's get out of here," she says. "I want to go back to that hamburger joint in town."

"You just ate there."

"I'm hungry again."

My fingers graze the edge of the switchblade tucked in my coat pocket. I palm it, keeping it close to my thigh as she steps toward the rocks and the setting sun's opulent red-gold light. "Let's do a selfie with my camera."

"I don't like them."

"Please."

"Just the one." She slides close to me, glancing over her shoulder at the rugged landscape and then back at the lens. Sometimes, it feels like I am leading lambs to the slaughter.

As she stares upward, angling her chin into the most flattering angle, my blade flicks open with a well-oiled whoosh as I click the camera button. The distraction holds her attention for a split second before her gaze drops to the glittering blade. Confusion creates a quick disconnect, and then the first flickers of alarm or panic on her face.

"What's with the knife?" she asks, nervously pushing hair away from her face.

My reassuring smile buys me a few more seconds before I thrust the knife, and the blade catches her directly in her midsection. We stare at each other, inches separating our faces, and time, which is always rushing, decelerates to a stop. Her smile falters. Her breath turns hot and labored. Adrenaline animates her gaze as it dips to the first sticky, warm droplets of blood dampening her shirt. Shock blossoms into panic.

Time starts moving again. I let her phone fall to the ground, pull the knife out, and jab it upward several times. More blood warms my hand and makes the knife handle slick. Readjusting my grip, I shove the blade in to the hilt.

The woman grips my shoulder and tries to push away, but the tip is buried so deep it scrapes the underside of her sternum. "Why?"

"You're on the list," I say in a voice husky with emotion.

It is not my intention to be cruel, so I twist the blade swiftly, carving through all the critical vessels and arteries in her gut. I help her step backward toward a sun-bleached orange rock. Her knees bow, and I keep twisting as I support her weight with my other hand. Deadweight or dying weight is heavy, and by the time her bottom grazes the rock on its way toward the dirt, I am breathless.

The rosy glow drains from her face, and blood soaks her Big Sky Country sweatshirt. The internal bleeding is weakening her fast, and soon her eyes will roll back in her head.

"Shh," I whisper. "It's almost over."

When bubbles of blood gurgle from her lips, I know she has crossed over the line, and there is no turning back. Even a medical team could not save her now.

I try to pull the knife from her body but find it is stuck. Removal requires several back-and-forth wiggles and then a hard yank. Finally, the blade slides free.

The sun's waning glow glistens off the knife's edge. After swiping the blade on her shoulder until it is clean, I close it up and tuck it in my pocket. I wipe my hands on a clean portion of her shirt and make sure I have not accidentally cut myself and left droplets of my own blood behind.

Flexing my fingers and working the cramping from the muscles, I imagine the next steps as I hurry to the car, open the trunk, and reach for the gas can and green trash bags.

We are alone on the trail, but this area is chock-full of hikers and cyclists, and it is still possible for us to be interrupted. I rush back to her, gasoline sloshing in the can and releasing an invigorating scent.

Kneeling beside her, I check her pulse. Her heartbeat still taps faintly, as if vainly pumping like the Little Engine That Could.

In the distance I hear the crunch of a mountain biker's wheels against the dirt path fifty feet below. As a precaution, I place my hand over her mouth and still my body, hoping the vanishing light hides all traces of us.

"Shh," I whisper. "It's okay."

Finally, the mountain bike wheels roll away down the mountainside. As if she understands all hope is truly lost, her heart stops, and the faint puffs from her nostrils cease.

I pull her away from the rock, lay her flat, and quickly strip the blood-soaked Big Sky Country sweatshirt from her and then unsnap her jeans and pull them off. Next, off comes her underwear. Mind you, all this is done in a professional manner and not in a sexual-deviant kind of way. There are killers who enjoy humiliating their victims pre- and postmortem, but I am not like that. I am not sick. I have a purpose.

Pocketing her cell, I shove the clothes into a garbage bag. They will go in the trunk of her car to be used at a later date.

The heady scent of copper wafts as crimson silhouettes the body in ever-widening shadows. In the distance, an animal howls as if the blood scent stimulates its hunger. Soon it will be circling. My unfamiliarity with this wild country and the creatures stalking the night prompt me to hurry.

Grabbing a fresh, finer-point knife from another pocket, I flick it open and carefully trace the outline of her face, which she uses to manipulate men.

I nose the blade tip under the skin along her hairline. It takes several minutes of angling and gently probing until I can grab a flap of skin. Once I have a fingerhold, the process quickens. With a tugging, blade-swiping motion, I work around the outline of the face, ripping away subcutaneous fat and fascia. Several times the skin catches, threatens to tear, and forces me to stop pulling and let the knife do its work.

The process takes ten minutes, longer than I had anticipated, but experience has taught me if I rush, my trophy will be ruined, because facial skin is thin and prone to ripping. Around the eyes is the tricky spot, because that area tends to snag and tear.

Skinning, like any task, improves with repetition.

Practice makes perfect.

Finally, I lift the skin mask from her skull and pull a bag from my pocket, snapping it open so it catches the air and inflates. Carefully, I tuck my trophy inside and lay it flat on the ground. Though satisfaction lurks close, I do not dare acknowledge it.

At her side, I kneel and carefully angle her body toward the sunset, because she had loved it, and then I douse the body with gasoline. When the can is completely empty, I jog back to her car. I strip my own clothes off, and the cool evening air sends gooseflesh rippling. From the trunk I grab fresh clothes, and I dress as efficiently as I kill. Thirty seconds later my bloodied clothes are in another garbage bag. I place the can, the bag of clothes, and my trophy in the trunk before fishing a box of matches out of my pocket.

It is growing dark as I dig a flashlight from the trunk and shine it on the path to make the final trip up the hill under the half-moon sky. The ground is wet from last night's rain, and several times I slip and stumble in the mud or on a rock.

Her body is saturated in shadows as I strike the match. A familiar sulfur scent, which I have loved since I was a child, rises up seconds before the flame appears and grows tall and bright. I toss the match onto the body.

The gas fumes light with a sudden hiss, illuminating the dark sky. A fire out here will be a beacon for the curious as well as the do-gooders. It will not be long before people come. But that is the point. I do not want the animals to consume her. I want her found.

The clock ticks in earnest.

The gravel shifts under my feet as I race down the hill and slide behind the wheel of the car. I start the engine, using the keys I told her not to bother carrying to the overlook. Smoke and flames, fouled with the scent of burning flesh, climb in the night sky. Forgoing headlights, I nose the car toward the old road marked with potholes and switchback curves.

In the rearview mirror the fire burns. Steady Montana winds whisk its embers toward the dry scrub brush hugging the hills. The damp ground will corral the flames, keeping the mountainside safe. No sense damaging the earth.

I settle back into the driver's seat, and my thoughts turn to the next town. And the next name on my list.

Flipping on the headlights, I press the accelerator, switch on the radio, and drive faster. This is more fun than I ever anticipated.

CHAPTER ONE

Forty miles east of Missoula, Montana
Wednesday, August 18
7:15 a.m.

When Sergeant Bryce McCabe of the Montana Highway Patrol received the call from the local sheriff in Deer Lodge County, he was at his ranch, stringing barbed wire along a hundred-yard stretch of pastureland. He hoped to be stocking cattle by next spring, but days off had been rare in the last few months, so progress was slow. The cattle might have to wait another year or two.

He cradled the phone between his head and shoulder and tugged off his work gloves. "Bryce McCabe."

"Bryce, this is Sheriff Harry Wexler." Anxiety sharpened the lawman's voice. "I need your help with a case."

Bryce dug his bandanna from his rear pocket and rubbed the sweat from the back of his neck. "What do you have, Sheriff?"

"Homicide. And as much as I'd like to tell you about it, seeing is believing." Wexler was a steady-as-he-goes kind of lawman, and for him to request assistance meant trouble.

"Is it like the last one?" Bryce asked.

"Seems so."

Bryce shoved the bandanna back in his pocket. "I'll be there in about an hour. Text the directions."

"Will do. Thanks, Bryce."

Bryce climbed into his '86 Ford ranch pickup and drove the dirt-packed road to the homestead he and his brother, Dylan, now shared.

The two-story house was constructed of hand-hewn logs resting on a stone foundation and sealed with chinking wedged between seams joined by notched corners. A weather-rusted red tin roof arrowed to a sharp peak to keep hefty winter snows off load-bearing beams. The eastward-facing front porch was shaded by a ten-foot overhang and outfitted with two handmade rockers made of lodgepole pine.

The house had been left to Bryce and Dylan by their late stepfather, Pops Jones, a former rodeo rider. Their mother had spent most of her life dragging her boys from job to job and town to town until she had hooked up with Pops. No one gave the union much hope, but as it turned out, Pops had been a real ray of sunshine for twelve-year-old Bryce and ten-year-old Dylan. And when their mother passed, the three had remained together on the rodeo circuit, wintering here at the cabin, until Bryce turned eighteen and joined the marines. Dylan remained with Pops two more years and then followed his brother into the service.

Coordinated holidays were rare, but both brothers had made it to the ranch three Christmases ago and enjoyed the last holiday the old man would see on this earth. There had been a good bit of barbecuing, bourbon drinking, cigar smoking, and more than a few jokes about the lady friends Pops had juggled.

The house was not fancy by any stretch, but it was built solid, set on fifty acres of decent land teeming with good memories.

As he got out of his truck, three old German shepherds came around the side of the house. The tall gray one that looked more wolf than dog was Chase. He was eight. The black one beside him was Max, seven years old, and the smallest, Conan, was six. They were retired military service dogs with handlers who were either dead or unable to care for them.

When an IED explosion killed his marine canine in January, Dylan had opted not to re-up. Shortly after he had separated from the marines, while he was preparing to return to Montana, his commander approached him about Chase. Dylan had accepted responsibility for the dog without a second thought, and together they had moved back to the ranch. Word spread that Dylan had the space and fortitude to take military dogs, and Max and Conan had arrived by March.

Each animal eyed Bryce warily, and he was careful to keep his body language relaxed. The trio was acquainted with him, but each had been chosen by the military because aggression came naturally. Best not to tempt their natural propensities or training.

"How's it going, guys?" Bryce asked smoothly. He paused at the top step and let each sniff his hand. "See, we're all still friends, right?"

When Bryce had been in Afghanistan a dozen years ago, a soldier in his platoon had found a puppy in one of the villages. Scrawny and tied to a stake in the ground, the pup had barked when he had seen Bryce and his men come into the village. His sergeant, a bear of a man, had pulled out a switchblade and cut the rope. One of the village elders had started yelling, and Bryce had offered him several MREs for the dog. A deal had been struck, and the mongrel, dubbed Buddy, was along for the ride.

Damn dog had turned out to be an island of sanity for the coming months. Almost none of the men could resist a smile when they spotted Buddy trotting through the camp. When the time had come for the unit to ship stateside, Bryce had created military service canine paperwork for Buddy, who now lived somewhere in the Virginia Blue Ridge Mountains.

Dylan came around the side of the house with a toolbox in his hand. His nineteen years of service had embedded a deep sense of routine, and he still rose at four, ate his chow three times a day at the kitchen table, and spent the rest of his time working with the dogs or building the new barn, which he intended to have fully heated and insulated by winter.

"You're back early," Dylan said.

"Got called in. There's a homicide," Bryce said. "Need to take a quick shower and head over to Deer Lodge."

"Anything I can do?" Dylan asked.

"Not really. If this case is like the one in Helena, it'll be a long day, so I can't say when I'll be back."

Dylan removed his hat and ran his hand over shorn dark hair. "Two is a pattern."

"Maybe."

"Time to call in the FBI?" Dylan's tone turned suspicious, as it did when outsiders were tossed into the mix.

"Rather not have the feds involved, but I'll have to see."

"We got the ranch covered."

Rusted front-door hinges squeaked as Bryce opened it. "I appreciate that. Nice having the company."

"By the way," Dylan said. "When you get back, there might be a new dog living here."

Bryce paused. "Another one?"

"Her name is Venus. She's a Malinois and has a reputation as a hard-ass. Unadoptable. A real bitch."

Bryce shrugged. "The more the merrier."

"Thanks, bro."

It took Bryce less than twenty minutes to shower and change into clean jeans, a fresh T-shirt, and worn cowboy boots. He had left his suits at his Helena apartment because he had banked on having a full day or two off. But if he was heading toward the mountains near Anaconda, a suit would be more trouble than it was worth anyway.

In his state-issued, black SUV, he drove west on US 12 for thirty minutes before turning south on I-90 toward Anaconda. Wexler's directions took him from the interstate to a series of progressively smaller roads. Sixty minutes after leaving the ranch, he spotted flares and a deputy's car.

Bryce parked behind the marked vehicle, reached in the compartment between the seats, dug out his badge, and looped it around his neck.

The deputy who approached Bryce's car looked barely out of high school. Efforts to look solemn did not hide his edgy, amped-up energy. "Sergeant Bryce, Sheriff Wexler is waiting for you," the deputy said. "Follow the dirt road up the side of the mountain."

"Thanks."

Bryce angled his vehicle up the barely paved road around tire tracks marked off with yellow crime scene tape. He drove up the hillside, gravel crunching under his tires, and eased toward a sharp turn that brought him to a dead end. The land around him was covered in a swath of blackened scrub grass swooping over the hill like an eagle's wing.

Bryce parked and reached for his worn black cowboy hat on the passenger seat. Out of his SUV, he settled it on his head and tugged the brim lower toward mirrored sunglasses. The wind carried persistent trails of smoke threaded with the scent of scorched flesh. He opened the back of his vehicle, grabbed a fresh set of latex gloves, and then walked beside the singed grass that had been drier than bone until Monday's soaking rain.

His gaze swept the hillside's base toward defined tire tracks. If not for the rain, the marks would have been faint, and obtaining an impression would have been difficult. Had the killer realized he had left this critical piece of evidence behind?

When he approached the ridge, he looked out toward the city, the foothills, and the jagged Anaconda Range beyond. The sun sent a fine trickle of sweat down his back as he strode toward yellow caution tape staked in a large square around the fire's point of origin, concealed with a blue tarp. If this was like the Helena case, the tarp covered a body, and he was not getting back to fencing anytime soon.

Resettling his hat, he strode toward Sheriff Harry Wexler, who was tall, broad shouldered, and sported a full belly earned in countless hours behind the wheel of a car. Bryce extended his hand. "Sheriff Wexler."

"Sergeant McCabe." The older man's weathered hands still packed a heavy-duty grip. "Caught you on your day off, didn't I?"

"It happens." He could not remember the last time he'd really kicked up his heels. Was it that Christmas with Pops and Dylan three years ago?

"I hear you inherited Pops's ranch," Sheriff Wexler said.

"That's right."

Montana was about 150,000 square miles, but Bryce had been in the field six years, enough time to meet most of the state's law enforcement officers, and if he was not acquainted personally, there was always someone to tell him what he needed to know. The flip side was his personal business had a way of making the rounds as well, which had not bothered him much until lately.

"Means a commute to Helena, doesn't it?" Wexler asked.

"Less than an hour. I don't mind the drive. And I still have several months left on my Helena apartment lease." A breeze rushed up the hill, and yellow tape rippled. "Who called it in?"

"A mountain biker who rides these trails every evening after work. He was finishing up his run when he smelled the smoke and saw the flames. He called my office as soon as he rode down the mountain and hit cell phone service."

"What time was that?"

"About ten p.m."

"Did he see anyone up here?" Bryce asked.

"Said sometimes he sees kids or tourists on the ridge taking pictures. Selfies, you know. But he didn't see anyone last night. I have his name if you want to interview him."

"Thanks." Bryce stared toward the fire's epicenter and braced. "I best have a look."

"I ain't seen a body like that before, but I heard about the other in Helena. Jesus H. Christ."

With a nod, Bryce worked his hands into the gloves. "Have any of your deputies been walking around up here?"

"No, sir," Sheriff Wexler said. "The responding deputy was focused first on the fire. We've had rain, but it's still dry. When the deputy saw the body, he suspected this case was connected to the other one, roped off the scene, and backed away. I'm afraid in the dark he trampled the tire tracks and the area around the body pretty good. He also had to wait for the body to cool before he could cover it."

"And the mountain biker? Did he come up here?"

"Said he didn't get near the scene. Just called in the fire."

Cases like this could be made or broken by a first responder. The scene could be altered and valuable evidence destroyed by untrained ignorance or police personnel struggling to secure the scene. In the latter case, there was no blame to hand out.

Bryce moved toward the blue tarp and, with the sheriff's help, removed it. Carefully, he crouched for a better look. The charred corpse lay on its back, its head pointed toward the valley and the distant mountains. The now-heavy smoky scent of burned hair, flesh, and bone swirled in the breeze. The blackened, marbled remains had withered appendages with snubbed fingers and toes consumed in the flames. The featureless face had a gaping jaw frozen in a ghoulish, toothy laugh.

Sheriff Wexler's voice rattled with unprocessed emotions. "Don't know what kind of person does this. I've seen bad things in my years, but this might be the worst."

"Always amazes me what humans do to one another." Bryce searched for clothing or jewelry. There was none.

Sheriff Wexler pulled off his hat and rubbed his forehead with his sleeve. "The medical examiner's office is sending up a death investigator. She should be here any minute."

Bryce rose, favoring his right knee, which he'd twisted on an Afghanistan march a decade ago. He took a moment to let the joint settle before he moved around the corpse to view what remained of the face. If he had not known what to look for, he might have missed the facial mutilation below the char.

"Did he do this to the other one?" the sheriff asked as he popped a mint in his mouth.

The other one had been found near Helena in mid-July. The medical examiner in Missoula had determined the victim had been female, Caucasian, and in her late twenties to early thirties. She had been stabbed multiple times, and her body had been stripped clean of clothing and jewelry; however, there were no signs of sexual assault. The killer had also removed the skin from the victim's face before dousing the body with gasoline and setting the remains on fire. The inferno had done an expert job of destroying forensic evidence and the victim's identity. DNA had been extracted from back molars and submitted for testing, but so far the victim had not been identified.

Gravel rattled under Bryce's boot as he flexed his knee. "It looks pretty damn similar."

The sheriff's radio squawked. The deputy stationed at the roadside below announced the arrival of the medical examiner's death investigator, Joan Mason. A former Philadelphia cop, Joan had relocated to Montana a year ago and taken the job in the medical examiner's office shortly after the New Year.

Approaching footsteps had Bryce turning to see the brunette with a lean, athletic build. She wore jeans, weathered boots, and a navy-blue wind slicker that opened to a white T-shirt. She pulled on disposable gloves as she moved with steady steps toward the scene. When she saw the body, her pace faltered a beat before she steeled herself and continued forward.

"Harry." Joan's Philadelphia accent drew out the sheriff's name as she shook hands with him and then Bryce. "Bryce, good to see you. Wish it could be under better circumstances."

"Unfortunately, it's rarely a good day when we cross paths," Bryce said.

Joan was not a sworn officer in Montana, but ten years in the Philadelphia Police Department as a beat cop and then later as a homicide detective had equipped her with keen investigative skills and a no-nonsense urban-street-cop directness that won her praise in Montana's law enforcement community. "Like the Helena victim."

"Seems to be," Bryce said.

As Joan circled slowly around the body, her expression turned grim. She cleared her throat. "Animal. No, I take that back. That isn't fair to animals."

She was right. Wilderness predators hunted for food and survival, not for sport.

Silence settled around Joan as she absently pushed up her sleeves, revealing the pink, puckered flesh on her forearm. Arson had been Joan's specialty back east, and the burn scars were living reminders of the monsters she had tracked.

Bryce remained silent, giving her time to mentally shore up her resolve brick by brick. There were scenes like this that they all needed time to process.

Bryce had needed time to process the first crime scene, which investigators initially had classified as a violent anomaly. The rescue and police crews who had worked the case had been stunned by the way the body had been savaged, and theories floating around included domestic violence, drug cartels, and human trafficking. Investigators hadn't reached any conclusions, so Bryce had sent the body to Missoula to Joan's boss, the state's best medical examiner, Dr. Peter Christopher.

Joan cleared her throat. "I assisted Dr. Christopher when he did the autopsy on the first victim. The doc determined the cause of death was stabbing."

"There's a lot of blood on the rock near the overlook and on the ground around it," Sheriff Wexler said.

Joan squatted near the victim's head and examined the skull. The slow rise and fall of her chest, coupled with unsettling uneasiness, suggested she was replaying her last brutal hunt for the arsonist who had nearly burned her alive.

"It looks like the face was removed in this instance as well." She pointed to a slight cleft along the hairline. "In my opinion, here's where the killer cut. Of course, that'll be for the doc to officially confirm. I assume you want the body sent to him?"

"Yes," Bryce said.

She rose with enviable ease. "The doc and I have had several discussions about this killer."

"And?"

"He's crazy as hell. And the consensus is to call Dr. Ann Bailey. Her background in forensic psychology could be of real use untangling this killer's mind."

"She's back from summer vacation?" Bryce asked.

"And moved back into Missoula and starts teaching at the university in a week," Joan said.

Dr. Bailey was in her early thirties and a professor at the University of Montana in Missoula. She was well respected in her field and had lectured to Bryce's police recruits in late May on the topic of abhorrent behavior. If the class she had taught was any indication, this case was right up her alley.

Red and blue lights flashed as the state's forensic van pulled off the gravel road and lumbered as far as it could before parking. The crew unloaded a tent and tables and established their base of operations.

“The forensic team is here mighty quick,” Sheriff Wexler said. “Takes pull to get them up here pronto.”

Bryce had made one call on the drive over. The fast results attested that this case did not require influence. Any officer who’d seen the file understood a dangerous killer was preying on their state. “Joan, what do you need from me?”

“Nothing either of us can do until I’ve processed the body and the forensic techs do their job,” she said, nodding to the three-person crew. “I need to radio my office and have my appointments canceled. It’s going to be a long day.”

“Most are,” Bryce said.

As she stepped away, Bryce stared at the hate-fueled devastation unleashed on this individual. Motivations for violence had never been much of an interest to him. Like any good hunter, he focused on following the physical evidence left behind by the killer. He left the higher reasoning to the doctors, defense attorneys, and judges. But if this scene was like the last, there would be precious little physical evidence, and he would need a specialist like Dr. Bailey to point him in the right direction.

He checked his phone and was not surprised to see he had no service up here. He would have to be nearer to the road for that. The silence this land offered was the reason he had returned home seven years ago. Far from the choppers, explosions, and endless gunfire, he had gladly disconnected.

But as he walked down the hillside, opened his contacts, and stared at Dr. Ann Bailey’s name, the idea of isolation was not so appealing.

CHAPTER TWO

Missoula, Montana
Wednesday, August 18
10:15 a.m.

Dr. Ann Bailey opened the front door of her former residence on Beech Street. She had purchased the house with her late husband more than a decade ago and had spent many happy and not-so-happy years in the one-story brick rancher. Ten years ago, she could not have imagined herself living anywhere else. And now it had been a year since she had stepped foot inside.

She peered into the shadowy interior, half expecting to hear her son's laughter, or smell the lingering scent of chocolate chip cookies, or see her husband's discarded work boots next to her son's sneakers. Instead, there was the hum of the refrigerator, the stale musty air, and the dust particles dancing in unwelcome sunshine.

Monthly mortgage payments, utility bills, and lawn care services now outweighed any anxieties about the past. Like it or not, it was time to clean the place out and put it on the market.

Ann clicked on the foyer light, hoping it would buoy her resolve. Instead, it drew her attention to the graphite fingerprint dust marring the pale-blue walls, the crumpled strand of yellow caution tape, and a discarded pair of evidence gloves.

Though tempted to walk away, she could not let the ghosts, demons, or whatever stalked the house win.

"Nothing ventured, nothing gained," she muttered as she picked up the moving boxes, tape, and box of plastic garbage bags.

This week's tasks were simple: clear out personal belongings worth salvaging, interview the woman who would deep clean the house, and get the place on the market. Simple tasks complicated by emotions.

She assembled her first moving box and then walked into the kitchen, where the sink still contained the empty coffee cup left behind by her late husband. Ann had painted the #1 DAD mug with her son several years ago, and from the moment Nate gave it to his father, it had been a favorite of Clarke's.

The cabinets were filled with dusty dishes that she had no desire to keep. Nor did she want the pots and pans or the **FAMILY MAKES THIS HOUSE A HOME** sign Clarke had given her on their first anniversary. A glance toward the basement door made her anxious to leave.

She crossed the living room and walked slowly along the hallway lined with a collection of pictures. The images featuring Nate were easy saves. Several made her smile, and she carefully dusted the glass with her sleeve and tucked each in her box. However, the portraits that included her husband triggered a complicated blend of anger and disbelief and were not so easy to salvage.

As much as she wanted to leave these pictures behind, she settled on one image she had taken of Clarke and Nate fly-fishing on the Bitterroot River under a flawless autumn sky. Both were laughing, radiating pure joy as Clarke helped six-year-old Nate hold up an eight-pound trout. She did not want to remember, but Nate might one day.

In Nate's room, the twin bed butted against the blue wall. The navy comforter was as smooth as the day she had made it, and the Power Rangers pillow remained perfectly centered. On his desk stood a globe and a LEGO airplane he had built. The clothes in the closet were all too small now and not worth harvesting, because boys grew like weeds. Still, she selected a few shirts associated with memories of soccer games, school pictures, and birthday parties.

Next, she packed worn copies of *Goodnight Moon* and *Where the Wild Things Are*. She grabbed a soccer trophy, the third-grade science fair blue ribbon, Nate's favorite fishing lures, and a small silver canister containing locks of hair from his first haircut.

The next stop was her bedroom. The bed had been stripped, Clarke's closet cleared, and the drawers emptied by the cops. Ann glanced in her closet and drew her fingertips along the bright floral shirts and dresses, realizing she had taken what she had really wanted eighteen months ago, when she and Clarke had separated. All these clothes, like the rest of this house, belonged in the past. Shoes were the same. She had no use for the heels, but she did grab a worn pair of hiking boots.

Perfume bottles, earrings, bracelets, and brushes scattered across her dresser. She raised a perfume bottle to her nose, inhaling and remembering Clarke. After he'd returned home from conferences in recent years, he had brought her expensive perfumes and jewelry. Looking back, she realized these splurges were intended to satisfy his own guilt.

"Ann, you're all that keeps me sane," Clarke said. It was hours after she'd left, and he had tracked her to her parents' house. They stood on the front porch, several charged feet separating them. Both had been careful to keep their voices low for Nate's sake.

"We need a break, Clarke." She could not articulate the tangled emotions that had chased her out of the marriage.

He gripped her arm in an unbreakable hold. Not enough to hurt but enough to remind her he was in control. "That's bullshit. I know losing the baby was hard. But we'll keep trying."

"Please, give me this time." In the cool air, her cheeks flushed.

"How much time?" he demanded.

Tears welled in her eyes. "I don't know."

He gently placed his hand at the base of her throat. Her pulse pounded under his calloused fingers. "I love you, and this cannot be forever."

"It's a break." She whispered the lie, hoping he would leave.

Turning from the memory, Ann hurried through the house and out the front door, drawing in a deep breath. She locked the door and settled her box of precious memories on the front seat of the car.

An older red Ford truck pulled up in front of the house, and the woman behind the wheel glanced at a piece of paper as if confirming she had found the right place. Ann raised her hand to signal her, and the woman waved back.

Ann moved away from her car, grateful to be interfacing with a real human and not ghosts. "Hi. I'm Ann Bailey."

"Hey, I'm Maura Ralston. We've traded phone calls about me cleaning your house."

Ann scrutinized the slim woman, trying to imagine her cleaning out closets and sorting through all her belongings and dividing them into charity and trash piles. She was turning this personal part of her life over to a stranger whom she had discovered on a flyer outside her office, and it smacked of cowardice. "I called the references you gave me."

Maura slid her hands into her pockets. "Awesome. All good, I assume, or I wouldn't be here."

"They were glowing. Methodical, neat, organized."

Maura grinned. "I'm all that."

"And you're not a reporter."

"No, I'm not." Maura laughed, her brow arching. "Where did that come from?"

"Never mind." Reporters had blown up Ann's phone last year, and she still received the occasional inquiry, which kept her vigilant. Last week it had been a guy named Paul Thompson, who was producing a podcast. She had ignored his three messages. "The house hasn't been really cleaned in over a year. All the closets need to be emptied out, major dusting, the appliances . . ."

"I get it. I've done all that before. All you need to do is tell me what you want saved, and I'll take it from there. A few days from now, the house will be pristine and ready to go on the market."

"You've been doing this work for five years back east. Why the move to Montana?" Ann asked.

"A fresh start. Divorce." Maura hesitated, as if gauging her words. "You too, right?"

"Excuse me?"

Maura looked toward the house. "I've done enough jobs like this to get a sense of my client. You're divorced or about to be. It was messy, and though you got the house, you really do not want it. But the property is worth too much to pass up, so you deal with the emotions and do the work."

Her clear-cut honesty was refreshing after a year's worth of family tiptoeing around Ann's feelings. "You sound like a psychologist."

"I want to be one," she said quickly. "And for the record, I know how rough the getting-on-with-your-life part can be. Mine cheated on me, which adds salt to the wound."

Ann liked the woman's candor. "I've already been through the house and taken what I want. Use whatever key pieces of furniture for staging. The rest, like I said, toss or donate. I don't care."

"Got it."

"The rate you quoted in your text is fine, so I'll give you the grand tour if you're interested in the job."

"Terrific."

Ann returned to the front door and opened the lock. As they stepped inside, Maura's gaze was drawn to the black graphite, crime scene tape, and gloves. "What happened here?"

"I'm surprised you don't know."

"I don't do the news or social media. Bad for the soul."

"Smart."

"Did anyone die here?"

"No."

"But . . ."

"An internet search will tell you what you want to know. And if you decide this job is not for you, no harm, no foul."

"No, I'll do it. I need the money, and the past is the past."

If only it were that simple. "If that's the case, any questions?"

Maura gripped the strap of her leather, fringed satchel. "I understand my marching orders pretty well."

"Good. Also, I mentioned I'm not fond of reporters. I don't want any in here. Only you in the house."

"No problem. Do you have a Realtor?"

"Yes. Her name is Stacy Winston, and if she wants to see the house, she's to let me know so I can call and give you a heads-up."

"Perfect."

Relieved, Ann fished a spare key from her pocket and handed it over. "I promised Stacy the house would be ready for market no later than the second week of September."

"No problem. I've seen enough so we can skip the tour. Looks standard."

"It should be." Ann produced a $200 down payment. It was a risk. Maura might take the money and run. She might turn the house into a party palace and ruin whatever value remained. She might sell tours to reporters. She might . . .

The list would roll endlessly in a negative loop, and it would go round and round for hours if she did not stop it. Ann reminded herself she had dutifully checked out Maura's references, which had all been great, and if Ann did not get someone, the work would fall to her.

"You have my number if you need to call," she said.

Maura followed her to her car and glanced at the box in the front seat. "That's all you want?"

"That's it."

"Okay. If you change your mind, call."

"I won't."

"I know I skipped the tour, but mind if I walk around the house?" Maura asked.

"Have at it. There's also a basement off the kitchen. There shouldn't be too much left there."

"Cool."

"I've got to get going."

Maura thrust out her hand. "Thanks for the job, Dr. Bailey. It really helps."

"Call me Ann, and thank you for taking this on." She opened her driver's-side door. "I work at the university, so I'm less than five minutes away. Seriously, any questions, call."

"I'm thinking about attending the university in the spring."

"If you want the tour, let me know."

"I'll definitely take you up on that," Maura said.

Ann slid behind the wheel, started the engine, and switched on the AC. The cool air brushed her skin as Maura vanished inside and passed in front of the display window.

What would that house reveal to Maura about Ann? All the small choices she had made, from the types of pans she had cooked with to the perfume she wore to the color choices on the walls, combined and told a story about her.

Her phone rang. Grateful for the distraction, she fished it out of her pocket, not glancing at the display. "Hello."

"Dr. Bailey, this is Sergeant Bryce McCabe."

"Sergeant McCabe. This is unexpected. What can I do for you?"

"I have a case I'd like to discuss with you," he said.

When she had spoken to the Montana Highway Patrol officers, McCabe had taken a seat in the back of the classroom and paid close attention to her lecture. His questions had been in-depth and displayed a sharp mind.

"Sure. Maybe sometime later this week?"

"I was hoping today."

"Today?"

"I'm at the crime scene now, and it'll be important for you to see it for yourself."

She checked her watch. Nate would not be home from computer camp for another five hours. The drive to the state police headquarters in Helena would take a couple of hours. "If I leave now, I can be at your office by lunchtime."

"The crime scene's not in Helena. It's about an hour and fifteen minutes east of you in Deer Lodge County. I can text you the address." His voice dropped, and the tone turned serious. "It's important."

"I can leave right now. I'm not dressed for work."

"All the better. The terrain requires a little hiking."

"Can you tell me anything about it?" Ann asked.

"Better you see for yourself, but if it will help, Joan said it would be your kind of case."

She cleared her throat. "I'll leave now."

"Good. See you soon." Seconds later her phone chimed with a text from Bryce.

The location was near a small town called Anaconda. It was a picturesque area known for the Anaconda Smelter Stack, a masonry structure that rose 585 feet out of a now-defunct ore smelter.

When she arrived, a deputy directed her to a gravel road toward a collection of cars on the top of a hill. She parked behind a dark SUV, gathered her box of mementos, and stowed it in her trunk. She changed out her sneakers for the old hiking boots.

After grabbing a wide-brimmed hat from the trunk, she settled it on her head, adjusted her sunglasses, and then rolled down the sleeves of her cotton shirt.

Ann spotted Bryce McCabe easily. He was taller than most men, standing at six foot five inches, and he had broad shoulders and muscled arms. He normally wore a suit, a tie, and his polished cowboy boots. However, he was dressed more casually today, as if the dispatcher's call had pulled him off the range on that wild patch of land that he had inherited last fall.

Anxious to see why he had called, she marched forward past the yellow evidence tents. A dozen steps into her climb, a gust carried the traces of decay and charred flesh.

CHAPTER THREE

Anaconda, Montana
Wednesday, August 18
12:15 p.m.

Bryce saw Ann Bailey walking up the hill toward the forensic team's tent and her long stride slow right about where the coiling scents thickened. She was a doctor of psychology, and though she had studied the criminal mind and understood patterns and practices, she had admitted in her training seminar that she had no real field experience. One thing to theorize about a serial killer and another to see, smell, or touch their vicious handiwork.

"The first homicide is always rough," Joan said as she stood beside Bryce.

"You think she'll make it?" Bryce asked.

"Even if it kills her."

To Ann's credit, she kept moving up the hill toward them. It was difficult to read her expression, shadowed by the glasses and the hat, but he suspected she had intended to shield her reactions as well as the sun. *I read you—you don't read me.*

"Joan," Ann said. "Sergeant McCabe."

She gave Joan a quick smile and extended her hand to Bryce. His calloused palm scraped against her smooth skin, and if he had still been on the rodeo circuit, he would have scoffed and teased her about being a greenhorn.

But Ann Bailey was not totally inexperienced, and she was nobody's shrinking violet. She had stood up to last year's shitstorm caused by her late husband, and many who'd been so betrayed and manipulated would have hightailed it out of Montana. She had stood her ground and kept her job, and was teaching her boy to hold his head high.

Bryce had always been attracted to Ann Bailey's looks. Blond, high cheekbones, full lips, and striking green eyes were damn nice in their own right. But combined with a stunning set of legs, full breasts, and a narrow waist, she had wheedled herself into his thoughts since he had first met her last year. Now that she was battle tested, she was all the more attractive.

"Thank you for coming so quickly," he said.

"You have me until two at the latest, and then I need to head back to town to get Nate." Drawing her shoulders back, she shifted her attention toward the body. "What happened?"

"Autopsy will confirm what I'm about to say, but I believe the victim was stabbed to death, and then her remains were set on fire," Joan said.

"Fire," Ann said softly.

"Judging by the smell, I'd wager the accelerant was gasoline," Joan said.

Ann regarded Joan, suggesting unspoken words passed between them. The women were survivors of a fire that had nearly killed them in college. So maybe later they would have a pointed discussion, but it would not happen in front of him.

She looked past them both to the blackened body lying out in the hot midday sun. "Joan mentioned a case similar to this one. It was in Helena, right?"

"Yes," he said. "As far as we know, this is the second victim killed this way."

"Two bodies in a little over a month. That's a short cooling-off period between kills," Ann said.

During the time between murders—the cooling-off period—the killer relived the crime, which energized whatever emotional payoff he enjoyed during the act. When remembering no longer satisfied his cravings, the search for a new victim began.

"Think we have a serial killer?" Bryce asked.

"Four weeks is a quick turnaround," Joan said.

"The interval between murders can last years or decades," Ann said.

"Or in this case, the guy burned through his memories in four weeks," Bryce said.

"It's not the fastest pace, but you're right—it's a short turnaround," Ann said. "Can I get a better look at the body?"

"It's rough," he warned.

"No doubt." Ann's lips thinned. "But unless you two want to simply discuss the theory of serial killers, which I can do for hours, I'll need to see this guy's handiwork. Do you have gloves?"

Bryce handed her a spare pair and watched her long fingers slide into the gloves as if she were dressing for a night at the opera. Brave face, but the extra seconds she took knitting her fingers together suggested shaky nerves behind the bravado. He had done as much when he had stared down the length of a rodeo bull or marched into a narrow canyon in Korangal Valley. The real test did not commence until you saddled up and it was go time.

Bryce took the lead, moving at a slower pace, giving Ann time to retreat as the scents strengthened and the buzz of black flies grew louder. Out in this weather, the sun and critters would turn this body to dust in a matter of days.

She edged close to the yellow caution tape and studied the body, which lay on its back, its charred skull angled toward the western, pale-blue sky. "Was the other body positioned to the west?"

"Yes. On the side, arms tucked close to the body, legs closed."

"Legs are closed in this case, but there doesn't appear to be any clothing. Were there signs of sexual assault on the first victim?" Ann asked.

"No signs of sexual assault, but she was also stripped naked."

"Also stabbed and then incinerated?"

"Affirmative."

"May I get closer?" Ann asked.

He lifted the tape, and she ducked under it. Her jaw tightened, but she kept moving until she was feet away from the remains. As she stared at the scorched figure, the silence that followed stretched to breaking. Finally, she moved toward the head.

There was no lingering this time as she instinctively drew in a deep breath and stepped back. "Does fire destroy the face like this?"

"It can do a lot of damage," Joan said evenly. "But we think the killer removed the face with a scalpel, like he did with the other one. There's an outline along the hairline, cheek, and jawline. Again, the medical examiner will have to make the call."

In the last two hours, Bryce had distanced himself from the images of the mutilated body. It was not intentional but a survival mechanism learned on the battlefield. During the mission, the dead ceased to be human and were reclassified as evidence. Later the images would return, reinvigorated and magnified, like all the other ghosts.

"I'd like to be present when the autopsy is conducted," Ann said.

Joan glanced toward Bryce, brow raised, but she said nothing.

"Sure," Bryce said.

"Was the first body found close to Interstate 90?" Ann asked.

"Relatively," he said.

"Close to bike or hiking paths?"

"Yes, but it was the fire that alerted locals and then the cops."

"There are plenty of places in Montana to bury a body so that it's never found," Ann said.

"Why draw attention to the remains?" Bryce asked.

"He wants his work discovered." Inhaling a steadying breath, Ann studied the face closely. "But the fires and the facial mutilations are connected. The killer is erasing the victim's identity."

"Look what I've done," Joan said. "Now guess who I did it to?"

"Maybe," Ann said. "Have you identified the first victim?"

"No," Bryce said. "This killer might want our attention, but he also doesn't want to get caught. I think stripping the bodies is a precautionary move. As destructive as fire could be, buttons, rivets, buckles often survive and later give clues about the victim."

"The first victim's face was not found, and so far, neither has this one's. Is it a trophy?" Joan asked.

"Trophies are common with serial killers," Ann said. "Whatever they take from the victims helps them relive the crime during that cooling-off period I mentioned. Often there's a sexual element. As the crime is mentally reenacted, the killer can masturbate."

"But remember, no signs of sexual assault on the first victim," Bryce said.

"Sexual stimulation comes in many forms," Ann said. "Sometimes the act of witnessing the victim's pain gets the killer excited. They can't achieve sexual gratification without another's suffering. Penetration isn't always required."

"That's why I've got you here," Bryce said. "You understand this kind of thinking."

She looked up at him. "I've studied it, comprehend it on an academic level, but I don't claim to understand this type of killer. If anyone says they do, they're lying." Defensiveness stiffened her tone.

"You still know more than me," Bryce said. "I've never had cases like these two."

"Do you have any theories about the Helena victim?" Ann asked.

"I've discussed it with the lead detectives at length. Our assumptions that the first kill was domestic don't fit anymore. Though we could still be dealing with cartels or human traffickers," Bryce said.

"I suppose this could be a message to rival gangs. Violence is often used in those organizations to control not just the victim but the survivors. But this kind of killing takes planning. The victim has to be selected, the materials gathered, and the site chosen," Ann said. "This killer is organized, and he's not stupid."

"You think the victims were chosen in advance?" he asked.

"Yes I do," Ann said. "He likely was stalking or grooming them for days or weeks. Are there any missing-person reports that match the first victim's approximate age and race?"

"No. We reached out to police in Wyoming and Idaho," Bryce said. "There were a couple that were possibilities, but the women have since been located."

"Will he do it again?" Joan asked.

"If I had to guess, I'd say yes," Ann said.

"Jesus," Bryce muttered.

"May I read the files from the first case?" Ann asked.

Bryce was pleased to see she was not running to the safety of her university office.

"I'll hand deliver them to you myself," Bryce said. "Name the place."

"I rented a house in town and will be there the next couple of days nonstop getting it set up before the school year starts. Tomorrow, Nate is going camping with his cousin, my brother, and Joan. That means four days of silence, so I'll have time to work."

Joan chuckled. "My first camping trip."

Ann smiled. "I'd trade places with you, if I could."

Bryce understood how solitude could coax the past and its demons out of the shadows. "I'll drop them off this afternoon."

"We should have the body out of here in under an hour," Joan said. "Likely the autopsy will be tomorrow. I wish I could be there. Maybe I could join Gideon and the boys later in the day."

"No, you go. It'll be good for you all. I'll attend," Ann said.

"You been to an autopsy before?" Bryce asked.

"First time for everything, Sergeant McCabe," Ann said.

Challenge hummed under her words, and he preferred her throwing punches instead of retreating.

"I remember my first," Bryce said.

She arched a brow. "If you're suggesting it won't be easy, you're correct, Sergeant McCabe. But don't worry about me. I don't bolt."

A grin tugged at the edges of his lips. "I wasn't suggesting you would."

"Yes, you were. But it's a justified worry. I'm untested."

"You'll hang tough," Joan said.

He sensed Ann was not as sure of herself as she pretended to be. "Exactly."

While Joan stayed with the remains, Bryce walked Ann down the hill. As they passed the tire tracks, she paused and studied them. They were covered in footprints.

"Most of the footprints belong to the deputy who came in on foot. The tire tracks were made by the killer, likely after Monday night's rain."

"Can you figure out what kind of vehicle he drives?" Ann asked.

"Might be able to."

They continued over the now sun-dried grass poking up from the soft dirt. Her long legs matched his strides easily.

"Thanks again, Doc," he said. "I'll see you later today."

She stripped off her gloves and shoved them in her pocket before she removed her hat, revealing a fine sheen of sweat banding her forehead. Blond hair twisted into a low knot. "Let's hope I can help."

***

Ann started her car and opened the window, breathing in fresh mountain air before she drove away from the crime scene. Scents of singed flesh lingered in her nasal passages and clung to her skin. Images of the mutilated body were branded into her memory.

A glance in her rearview mirror caught Bryce McCabe watching her drive away. His grim expression had suggested that he fully expected her to rethink her involvement in the case and decline to help. That was not going to happen, but he did not know that. Yet.

Known for his direct, if not abrupt, style, Bryce McCabe had been on tenterhooks around her, as if he were juggling a dozen fragile eggs. His underestimation irritated her, but of course he really was not so different from everyone else in Missoula. Since her husband's death in the fire he had set, those who knew her, as well as strangers, tiptoed around her. Most did not know what to say. They wanted to be kind, but they were also curious about Clarke. *How are you feeling? Did you know what Clarke was doing? Tell us all the dirty little secrets.* Bryce had never once brought up Clarke when she'd visited his office, and that was a point in his column.

Lecturing a classroom of police officers was far different from fieldwork. Regardless of the personal demons a case like this might summon, she was here to stay.

And most surprising, now that the initial shock was wearing off, she realized she was fascinated by this crime.

As she turned onto the highway, her thoughts drifted to the body and possible theories. This killer had a distinct message and mission and a specific victim in mind. Murder was not enough for him. He was bent on eradicating their identities on all levels.

She gripped the steering wheel tighter as she slowed for a stop sign at a T intersection. She flashed to the blackened skull's slack jaw welded into an unending silent scream. *"Help me!"*

Ann trusted that the killer was paying close attention to this investigation. He had deliberately drawn attention to his work, suggesting he craved the fame and notoriety. There had been a media blackout on the first murder; however, a second killing would establish a trend and set off alarm bells in the press. The killer wanted his bodies found.

Had the killer already posted pictures hinting to his crimes? Uploading direct images or videos could trigger warnings with viewers and inquiries from law enforcement, but partial photos of the body or vistas around the crime scene could go unidentified for a long time.

If her university students had taught her anything, it was that everyone now lived in the fame-hungry world of social media. Nothing, including a meal, a drink, or a communal gathering, *really* happened unless it was documented online.

I'm right here. Can't you see me? Find me.

A truck whistled by her car in the adjacent lane, snapping her mind back into focus. She turned on her blinker and headed toward the interstate.

With three hours until Nate was finished with camp, she had a bit of time to work on setting up the new house she had rented on Turner Street. The basic pieces of furniture had arrived, but all the little things, including dishes, glasses, sheets, bookshelves, even her bed frame, needed buying.

She was living in chaos, and as tempted as she was to return to her parents' ranch house, to do so would be admitting they were right—and that she was not ready to live alone.

"Let us protect you and Nate. You're safer out here on the ranch," her father had said.

But her mother and father had put their lives on hold last year, and she refused to let them continue. Two weeks ago, when her brother and she had gratefully sent them off on another motor home adventure, she had moved back into town.

As she pressed the accelerator, her last words to her parents rattled in her head: *"I've been through the worst. I'll be fine."*

CHAPTER FOUR

Missoula, Montana
Wednesday, August 18
3:45 p.m.

After an hour spent racing through the box store, Ann had managed to buy sheets and a comforter decorated with stars and planets for Nate's bedroom, glow-in-the-dark stick-on stars for his ceiling, and two high-wattage bedside lights for reading. Also in the cart were plain white towels, bath mats, shower curtains, and a blue-and-white quilt marked 50 percent off. She did not have the energy to choose glasses and plates, so she bought long sleeves of durable paper plates and cups. It had been easy to make basic decisions last year, but now they felt insurmountable.

Analytically, she recognized her behavior as classic avoidance based on a fear of the future. If she were counseling an individual like herself, she would have praised them for the small steps they had accomplished. But she was not a patient, and she was stronger than any stupid anxiety that, honest to God, could not have been worse than it was last year.

As the clerk rang up her order, she noted the young man kept glancing at her as if he recognized her. She injected her steady gaze with challenge until he stopped sneaking looks. When her total rang up, she suppressed a grimace. Until she sold the house on Beech Street, finances were going to be tight.

The shopping cart's wheels rattled as she pushed her purchases across the parking lot and loaded them in her trunk. At the university, she parked outside the building where Nate was attending a computer camp. She still had a minute to spare.

She savored the warmth of the sun on her face as she watched the side of the gym door, waiting for it to open and the kids to be released.

Her phone rang. She did not recognize the number. Wondering if it might be from the police department, she took a risk and answered. "This is Dr. Bailey."

"Dr. Bailey? Ann Bailey?" The springs of a chair squeaked as if the caller were shifting forward.

"That is correct."

"This is Paul Thompson. I'm working on a story about Elijah Weston."

"How did you get this number?" she asked.

"I'm good at what I do."

His arrogance scraped her nerves. "Good for you. Don't call me again."

"I want to talk. You name the time and the place. I have a few questions."

Ann hung up and then blocked the number. Her hands were trembling as she thought about Elijah Weston. She had known him in college, slept with him twice, and then, when he was charged with arson, she had testified against him.

Elijah had been out of prison a year, and not a week went by that she did not spot him at least once. He rarely approached her, but his mere presence was a message: *"I haven't forgotten. And you won't, either."*

The gym door burst open, and the ten kids, ranging in age from ten to thirteen, strolled outside. Some carried their backpacks, others dragged them, all with a tired but contented expression suggesting it had been a good day.

She did not see Nate immediately, and whenever he dallied, adrenaline rushed her body and her relaxed status switched to a full-blown red alert.

Her heart was fast-tracking to fifth gear when she saw her son making his way out of the building. He was sporting his new wire-rimmed glasses and a short haircut that was identical to his cousin Kyle's and uncle Gideon's. The combined effect made him look older than the ten-year-old boy standing in front of her.

He spotted her, raised his hand, and tossed her a halfway smile. Not the full-on grin he had a year ago, but not the dismissive smirk of a teenager.

Ann waved back and watched as the other boys hurried to their rides. A couple of twelve-year-olds, Roger and Ben, rushed up to speak to Nate, and her boy actually grinned. Then the boys looked toward Roger's mother, who shook her head no. There were some exchanged words between the trio, and then Nate nodded, adjusted his backpack, and headed toward Ann's car.

Her heart twisted. He opened the back door and tossed in his backpack.

"How did it go today?" she asked a little too brightly.

"Fine." He clicked his seat belt.

"Did you make your solar system presentation?" she asked.

"Yes." He pushed up his glasses and looked out the window.

"Want to get ice cream?"

"No. Did you get my fishing lures from the house?"

"I did. They're in the back."

He glanced over the seat at the bags of newly purchased items. "What about my globe from the house?"

"No, did you want it?"

"Yes. I told you that."

"I don't remember. Sorry."

"You didn't get it?" he challenged.

"I'll go by tomorrow."

"Why can't we go now?" He shifted his gaze, his eyes ripe with a dare.

"What's the rush?" she asked.

"What's the big deal?"

"What's with the attitude, kid?"

His shrug was not as surly as his defiance. "I told you—I wanted to see the house, Mom, but you went by without me. I'm not a baby."

"I didn't say you couldn't see it."

"Then let's go now." He cocked his head. "I want to get my globe."

"I have a house cleaner there now."

"How much mess can we make retrieving a globe?"

He was not arguing about a globe; he was asserting his need for closure. She'd thought that by going to the house alone, she was protecting Nate, but in reality, there was no foolproof way to do it.

"Okay, but we can't get in the cleaning lady's way."

Shock widened his eyes. "I thought you were going to fight me about seeing the house. I had arguments prepared."

She put the car in gear. "You'll have to save them."

"Why now? You haven't let me see the house at all in the last year."

"Might as well do it now. As soon as it's clean, it's going on the market."

He did not press about keeping the house or moving back in, which led her to believe he did not want it any more than she did. But still, he needed to say his goodbyes. "Okay."

She drove to the old house, wishing it were a hundred miles away. But in five minutes they were both parked in front of the residence. Maura's truck was in the driveway, the garage door was open, and it was filled with at least a dozen packed green garbage bags and another ten moving boxes filled with books, dishes, and lamps.

"She works fast," Ann said.

"I hope my globe is not in one of those trash bags."

Ann shut off the engine. "Let's go see."

Nate waited for her to come around the car, giving her some comfort that he was not fully grown up. They walked up the sidewalk and through the front door together. She was grateful that the graphite powder had been cleaned off, all the shades and windows in the house were open, and a cross breeze had chased away most of the staleness. In the kitchen, a portable radio blasted out a country-and-western song.

"Whose radio is that?" he asked.

"The lady who's cleaning the house." Ann rounded the corner and was relieved to see Maura wrapping the dishes from the cabinet in newspaper. "Maura?"

The woman turned quickly, as if she did not expect to hear her name. However, her smile was bright and welcoming. "Hey, Dr. Bailey."

"How's it going?" Ann asked.

"Slow and steady." Maura turned down the music. "I started in the foyer, moved to the closets, and then decided to tackle the kitchen. Good time of year to get kitchen items to the secondhand stores. New students are looking for dishes, plates, and lamps." She grinned at Nate, turned around, and produced a Superman cup. "Is there anything here you want me to save?"

Nate's eyes widened. "That's my favorite cup."

Maura handed it to him. "I thought it might be."

"It's okay if I keep it, right, Mom?" he asked.

"Of course, pal. That's why we're here. To retrieve whatever you want to keep."

"Okay. Thanks, Maura."

Maura's relaxed grin spoke to her laid-back demeanor. "You're welcome, Nate. Is there anything else you want?"

"My globe."

"Still on your desk," Maura said.

"Thanks." The boy hurried along the hallway, his thudding feet echoing behind him.

"I should have this room cleaned out and emptied today," Maura said. "I noticed you've left a lot of clothes, makeup, and jewelry behind. I did not bundle those up. Do you want any of that?"

"No. I packed what I wanted." The blue stoneware dishes Maura was wrapping reminded Ann of the day she and her late husband had bought them. Barely out of college and newly married, she'd been pregnant with Nate. She had been drawn to the color because it looked calming. Foolish reasons to choose everyday dishes, but she had needed something to settle her nerves, which had been on overdrive since the day she and Clarke had exchanged vows. Even then, her subconscious had recognized her mistake.

Ann rattled her keys in her hand, already anxious to leave. "Do you need anything, Maura?"

"Nope. All set."

"It all looks great. And thanks for wiping off the graphite."

"Figured it's not the kind of message to send to new buyers."

Ann braced for the questions that always followed, but when none came, she allowed some of the strain to bleed off. "Okay, I'll check on Nate."

"Sure."

As Ann moved along the hallway, she noticed the family pictures had been removed from the walls, leaving behind their shadowed imprints. She was not sure where Maura had put the portraits but was glad that they were not displayed for Nate to see. She found the boy in his room, standing at his desk and spinning the globe.

"It looks so much smaller," Nate said.

"You're bigger. A year is a long time." She leaned against the doorframe, determined not to rush him. This would be the last time they came into this house.

As the globe rattled on its axis below a Power Rangers poster, he opened a desk drawer and removed a wooden cigar box. He studied the contents.

"What's in the box?" Ann asked.

"Rocks. Dad always brought me back a rock when he traveled." He rooted around and removed a smooth black stone.

"Where's that one from?"

"San Diego. Dad was there for a conference in 2016."

Clarke had been a firefighter and arson investigator for the city. He often traveled out of state to seminars and conferences and had become one of the nation's leading experts on fire. Ann wondered what he would have said about the body she had seen on the ridge near Anaconda today.

"You should keep those," she said carefully.

"There's no fingerprint dust on the box."

"Fingerprint dust?"

"There was some on my window," he said. "Maura must have cleaned off the rest."

"She did," Ann said softly.

"You really think I should save the rocks?"

"Do you have good memories when you look at them?" she asked.

"I do."

"Then you should keep them." She laid her hand on his shoulder. "Your dad did love you very much, Nate. Never forget that."

Nate closed the box and tucked it under his arm and retrieved his Superman mug. "This is all I want."

"What about the globe?"

"It's not that accurate. The sizing of the countries is not as precise as it should be."

"We can get you a new one."

"Maybe."

When they reached the front door, Maura was carrying a box to the back of her truck. She waved to Ann and smiled.

Ann wanted to believe that life had shifted for the better. But as she looked at the house, she wondered if anyone could escape the past.

***

Elijah Weston stood across the street from the one-story house, watching Ann and her son get into their car. He tried not to follow her too much, but there were days when his curiosity was overwhelming. Today, he had come to see the Beech Street house, but he had lucked out and seen her and the boy.

He had first noticed her on campus as she raced across the front courtyard on a cool September day. He had been a freshman and she a senior. Leaves had caught in a gust of wind and swirled around her feet as her blond hair flew behind her like a golden wave. She had taken his heart that second, and despite a decade behind bars, he still loved her.

And the boy. He was growing so fast. He had to be an inch taller than he had been at the beginning of the summer.

As Ann backed out of the driveway, she glanced in her rearview mirror, seemingly making sure the boy had hooked his seat belt. But she let her gaze roam. She was always checking. Always vigilant. She drove off.

He was glad to see her cleaning out the Beech Street house and moving on. That was healthy. The reporters who had deluged the city after her husband died were gone, and the calm was returning to her world.

He lingered, watching the cleaning woman load up her truck with more boxes, and when she finally drove off, he glanced from side to side. It was five thirty in the afternoon, and most of the folks in this neighborhood were still at work. There were no unexpected cars in any of the driveways, hinting that someone might be home and available to see him.

He trotted toward the house and tried the front door, discovering it was unlocked. Grateful for the cleaning lady's sloppiness, he slipped inside and closed the door behind him.

After the police had finished their investigations in early winter, he had been tempted to slip into the house several times, but there had been too many reporters and too much curiosity about the house. Now he had it all to himself.

He had never been impressed by the rancher and did not picture Ann living here. But she had been young when she chose it. He wondered when her husband's frequent absences had turned into disquieting questions and unconscious worries. Had she sensed the depth of his evil? What had finally driven her out of this place?

He walked into the boy's room and smiled. The periodic table poster reflected the child's intelligence, whereas the Power Rangers poster and glow-in-the-dark stars on the ceiling marked his youth. The boy had chosen the Red Ranger, same as Elijah had as a boy.

Ann had done a good job with the child, and she had kept their little family afloat during the storm.

He spotted a globe on the desk and picked it up. It was not expensive, but the boy had scratched his initials in the plastic base. The sizing of the countries was incorrect in a charming way.

He turned to a dresser, where a comb stood tucked in a brush, as it must have for the last year. As he should have noted before, there were strands of hair on the brush. Scientists had tested DNA in hair follicles that dated back to the time of the caveman, meaning there had to be enough material here to get a full read on the boy's DNA.

Elijah pulled a plastic bag from his pocket. He had been drawn to the house because of Ann, but he had come prepared, hoping to find proof of the boy's paternity.

He put multiple strands of hair in the bag and tucked it in his pocket. Since he had first seen pictures of the boy, he had suspected the child was his. But his priority had been leaving prison, getting established, clearing his name, and suing the state of Montana for wrongful imprisonment. Now that he had both settlement money and a reputation that would mend over time, he could claim what was his.

He tucked the globe under his arm and moved into the room Ann had shared with Clarke. The mattress was askew, and several portions had been cut out of the tufted fabric by the forensic team, looking for samples.

He crossed to the dresser still sporting Ann's perfume bottles, raised the one with a butterfly glass top to his nose, and inhaled, imagining Ann dabbing it on her bare neck. He put the bottle in his pocket.

Outside a vehicle pulled up and a car door slammed. There would be time to return and see what else he could find. But for now he hurried to the back sliding door, opened it, and carefully closed it before jogging across the small patio and ducking into the woods. He would return soon.

CHAPTER FIVE

Missoula, Montana
Wednesday, August 18
6:15 p.m.

Bryce pulled up in front of Ann's new house in the quiet residential neighborhood. It was like many in Missoula. Brick, one story, surrounded by tall shrubs by the front windows. He assumed she was also in a good school district.

Out of the car, he grabbed the file box and strode toward the house. As he rang the bell, several loud thumps echoed inside. His hand slid automatically to his sidearm.

The front door snapped open to a flustered Ann. "Sergeant McCabe. Please come in."

Thump. Thump.

"What's that?" he asked, lowering his hand.

"It's my son. He's packing for his camping trip." She brushed back a strand of hair and stepped to the side. When he entered, she closed the door behind him. "The trip is four days, but in Nate's mind, it's a yearlong expedition."

He removed his Stetson, followed her around the corner, and found the boy sitting in the center of the living room rimmed in moving boxes. The kid sat cross-legged, surrounded by what looked like every stitch of clothing he owned. There were also several new fry pans, three flashlights, and a large bag of Twizzlers.

"Nate, this is Sergeant Bryce," Ann said.

The boy appeared to shift mental gears, stood up, and extended his hand. It might have been the last thing he wanted to do, but his mother's training ran deep.

Bryce took his hand and shook, discovering the kid had a strong grip. "Good to meet you, Nate."

"Yes, sir."

"Looks like you're headed on a big trip," Bryce said.

"It's a four-day camping trip with my uncle and cousin. And Joan. We leave in the morning."

Bryce could not picture city slicker Joan Mason camping when she regularly complained about the lack of restaurants and bars in Montana. Still, she was going, and in his book got an A for trying to make her relationship with Gideon and his family work.

"The weather is supposed to be nice," Bryce said.

"The temperatures will range from eighty-five to ninety degrees, and the skies will be partly cloudy," Nate said. "Zero percent chance of precipitation."

"A little cloud cover helps when you're near the water. Cuts the reflection."

"That's what Gideon says. What's in the box?" Nate asked.

"Files for your mom to look over."

"Let me take those," Ann said. "I'll set them in my office."

"Best to keep the lid on," Bryce warned.

"Understood."

As she stepped away, Bryce set his hat on an unopened box, rested his hands on his hips, and inspected what Nate had chosen. "How do you plan on transporting this?"

"I have two big suitcases. It'll be tight, but I'll make it work."

"How far in-country are you going?" Bryce asked.

"The cabin is seventy-one miles northwest of here." The boy stood back, also placing his hands on his hips.

Bryce shook his head, pretending to consider the value of the suitcases. "I never had much luck in the mountains of Afghanistan with a suitcase. The wheels kept getting stuck in the mud."

Nate arched a brow. "Is that a joke?"

"It is." When the boy continued to stare, he went on, "All right, I did not take a suitcase on the marches, but I sure did overpack my rucksack on the first expedition. Do that once, maybe twice, and you never forget." He plucked a backpack discarded to the side. "I can help, if you don't mind."

"I can barely get anything in that backpack."

"You might be surprised. Hand me those three shirts and two pairs of shorts. And I'll take six pairs of socks."

"Six?"

"A soldier has to take good care of his feet. Makes all the difference in the world."

"That's what Uncle Gideon said."

Bryce carefully folded the first shirt in half and then rolled it up into a tight cylinder. He handed the second shirt to Nate. "No sense in me doing all the work."

The boy copied Bryce, though he had to redo his roll twice to get it as small. Next the shorts were rolled, and the socks were turned over on themselves into snug balls. He lined the bottom of the pack with socks, pants, shirts, and underwear. "What shoes are you wearing?"

Nate pointed to a pair of worn sneakers. "And my hiking boots."

"Good choices." He skipped over the snacks and fry pan, knowing Gideon was always prepared, and grabbed a paperback. "*King Lear* by Shakespeare. That's mighty tough reading."

"It's not too bad, once you get used to it."

Bryce's knowledge of English literature was limited, but he remembered the basic theme: father betrayed by a child. "Never hurts to have a book. Hand me two of those flashlights."

Nate handed him the flashlights. Next came an empty gallon ziplock bag, which Bryce filled with bug spray, tissues, matches, an extra pocketknife, and sunscreen. By the time he had picked through the items, he had selected 5 percent of what Nate had hauled out.

As Bryce rose and hefted the pack, he judged the weight to be acceptable. Floorboards in the hallway creaked, and he knew Ann was watching. "Let's try it on."

Nate adjusted his glasses and eagerly fed his arms into the pack. The weight sat low on his back, so Bryce adjusted the straps until the pack supported his spine. "How does it feel?"

Nate walked around. "Not bad. Are you sure it's enough?"

"It's enough for five or six days, just in case."

Tugging at the shoulder straps, Nate asked, "How do you know so much about packing?"

"Fourteen years in the marines made me an expert. Like I said, once you've had to ruck two hundred pounds up a mountain, you lighten your load any way you can."

"How many times would you say you've packed like this?"

"Thousands."

Nate nodded slowly. "That's enough time to reach proficiency levels."

Bryce chuckled. "I'd say so."

"Mom!" Nate said.

"Yes?" She was leaning against the living room wall.

"I'm ready to go," Nate said.

"Looks like it," she said.

"Can I call Kyle?"

"Sure."

"I bet he's overpacked."

"Better check and see."

The boy left the room, easily shouldering the weight.

"Thanks," she said softly. "He wasn't listening to me."

"Don't take it personally."

"I get it. It's a father-son kind of thing." A sweet bitterness tangled around the words.

"Does he talk about his father much?"

"Not really." She ran long fingers through her hair and smiled. "But that's not what you came to talk about. The files are in my office. This way."

He followed her to a small room that was not much bigger than an extra-large closet. But she had managed to fit a tiny desk and computer in the corner and a compact couch behind her. Leaning against the wall was a large framed print featuring the sunrise over the eastern mountain range. Pencils, papers, magazines, and files were all neatly arranged, but he would have been surprised to find otherwise.

Ann removed the box top. "Is there anything I should be aware of?"

"Goes without saying, it's nothing you want the boy to see."

"I'll keep the office locked when I'm not here."

"Read through the officers' reports and the forensic files and give me your best theories. I'm trying to figure out who the hell this guy is and what's driving him."

"I'll get on it as soon as Nate goes to sleep."

"I appreciate it." When they were away from the chaos of the crime scene, his unasked questions turned more personal: How was she really doing? Had any more reporters tried to break into her university office or ambush her at the grocery store? And how was it going with the community at large? Had they rallied around or taken a step back, as many do to victims of violence? "You take care. Call if you need anything."

"Thank you."

Under the politeness, he sensed a rigid streak of independence. "I mean that. Call me if you need anything."

"You're kind. But I need to figure this one out alone."

He followed her to the front door, offered his thanks one last time, and then headed to his vehicle. Too bad Clarke Mead was dead. He should have been punished for murder and arson and the pain and suffering he had caused Ann. Death had robbed Bryce of the pleasure of seeing him rot behind bars.

***

I pin the top half of the delicate skin to the board and stretch the chin section as deftly as I can. I am not known for a subtle touch, but I am going slowly here. It is important to be careful. Meticulous. Still the skin, which is starting to dry out, is getting more difficult to handle.

I am getting better at all this. Practice does make perfect, as Mom used to say.

When all four corners are finally pinned, I wash my hands, dry them, and reach for the scalpel. If it were a deer hide, I would use a pressure washer and skim off the underlayer of fat and flesh with it. But human hide is more delicate and requires a subtle touch. Which, as I said, I do not have. But I have discovered a quiet, meditative quality in the work.

My blade picks up the pink flesh and gently pulls it away from the skin. Spray from a water bottle rinses away the blood. Next will come the salting and after that the tanning solution.

It's not a pretty process and would turn the stomachs of most who wear leather belts, shoes, or rawhide vests without a second thought. It's dirty work, but the end product—a prized trophy—is going to make big headlines one day.

I am excited about the coming attention my little crime spree is going to garner. You might think less of me for craving notoriety, but we all want to be famous. We might demur and insist we do not like the attention, but we all crave it.

I examine the taut skin, and satisfied, I grab wipes and wash my hands again. Restless, I remove a beer from the mini refrigerator and then dig a DVD from my backpack. I pop it in my computer and hit "Play."

The footage is not terrific. The lighting was terrible, and the focus went in and out. But there is enough to remind me of a special night.

The camera captures my hand reaching for the doorknob.

Twisting it, I slowly push open the door. The interior is dark, but I hear the scratching of feet and metal against wood.

I flip on the light switch, and the single bulb in the center of the room dangles from a wire and spits out enough light to illuminate the woman. I have stashed her in this small shed in the country because I have not found the courage to kill her yet. This is my second murder, after all. The first time happened in the heat of anger. No planning, no thinking. Now I am going to kill with intention, and it's daunting.

This place is not more than a hunting shack, and the structure is not sound. Still, there is a heavy wood-burning stove fixed to the floor that gives me an anchor for the rope securing her.

I hold up the grocery bag. "I brought you ginger ale like I promised."

She looks at me wild eyed. Her long hair is all tangled around her dirt-smudged face. She has cried a lot these last few days, but now is ominously silent.

I twist off the top and approach her. She flinches and does not reach for the soda.

"Go on and take it," I say. "It's real soda, not that diet stuff that tastes like chemicals."

Dark eyes cut to the bottle and then back to my face. The prey is summing up the predator, wondering whether fear is more powerful than thirst. Finally, grimy fingers wrap around the bottle, and she raises it with trembling hands to her mouth.

I am glad to see her enjoy the cool drink. As I have said before, my intent is never to hurt anyone. Causing pain is a needless cruelty, and seeing her like this reminds me I have to get on with it.

She gulps the last of the drink, swiping her moist lips with the back of her hand. "What are you going to do now?"

"Let you go. I told you I needed time to think."

"I want to go home."

"You will. Today."

"Why did you do this?"

"It doesn't matter." As I approach, she looks up at me with eyes filled with a blend of fear and hope.

I remove a knife from my pocket and open it. The blade glints in the moonlight seeping in through the cracked chinking sandwiched between the logs. She tenses and scurries back as far as her rope tether allows. "Are you really going to let me go?"

"I said I would."

"I know that look on your face."

Though curious about my telling expression, I ignore the comment. "You swore you wouldn't say anything, right?"

Her bobblehead nod is comical.

"See?" I say. "You and I have nothing to worry about."

Her lips falter into a smile. "Yes. Yes."

I reach for the rope. The soda will have given her some energy, and she is scared. Never underestimate scared.

She gazes up at my steady hands sawing the blade back and forth over the hemp. She nibbles her bottom lip and tries to remain still. As the rope frays, the stress in her body eases a little.

The soda and this new hope are my last gifts. No sense being mean.

Without hesitation I jab the blade into the side of her neck. The spray of blood tells me immediately that I have hit a big vessel. I dig the sharp edge deeper, and her body arches as pain and shock rocket through sinew and bone. I step back and take a seat in an old rusted lawn chair in the corner, knowing Mother Nature will take her course.

"No sense in fighting, Sarah," I say. "Lean into it. It'll be over before you know it."

Blood gurgles from her mouth, streams down her neck, and soaks her shirt. Her eyes transmit shock and then finally a resigned acceptance. When her eyes close, I sit for a moment, listening until her breathing slows to a stop.

Finally, I rise and press my fingertips to her neck. When I am certain she is dead, I cut the rope loose.

I watch the recorded image of my hands clumsily working around the contours of the woman's face. I botched that job, and by the time I was finished, there was nothing worth saving.

I made a lot of blunders that day, which I suppose is why I watch the video over and over. I am never going to make those mistakes again.

CHAPTER SIX

Missoula, Montana
Wednesday, August 18
10:15 p.m.

Ann had been staring at the gruesome images of the bodies found near Helena and now Anaconda for close to two hours. Classical violin played softly from her phone as she jotted more thoughts on a yellow legal pad already half-full.

According to Bryce's notes, there were no missing-person reports filed in any of the jurisdictions around the time of the murders or in the months since. However, the hypothesis that someone might have reported these people missing assumed the victims lived locally, which at this point she believed was not likely. They either were tourists or seasonal workers who were here today and gone tomorrow.

On a map she traced her finger along the interstate from Helena to Anaconda. "Are you headed south or southwest? Is this some kind of journey?"

Assuming the westward progression was correct, she theorized that this killer could be accustomed to working across county and possibly state lines. Many prolific serial killers had jobs that required travel. Truckers, salespeople, road crews. All were gone for extended periods of time, which gave the cover they required to hunt and kill. She pulled up Bryce's name on her phone and texted:

Ann: Have you fed these cases into ViCAP?

Bryce: Yes.

ViCAP was an FBI database of violent offenders, but the repository depended on local law enforcement submitting detailed questionnaires on the crimes they saw. Given that most officers were overworked and underpaid, this extra layer of paperwork often led to offenses not being tracked.

Ann: Killers evolve. What about bodies that were burned but not mutilated? Or mutilated but not burned.

Bryce: Thirteen fit that criteria. Six have been solved. Seven pending.

Ann: Where?

Bryce: East Coast.

Ann: Dates? Locations? Is there a directional pattern in any of the cases?

Bryce: Stand by.

A rustling sound had her looking over her shoulder. She expected to see Nate, but when she did not see the boy, she rose, phone in hand, and stepped into the hallway, glancing toward his room and the bathroom.

She peeked in his room and saw him lying curled on his side fast asleep. Quietly, she noted the gentle rise and fall of his chest and relaxed.

She moved to the front door and confirmed the dead bolt was locked. As she stood in the darkness, her heart foolishly pounded as she pushed back the curtains covering the front window.

Moonlight slashed across the yard and her car where she had left it hours ago. The trees swayed in a breeze. A cat howled and a dog barked. No signs of a reporter or that blogger Paul Thompson looking for an exclusive interview. Just the night, doing its thing.

"Nothing," she breathed.

Her phone chimed with a text, startling her. She let the curtain fabric slide from her fingertips.

Bryce: Two cases include stabbing and mutilation. One in Kansas and another in Knoxville, TN. Both victims were female. Both stabbed. Neither victim was burned but the Tennessee victim suffered significant postmortem facial mutilation indicated by marks on the skull. She vanished in May but her body wasn't found until early June.

Ann: Can you access the case files?

Bryce: Consider it done.

Floorboards creaked and she whirled around to see Nate. He stood in the middle of the hallway, dressed in blue pajamas that hit well above his ankles. His hair was sticking up as he knuckled his right eye.

"What are you doing, Mom?" He yawned.

"I heard a cat outside," she lied.

"That must be Whiskers. He belongs to the people across the street."

She did not bother to ask how he knew. Her kid had a talent for absorbing details. "What are you doing up?"

"I heard something outside."

"Maybe it was Whiskers," she said.

"What I heard didn't sound like a cat, Mom."

She stepped away from the window, laying a deliberately calm hand on his shoulder. "What did it sound like?"

"Footsteps."

She did not want to stoke his worries because of her active imagination. "There's a lot of wind out there tonight."

"I also know what wind sounds like." As they moved toward his bedroom door, he stopped. "I don't want to sleep in my bed tonight."

"Well, then you can doze on the couch in my office. I've a little more work to do."

"Okay." He rushed into his room, grabbed a blanket and pillow, and quickly brushed past her to claim the couch. He arranged his makeshift bed and opened a paperback.

"What are you reading?" she asked.

He held up the cover. "*King Lear*."

"Wow."

"That's what Bryce said when we packed it. But I dug it out so I could read it before bed. Have you ever read it?"

"Sure, in college." And never for fun.

He settled under the covers, and she tucked the edge close to his chin. "Did you like it?"

She dodged the question with another one. "What do you think of it?"

"I don't know. Weird."

She waited for more.

"Children play a part in their father's death. It's kind of odd."

The play struck too close to home. "Where did you get this book?"

"At computer camp. There was a big pile of books for free."

"Oh. Let me know if you want to talk about it."

"Okay."

She kissed him on the forehead and turned back to her desk, but found concentration impossible as she listened to him turn the pages, which grew slower and finally stopped. When she looked over her shoulder, he was asleep, the book resting on his chest.

As he slept, she searched for little hints of herself in his features. The shapes of his ears and feet were hers. His sense of humor was all Bailey, and until recently, she had attributed his intellect to herself. Clarke had been blessed with raw cunning, which had served him too well, but he was by no stretch a scholar. He never would have read a copy of *King Lear*.

Nate's intelligence now reached far beyond hers and Clarke's. Nate was reserved, he loved science fiction and fantasy, he did not enjoy crowds, and he obsessed over the arrangement of his bedroom. He had eaten the same cereal for breakfast for the last five years.

She had slept with two men in her life, Clarke Mead and Elijah Weston. She had been faithful to Clarke, but during their brief breakup in college, she'd had sex with Elijah twice. When she found out she was pregnant, she was certain the baby was Clarke's, and she had willingly returned to him.

She tipped her head back and thought about Elijah Weston. Even without a DNA confirmation, she acknowledged Nate and Elijah were carbon copies of each other. Anyone who saw Nate and Elijah together now could not miss the truth.

Outside, the wind whipped up, cracking tree branches that scraped against the side of the house. She gently picked up Nate's book, replaced the bookmark, and closed it.

Ann had protected her son from one monster. And now she worried there might be another circling close.

Elijah had not approached her about the boy, but it was a matter of time before he claimed his parental rights.

CHAPTER SEVEN

Missoula, Montana
Thursday, August 19
9:15 a.m.

The hustle to get Nate up, dressed, and ready for his camping trip had begun early, and by the time Ann had him fed and ready to go, her brother and Joan were approaching her front doorstep. Nate ran past Gideon and Joan to his cousin, Kyle, and the two boys chatted as if they had not seen each other in years.

Gideon, a homicide detective with the Missoula Police Department, was two years older than Ann. He had a tall, lean body with broad shoulders. His dark hair had turned salt and pepper, and the lines around his eyes had deepened more in the last couple of years. Joan was short, petite, fit, and for as long as Ann could remember, had walked with a cop's confidence.

Gideon hugged Ann. "Ready to go it alone?"

"I'm not sure about me, but Nate's been ready for days," Ann said.

"You can always come with us," Joan said.

"I'll be fine. There's still a lot to get done here at the house and prep for the new school year. And I'm attending the autopsy of Jane Doe today."

"I hate to miss it," Joan said.

"I told you to stay behind," Gideon offered.

"No, the whole point of this fresh start is not to let the job drive my life. I'm camping with you boys."

Gideon winked at her. "It'll be fun."

Joan shook her head. "From your lips to God's ears."

Gideon looked at Ann. "Come with us. All this can wait. You can read the autopsy report later."

Since Ann had stepped onto her first crime scene, the thrill of the hunt had infected her blood. "No, camping is your thing. Never was it mine." She handed him Nate's pack.

Gideon hefted it. "Is this all? The way he was talking, I thought I'd have to hitch the trailer on the back of the truck."

"Sergeant McCabe dropped off files for me yesterday. He helped Nate prioritize."

"I hear you held your own at the crime scene yesterday," Gideon said.

"I'm fascinated by the case," Ann admitted.

When Gideon looked as if he would argue, Joan nudged him. "We need to get going. And your sister will be fine."

"I won't be within cell service range, so if you need anything, call the station," he said. "Officer Smyth will be on call this week."

"I'm fine, really." She turned him around and gave him a gentle shove toward the boys, who were in the back seat, belted in and ready to go.

Gideon and Joan settled into the truck. Her brother tossed her one last worried look, and she scrounged for one last smile before he pulled away. She stood on the porch, waving as she watched the vehicle vanish around the corner. When it was gone, a breeze caught the ends of her hair, conjuring memories of last night's noises, which had not been Whiskers or the wind.

She walked around the side of the house toward Nate's bedroom window. There were a few sticks, likely culled in the wind, but nothing out of the ordinary. She tugged on the lower sash and discovered it was indeed locked.

As she turned, she felt a little foolish until she spotted a flicker of silver glimmering in the mulch bed. She knelt and picked up what looked like a chewing gum wrapper folded into the shape of an airplane.

Ann stepped back, held it up to the light, and studied the sharp, clean angles. As tempted as she was to crush it, she carried it into the kitchen. She carefully set it on the windowsill and poured coffee into a paper cup. As she sipped, she stared at the tiny plane that honestly should not have been threatening in the least. But it had been under her son's window, and the precision folds and razor-sharp angles reminded her of Elijah.

Ann set down her cup. "It could have been left by a contractor or the real estate agent." As the possibilities swirled, she realized she needed to get out of the house and clear her head.

She quickly brushed her hair, pulled it up into a sleek ponytail, and then put on lipstick to brighten her lips. She moved back into her office and stared at the case files she had carefully tucked away after she had guided Nate back into his room last night.

She had glimpsed the crime scene yesterday, but with all the controlled chaos of the police personnel, coupled with the shock of seeing the body, she had not processed as many details as she could have.

She laced up her hiking shoes, stuffed her credentials and cell into a cross-body purse, and headed out the front door, which she locked and then double-checked.

The drive to the crime scene was uneventful. She parked on the gravel road, tugged on a hat over her aviator sunglasses, and followed the grass path beaten by the forensic team and police up to the spot where the body had been found.

The rain three nights ago had washed over the grass and softened the brittle brown with lighter shades of green. The Montana grasslands were clever. In drought they went dormant and waited, patient and silent, under cloudless skies. And when the rains came, they soaked up the moisture and rejoined the living until the next drought.

The police estimated that the murder had occurred here after the rains. Was that a calculated choice by the killer, or was it merely an accident of time?

She looked back toward the path and noted the flecks of white plaster that remained where technicians had taken tire and shoe impressions. Luckily, given the trampling in the dark, the first responders had not destroyed those forensic details.

Ann ducked under the yellow tape and stood at the edge of the blackened grass. Setting the body on fire had many strategic advantages. It masked the victim's identity and destroyed evidence. And the removal of the victim's clothes, if not related to a sexual fetish, was another way to delay identification. Why draw attention to a body that would be difficult to identify?

DNA had been extracted from the back molars of the last victim and was at the state lab now for testing. If the DNA was not found in a database, it could be used for reverse genealogy, which had been a critical tool in recent years and had helped solve several high-profile serial murders. Conceivably, genealogists could backtrack through public ancestry sites and identify the victim. But that took time, money, and resources. Perhaps, if authorities did not make identifications soon in the first and second cases, mapping might be an option.

She rose, moved to the steep hillside, and looked toward the valley, allowing the wind to push against her. Tuesday's moon had been at half strength, and the lights from the small town below would have winked like gems. Was this location important to the killer or random?

As she turned to leave, she spotted what looked like a narrow path and, in the distance, the flicker of white paper. Adjusting her purse, she made her way slowly down the mountainside. Several times small rocks rolled out from under her feet, and she struggled to catch her balance. Each time she looked back, she visually retraced the steep path and questioned whether this was wise.

Drawn by the paper, she half stepped, half scooted over the loose rock until she reached it. Squatting, she realized it was a Polaroid picture. It was rumpled and dirty, but there was no missing the smiling young woman's face staring back at her. She looked up the hill and thought about the body she had viewed yesterday. Was this her?

The gravel on the steep grade slid under her feet, and before Ann could react, she fell backward and hit hard on her backside. She had to dig in her heels to stop herself from tumbling over the side.

When she came to a complete stop, she sat still for several moments as her heart rammed against her ribs. No one knew she was up here. She had no cell service, and a fall would put her in life-threatening trouble.

She could picture the headlines now: CRAZED WIDOW PLUNGES OFF SIDE OF ANACONDA MOUNTAIN.

As her adrenaline spiked, she searched for the Polaroid image. At first, she thought she had lost it, but then she caught sight of the white corner. It was trapped in the grass. She carefully leaned over and picked it up.

Pinching the paper between her fingers, she inched her way up the hill, moving slowly and avoiding loose rock. The return climb took three times as long as the descent, and when she reached the top of the hill, she lay back on the grass until her nerves settled.

Rising, she allowed herself one last look at the surrounding area and the crime scene. Why this place? She did not know. Yet.

Her hands were both scraped raw, but instead of dwelling on an injury she could not fix here, she hurried toward her car. Relief washed over her when she reached the vehicle.

From her glove box, she removed a plastic shopping bag, which, like napkins and wipes, she kept stocked because, well, you never knew when you might need one. She carefully placed the picture in the bag and laid it on the passenger seat.

The engine started easily, and the rush of cool air-conditioning felt good against her skin. She grabbed a wet wipe from the glove box and cleaned off the dirt as best she could. The deep scrapes burned, but they were a small price to pay for the picture.

She drove a mile before she checked her phone. It would not be like Nate to call three hours into his own adventure, but better to know. No calls from Nate but two from Bryce.

She hit "Redial," and he picked up on the second ring. "Hey, sorry I missed your call. I was out of cell service."

"Did you go on the camping trip with Nate?" Bryce asked.

"No. I hiked up to the crime scene." She stopped at a T intersection, looked both ways, and took a left toward the interstate.

"Not the best place to be alone."

She could have made a statement about independence and her ability to make sound decisions, but her aching palms said otherwise. "I did find something. A Polaroid picture."

"Of what?"

"A woman's face."

"The crime scene went over every square inch of that site."

"It was down a pathway."

"They hiked until it was too steep to continue."

She flexed her left hand and frowned at the traces of dirt still embedded in her scrapes. "Not that steep."

"Yeah, that steep. Are you okay?"

"Of course. I grew up climbing these foothills."

He sighed. "I'm headed into Missoula now and about an hour out. The medical examiner is ready to do the autopsy. Do you still want to attend?"

The memories of the burned, mutilated body rushed her. "I'll see you in an hour."

CHAPTER EIGHT

Missoula, Montana
Thursday, August 19
1:30 p.m.

Bryce leaned against the side of the forensic science building, watching the parking lot for Ann's vehicle. When she pulled up, he was pleased and relieved. She did not need his permission, but he had not liked her being at the crime scene alone.

As she rose out of the car, he noticed her lipstick looked fresh and hair just combed. There was also a faint swath of dirt along her right pant leg.

He considered holding back a comment, then did not. "You fell on the hill."

"The rocks can be slippery. No big deal." She held up a shopping bag. "Not exactly an evidence bag, but I put the picture in here."

He looked in the bag. "Where was this?"

"About a hundred and fifty yards from the top."

As he pulled a fresh evidence bag from his pocket, he noted the red scrapes on her hands. He was not her boss, her brother, or her anything, and it was not his place to lecture.

She gingerly pinched the edges of the paper and dropped it in his bag. "It's been in the elements, so it's pretty beaten up. But you can see the picture of a woman. She might be the victim."

He studied the image and snapped a picture of it with his phone. "I'll turn it over to forensics." His tone remained even. "How are the hands?"

She involuntarily flexed them. "A reminder to be more careful."

He opened the door to the medical building and waited for her to pass. Removing his hat, he showed his badge to the guard at the front desk, and the two took the elevator down to the basement floor.

"Dr. Christopher is waiting for us," he said. "He should have the body prepped and ready to examine."

"Right."

"Are you sure you're up for this?"

"I'll be fine. Any luck on those files from Kansas and Tennessee?"

"They're on the way. Too big to fax, so each jurisdiction overnighted them. Should be here first thing tomorrow."

"I know the cases aren't identical, but killers learn as they go. They evolve. The first time is usually planned over a long time, but the killer is also inexperienced, and the killing doesn't always go as expected. Afterward, the offender generally evaluates his work. What could he have done better? How could he avoid mistakes in the future? Should he have chosen a different victim?"

"He's doing a mission debriefing."

"Exactly." When the elevator doors opened, she stepped into the hallway. "What's the timeline on those cases back east?"

"Kansas was last October and Knoxville in May," he said.

"If we're assuming the two cases are connected, Kansas to Knoxville is a west-east direction," she said to herself.

"What's that have to do with it?"

"Nothing yet. Just a theory that the killer could be moving west. I could be wrong."

"Regarding the Kansas case, the victim was a sex worker, and the primary suspect is her pimp. He cut her face before he killed her. The Knoxville case involved a local Realtor. She went missing for ten days, and when her body was discovered, the medical examiner noted the facial mutilation was done postmortem."

"Dr. Christopher made a similar comment about the Helena victim in his autopsy notes. He noted the straight lines of the blade."

"The body in Knoxville wasn't burned, and the victim was identified by her clothes and jewelry. Maybe he's learned a few tricks along the way," he said. "Assuming the killer is connected to the Knoxville case, he arrived right at the beginning of tourist season, when out-of-state plates often go unnoticed."

"Careful and meticulous," she offered. "He doesn't appear anxious to stop."

Bryce frowned as she echoed his worries. "Then we stop him."

She tucked a strand of hair behind her ear and followed him into the locker room outside the autopsy suite. As he gowned up, he glanced toward her as she dutifully turned off the ringer on her cell phone and placed it in her purse hanging in a locker. She slid into her gown quickly, and he handed her gloves.

As she gingerly worked her fingers into the gloves, he noticed the scrapes and gashes on her palms. A fall in a location like that was a fast track to ending up a statistic. But again, not his place to say.

"I can hear you thinking," she said.

"Really?"

"It wasn't smart to go up there alone." She winced a little as the glove's thin skin settled on one of the deeper wounds.

"No, it was not."

Her gaze held a mixture of defiance, independence, and maybe a little relief that he was not lecturing. It did not take a big stretch to imagine how her late husband would have handled this. He had worked with Clarke Mead once on an arson case. Bullish, determined, and focused, Mead had a tendency to lecture. Though Bryce was willing to bet that Ann had gone toe to toe with him more than once.

She was the first to the door and held it for him. Nodding his thanks, Bryce passed into the sterile tiled room perfumed with the faint scent of chemicals and charred flesh.

A sheet-draped gurney butted against a chrome sink-counter combo that was the medical examiner's workstation. Beside the gurney was an instrument table holding a closed packet of sterilized tools. Soft classical music played from a speaker on the shelf above the sink.

Ann knitted her fingers together, her gaze magnetized on the draped body. "Doesn't look like there's much left."

"Hopefully more than the killer planned on leaving," Bryce said.

Swinging doors opened. Dr. Christopher was a tall, lean man in his late thirties who wore a tie-dye surgical cap and light-blue scrubs. He was a graduate of the Yale School of Medicine and had relocated to Missoula in his late twenties. Etched lines around his eyes and mouth were the mark of a man who spent his off hours in the sun, working a small ranch outfitted with a collection of cattle, horses, and chickens.

"Doc," Bryce said. "How's the posse back at the ranch?"

"All doing well. The calves born in the spring are thriving. I hear you've got a herd as well."

"As a matter of fact, we are about to get a new addition to the herd, Venus. She's five or six."

Dr. Christopher smiled as he shook his head. "I've got to hand it to your brother. That's a hell of an undertaking."

"Dylan doesn't mind four-legged creatures. It's the two-legged ones that frustrate him."

"Dr. Bailey," Dr. Christopher said, extending his hand. "This is new for you."

Her grip was firm, and she gave no indication her hand was tender. "It's the theme in my life."

"Still out at your folks' place?" he asked.

"No. Nate and I moved into town about two weeks ago."

"Just in time for the school year," Dr. Christopher said.

"That's the plan."

Dr. Christopher's easy banter softened the worry lines on Ann's face as she followed the doctor toward a large computer screen. Bryce had been to his share of autopsies, but he was still shocked by what a human could do to another.

"First, let's look at the X-rays." Dr. Christopher pressed several keys, and the image of a human skeleton appeared. "As you can see, the victim suffered no broken bones during her murder, but about ten years ago, she suffered an ankle fracture. There is a plate in place, which I'll remove during the autopsy and determine if there's a serial number."

"That might help with a faster identification," Bryce said.

"It might. Any luck with the first victim?" Dr. Christopher asked.

"None," Bryce said.

Dr. Christopher indicated three different marks angled on the underside of the breastbone. "These marks on the rib cage were made by the murder weapon. I believe the knife was a long narrow blade with smooth edges."

"How can you determine the knife size?" Ann asked.

"I can't exactly," Dr. Christopher said. "But I can say a larger hunting knife, say with a serrated edge, would have left a different mark."

"How many times was she stabbed?" Ann asked.

Dr. Christopher switched screens to a photograph taken of the body. "I'd say five times. I'll know better when I open her up, but I believe this cut," he said, pointing to the largest on the left side, "was her last, and it finished her off. Even if she had been close to a hospital emergency room, she wouldn't have survived."

"How do you know it's the last cut?" Ann asked.

Dr. Christopher swiped to another image. "You'll notice a small triangle of metal on the underside of the breastbone. I'd say that's the tip of your murder weapon. If he continued to stab with the damaged blade, the shape of the cuts would have varied."

Ann leaned closer, studying the image with a keen curiosity. "I would think she would have had time to see the knife coming."

"It's easy to underestimate the speed of a knife blade," Bryce said. "Cops are trained to follow the Twenty-One-Foot Rule when dealing with an offender armed with a knife."

"Meaning?" she asked.

"In the time it takes the officer to identify the threat, draw his weapon, and fire, the offender can travel twenty-one feet and deliver a lethal thrust of a knife."

"If the picture I found is the victim," she said, "it suggests she was acquainted with her killer."

"That's an interesting point," Dr. Christopher said. "All the wounds are angled upward. If the killer had been rushing directly at her, it's likely the slashes would have been downward." He raised and lowered his arm to illustrate.

"A well-placed knife jab isn't easy," Bryce said. "The target is often moving and fighting back. Does she have any defensive wounds?"

"No," Dr. Christopher said.

"Over fifty percent of murdered women are killed by an acquaintance or an intimate partner," Ann said.

Killing via knife was messy. Blood spatter often sprayed the attacker, surrounding walls, and ground. Blood also could embed into the knife handle's crevices and remain despite a careful cleaning. That, combined with a broken tip, meant it would not be hard to link the weapon to the crimes if and when Bryce found it.

As the doctor motioned them toward the body, each donned masks and protective eye gear. A medical technician, Jessica Leonard, entered the room. In her late fifties, Jessica had salt-and-pepper hair and olive skin. She was a fourth-generation Montana native and a retired emergency room nurse.

"We've drawn blood and sent it off for drug testing," she said.

"Results will take a few weeks," Dr. Christopher said. "The July victim's toxicology results came back late yesterday. No drugs in her system, but she had a high blood alcohol count."

Jessica opened the instrument packet and then removed the sheet draped on the body. The remains were blackened, twisted, and the limbs had grown rigid from rigor mortis. What remained of the victim's hands and feet had contracted inward, and the victim's hair had been scorched off. The face was barely recognizable as human.

They all went silent, and Bryce was aware that Ann's breathing had grown shallow. As tempted as he was to offer words of encouragement, there was little he could say to soften this blow. She would have to gut this one out, as all cops did during their first autopsy.

The doctor ran his gloved finger along the blackened and cracked skin of the right biceps. "If you look closely, you'll see the remains of a sleeve tattoo. The technician took multiple pictures, so hopefully we'll be able to digitally enhance it."

"Smells like the killer doused her body pretty good with accelerant," Bryce said.

"I can't imagine carrying gallons of gasoline up to that spot," Ann said. "Could the killer have transported the gas up earlier?"

"Very possible," Bryce said. "Or maybe he had the victim carry them."

"Did you find the accelerant containers?" Ann asked.

"No." The only solid clue Bryce had now was the bent and twisted photo Ann had found. He would drop it off with the forensic department as soon as they left here. It was a long shot, but it could not be ignored.

The doctor walked around the body, taking time to conduct a visual inspection, which revealed no shadows of ligature marks or additional injuries.

Jessica set down her camera and worked the limbs until the rigor broke up and the muscles and sinew loosened, allowing mobility in the joints. She then placed her hands on the body's curled shoulders, pressing gently until they lay flatter against the gurney.

With the body now more fully supine, the doctor made incisions on either side of the breastbone and then over the rib cage and the abdomen. The Y cut made, he peeled back the dark flesh to reveal the pink-gray underside.

Bryce homed in on Ann's blank expression. He could read her no better than when she'd been wearing the mirrored sunglasses at the crime scene. However, her deliberate, slow in-and-out breaths suggested a struggle behind the cool, detached facade.

With the media on her tail most of last year, she could have remained sequestered on her parents' ranch or left town for good. But not only had she stayed—she was here, facing what he guessed were some of her own demons.

The doctor reached for large bolt cutters and snapped each of the ribs. The rib cage, the body's natural armor for vital organs, was finally freed, and he lifted the arching bones and cartilage as one unit and set it on a tray Jessica held out.

Bryce had stood at many autopsies and witnessed all manner of trauma—organs lacerated by a knife blade, a liver or gut chewed up by a hollow-point bullet, bones crushed by blunt-force trauma, or body cavities discolored and swimming in pools of poisoned blood. This was the second time he had seen internal organs cooked and shriveled.

The doctor pointed to a darkened mass. "This is the liver, and as you can see, it's been sliced several times. The victim would have bled out in minutes." He shifted his attention to the victim's heart. "The knife blade nicked it slightly."

"She was inches from her killer when he struck," Ann said. "Jane Doe was comfortable with him."

Dr. Christopher continued the examination, removing the heart and then the lungs, which showed no signs of smoke inhalation. That suggested the fire had been set postmortem. The doctor extracted contents from her stomach. "She had a hamburger and fries within ten to twelve hours of her death."

"There are a couple of fast-food establishments in Anaconda that serve burgers," Bryce said.

"Maybe someone will remember her, assuming the killer didn't purchase the food," Ann said.

Without comment, the doctor shifted his attention to the skull and traced his finger along the top of the forehead. "Note the scalpel marks along what would have been the hairline," he said. "And also notice that the lines are neat and straighter than the last."

"Practice makes perfect," Ann said.

"This killer appears to be a quick study," Dr. Christopher said. "His work was not as clean on the Helena victim."

"But we are definitely dealing with the same guy?" Bryce asked.

"Unofficially, I'd say it's the same guy," Dr. Christopher said. "Note the way the scalpel imprint hooks sharply around the ear toward the cheekbone. It was the same in both cases. It's an unintentional pattern or tell."

The autopsy continued for another hour. The doctor confirmed the victim had not been sexually assaulted, and there appeared to be no signs of torture. He removed the plate from her ankle and wiped it. "I'll have to clean it up to get the full serial number. I'll track it."

"Anything else?" Bryce asked.

Dr. Christopher shook his head as he looked at the body. "Until her death, Jane Doe had been a healthy young woman."

"Thanks, Doc," Bryce said.

"Yes, thank you," Ann added.

Bryce met Ann in the changing room and noted she was quick to strip off her gown. Pulling off her gloves appeared painful, and he bet the latex had stuck to her wounds and was taking fresh skin with it. However, she did not complain and carefully, as if to prove she was fine, removed her purse from the locker.

Neither spoke as they made their way through the building's lobby. He pushed open the main door, and he followed her into the bright sunshine. The air smelled sweet and pure.

"You okay?" he asked.

"When Gideon said he was taking Nate camping, I pictured a movie, wine, maybe reading a book for pleasure. I was thrilled because I don't think I've had a moment to myself in a couple of years."

He did not respond, letting her coiled emotions unwind.

She cleared her throat. "However, I can't imagine doing any of those things now. As tragic as I find this case, I also find it fascinating."

"Really?"

"It's one thing to read journals and theorize about killers in a sterile office, but it's another to see, smell, and touch their handiwork." A faint smile tipped the edges of her lips. "I wonder what that says about me."

"Maybe you're more cop than scientist. Do you have conclusions?"

"I do." She went silent, as if ordering her thoughts and assessments. "I don't believe this killer was motivated by the fire. As we know, there are offenders who are sexually and mentally stimulated by flames. This killer used the fire to both destroy the victim's identity and, as we have theorized, attract attention."

"Go on."

"The fatal cuts were to the heart and liver. The killer was standing close and thrust the knife upward quickly. She bleeds out in a manner of minutes. It's quick and efficient. No signs of sexual assault, no broken bones, no apparent trauma that would have caused excessive pain. The killer was not motivated by the victim's suffering."

"What juices his batteries?" Bryce asked.

"Perhaps the victims look like someone familiar to the killer, such as a mother, wife, or girlfriend. The killer may or may not have stopped to analyze his motivations, but he keeps killing because the act is fulfilling." She stared up at him. "All theory at this point."

"Killer male or female?"

"Ninety percent of serial killers are male. But ten percent means a female is possible."

"Local or passing through?"

"When I see the files of the Kansas case and especially the Knoxville case, I might know better."

"Do you have theories regarding the removal of the face?" he asked.

"Our faces are a big part of our identity. All you have to do is look at social media. Destroying the victim's face is stealing something very intimate."

"The picture you found doesn't appear to be a selfie. And it can't be posted."

"Maybe that's exactly why the killer used a Polaroid camera. The images mark the event, but they are untraceable. He likely has pictures of his Helena victim."

"The pictures are also trophies?" Bryce asked.

"Yes. That's one of the easiest prizes to collect," she said.

"I'll deliver the picture to the lab now, and then I'll head into Anaconda, visit the burger joints, and determine if anyone saw Jane Doe." He nodded toward her hands. "How are they doing?"

She held them up and gave him a view of her palms. "They sting, but I'll survive."

They were scraped raw, and the right hand had a gash. "Damn. I have a first aid kit in my car."

"They'll be fine."

He shook his head. "It'll take five minutes to clean them and put on ointment. Car's right here."

The expected argument did not materialize, and she walked with him to his SUV. He opened the back hatch and reached for a red first aid tackle box he always kept stocked. Since the marines, he had been a stickler for having his kit ready.

He tore open a packet of cleansing wipes and motioned for her to extend her palms. She did, looking a little chagrined. Her uneasy expression vanished as soon as the pad touched her flesh. She hissed, and she tried to draw her hand back, but he held it steady, feeling the rapid beat of her heart thrumming in her wrist.

"That's the worst of it," he said as he carefully wiped around the largest of the gashes.

"Serves me right. If Nate had done something like that, he'd be in time-out until he was thirty."

"Thirty? That's mighty harsh."

"Maybe, but it was stupid, and I'd hate to see him do something like that on this camping trip."

"Gideon will keep a close eye."

"You're not saying anything I haven't told myself one hundred times since they left. He needs to get out and enjoy himself. He needs to be a kid."

He discarded the wipe and opened a second, and this time she raised her other hand without prompting. This palm was not as badly scraped as the first.

He smoothed antibiotic cream on her palms, careful to hit all the spots, before he replaced the cap. "Good as new. Do you have antibiotic cream at home?"

"I'll grab some at the store this afternoon. I'm still stocking the new place."

He handed her the tube. "Take this."

"Not necessary," she said.

"If you buy new cream, give it back to me. If you don't, you're covered."

"You've done first aid before," she said.

"When you command young men in the field, you've got to be ready for anything." He shook his head, a grin tugging his lips. "They're pros at finding ways to get hurt."

"Do you miss commanding men?"

"Sometimes. Keeping up with that many eighteen- to twenty-year-old soldiers is a younger man's game."

"What about the travel?"

"For the most part, I'm right where I want to be."

"Good."

"And you?"

"Me?"

"None of my business, but I'm surprised you stayed in town after last year."

She reached for her sunglasses. "This is my home. Nate's home. And I don't scare easily."

"No, ma'am, I don't believe you do."

"You'll call me if you pull a print off that photo."

"You'll be the first," he said.

***

Elijah Weston stood in the unfurnished home that smelled of fresh paint and pine cleaner. As he crossed the glistening hardwood floors of the living room, his footsteps drifted up toward a vaulted ceiling with faux beams. The fireplace was not large and was covered in a veneer of stone, but it was impressive to look at. The kitchen was not the eat-in kind, but it was a hell of a lot bigger than the small, greasy kitchenette of his mother's trailer and the cramped 1970s avocado-green version at the halfway house. The gleaming windows let in lots of natural light, and the wide patio doors looked out onto a lush backyard that was enclosed by a white privacy fence.

"What do you think, Mr. Weston?" the Realtor asked.

Her name was Sue or maybe Susan, and she lingered by the open front door. Curiosity combined with traces of fear, suggesting the desire to make money warred with the temptation to run away from the town's convicted arsonist.

Sue or Susan knew as well as most in town that he had sued the state of Montana for wrongful imprisonment. The state, instead of taking the case to trial, had settled for $2 million. The monetary payout may have seemed large, but given that he had spent a decade in prison, it felt paltry. As much as he wanted to fight the state and bloody its nose, he'd opted to take the money. Time to get on with living.

"I will buy it," Elijah said.

"Buy it?" she asked.

"Time to invest."

"Do you want to discuss financing?" she asked.

"It'll be a cash offer."

"Seller is asking five hundred and twenty thousand dollars."

"I'll pay four hundred and eighty thousand if they agree to sell it to me by close of business today."

"That's forty thousand off asking. Will you negotiate?"

"The house has been on the market sixty-one days, which in this town is a lifetime. It'll cost me at least fifty thousand to bring the house into this century, and given that the seller has removed the furniture, I'd say he is already on to his next property. Do you want to put in the deal, or do you want me to find someone else who will?"

"No, I can do it," Sue/Susan said quickly. "I'll draw up the papers right now."

"Perfect." He turned his attention to the backyard. There were trees to be cut and weeds to be pulled, but the idea of being outside appealed to him. Being in a box had created a new addiction to sunshine.

"Why this house?" the Realtor asked. "Single men don't usually move into suburban neighborhoods."

"It's an excellent school district, and there's a large yard that backs up to woods. When it's renovated, I can flip it for thirty percent more."

Her face relaxed, as he had expected it would. He had fed her the explanation that she needed to hear. It would also be the story she would tell her friends.

The truth was, he had chosen the house for one simple reason.

It was close to Ann and Nate.

CHAPTER NINE

Missoula, Montana
Thursday, August 19
7:15 p.m.

What was it about the victims that had drawn the killer?

The question rumbled in Ann's mind as she walked toward her front door, carrying two shopping bags. She had finally made it to the home goods store and bought the rest of what she needed. What was not in stock the cashier had ordered online, which meant she should have her items in a couple of days. That suited her. She had no desire to spend the evening unpacking dishes.

A soft breeze brushed her skin as she fished in her purse for her keys, which had already sunk to the bottom. Her fingers finally brushed the metal, and she quickly unlocked the door.

Tonight, she would chill. Have a glass of wine. Heat up the to-go meal from a small Italian restaurant and think about the two murder cases that would not leave her alone. She flipped on the lights and tunneled through the room between the unpacked boxes. *It takes time to make a house a home,* she reminded herself. Rome was not built in a day.

She set her bags on the kitchen counter. The pasta dish went in the microwave, and she twisted the wine bottle top off with a quick turn.

She filled a paper cup with the red and, after a sip, determined it was passable. Moving around the first floor, she closed all the curtains and shades. Other than the school district, the instant privacy of the existing drapes had been a big selling point for the house.

Her phone buzzed with Maura's number. Grateful for the distraction, she answered, "Maura, how's it going?"

"It's great. I found a few items at the Beech Street house I thought you might like to have. Can I stop by?"

"Sure." What did this near stranger think was important to her? "I'll text you my address."

Fifteen minutes later, headlights swept across her front window as the cleaner parked behind her car. Ann set her wine down and opened the door to see a smiling Maura carrying a box. "Come on inside."

"Great." Maura stepped into the foyer, her gaze sweeping the barren room. "I thought you might like these. They seemed personal."

"Set them on the kitchen counter. I'll go through them later."

"I have the truck loaded, and I'm headed to the charity center. If you have a quick look, I'll haul off what you don't want."

She could not imagine wanting anything. It was all she could do to save what she did. "You don't have to wait."

"Honestly, it'll be more efficient if you have the time to do this now. I've done enough of these moves and know the faster you can get through miscellaneous items, the better. They have a tendency to clutter our lives."

That was why she had left them behind. "Can I pour you a glass of wine?"

"Yeah, sure. It's been a long day."

"Does red suit?"

"Always."

Ann filled a paper cup and handed it to Maura. "No glassware yet."

"Thanks." Maura held up the cup. "I have boxes full of real glasses in the truck. I can bring them in now."

"No, I don't want them. Making a clean break, if you know what I mean."

"I hear you. I'm on a journey of self-discovery myself." She took a sip of wine.

Ann held up her cup. "Here's to one foot in front of the other."

Maura gently tipped her paper cup toward Ann. "Amen."

Ann peered in the box, and her gaze went directly to a small teddy bear. Nate had named the bear Montana Mac, and it had been his favorite when he was four or five. Guilt jabbed her as she wondered how she could have left Montana Mac behind. "Where did you find this?"

"It was in the kitchen in one of the lower cabinets. I figured it was a favorite hiding place."

She straightened the bear's black, off-kilter nose. "The bottom kitchen cabinet was Nate's space. He used to pretend it was a spaceship."

"He and his little buddy must have been on a trip when he forgot about him."

When Ann had made the decision to move out, she had done it quickly, fearing if she thought too much, she would change her mind. She had packed some of her clothes and Nate's and driven straight to her parents' ranch. In all the confusion, Nate had never asked about Montana Mac or, if he had, the request had been lost in the noise of her own guilt and worry. "Thanks, Maura. Good save. What else do you have?"

"Silver pieces that look like they belong in the family."

"No. Yard sale finds. They can go."

Maura rummaged in the box. "Earrings in the kitchen drawer. Look like real pearls."

A gift from Clarke. "No, they can go."

Maura looked a little surprised but kept going through the box. There was a small photo album featuring all Nate's visits to Santa. In the first he was eleven months, but in the second, at twenty-three months, he had learned stranger danger and would have nothing to do with the big guy in the red suit. Clarke had offered to hold him, and the photographer, who had dozens of children waiting, had snapped a picture of a stressed-out Santa and a grinning Clarke holding a red-faced Nate.

In the end, she kept the photos and the bear, but everything else she let go. "Thanks, Maura."

"Sure, no problem."

"Would you like to visit?" Ann offered. "I don't have much yet, but I have pasta I'm heating up, and we can eat on the couch in the living room."

Maura checked her watch. "The charity center closes in an hour, but the truck is covered with a tarp, so it can sit until morning."

Each settled on either end of the couch with a paper cup of wine and a bowl of penne pasta covered in marinara sauce.

"This is amazing pasta," Maura said.

"It's from a little out-of-the-way place called Tony's. When I want to treat myself, I go there." Ann slipped off her shoes and curled her feet up under her.

"I should have all the closets, cabinets, and bathrooms cleaned out by the end of the week," Maura said as she finished off her pasta.

"You're efficient. At the rate I was going, it would have been years before the house was sold." Ann found a clear spot on the coffee table for her bowl and retrieved her wine.

"Easier when you're on the outside looking in. Outsiders don't take time to ponder or second-guess."

Ann had done more than a lifetime of each. "I think you're right."

"You teach forensic psychology." Maura sipped her wine. "Do you solve cases with the cops?"

Ann laughed, not willing to discuss any of her work with the state police. "I grade papers and hand out homework assignments."

"If I wanted to take a class at the university, could I still sign up?"

"Yes, at the registrar's office. I'll be in my office the next couple of days, so if you want a tour, I'd be happy to give you one. I can also introduce you to the registrar."

"I might take you up on that. What kind of class would you recommend?"

"Come and see me, and we'll figure it out." Ann finished her glass and discovered she wanted a little more. It felt good to relax and have a normal conversation, even if it was superficial. "Would you like a little more?"

Maura glanced into her empty cup. "I better get going. Tomorrow's a long day."

"Of course." Ann followed Maura as she made her way around the boxes to the door. "Maura, remember there are people who are still really curious about me. What's in that house is for your eyes only. I'm not feeding anyone's morbid fascination with my life."

"Of course," Maura said quickly. "I understand the importance of privacy."

"Good."

Ann stood at the door and watched Maura load the box and then get back in her truck. As she backed out of the driveway, Ann noticed that Maura's truck sported Wyoming plates. She had said she'd worked back east for several years but had not mentioned when or where she had arrived out west. She would not have been the first to put off a visit to the DMV.

Ann walked to her mailbox and retrieved a handful of ad flyers and bills. Her father always said salesmen and bill collectors were the most efficient at finding a new address.

She returned to the kitchen and poured the last of the wine in her cup as she stared at Montana Mac. "Sorry, big fella. I didn't mean to leave you behind."

Mail and Montana Mac in hand, she went to her office and sat at her desk. Sipping her wine, she settled the bear on the couch behind her and then opened the Helena murder investigation file.

The gruesome pictures reached past the haze of the wine and reminded her that there was a monster in town. And as much as she wanted to get on with her life and find happiness, or whatever, it would all have to wait. She would search every detail in this case, and maybe make up for all the warning signs she had missed with Clarke.

As she flipped through the mail, a handwritten envelope fell out. It wasn't stamped, and the address was simply "Ann."

Curious, she pulled out the note card and opened it.

Ann, it's time we met and talked.

Find me or I will find you.

Elijah.

Her office chair squeaked as she sat back and studied Elijah's bold, direct script. Finding her here would not have been a difficult task, especially for someone as smart as Elijah. A call would have been more efficient, but a note carried greater impact. It was a tangible reminder that he knew exactly where she lived.

She crumpled up the note and tossed it toward the new small brown trash can. The unwieldy ball bounced off the rim and hit the floor, rolling back toward her. The note refused to be tossed away, just as she suspected Elijah was not going away easily.

PAUL THOMPSON'S CRIME FILES

The woman across from me is successful, attractive, and poised. She is the kind of woman most females envy and most men want. And she has been writing to a man locked behind bars in Montana for four years. If you guessed the man was Elijah Weston, then you would be correct.

"You must be wondering why I started writing him." The Realtor is dressed in neatly pressed black slacks and a red shirt that offsets her shoulder-length blond hair. Her nails are manicured, and a charm bracelet given to her by her grandmother dangles from her wrist and complements discreet gold hoop earrings.

"You're not what I pictured," I say.

"I never would have seen myself doing anything like this."

"So why do it?"

She leans back and picks an imaginary piece of lint from her slacks. "Five years ago, I was in a low point in my life. My boyfriend and I broke up, and my father died. There was an article on the internet about a prisoner in Montana. He had just earned his college degree while behind bars and was touted as a model prisoner. It was a second-chances kind of story. That appealed to me, but when I saw his brief interview, I was kind of amazed."

"He's a good-looking guy."

"To say the least." The silence settles around her. "I needed to believe in second chances then, and he was an inspiration to me. I decided to write and tell him so. It's important to acknowledge when people try to clean up their mistakes. I didn't think he'd write me back, but two weeks later there was a letter in my mailbox."

"What did you think?"

"I was shocked. A little afraid."

"Why were you afraid?" I ask.

"He now had my home address. Which I had to give in order for the prison to accept the letter."

"What did he say?"

She reaches for a letter sitting on the table beside her. "I'll read just a little."

"Whatever you're comfortable with."

She clears her throat, crosses and then uncrosses her legs. *"Dear Sarah. Your letter really touched my soul. I'm sorry for your losses and the challenges you've faced this last year."* She looks up. "The next part is personal, but he ends the letter with, *'Life's next second chance is waiting for you. It's called Tomorrow, Firefly.'*"

"It's nice."

"Sounds like an internet meme, but it really meant something to me. Because of that, I picked myself up. I got my real estate license, and I began building a really nice career. His words helped me. He made me realize I was a fighter."

"And you kept writing him?"

"Yeah. He became a friend. A confidant."

"When did you first hear about the Fireflies?"

She smiles. "Not until last year, when that woman in Montana died. The press called her a Firefly. I didn't realize Elijah had been writing to twelve or thirteen different women."

"There were thirteen in total. How do you feel about the others?"

"It made sense that there would be other women who were drawn to him. And I understood he needed more contact with the outside world than I could give." Her smile widens a fraction. "I like to think, though, that I was his favorite, and that no matter what, we would always be connected."

"Do you believe that?"

"Yes, I do."

CHAPTER TEN

Missoula, Montana
Friday, August 20
6:15 a.m.

Whatever plans Ann had for an early-morning run were canceled as soon as her phone alarm buzzed and she sat up. Her stomach rolled, her head pounded behind her left eye, and her mouth felt like she had eaten a sock. Finishing up the bottle of wine had not been a genius move.

Her first impulse was to push through the sickness and check on Nate. And then she remembered he was camping. She was alone. There was no agenda.

She could fall back to sleep, but when she eased back against the pillows, her head pounded harder, and the bed swirled as the drumbeat of recrimination thudded under her temples. The wine had allowed her to doze, but it was a restless, uneasy sleep filled with images of Elijah.

Drawing in a breath, she forced herself up off the mattress and moved into the bathroom, where she grabbed aspirin, which she swallowed dry. The next fifteen minutes became a study in will as she showered, dressed, and applied some makeup to brighten her pale complexion.

Feeling a little more human, she went into the kitchen and made coffee. The machine had barely gurgled out a half pot when she poured the first cup and drank. "Welcome back from the dark side, Ann," she muttered.

As she refilled her cup, her phone chimed with a text.

Bryce: The Kansas and Knoxville files arrived. I'll be in Helena today.

It was a two-hour drive to the state capital. She checked her watch. If she left now, she could be in Bryce's office by nine. That would give her a full day to review the cases. She did not need him present—in fact, it would be better if he left her alone to her thoughts in a quiet conference room stocked with more coffee. She checked her calendar. Her bed frame, along with several carpets, was scheduled to arrive by nine. As tempted as she was to have the delivery person leave them on the front porch, she needed to wait.

Ann: I can be in your office by noon.

Bryce: Here all day. If I'm in a meeting, have them page me.

Ann: See you then.

Bryce: Roger.

The chance that the other crimes back east were related to the Montana cases was slim. But a small chance was greater than none.

***

Elijah sat behind the registrar's desk, ready to face the endless mundane tasks that awaited him. Most would be problems that could have been avoided with careful planning beyond the next five minutes. But no one planned, so he ended up with harried students who believed he could magically fix incomplete schedules, bestow missed credits needed for graduation, or create spots in classes filled two weeks ago.

He had taken the volunteer job not to help his clueless fellow students, but to be close to Ann. He had kept his distance this last year for strategic reasons. Not only did he have to deal with the state and get his settlement, but it always took time for media attention to die down. Both goals had now been accomplished, so it was time to reassert himself and remind her the time for reckoning had arrived.

He sensed a woman approach his desk. She stood patiently for a second before she began to shift back and forth on her feet. He did not raise his gaze immediately, denying her immediate gratification.

Finally, he looked up, knowing impatience snapped in his gaze. She was midsize, lean with light-brown hair. She was older than the average student, maybe late twenties. "May I help you?"

Her stare lingered on him, and a quiet warning rang in the back of his head. Was she a reporter or a cop, or a woman who was curious about his story?

She held up the campus brochure. "I'd like to audit a class."

"Audit?"

"I'm dipping my toe back into academics. Thought an audited class would knock the rust off my brain cells."

"What kind of class do you want to take?"

"Intro to Forensic Psychology. Dr. Ann Bailey teaches it."

His interest was piqued. "You know Dr. Bailey?"

"I'm actually working for her. I have this cleaning business, and I'm getting her Beech Street house ready to go on the market. By the way, my name is Maura Ralston."

He was not surprised that Ann was selling, and he took it as a good sign. She was moving on with her life.

Elijah studied the woman more closely. She had a wide smile, a cute face, and her long brown hair had streaks with blond highlights. Her floral scent reminded him vaguely of Ann. She looked almost familiar, but he couldn't place her.

"Maura, the class is full," he said. "Dr. Bailey is a popular teacher, and this is the first time she's taught a freshman class in five or six years."

"Damn. Does she teach anything else?"

"We have other classes like that. I know the professors, and they're decent instructors."

"I'm sure they are. I really liked talking with Ann yesterday."

He leaned forward. "She teaches a graduate class, but that's not the place to start if you're rusty."

"No, I suppose not." She grinned. "Would I be considered officially enrolled if I'm auditing? I won't take the tests or write papers. I want to hear the lectures and do as many of the readings as I can. Like I said, knocking the rust off the brain."

"Sorry, the school limits how many bodies can be in a room at one time."

"But not everyone always shows up all the time."

"True." The woman knew how to work the angles. "But I still can't let you in the class."

She shoved out an impatient sigh. "Well, it was worth a try. If I get enough work in town, I might be here next semester." She fished a card from her fringed purse. "And in case anyone is asking, I'm a crackerjack cleaning lady. No job too big or too small."

"I've seen your flyers around."

"The university is a target market."

"I'll hang on to the card."

The grin, which now reminded him a little more of Ann, blurred his initial concerns about her. "Good to meet you, Maura. I'm Elijah Weston."

"Good to meet you, Elijah." That grin brightened. "I think I'm going to like this town. I've only met you and Ann, but you've both been great. Is everyone this friendly in town?"

"Not everyone," he said.

"Well, I like you." She checked her watch. "Got to go, Elijah. Off to Ann's for more decluttering."

"What's she doing with her stuff?" Having pieces that had been hers might make his house feel like a home.

"She doesn't want any of it."

"I bought a house. And don't have a stick of furniture. Mind if I take a look?"

"She's not crazy about strangers being in the house."

He smiled. "I'm not a stranger. We're old friends."

"Okay, I don't see why not. Ann doesn't want anything, so if you see something, take it. It'll save me a trip to the dump or salvage shop."

"Understood."

"Great. I'll be there all day. Maybe I'll see you."

"Maybe." He watched her walk away, admiring the way her ass filled out her jeans. Ten years in jail had left him with an appreciation for views like that.

His phone rang, and he picked it up. "Registrar's office."

He answered more uninspiring calls. But as he hung up the receiver each time, he was not as irritated as he normally was. Maybe it was the idea of seeing Maura's ass. Or Ann's old house.

Clipped footsteps drew his gaze back to the lobby as a woman in her late forties crossed the room. Her name was Edith Scott, and she was a petite woman with a slim build that made her look at least a decade younger. A gold headband tamed dark-brown hair that skimmed her jawline.

The last decade had been kind to her, and she looked like she had when she'd sat in the jury box at his trial. She had worn a smug expression as the jury filed back into the courtroom after their short deliberations. She had risen and read the verdict to the judge and court.

On the charge of arson in the first degree. Guilty.

On the charge of malicious wounding. Guilty.

Elijah had stopped listening, but he had been laser focused on Ms. Scott's face. Her eyes had telegraphed a brightness that hinted of righteousness. She'd believed she was saving the community from him.

As Edith now crossed the lobby, he said, "Good morning, Ms. Scott."

She stopped and faced him. Her complexion paled and her smile faded. "Elijah."

"Good to see you, Ms. Scott."

He was pleased his presence scared her. Eleven years ago, she likely had never considered the day there would be no bars separating her from The Monster.

She did not respond but turned toward the elevator and pressed the button with a hand that trembled slightly.

"I haven't seen you around much," he said.

Her shoulders stiffened, but she did not turn.

"Not to worry," he said easily. "I'll be around for a long time."

The doors opened, but when she turned as the doors closed, her gaze was planted on her feet.

"Have a nice day, Ms. Scott," he said.

He had heard that living well was the best revenge. That might be true, and he hoped to find out. But in the meantime, payback was also a bitch.

CHAPTER ELEVEN

Helena, Montana
Friday, August 20
11:15 a.m.

The hangover still lingered when Ann arrived at the Montana Highway Patrol offices in Helena. Out of the car, she tipped her face to the sun, drew in a deep breath, and slung her large purse on her shoulder.

Inside the building, she was greeted by the hum of conversation blending with ringing telephones. Several officers came and went as she walked up to the thick glass window and showed her identification to the guard on duty.

"I'm here to see Sergeant McCabe," she said.

"Wait a moment," he said.

She replaced her identification in her wallet and stood in the small glass reception area. She had minutes to wait until the elevator doors on the other side of the lobby opened and Bryce strode out. He wore a dark suit, white shirt, yellow tie, and polished black cowboy boots.

He nodded when he saw her and quickly opened the door. "Good to see you."

"I made better time than I anticipated."

"Good weather always helps. Come on upstairs, and I'll take you to the conference room. I've got the files set out there."

She tightened her grip on her purse strap, and she quickened her steps to match his. "Have you had a chance to go through the first murder book?"

"I've spent the last couple of hours reading through it. I'll let you do the same, and then we can compare notes."

"Fearing confirmation bias?"

Sun-etched lines at the corners of his eyes deepened as he smiled. "I've seen men get killed because they locked onto a conclusion before they had all the facts."

Elevator doors opened, and inside he pushed the button for the third floor. Standing close to him in a confined space reminded her of his height.

"How's that fence going at the ranch?" she asked.

"On hold for right now, but sooner or later I'll get back to it."

"You're planning to build out there?"

"There's a house on the land—it's habitable, but it's small. Means all my days off for the next decade are taken."

"But you'll leave your mark on it, and that's saying something."

"Nice to see a job go from starting line to the finish. That doesn't happen in law enforcement all the time."

"I could say the same about teaching."

The doors opened, and he held them as he waited for her to exit the elevator. "How does Nate feel about being back in town?" He paused at a closed door, opened it, and switched on the light.

"He seems to be adjusting. We went by the Beech Street house, where we used to live, so he could pick out what he wanted."

"How did that go?"

"He's not talking much. Plays his cards close to the vest."

"Apple doesn't fall far from the tree."

"How so?"

He paused in front of her, feet slightly braced. "You're a hard one to read, Dr. Bailey."

"Maybe." She set her purse on a long conference table and looked to the neatly bound case files. "These are the murder books?"

"Yes. There's fresh coffee in the pot, bathroom down the hallway, and you'll have all the privacy you need. My office is two doors down on the right."

"Did you find out if your Jane Doe had been in Anaconda?"

"I stopped by the two burger stands in town. I asked about a Caucasian woman in her late twenties and showed the picture. Neither place reported seeing anything that they considered odd."

"Nothing conclusive." She opened the first book. "Then let me get to it."

Bryce strode toward the door, glanced back as if he had something to say, but in the end left her alone with the files.

She filled a mug with black coffee, then pressed the warm cup to her temple before she sat and opened the first case file from Kansas.

Bryce had been correct. The Kansas murder did not appear to match either the Knoxville or Montana cases and was easy to rule out. Not only did the police suspect the victim's pimp, but they reported that her clothes had not been stripped off, the remnants of her wallet had been found on the passenger-side floorboard, and there'd been little facial mutilation.

The Knoxville murder victim had been identified as Sarah Cameron. She had been twenty-eight and a Realtor. She had been summoned to one of her listings and had told her boyfriend she would be home by seven. She'd never made it home. Search crews had been dispatched within twenty-four hours, but the cops had focused originally on the boyfriend. Sarah and David Brown had been seen fighting in public several times. However, after several days of questioning David, the cops could not unearth anything tying him to Sarah's disappearance.

The cops put a trace on Sarah's phone and alerts on her credit cards. They did get a hit on the phone four days after Sarah vanished, and her credit card was used to purchase gas. The strip mall and gas station were thirty miles west of Nashville, and the cops found the phone in a trash can in the gas station's men's room. The phone was wiped clean of prints, and its digital history revealed that whoever had taken the phone had made several nondescript social media posts while traveling to the current location. However, there was no sign of Sarah or her abductor.

Two weeks after Sarah vanished, hikers in the Smoky Mountains near Knoxville found her partly decomposed body near a mountain path. Identification of the remains was made easy because of a bracelet Sarah had been wearing. No suspects were ever arrested.

Sarah's autopsy report showed she had been murdered thirty-six hours before the discovery of her body, suggesting she had been held for almost two weeks. There were no defensive knife wounds on her hands and forearms, implying she didn't expect an attack. What caught Ann's attention was the facial mutilation. The medical examiner wrote, *"It's as if the killer were trying to remove her face."*

This case drew massive media attention. Young and pretty, Sarah had captured the press's headlines, which focused primarily on the unknown assailant who had held her captive. Some reports tried to link her death to a robbery gone wrong, while others suggested a sex-trafficking ring was responsible. The theories were endless; however, the police never found the location where she had been held or dug up any substantial leads on her killer.

Ann sat back in her chair, wondering if the killer had been paying attention to these news articles and enjoying the attention.

She reread the Knoxville file and discovered a small detail she had missed the first time. Polaroid paper had been found near the body, but no fingerprints had been pulled.

The delay between Sarah's kidnapping and murder fit the profile of a first-time killer. She guessed murder had not been on this killer's mind initially. Maybe the killer was stalking her. Maybe he got too close. Maybe she threatened to cause trouble. Whatever happened, the killer knew she could not be let free, so Sarah had been taken somewhere until the killer found the resolve to carry out his fantasy.

She rose and made her way to Bryce's office. She found him deep in thought behind his desk, phone pressed to his ear. When he saw her, he waved her inside.

As he spoke to someone about a highway patrol matter, she had a moment to look at the wall where he displayed several service awards and a few military citations. There was also a picture of him with a group of men wearing fatigues, thick beards, and full military gear. She guessed by the terrain that it was Afghanistan.

"That was taken about fifteen years ago," Bryce said, rising.

She looked quickly away, as if she had been caught staring, which was exactly what she had been doing. "How old were you?"

"Twenty-four. A lifetime ago."

Fifteen years ago, she'd been a freshman in college. And by twenty-four she was a new mother trying to balance life with a husband, toddler, and a master's degree program.

"You miss it?" she asked.

"Sometimes. But less and less." He slid his hand into his pocket. "Did you find anything?"

"Wondering if you had that Polaroid paper tested for prints."

"It's at the lab now. I called an hour ago, and it's not looking good. The prints are badly smudged, but the techs are taking another pass at it."

"The Knoxville murder file noted that Polaroid paper was found near the body's location."

"Really? I haven't had a chance to read the file in great detail."

"If I'd not found the picture near the Anaconda scene, I would have missed it."

"What about the other case?"

"I would say it's not related. Too many inconsistencies, and the police believe they have a suspect."

"Your conclusion?" He sat on the edge of his desk and folded his arms over his chest.

She felt the full weight of his attention as she recapped her theories about the Knoxville case. "Also, Sarah Cameron's quick identification and local prominence led to wide media coverage. Maybe the explosive scrutiny was overwhelming."

"It's also exhilarating to be on the knife's edge," he said. "And it's no fun if there's no one to admire your masterpiece. Which sets up the current scenario. He sets them on fire so everyone knows exactly where they are but not who they are."

"Perhaps the victims share a connection he doesn't want us to know about," Ann said.

"But I now have Sarah Cameron's name."

"Find out about the people who appeared in her life shortly before her death. Also talk to the boyfriend. He might know something," Ann said.

"Sarah Cameron was attractive, and the woman in the picture you found is also good looking. I'll wager the same on the woman in Helena. Maybe he's not taking their identity when he mutilates them. His last act is simply to make them ugly."

"Maybe," Ann said.

Bryce reached for his phone and dialed. "This is Sergeant McCabe. What's the status of those prints?" He frowned. "Only a partial. It's something." He ended the call. "The partial is being run through AFIS. With luck we'll get some kind of hit."

She smoothed her hands over her pants. "Focus on Sarah Cameron."

Bryce rose. "Ann, what kind of monster are we dealing with? Is this guy a sociopath or psychopath?"

"Both share traits. They both lie and lack remorse for the feelings of others. A sociopath or someone with antisocial behavior tends to be impulsive and irresponsible. But this killer is organized. And so far, he has not left behind any substantial forensic evidence, which takes planning and forethought. That leads me to believe we're dealing with a psychopath. And for the record, both types of offenders represent less than five percent of the general population. In prison the rate is closer to sixty percent."

"What are we looking for in this killer?" Bryce asked.

"This person is going to be charming, manipulative, callous, and he'll require lots of stimulation mentally and physically." She drew in a breath. "They're harder to spot than you might imagine."

"What about physical traits?"

"Anatomically, MRIs reveal irregularities in the brain specifically in the amygdala, located in the center of the brain. This portion of the brain should activate when the subject is faced with emotion or empathy. Not surprising, but it's underactive in psychopaths."

Bryce held up his hand. "What about characteristics I can see?"

"Psychopaths come in all kinds of shapes and sizes. There's no way of looking at a person and telling."

***

Elijah pulled up to the house Ann was selling and spotted the red pickup truck in the driveway. He thought about the free spirit, Maura, and how good she had smelled. He wondered if her skin was as soft as it looked.

He parked down the block and walked toward the house, knowing folks in this neighborhood normally paid attention to the comings and goings of people. He wagered they were on high alert after last year, and Ann had warned Maura about letting anyone in the house. Perhaps he should stay away. Had not his mother always said that when you go into the house of the dead, you risked stirring their souls?

The last time he had been alone with Ann, it had been in the small two-bedroom she had shared with Joan Mason in college. They'd had sex in her foyer, and when he had left her, she had been panting and satiated, and he had been hopeful they might have something.

Then the college house had caught fire shortly before graduation. Ann's brother, Gideon, had rescued Ann, and Clarke Mead had barely saved Joan. The cops found the three incendiary devices. One had failed and not burned properly, leaving the torn shreds of a sweatshirt covered in Elijah's DNA. He was in handcuffs before the embers cooled. The jury's verdict had been as swift, and at the turn of the new year, he was in prison.

But there'd been a reason that device had not burned fully. It had been meant to be found. The evidence against him had been a plant. He had been set up. And ten years had been stolen from him.

Burying his anger, he got out of the car and strolled up the front walk, taking in the small house that backed up to a bank of woods. As he approached, music echoed from the interior. He tried the door, discovered it was unlocked, and opened it. Dust particles danced in a thick band of sunlight streaming in from the patio window.

"Hello," he said.

The music grew louder as he walked toward the bedroom. He made his foot strikes louder, hoping to alert her that he was here. The last thing he needed was for her to panic and call the cops. His past record might have been expunged, but if the two speeding tickets he'd had in the last six months were any indication, the cops were looking for an excuse.

He walked to the main bedroom doorway and saw the collection of overstuffed garbage bags. He peered into one and noted more of Ann's clothing.

"Maura!" he said. When she still didn't respond, he knocked on the wall.

The music went silent. "Hello?"

"Maura. It's Elijah."

She peered out of the bathroom, her expression a mixture of shock and happy surprise. She had changed into a light-blue dress that skimmed below her knees. The neckline scooped along her collarbone, and the sleeves floated above her elbows. She also wore three-inch beige heels and a gold, chunky bracelet.

"You dress up like this to clean?" he asked.

Nervous laughter bubbled. "God no." Blushing, she leaned slightly forward, and he caught the aroma of lilacs. Ann's scent. "These are Ann's," she said.

The clothes fit her well and showed off the full curve of her breasts. "And she's okay with this?"

"She doesn't want anything from the house. I checked with her. And as I was bagging up her closet, I came across a couple of really nice dresses. I thought I'd try a few on."

"And you decided to help yourself."

"I know it looks weird. But they're all going to the thrift store anyway."

He had never seen Ann wear this dress, but he doubted he had seen her in anything from any closet in this house. She had left Clarke by the time he had been released from prison.

"What do you think of the dress?" Maura asked.

"It looks good," he said quietly.

She smoothed her hand over her flat belly. "Thanks."

He was smarter than almost anyone, but he lacked direct experience with women. The women who had reached out to him in prison wrote him sensual, exciting letters, but they were all distant. Even the ones who had visited him while he was behind bars had been separated by a thick glass partition.

Now, all that stood between Maura and him was inches of air. It took control not to run his hand along her cheek. Was her skin as smooth as it looked?

Her brows gathered as she moved a step toward him and then slowly turned with her arms outstretched. "What do you think about me in this dress?"

"It's hot," he growled.

She moistened her lips.

How would Ann's breasts fill out the dress? Would her soft mounds strain against the delicate fabric? And the hem—would it skim above or below her knees? Ann had long legs, so he guessed several inches above.

"How about dinner tonight?" he asked.

"Yeah, sure."

This was the mating dance, he supposed. He had never had much practice as a teenager, and now fast-forward ten years, and he was as clueless. One thing to read one of his Fireflies' letters, process their words, and craft his response. Now here, with a woman so close, it wasn't as easy.

She fingered the soft folds of the dress's skirt. "I'm working here until at least five. I can meet you. You like Italian?"

"Sure."

"There's a place called Tony's."

He knew the place. He had been there many times, mostly grabbing takeout, but he had gotten to know the owner, who did not care about his past. "Sounds perfect."

"Terrific. What about the furniture?"

"I don't want any of it." He turned but paused at the door. "Wear the dress."

CHAPTER TWELVE

Missoula, Montana
Friday, August 20
6:15 p.m.

Ann was ready to kick off her shoes and drink maybe a small glass of wine when she pulled into her driveway. It still felt odd not to have Nate, but for tonight, she was glad for the quiet. Time to process was rare these days. She fumbled with a large pizza box, her purse, and her keys.

As she searched the ring for the new key, a car pulled up behind her. Tensing, she located her house key and opened the door before she turned.

"Ann!" a woman shouted.

She recognized Edith Scott as she climbed out of her parked car. Judging by the woman's tight, defensive body language, this was not a social call. "Edith."

"I need to talk to you," Edith said.

"Can it wait until morning, Edith?" Ann asked. "It's been a long day."

"It's about Elijah Weston, and it cannot wait."

The sound of his name soured her mood. "What about him?"

"Did you know he's volunteering at the registrar's office at the university?"

She did not. There was no logical reason for him to take on a role like that. It did not pay anything, and given his recent settlement, the position was not worth his time.

She refused to delve into Elijah's motivations. Each time she did, she ended up with insomnia and a headache. "Okay, what do you want from me?"

"Talk to him. Figure out why he keeps sticking around."

She set down her purse and swiped away an annoying strand of hair. "What makes you think he'd listen to me?"

Dark eyes narrowed. "You're joking, right?"

"Why would I joke?"

Edith blew out an aggravated breath. "Everyone on the jury knew he had a thing for you. He barely looked up during his trial until you came in and testified. Then he could not take his eyes off you."

She remembered how his intense gray gaze had reached across the room and all but wrapped around her. By then, she'd been married to Clarke and visibly pregnant. She had worn a large coat, hoping to hide her growing belly. "I can't help that, can I?"

"He's still here because of you. You do understand that, right?" The pitch of her voice rose with the color in her cheeks.

"I have no control over Elijah, and why do you care?"

"Because he scares me! He's going to come after me."

"Why?"

Edith gripped her car keys tighter. "I voted guilty. I sent him to jail for ten years."

"Given the evidence, it was a logical choice. We all thought he was guilty."

Edith's lips pursed. "Well, he wasn't, and now he's out. And ten years is a long time to foster a grudge."

"Has he made any threats?"

"He doesn't have to. He has a way of looking at me that makes my skin crawl."

"You had no way of knowing he was set up. You voted on the evidence presented to you."

"I didn't believe him. He said he was innocent over and over, and I thought he was a liar. I said as much to the media after I sent him to jail. And I'm afraid he's going to come after me sooner or later."

"I think you're giving yourself too much credit." Edith might have sent him to prison, but Ann was denying the man the truth about his child.

"How can you say that?" Edith shouted. "He's coming after me."

"He's free. And he doesn't want to return to prison. He's not going to endanger his liberty."

"Do us all a favor and find another place to live." Edith gripped Ann's arm in a tight hold. "You have a talent for picking troubled men, and we're all suffering for it. God help us when Nate gets a little older."

The rage that surged in Ann was instant. She ripped her arm free, feeling the scrape of Edith's nails against her skin. Instead of retreating, she closed the gap between them. "Don't you ever speak against my son. He is innocent."

"How can he be? He's already proven he's smarter than any boy his age should be. It's not natural, and it's going to lead to trouble."

"Get off my property!" Ann stepped so close the pizza box bumped the woman. "Get off now, or you won't have to worry about Elijah. You'll have to fear me."

Edith took a step back. "Is that a threat?"

"It's a promise," she warned as she jabbed the pizza box again into Edith, forcing her back several more steps. She kept pushing until the woman turned on her heel and got back into her car.

"I'm calling the cops!"

"Be my guest," Ann said.

Ann did not budge from her corner of the yard until Edith's taillights had vanished around the corner.

As she stood at the edge of her property, she gripped the pizza box so tightly that her fingers dented the cardboard. Her constricted chest muscles made it difficult to breathe, and she had to force herself to pull in air. A car door three houses down closed, and someone's front door opened. She had become a spectacle for the neighbors. Terrific.

Ann retraced her steps, picked up her purse, and set it in the foyer before she slammed her front door. She carried the pizza into the kitchen and tossed it on the counter, her appetite gone.

She poured herself a full cup of wine. As she sipped, her temples pulsed. "Bitch."

Her phone rang, and when she glanced at the display and saw Bryce's name, she let it go to voicemail. He was a sharp enough cop to detect the stress in her voice if she spoke to him now.

She kicked off her shoes, walked to the window, and took another sip. There were elements of truth in Edith's words. She had chosen men who lived in the shadows, men who kept secrets, and men who were dangerous. If she were her own patient, she would have suggested a convent.

Her phone beeped: *1 Voicemail.*

Worse still, she was attracted to Bryce. He excited her in ways she had not felt in years. Alive, hopeful, sensual. She drank more wine. "Based on my history, he's probably a serial killer."

She pressed fingertips to her temple. And if he was not a murderer, he was at the very least better off without her. She took a gulp of wine and then played back the message.

"Ann, it's Bryce. The Helena victim has been identified. You're welcome to join me at the forensic center tomorrow in Missoula."

She set the phone down and considered refilling her glass. However, at the rate she was going, she would end up with another hangover, and she needed to be sharp. Catching this killer might provide an outlet for her anger and frustration.

She grabbed a piece of pizza and took several bites. Her nerves settled a fraction, and she realized she wanted in on this case. She could not do anything about Clarke or Elijah, but she sure as hell could catch this monster.

Wiping her fingers, she texted Bryce: Give me a time and place, and I'll meet you.

He responded immediately. I'll pick you up. See you at 7:30 a.m.

***

Paul Thompson sat on the Deer Lodge motel bed as the muted television broadcast the local news. The room was decorated in a 1980s cowboy vibe with a picture featuring racing horses, wallpaper that mimicked the interior of a log cabin, and bedspreads that were a muddy brown with a white trim. This was traveling on a budget.

His phone chimed with a text, and he was a little surprised to see the sender's name.

Nena: Keep thinking about our interview.

Paul: What about it?

Nena: You kept asking me about why I had a thing for Elijah. Now I know why.

Paul: Why?

Nena: It was comforting to know he was locked away. I was his link to the outside world. I was in control.

Paul: You like control.

Nena: Yes, very much.

Paul: How did it feel to know there were other women?

Nena: Maddening.

As he fluffed the pillows behind his back, he changed the channel to the other news station. He was waiting for the reporter to say something about the fire near Anaconda. Back in Nashville, a story like that would not have been big news, but out here, where the land could be drier than tinder, everyone paid attention.

And he made note of fires because he was here to interview Elijah Weston.

Nena: I'd like to see you again.

Paul: Why? We covered it all in the interview.

Nena: There's more I want to tell you.

Paul: What?

Nena: Only in person.

Paul: I'll get back to you.

Paul used this phone exclusively for interviewees, because he never knew when he might end up with a crazy one. Tossing it aside, he reached for his personal phone and scrolled through the texts. Nothing from his ex-girlfriend, thankfully. She had been a pain in the ass after the breakup. And nothing from his agent, who thought he might have a line on sponsorships for the Weston podcast.

A smile tugged at his lips. He had known he'd struck gold from the moment he had heard about Elijah from an old girlfriend. He had spoken to six of the Fireflies, and as soon as he scored interviews with Ann Bailey and Elijah Weston, he would have all the audio he needed.

He had leverage, which he was certain would force Ann to talk to him.

***

Elijah rose from his booth in the Italian restaurant when Maura walked in. She was wearing not the blue dress but a sleeker black jumpsuit that dipped down between her breasts. Rhinestone earrings dangled from her ears, and Ann's scent lingered around her. He grew hard and this time was glad they were in public and there was not a bed five feet away.

He wondered whether Ann had worn the jumpsuit and hoped it had not been selected for Clarke's benefit. "You look great."

She squirmed into the booth and, when the waitress came, ordered a red wine. "Thanks."

Courtship was proving harder than he imagined when all he wanted to do was strip her naked. "You been in town long?"

"A few weeks. It's a nice town."

"I suppose."

"You suppose? If you don't like it, why are you here?"

"It serves a purpose for now."

"I saw you talking to that Edith lady at the university." She blushed and then, as if revealing a dark secret, said, "I snuck back and watched."

He said nothing.

"She seemed pretty unnerved to see you. It made me wonder about you, like if you had done something bad, so I did an internet search."

"And you found out that I'd done nothing."

Maura smiled as she raised the glass to her lips. "That we know of."

"What's that supposed to mean?" he snapped.

Her grin widened. "Just kidding. Honestly. Don't be so sensitive."

"Ten years in jail has that kind of effect," he said carefully.

Amused, not chagrined, she tapped her finger against the side of her glass. "Grumpy?"

"Not at all."

She leaned forward, clearly knowing he would get a better view of her breasts. "When's the last time you got laid?"

"Excuse me?"

"Come on, no judgments. It's been a while, hasn't it?"

"Not as long as you think."

She sat back, regarding him as she held the glass up to her lips. "How long?"

"Do you want to get out of here?" he asked.

"I thought you were hungry," she said.

"I am. But not for pasta."

"Yeah, let's go."

He reached in his wallet and tossed two twenties on the table.

"It'll have to be your place," she said. "I'm kind of living out of the truck right now."

"As long as you can handle a mattress on the floor."

"You would be amazed what I can handle."

Fifteen minutes later, he pushed open his front door and pulled her inside. She closed the door behind her with a kick. Slowly, she ran her fingers through her hair and moistened her lips. She smelled like lilacs.

In the dim light, she looked like Ann. Not the sweet Ann, but the woman who had let him into her house all those years ago and allowed him to put her against a wall and take her. In that moment, the darkness in Ann had reached out to him.

Maura let the purse dangle from her fingertips before she gently dropped it. "You'll have to get the zipper in the back," she said.

She turned toward the wall and scooped her hair around, exposing her neck. He traced his fingers over the nape and then tugged on the zipper until it stopped above her bottom.

He slid his hands under the fabric, reaching around and grabbing her breasts. They were soft, supple, and almost the right size. She hissed and arched toward him.

He pushed the top of the jumpsuit down over her shoulders, and then she grabbed the fabric and wriggled out of it. She stood naked, glancing over her shoulder. "What are you waiting for?"

His erection throbbed. "You in a rush?"

She faced him and reached for his belt buckle. As her breasts brushed the cotton fabric of his shirt, she unhooked the top of his pants and reached for him. "Always. Now are you going to do this or what?"

He turned her toward the wall, separated her legs, and, grabbing her hips, shoved into her.

"That's better," she said. "But it's not enough."

He thrust hard several times. "What do you want?"

She arched her back, cupping her breast. "I'll let you know when I've decided."

The light caught her hair in just the right way, and Maura was transformed into Ann. The last ten years melted away, and they had found their way back together. "Ann."

Her mews and moans grew louder, and if she had heard him, she did not seem to care. His pace quickened, and when he came inside her, there was a split second of utter bliss.

Control had always been important to him. Even in prison, he had mastered his world and the people around him because he understood the value of self-containment. But Maura had momentarily stripped away that control. And for now, he allowed it to drop.

***

I do not like to hurt people.

I like to make people feel better.

But there are those moments when there is a need inside me that is so powerful it blurs the lines between good and bad.

I am outside Ann Bailey's new house, watching her as she paces among the unpacked boxes. Finally, she chooses a bookshelf kit, opens the end, and dumps out the pieces. As she reads the instructions, a frown tugs down the edges of her lips. Poor Ann. Too smart to decode a set of instructions. As if sensing someone watching, she moves to the window and closes the drapes.

She is the kind of gal who has lots of books and loves to read, so she will need a lot of shelves. It is too bad that I cannot knock on her door and help. I am pretty handy with most household tasks, and I could volunteer and help for an hour.

But Ann clearly would not like knowing that I have been watching her. She would want to know why, and I would have to tell her that she is on my list.

It has been days since I checked the last woman off my list. My thirst should be quenched. But it is not.

I know I have to wait. And I will. For now. But it will not be long before the next one.

CHAPTER THIRTEEN

Missoula, Montana
Saturday, August 21
7:15 a.m.

When Ann stepped outside her house, Bryce's dirt-dusted vehicle was parked in her driveway. He was behind the wheel, reading his phone when she walked up and knocked on his window. He smiled and motioned for her to get in. As she moved toward the passenger-side door, she sensed he was watching her. And she liked it.

"You're early," he said as she opened her door.

"You're earlier," she said.

"Couldn't sleep."

She clicked her seat belt, not sure how she fit into this investigation but ready to be a part of it. "You said you have an identity on the Helena victim?"

He put the SUV in reverse, backed out of the spot, and headed away from the neighborhood. "Her name was Dana Riley. Doc pulled DNA from her molars when he did the autopsy in July, ran it, and we finally got a hit in the CODIS system. Dana Riley did a year in a Maryland prison for stealing."

"What brought her to Montana?" Ann asked.

"Don't know yet. Hoping to get a line on where she worked and stayed. I need coffee. You?"

"Always."

He pulled into a drive-through and ordered two coffees with extra cream and sugars. He handed her a cup, settled his in the cup holder, and drove.

She pried off the lid, savoring the scent. "Bless you."

"Looks like you didn't sleep too well last night."

She opted to treat herself and poured the two creams into her coffee. "I was up late trying to put together a bookshelf. I'm fairly certain the Swedes designed the unit to drive me insane."

Out of the parking lot, he wound his way through town. "What happened to the extra sleep you were going to grab while Nate is out of town?"

"Best-laid plans." She dumped in the sugars. "Turns out, I don't sleep well when Nate's not home."

Out of habit, she pushed up her sleeves, inadvertently revealing the scratches left behind by Edith.

"What happened to your arm?" Bryce asked.

"I got into it with a woman who works at the university," she said.

"She grabbed you?" His voice deepened with annoyance.

"She confronted me when I arrived home. She thinks I should leave town. I suppose she thought she was emphasizing her point."

A muscle in the side of his jaw pulsed. "Why? You have every right to be in Missoula."

"She thinks Elijah Weston is hanging around town because of me, which he is not." She sipped her coffee, wondering why she was being so candid.

"Has Elijah Weston given you any trouble?" he asked carefully.

"Nothing explicit."

"Meaning?"

"He has a way of showing up. He left a friendly note in my mailbox."

"He was on your property?" Bryce's jaw tightened.

"Yes. And he's taken a volunteer job at the university. I'll be seeing more of him."

"You weren't on his jury."

"No, but I testified against him at the trial." She blew on the hot coffee. "I'd rather talk about Dana. Do you have a picture of her?"

"Nice deflect."

"I'm tired of worrying about me."

He scrolled through his phone and pulled up Dana Riley's mug shot. "Not the most flattering."

Ann settled her cup in the holder, took the phone, and studied Dana's picture. She had pale skin and light-brown hair. Her light eyes were downcast and her cheeks hollow. She handed the phone back to him. "When was that taken?"

"About three years ago."

On a hunch, she opened the latest and greatest social media app on her phone. She had several, not because she enjoyed posting, but to stay abreast of the culture and trends, which some serial killers used to find victims. She searched for Dana Riley. None of the images attached to the accounts resembled their Dana.

"We get lots of seasonal workers that come to the state," Bryce said. "Dana could have been working at a local bar for tips. The sheriff is talking to the area bars and restaurants first."

"I'd also like to see where her body was placed," she said.

"That can be arranged."

He pulled into the parking lot of the regional forensic building, and after both were out of the car, he escorted her inside. He showed his badge to the officer on duty, and when the door buzzed open, he followed her into the small back offices. They were met by a midsize man dressed in a Montana Highway Patrol uniform. He had a round belly, muscled legs, and a thick mustache.

"Bryce," the man said, extending his hand.

"Matt, good to see you." He nodded toward Ann. "Matt Towzer, meet Dr. Ann Bailey. She's consulting on the case."

"Doctor of psychology, I hope," Towzer said. "Whoever murdered Dana Riley has some odd views about murder."

"Forensic psychology," Ann said. "And you're right about the killer. He's not typical."

"Last murder I worked was a barroom fight. Man knifed another. Two drunks fighting over a woman. But this case, hell, I've never seen anything like it."

The curled, blackened images of the Helena victim, or rather Dana Riley, pushed to the front of Ann's memory. The cuts around her face had been jagged and halting, an indication that the killer had not yet perfected his ritual.

"What can you tell us about her?" she asked Towzer.

"Bryce called me when he received the victim's identity last night. I was in Helena, so I made the rounds of the local bars and restaurants. I showed her mug shot around for about an hour, and as luck would have it, a local bartender at the Red Horse recognized her picture. The guy's name is Tate Andrews, and he said Dana worked there for about a month. She was popular with the customers, and then one day she did not show up for work. He said that thing happens all the time with seasonal workers. I told him more cops might be stopping by."

"You said you also located Dana Riley's truck?" Bryce asked.

"Once I had her name, I did a vehicle search and came up with the VIN for the Ford truck. I visited the two tow lots in Helena and spotted the truck. The VIN matched."

"Good work," Bryce said.

"Lucky I found it when I did," Towzer said. "It was scheduled to go on the auction block in a couple of weeks."

"Have you searched the vehicle yet?" Bryce asked.

"No. The vehicle just arrived here about an hour ago on a flatbed. The technicians are getting ready to work on the truck now."

The trio took the stairs down to the basement level, where the vehicle bay was located. Impatience and excitement surged as Ann thought about searching the truck for evidence. More than ever, she wanted to catch this killer.

"Dr. Bailey, you know better than me," Towzer said when they exited the elevator. "Why would a person do this to another? I have seen people mess up each other, but it's generally in the heat of emotion. Whoever did this was cold and deliberate."

"There are some people who feel no remorse," Ann said. "It's basically a faulty wiring system in their brains. And there are some who feel guilt, but simply can't stop themselves. Their violence is a compulsion."

"What's driving this guy?" Towzer asked.

"I'm not really sure," she said.

"Holy hell," Towzer said.

"Now that we know the victim's name," Bryce said, "it's a matter of backtracking her steps and figuring out when she might have hooked up with this person."

The three made their way down a hallway to the loading bay, where they got their first look at Dana Riley's Ford truck. The vehicle had Maryland plates, a rusted bumper, and worn tires that would not have made it through a Montana winter.

A forensic tech was photographing the truck, while another had opened the cab and was laying out the vehicle's contents on a blue tarp. Included in the growing collection of items were a suitcase, gas cans, jugs of water, food wrappers, and a worn black leather purse.

Odd to see all the woman's belongings on display. Whatever secrets Dana Riley had carried with her would soon be laid bare.

Ann walked over to the purse. Its braided shoulder strap was tattered near the silver hook that attached it to the pouch. "Has anyone gone through this?"

"Not yet," the tech said. "I can do it now if you'd like."

"That would be great, thank you," Ann said.

The technician switched on a light table and removed the items in the bag one by one. The contents were standard. Red lipstick, drugstore brand. A comb and small brush. Tissues. Dozens of crumpled receipts. Gum.

"What about a wallet?" Ann asked.

"No sign of one," the technician said.

Was the wallet another trophy? Or had the killer taken it to slow the identification process? That supported the theory that the victims could be connected.

The technician reached in the side pocket, removed a Polaroid picture of Dana Riley, and carefully laid it on the table.

"A Polaroid picture," Ann said.

Bryce studied the image of the smiling woman's face. "This was taken at the crime scene."

"Are you sure?" Ann asked.

"Very. I've walked it several times."

It was jarring to see the dead woman's smiling face and bright eyes looking directly into the camera. Her skin had a rosy glow, and her full lips bore the red lipstick. Silver earrings dangled, and her long light-brown hair was swept up into a ponytail. The print's background captured an obscured sunset marred with haphazard scratches.

"What's with the marks on the image?" Bryce asked.

"Some Polaroid artists do that to create an effect," Ann said. All the marks angled toward Dana's face, hinting at the knife wounds that would soon take her life.

Ann was convinced more than ever that the image she had found near the Anaconda site was of Tuesday's victim.

"Be sure to dust that for prints, ASAP," Bryce said.

The technician acknowledged him with a nod and bagged the picture.

The collection of receipts proved Dana had indeed stopped for gas multiple times between Maryland and Montana. There was also a receipt from Nashville dated two weeks after Sarah Cameron died. Dana had been within driving distance of Knoxville around the time Sarah had vanished. All the receipts were signed D. Riley.

Ann reopened the social media app on her phone. She typed *D. Riley*. She pulled up a profile picture featuring a woman who matched the mug shot. "Here she is."

Bryce leaned toward her and studied the image. "Damn."

She scrolled back through D. Riley's account, finding pictures that detailed the story of someone who was going on a trip. The journey appeared to begin in June in Maryland with the image of a suitcase in the bed of this truck. The caption read: **WESTWARD HO!**

The next pictures were selfies taken on Lower Broadway, the music district of Nashville, and then more images marking Dana's path through Missouri, Kansas, Nebraska, and Wyoming. The images were not particularly remarkable, but they all featured her smiling face.

"The posts continue into early July with Dana," Ann said. "But after the day her body was found, the pictures continued but were of random shots of food, flowers, and road signs."

Bryce studied the images. "That land's west of Helena. I've driven across this state enough to know most of it by heart." He pointed to the last shots. "Those images were taken right outside of Missoula."

"You think this Dana Riley was traveling with her killer all the way from Maryland?" Towzer asked.

"Maybe," Ann said. She scrolled back through the pictures, retracing the soon-to-be-dead Dana back through time. The pictures would have to be analyzed in detail, but at first glance she saw nothing indicating the identity of Dana's traveling partner.

"As soon as I have her Social Security number, I'll search her credit history and get a warrant for her financial transactions," Bryce said.

It was a trail of digital bread crumbs, but it was at least a path they could follow.

"Helpful to know if Dana had family or friends back in Maryland," Ann said. "I'd like to talk to them."

"That is already in the works," Bryce said.

"Good."

She approached the vehicle and peered into the dirt-streaked window. The forensic tech was clearing the vehicle's interior, but it still contained discarded clothes, fast-food wrappers, an unopened box of Twinkies, and a couple cases of beer.

"There has to be someone living who can speak for Dana," Ann said.

"Going to the bar will mean a two-hour trip to Helena," Bryce said.

"That'll be worth it," Ann said. "Drop me at my house, and I'll drive up there."

"You can ride with me."

"Then you have to double back."

"Not a problem," he said.

The two thanked Towzer and the technicians, then left the forensic center. They climbed into Bryce's vehicle. He switched on the radio and started driving.

As Bryce drove, Ann glanced out her window, watching Missoula buildings be replaced by the jutting rocky landscape along I-90. "Are we going to pass your ranch? You said you're between Helena and Missoula."

"When we get on Route 12, we'll be close to the turnoff."

"I never get tired of seeing this land," she said. "There was a time when I dreamed of living anywhere but here. Now, I can't imagine anywhere else."

"I've seen a lot of the world," he said. "I can say it doesn't get any better than Montana."

"Spoken like a true cowboy."

Bryce easily found the barn-style building that housed the Red Horse when they arrived in Helena.

Out of the car, Ann checked her watch. "It's eleven thirty."

"Best time to talk to a bar owner. They're usually the one on-site, and the music isn't blasting, so you can hear yourself think."

"You've been here before?" Ann asked.

"A few times."

They crossed the sidewalk, Bryce opened the front door, and, removing his hat, he followed behind her.

The bar was still, the jukebox silent, and the barstools, leather booths, and floorboards were soaked with the lingering scents of whiskey and cigarettes. She had not been in a bar since college and had forgotten the thrill of walking into a place alive with music and people. After Nate was born, she had been too busy caring for him and going to school. Late nights at the bar with the other graduate students required time she did not have. And now, the last thing she wanted was to show up in a bar filled with university students.

"Hello," Bryce said as he rapped his knuckles on the bar.

Glasses clinked in the back room, and a young woman holding a tray of tumblers appeared. She had on shorts and a snug tank top, and she sported a tattooed sleeve on her right arm. "We don't open for another six hours."

Bryce held up his badge. "Looking for Tate Andrews. I have questions about Dana Riley."

"Tate said the police came by last night. Tate won't be in until three. But I know Dana. I'm Stella Andrews, Tate's sister."

"What do you know about her?" Bryce asked.

"She arrived at the beginning of the tourist season and said she'd work for tips. Normally, we don't do that, but it had been a long, cold winter, folks were coming out in droves, and we were slammed. We needed the help."

"What was she like?" Ann asked.

"Friendly and got along well with the customers. Worked hard enough. Made good tips, but the pretty ones usually do."

"Did she talk about herself at all?" Ann asked.

"Not really. Gave me the impression she was going to be here awhile. She liked it. But most folks do in the summer. It's the winters that chase them off."

"Was she traveling with anyone?" Bryce asked.

"Not that I know of," Stella said. "She kept to herself. Worked long shifts, and I don't know where she went when she wasn't working. Likely slept in her truck, which seasonal workers do."

"Did she ever mention Sarah Cameron?" Ann asked.

"I don't remember who she talked about," Stella said.

"Do you have any video footage from around that time?" Bryce asked.

"No, sir. Long gone," she said.

"What brought her here?" Ann asked.

A half smile tugged her lips. "She said it was a man who was just out of prison. I never pressed for details. I stay out of my employees' lives."

Bryce handed her one of his cards. He asked her to call him if she thought of anything else. They stepped outside.

"Is that what police work is like? Bits of information that don't appear to connect?" Ann asked.

"Basically. If I'm lucky I join enough pieces to get a picture."

***

Elijah did not wake until after eight and was surprised he had slept so late. He was also relieved to discover Maura was gone. Once his lust had been satisfied, her hold on him had dissolved. One thing to have sex with a woman in his bed, but another to wake up to her. He was reserving those personal moments for Ann.

He rose and turned on the shower's hot spray. He stripped the sheets from his bed, dumped them in the washing machine along with a liberal amount of soap, and turned it on. Returning to the steamed air of the bathroom, he stepped inside the stall and allowed the water to wash over him. He lathered his entire body, scrubbing until scents and persistent memories swirled down the drain.

He dried off quickly and, wrapping a towel around his waist, approached the clouded mirror. Carefully, he wiped away the fog and stared at his expression. He summoned a smile, hoping it would soften the coldness, but found it conjured Joker-like images. He lathered his face with shaving gel and carefully placed the razor at his throat. Pulling the blade in a straight line, he slowly removed the stubble and then rinsed away the excess cream.

Again, he looked into the mirror and opened his mouth wide, like an opera singer prepping for a solo. He smiled a second and then a third time. Neither attempt felt sufficient. And if he was going to blend in, he would have to develop a pleasant, easy expression.

He closed his eyes. Very quickly, his thoughts settled on Ann. When he pictured her, she was always smiling. Her long hair was around her shoulders. And she smelled of the right balance of perfume and woman.

When he opened his eyes, his gaze had softened, and his lips naturally curled into a passable smile.

As with everything in his life, all roads led back to Ann.

PAUL THOMPSON'S CRIME FILES

Dana Riley is a self-described gypsy. She has been on the go since she could walk and likes moving frequently. In recent years, home has been in a small coastal town in Maryland, the foothills of North Carolina, and in Music City—Nashville, Tennessee—where we sit today. We are in a honky-tonk on Lower Broadway. It is a warm May day, the sun is shining, and Dana admits that these are the days she lives for.

"You want to know why I wrote Elijah?" In the thirty minutes we have been chatting over cold beers, she has already established a charmingly direct style.

"I do."

"Saw him in the paper several years ago. The story was something about him being a genius and a success story of the prison system. But I was taken that instant. His eyes leaped off the page. I had a few too many beers, so I jotted him a note and told him so. I have written 'fan' letters to men in prison before, but you never know what to expect."

"Why do you write men in prison?"

"They are lonely. And I feel bad for any animal, even a mean one, when they are caged. I cannot think of a worse thing."

"You only wrote him a few letters, right?"

"Three while I was in Maryland. I had just gotten out of jail, and I knew I understood what he was going through." She takes a sip of beer and swipes away foam coating her upper lip.

"Now that he is out of prison, what do you think about Elijah?" I ask.

"I think about him a lot," she says softly. "I'm glad he got money from the state."

"Are you worried about your safety now that he's out of prison?"

"I'm not afraid of him, but others should be," she says.

"What do you mean?"

"He knows who took what from him, and he wants it back."

"Anyone in particular he's going after?"

She sips her beer. "Dr. Ann Bailey."

"What is it about her?"

"She *knew* him in college, if you know what I mean, and she got knocked up about that same time. Have you ever compared a picture of her kid to Elijah?"

"No."

"If you've seen a picture of her boy, it ain't a stretch to wonder, 'Who is the daddy?'"

CHAPTER FOURTEEN

Missoula, Montana
Saturday, August 21
4:15 p.m.

Bryce pulled into Ann's driveway. "I appreciate the help. I should have Dana Riley's credit card transactions by tomorrow."

"Call me when you get them. I'm wondering if the killer used her card like he did Sarah's."

"If he did, that increases the chances that there will be a surveillance camera that captured his image." His wrist rested on top of the steering wheel. "You'll be the first I call when I know anything."

"Terrific." A part of her wanted to linger and say something more to him. She was attracted to him but was not sure how to articulate it. Direct, coy, or subtle hints? Most women her age knew the ins and outs of romance. Her dating experience had stalled her senior year of college, and her two sexual experiences with Elijah had resulted in pregnancy. She wanted to explain some of this to Bryce, but even her out-of-practice self knew it amounted to information overload.

She reached for the door handle. "Have a good day."

His gaze lingered on her. "You do the same."

She got out of the car. Bryce waited until she pushed open the front door before he backed out of the driveway and drove off.

Frustration simmered inside her. "For God's sake, Ann. You can observe an autopsy, but you can't have a normal conversation with one man."

The sun hovered overhead, and an edginess rippled through her body as she looked at the collection of boxes. She turned and left her house, locked the door behind her, and drove to the Beech Street house to check on Maura's progress. The red truck was not in the driveway.

She parked. As she looked at the house, her nerves reflexively tightened, as if an archer were drawing them back like bowstrings. Her mind shifted to the last time she was in the house alone with Clarke.

"Come into the basement," Clarke said.

"Why?" She had made the decision to leave him and was now waiting for the right time. Had he somehow figured out she was planning to take Nate and move out?

"I want to show you something." His wide grin softened his masculine features, and on some level her worries eased. She had been in the basement a million times before.

She went down the wooden steps, heard the door close behind her, and looked up to see her husband following. At the bottom, she saw the mattress on the floor made up with white sheets. Soft music played. Beside the makeshift bed several electric candles burned.

"What's that?" she asked.

"I know you want to go to Hawaii, and I know I've been putting you off. And since we can't get away, I thought it might be fun to create our own vacation spot."

She looked up the stairs toward the light shining under the closed door. "Nate will be home soon."

"Gideon has the boys." He took her by the hand in a firm, unbreakable grip. "It's just you and me. We have several hours all to ourselves."

"I can't, Clarke," she said.

He ran one hand up her flat belly and cupped her breast. The second hand fisted her hair. "I promised you we'd get to making another baby as soon as we could. No time like the present."

"I can't think about that right now." When she'd lost the baby last year, she had been shocked to realize that she had been relieved. Giving birth to Clarke's baby would have anchored her more tightly to him. That was when she'd begun to face her unconscious fears about her husband, and she had started to think about leaving him.

He leaned over and kissed her and then the hollow of her neck. Accustomed to his touch, she did not resist. "I want you, Ann. I've missed you."

She swallowed the tightness in her throat. "I can't do this right now."

"Why not?" He gently nibbled her neck with his teeth. "Prove to me I don't have to worry. Prove to me you'll never leave me."

Tears welled in her eyes, and she allowed him to lower her to the mattress.

Avoiding this place was cowardice. She owed it to herself and Nate to make sure the house was getting a proper cleaning so it earned top dollar on the market.

She shut off the car and hurried to the front door. The worn key slid easily into the lock, and when she stepped inside, she reached automatically for the foyer light switch. A decade of muscle memory was hard to shake.

The scent of pine cleaner lingered in the air, and as she walked down the hallway and looked in each room, she could see they had been completely decluttered, the closets emptied, and the beds staged for the new buyer.

In her old bedroom, the king-size bed conjured images of Clarke sitting on the side, his shirt unbuttoned as he unlaced his boots and grinned up at her. He always smelled of smoke and cinder, but in the early days, it was sexy. Pulling off his boots, he would rise and walk toward her. His muscled frame always towered over her.

When Ann shook off the memory, her breathing was rushed and panicked. She shifted her focus to the closets, now empty and pine scented. The bathroom sparkled, better than she had ever managed when she lived here. The kitchen was also clean, the refrigerator wiped out, and the magnets, flyers, and pictures once on the outside had been stripped. All traces of humanity had been erased with garbage bags, cleaning supplies, and Maura's yellow rubber gloves. She had done her magic and exorcised the personality from the rooms. And there was a part of Ann that would mourn this lost life.

The furniture would have to be sold, but that came later, after the house. Who knew—maybe the buyer would take some of it.

A hard knock on the front door startled Ann. She turned, heart thrumming in her throat. The oval glass cutout obscured the man on the other side, but she did not recognize him.

Fishing her cell from her purse, she readied to dial 911 for help as she opened the door. The stranger was tall and lean. He had light-brown hair tied back in a ponytail, penetrating green eyes, and an angled face covered with several days' growth of beard. His gray T-shirt sported a deco-style logo that read **Radio** surrounded by lightning bolts.

"Yes?"

"Dr. Bailey?" The deep timbre of the man's voice hit a familiar chord.

"Who are you?" she challenged.

"My name is Paul Thompson. I've left you several voicemail messages."

She recognized the name. He was the one producing the podcast. "I don't want to talk to you, Mr. Thompson."

"Can I come in and talk to you?"

"I said no, Mr. Thompson."

"Please call me Paul."

"Doesn't matter what I call you, Paul. I'm not talking to you about my late husband."

"I don't want to talk about Clarke Mead," he insisted. "I want to talk about Elijah Weston."

"I don't know him that well."

"That's not what I heard. Some say you were pretty close in college."

"I don't care what you've heard," she said quickly. "I'm not talking to you."

He reached in his pocket. "Let me give you my card."

"What part of *no* don't you understand?"

As if she had not spoken, he scribbled something on the back of the card. "I've written the name of my motel on the back. I'll be in town a few more days getting background material and doing general research. I think it would be good for us to talk." He held out the card for her.

He was clever. He was smooth. But she was not swayed.

When she did not take the card, he tucked it in the seam between the front door and brick wall. "Call me."

She waited and watched until his car lights swept the house as he pulled away.

When she was certain he was gone, she snatched up the card. She was tempted to toss it, but she feared this was not the last she would see of him.

She locked the front door and jiggled the handle several times until she was convinced it was locked.

Time to find Maura, get her key back, put this house on the market, and then bury the past forever.

***

I hurt people, but I do not enjoy it. And like it or not, pain is unavoidable. In this case, a lesson needs to be taught.

As I sit beside the sleeping woman's bed, I'm struck by how soundly she sleeps. I remember when I was younger, I slept that hard. But as I got older and the Need inside me grew, sleep abandoned me. Once, seven hours of sleep a night was the norm. Now it is closer to one or, if I'm lucky, two hours.

Tonight is no different. The catnap lasted all of forty-nine minutes, and my eyes popped wide open, and I was ready to go. Feeling at odds, I spent some time driving, looking for an all-night coffee place. And when I found one, I ordered a double latte with extra sugar. Images of her grew stronger until I knew I had to act.

Leaning forward now, I stare at her closed eyes, knowing her lizard brain will soon sense my presence. It is one of those evolutionary quirks. We think we have dragged ourselves out of the primordial ooze, but in reality, that lizard brain is as it was during our ancestors' time. It's always on the lookout for danger.

With gloved hands, I tug at her sheets, slowly pulling them off her body until I see her gray flannel nightgown covered in purple flowers. Christ, how does a grown woman end up wearing something like this?

Her nose twitches, and she reaches for the covers. When she does not find them, her eyes flutter open. She was not expecting to wake. But when those beady little eyes crack, they do not see empty darkness. They see me. And I am smiling.

"Hello," I say softly.

Alert, her eyes blink like a newly installed stoplight. She wants to clear her vision and convince herself this is a nightmare.

"No, I'm still here," I say.

She scrambles to a sitting position, her full breasts flopping under the flannel. More blinking and then: "What do you want?"

"Not much," I whisper.

"Don't hurt me."

She reminds me of my aunt who brought me the marshmallow chocolates I hate at Christmas and who always smelled of coffee and cigarettes.

"I have money," she adds.

"Do you? How much?"

"A couple hundred dollars. It's in my purse."

Cash always comes in handy. "Could be of use."

Her gaze darts to the door, as if she's calculating an escape. "You'll take it and leave?"

"You won't tell the cops I was here?" I tease.

She shakes her head. "No. I swear."

Ah, she *swears*. That means I'm in the clear, right?

I rise, knowing this is a mini fakeout. I love those. As I stand, she relaxes, believing after she has seen my face that I am going to take a couple hundred bucks and be on my merry way.

As she unclenches her fists a fraction, I take the moment and move quickly to grab the other pillow and press it against her face. I am on top of her like a cat, smashing the down pillow against her nose and mouth. She grabs my arms and digs fingernails into my skin. That pisses me off, and I thrust a knee into her gut twice.

Pain makes her go limp, and I press the advantage and the pillow harder, gripping her sides with my thighs.

It all takes four minutes of holding her down before I feel her energy evaporate. Finally, when she goes limp, I am breathless, and there is sweat beading between my shoulder blades.

It is not so easy to suffocate a person. It causes undue stress for both of us, and I am not happy about that. As I rise, I sense she is still breathing. "Damn it. What does it take?"

I finger the knife in my pocket as I watch for any signs of life. Her chest moves slightly. I open the knife.

Raising it above my head, I jab it hard into her chest three—no, four—times. The blood splashes my hands and stains her nightgown. When I rise off the bed, I wipe the blade on the sheets and replace it in my pocket. I will not be taking this face.

I pick up the pillow and fluff it, taking a moment to remove the imprint of her face.

My clothes are not too bloody, plus it is night. As I leave, I pause to turn the air-conditioning down to fifty degrees. Obscuring the time of death means it will be harder for the cops.

Did she die on Saturday or Sunday?

Either way, I will have an alibi.

CHAPTER FIFTEEN

Missoula, Montana
Saturday, August 21
9:15 p.m.

Bryce spent a couple of hours at his office calling in requests for Dana Riley's phone and credit card records. Both would re-create her travel patterns and tell him where she had been before she died. Then it would be a matter of locating surveillance footage from the establishments she had patronized. Likely many had been erased, but he would at least have a beginning.

He parked and eased out of the car, looking for the trio of German shepherds illuminated by the porch light glow. When his mother, his brother, and he had moved onto the ranch with Pops, there had always been rescue dogs on the property. Whenever he came home from school or a rodeo event, they had raced to greet him. This new brood did not greet him, nor did they wag their tails. But on the bright side, no one was growling, and so far, they had not bitten him, which, according to Dylan, was high praise.

He passed by the dogs, who sniffed and eyed him closely, and then he went inside. Around the side of the house, the clank of dog bowls was followed by the thud of paws and then Dylan's steady, stern voice.

Shrugging off his jacket, Bryce reached in the refrigerator for two cold beers.

He found his brother standing in the center of a circle of bowls as four dogs ate. The newest was smaller than the males, but she possessed an edgy energy that hinted at a hair-trigger temper.

"The badass, Venus, has arrived," Bryce said, handing a beer to Dylan. "How's it going?" He loosened his tie and twisted the top off the bottle.

"As long as none of the guys get in her face, I think she'll be fine."

He watched Venus gobble up her food, and when she was finished, she sat and looked at Dylan. "What's her story?" Bryce asked.

Dylan fished a treat from his pocket, gave it to her, and rubbed her between the ears. "Handler couldn't take her. Like the rest of my pack, she was deemed damaged or high maintenance."

He studied Venus, who was not concerned by her reputation. "Welcome to the club, Venus."

Dylan pulled four red rings from his back pocket. He tossed one, called out a dog's name. Each waited their turn and then gleefully chased down their rubber prey.

"I wanted to talk to you about something," Dylan said.

"Have at it." The cold beer tasted good.

"It's time I became gainfully employed," he said.

"I told you there was no rush."

"Well, I'm like you. I need to work." As he spoke, he retossed the rings for each dog. "I'm thinking about creating a breeding and training camp for service dogs."

"You going to breed any of this crew?"

"Hell no. Venus is too old, and if she did produce a pup with any of these guys, I'm afraid we'd have a modern-day Cujo."

The image prompted a grin. "I don't suppose there's a market for that."

"No. But there's a need for service dogs for retired military."

"I say go for it."

"Just like that? No discussion? You understand it's going to require more than the barn renovation."

Bryce took a long sip, trying to imagine the yap of puppies in the yard. "Do it, if it suits you."

"I have plenty of savings," Dylan offered.

"And I might kick in."

Dylan eyed his brother. "I thought you wanted to get some cattle."

"At the rate I'm going, the back fence will never be installed, and I'm not ready to tie myself to the land yet. Maybe in a decade or two."

"If you're really okay with this, I'll be making calls first thing Monday to contractors."

"I get to name the first puppy."

Dylan grinned. "You can name the whole damn litter."

"Will do."

Dylan tossed a ring for each of the dogs again. "Where were you today?"

"In Helena, investigating the July murder. Took Dr. Ann Bailey with me."

Dylan cocked his head. "Didn't I read something about Dr. Bailey's husband?"

"Late husband. Yeah. He was in the news last fall."

"How's the doc doing?"

"She's doing well." He took another sip of beer, wondering if he might get a chance to spend time with her that did not involve homicide. "She's a strong woman."

"Doesn't she have a kid?" Dylan asked.

"Nate. He's ten."

"How's he faring?"

"He's camping with his uncle now."

"That's not what I mean." He threw the rings several more times.

"According to his uncle, he's smart enough to audit classes at the university. He's edgy by nature and worries. But given what he's been through, I'd say he's doing well."

"Any signs of his old man in him?"

Bryce frowned. "He's a kid."

"Jury is still out on the nature-versus-nurture match."

"Are we talking about Nate or us?" Bryce asked.

His brother regarded him with the open honesty of blood. "You sound a little defensive."

"Let's face it. We both worried that we'd end up like our old man."

"But we didn't."

His brother had always keyed into genetics. Their father had been a drunk and a wife beater, and witnessing violence in their home had left them both wary. Since his return to Montana, Dylan had shifted his obsession with genetics to the dogs. He knew better than anyone there were traits to encourage and ones to avoid.

"And neither will Nate. The kid has spirit, he wants to learn, and he's willing to work," Bryce said.

Dylan's grin was sheepish. "And the mother? What do you think about her?"

"She's smart. Determined. Unafraid."

"And attractive, from what I remember."

"Can't fault the woman for that."

Dylan laughed. "And you like her."

"I didn't say that."

"Yes, you did." Dylan held up his hands, laughing at Bryce's frown. "Hey, if you like her, ask her out."

"She's gun shy."

Venus ran up to Dylan and dropped her ring at his feet. He flung it and watched her lean, sleek body race across the tall grass. "The best take time and patience."

"Maybe."

"Flowers don't hurt, either, or so I've heard."

"Thanks for the advice."

Growling drew Dylan's gaze to the field. A snarling Venus now had all the rings and was facing the males. Dylan broke away immediately and, speaking German, ordered them all to stand down as he put himself between the dogs. His voice raised, he commanded all to sit.

"Some take more patience than others?" Bryce goaded.

Dylan kept his gaze on Venus, who looked ready to spring into the air. "Rome wasn't built in a day."

***

It was after midnight when Ann pinned a long white piece of paper on her wall and, with a black marker, wrote out the dates of the three murders: June, July, and now August. Under each she wrote the city and then jotted down Sarah Cameron's name under *June*, Dana Riley's under *July*, and, beneath *August*, Jane Doe. She printed off pictures of the two identified victims as well as the Polaroid, then taped each under the corresponding month. Next came a collection of sticky notes with scribbled notations. Stabbing. Facial mutilation. Polaroid images. Social media posts on Sarah Cameron's and D. Riley's pages that appeared days after either their disappearance or death.

She stood back, knowing the killer had linked these murders for a reason. Based on these images, he preferred young women with light-colored hair. He did not sexually abuse his victims, took untraceable pictures of their faces, which he mutilated postmortem. The sections of skin, along with the pictures, were souvenirs.

"Why these women?" she asked.

Her doorbell rang. Stiffening, Ann rose and moved to her front window. Carefully, she drew back the curtain and searched her porch. No one was there.

Strain crept up her back, banding around her scalp. She hesitated and then unhooked the security chain and opened the door. She looked left, right, around the curb, and then toward her mat. But there was nothing. No Elijah. No Paul. Not even Clarke's ghost.

She rubbed her arms and closed the door, hooking the chain and throwing the dead bolt.

As she stepped away from the door, her phone chimed with a text. Startled, she was relieved to see Bryce's name.

Bryce: I have financials for Sarah Cameron and Dana Riley.

Ann: What did he buy?

Bryce: Gasoline. Fast food. Rang up tabs at grocery stores. Reaching out to stores now for surveillance footage.

Ann: Any leads on Jane Doe's identity?

Bryce: Searched surrounding towns and counties for missing-person reports. No hits.

But there was a missing woman. Her family might not realize it yet, but Jane Doe was never coming home.

Ann: What about women who were supposed to be on vacation or a business trip? Departure expected, but they are late returning.

Bryce: Will alert surrounding jurisdictions.

There was a pause, and then the text bubbles rolled: Go to bed.

Ann: Back at you.

Bryce: What are you doing tomorrow?

Ann: Looking over financials with you?

Bryce: See you in Missoula at 11:00 a.m.

Theoretically, they both could get enough shut-eye during what remained of the night. He might be able to function on little to no sleep, but she could not. At this rate, she was going to develop double vision and start bumping into walls.

Ann: My house. Will have coffee.

Bryce: Roger.

Under Jane Doe she wrote: *Killer still in Missoula?*

***

I do not like to hurt people, but I really do enjoy screwing around with them. Amazing how the little things freak people out. A note on a windshield. A planter that has been moved. The ring of a doorbell.

If I ever get caught, which I never will, I will call it harmless fun. A joke. A prank. No harm, no foul.

But I know what these little tricks really mean. They are a warm-up for the main event that is coming soon.

CHAPTER SIXTEEN

Missoula, Montana
Sunday, August 22
6:15 a.m.

Ann woke early, rising before the sun. She rolled onto her side, noted the time, and groaned. She pulled the covers up, willing herself to sleep a couple more hours, but her brain quickly revved to fifth gear.

Frustrated, she stepped into the bathroom and turned on the shower's hot spray. When she stepped under the water, she moaned as heat beaded against her chest. She tipped her face toward the nozzle.

Out of the shower, she dressed, properly dried her hair, and put on makeup. The simple routine was followed by a good cup of coffee. She started to put away her books, but found herself reading or thumbing through each, as if reacquainting herself with old friends.

When her doorbell rang, she had barely put a dent in the first box of books. Bryce was early. Rising, she pursed her lips and ran her fingers through her hair before she reached for the doorknob.

Smiling, she yanked it open and found Paul Thompson on her front porch. Her smile vanished. "What do you want, Mr. Thompson?"

He raised two smooth hands more suited for a keyboard than manual work. "I should have called first, but I wanted to give you another chance."

"For what?"

"To talk to me. I felt like we got off on the wrong foot. It's important that my story has your perspective."

"We didn't get off on any foot, Mr. Thompson. I'm not going to sit for an interview or have any kind of discussion with you."

"I'll steer clear of any questions you don't want me to ask. I'll talk to you whenever or wherever is convenient for you. This can all be on your terms."

"No." She began to shut the door.

"Do you think Clarke Mead knew the truth?" he rushed to say.

She stilled. "What are you talking about?"

"You know."

"You're being vague and not giving me any hard facts."

He studied her a moment, like a poker player trying to decide whether he should show his hand.

"I can read your expression," she said. "*Overplay and she'll slam the door in my face. But if I don't lay it all out, she'll still slam the door in my face.* Basically, you have nothing to lose." Her heartbeat jacked up a notch; she hoped this was simply a bluff.

"It's about your son," he said, dropping his voice.

"My son?" A swift chill swept over her, freezing her muscles, her lungs, her heart. "What about him?"

"I didn't bring this up the last time because I don't want to have this conversation on a porch," he said. "This is going to be awkward for both of us."

Ann raised her chin, did her best to look annoyed, and hoped the expression did not betray the fear clawing at her insides. "What is so awkward for us?"

Again, in a hushed tone: "Did your late husband know Nate was not his biological son?"

"Who told you something like that?" she said quietly.

He adjusted his backpack on his shoulder. "I've interviewed several of the Fireflies."

"Fireflies." Her laugh was mirthless. "Elijah Weston's groupies."

"Yeah."

"What do any of them know about my son or me?" She shook her head, forcing her gaze to challenge him.

"More than you realize."

"Honestly, Mr. Thompson, it takes balls to knock on a woman's door and accuse her of cheating on her dead husband."

"The boy was born seven months after you and Clarke married."

Her heartbeat pounded in her ears. "So? Clarke and I dated our senior year."

"You testified at Elijah's trial. I read the transcripts. You and Clarke were broken up at the time of the fire."

Her eyes narrowed as she clung to her bravado. "This feels like a fishing expedition, Mr. Thompson."

"The Fireflies believe Elijah Weston is the boy's father. If they saw the resemblance, then Clarke must have known it. I've seen pictures of your late husband. He doesn't look anything like the boy."

As her stare locked on his green eyes, whatever words she had assembled scrambled away. Her skin puckered with an uneasiness as she thought about crazy groupies discussing her son.

A dark SUV pulled up in front of her house, and Bryce got out, holding a manila file. He was wearing jeans, a black T-shirt, boots, and a hat. His service weapon was holstered at his side. Mirrored sunglasses hid Bryce's eyes as he approached, but his lips flattened, and his jaw tensed as he looked from her to Paul Thompson.

"Dr. Bailey," Bryce said carefully. "There any trouble here?"

Thompson took a step back, his gaze still locked on Ann. "No trouble. We were having a conversation."

"Judging by Dr. Bailey's expression," Bryce said, "she's not liking what you're saying."

"It's fine," Ann said. "Mr. Thompson is producing a podcast about Elijah Weston, and he wants my input. I've declined, but he's trying to sway me."

"No means no, pal," Bryce said.

Thompson removed a card from his pocket and handed it to Ann. "In case you lost the other one. I'm in town now for another week. Call me anytime."

She accepted the card. "Have a nice day, Mr. Thompson."

"You as well, Dr. Bailey." Thompson turned, his long strides eating up the distance to the gray four-door rental car.

When Thompson drove off, Bryce's gaze still lingered on the street as he spoke. "What did he want?"

"He's like all the others." Weariness dusted the words. "He wants an interview."

"You've had requests before. Whatever he said rattled you."

"I'm a little sleep deprived." It wasn't far from the truth.

Bryce shifted his gaze to her, his mirrored glasses tossing back her own reflection. Silent, he regarded her.

"Is that how you look at suspects?" Her attempt to flip this back on him fell flat.

He nodded slowly. "It's a warm-up."

"It's not working."

He shook his head. "I'm not going to interrogate you, Ann. But I can see that the man upset you. And after the last year, that's saying something. If you need to talk to me, you can trust me."

Oddly, she believed him. "I wasn't expecting him. He caught me off guard." She stepped back. "Come on inside. Murder is far more interesting than me."

He hesitated another beat and then crossed the porch into the house. Removing his hat and glasses, he kept the file tucked under his arm as he surveyed the living room, which was more cluttered than when he had last seen it. "How's the unpacking going?"

"Slow. And Hurricane Nate will be home tomorrow night, so I'm running out of time. School starts next week, and then life really gets crazy, and yet here I stand in chaos."

"Couple of days' work should take care of all this."

"But it's finding the desire to unpack." Shaking her head, she tried to summon a smile.

He traced the silver buckle on the leather hatband as he walked toward the stacks of books. Most of the books were about all manner of death and crime. There were a couple of fiction ones, and those were murder mysteries. "What would you be avoiding, Dr. Bailey?"

"The rest of my life?" she asked lightly. "It scares the hell out of me."

A half smile tweaked his lips, as if he were familiar with the feeling. "You can try to hide from it, but either way, it's going to keep coming toward you like a stampeding herd of horses."

She flicked the edge of Thompson's card. "I know."

"Can I help? I'm handy with assembling bookcases."

Silence settled, and normally she used it to her advantage. Students often rushed to fill the quiet, and when they did, she always learned important tidbits. However, now the stillness coiled around her nerves. Paul Thompson's words had rattled her, and Bryce knew something was off. She did not care what people might say about her, but she worried about Nate losing the last pillar of his shattered family.

Ann looked at Bryce, wanting to confess all this to him so he could point her toward the clear path. But finding the words was her problem. "You can help me drink the pot of fresh coffee I made. I did promise you coffee."

He considered her. "Yes, you did."

"This way." She guided him past more boxes and into the small galley-style kitchen sequestered from the dining area by a small island. The preset coffee machine gurgled, and the coffee cups were set out, along with sugar and milk.

"Just black," he said.

She poured him a cup and set it on the island, not trusting her composure if her fingers touched his. It might be that small contact that rattled open the lock that kept her secrets and desires boxed. She poured her own cup.

"Thanks." Long fingers wrapped around the mug, unmindful of the heat.

"Let's go back to my office," she said. "I put up a grid that I've been filling out slowly but surely."

"I'd like to see it."

He followed her down the hallway, and as soon as he stepped into her office, his gaze was drawn to the timeline that she had stretched across the long blank wall.

"The good thing about not being unpacked is that you have plenty of blank walls," she said. "The clutter that life brings has yet to really take over."

He sipped his coffee, nodding his appreciation, and then set it down on the edge of her desk. He opened the manila file to the top page, covered with his own scrawled notes.

"I traced the postmortem purchases made on Dana Riley's card all the way to Missoula. The last one was made six days ago."

She scrolled through Dana's social media feed. "What did she buy?"

"Gas, food, and there was a single purchase for $825.14."

On D. Riley's feed, Ann discovered a picture of blue snakeskin boots sitting on a rock overlooking Missoula. The setting sun dipped toward the mountainous horizon, painting the land in fiery reds, startling oranges, and vibrant yellows.

She turned the phone toward him. "Maybe the killer bought a very expensive pair of boots?"

He took the phone and enlarged the image. "That's taken here in town?"

"Yes. What was the name of the vendor?"

"The Classy Cat."

"They don't sell anything on the cheap." She searched for the name, found the website, and clicked on the store hours. "They're closed today."

"Then we'll be there first thing in the morning."

"Why expensive boots?"

"A present for a woman?" he offered.

"But it's such an extravagance."

"Best bait is not cheap."

"Feels more like showing off."

Her gaze wandered from the fiery colors in the post to the grainy picture of smiling Jane Doe, and then her mind wandered back to the autopsy. "Shifting directions to the burning of bodies."

"Okay."

"It's more than destruction of evidence. This killer is not just destroying evidence of the victim's identities, but he's communicating with someone."

"Why do you say that?"

"There's no purpose to the fires. They may delay identification for a brief period, but anyone who watches TV knows about DNA and dental records. If anything, the fires increased the killer's chances of being caught."

"Another arsonist would notice that the fires had been set."

"Exactly."

"Elijah Weston?"

"Maybe. He's certainly been in the news this last year. And he has a fair number of groupies."

Bryce studied her closely, as if peeling back the layers. "Did Thompson mention Elijah's groupies?"

"He did. He asked me about the Fireflies."

"Elijah's groupies."

"Yes." How many times had her brother said that coincidences associated with crimes were rare? "What if this is all connected to Elijah?"

"How?"

"Dana told folks she was here to see a man who'd been released from prison."

"Elijah."

"Maybe. And remember one of Elijah's Fireflies was killed last year."

"Lana Long, I remember."

"She died by fire, and her death was widely covered, and Elijah attended her funeral." She had been shell-shocked at the time and too busy protecting Nate and unraveling the web of lies Clarke had spun. "Maybe the fires are more than simply getting Elijah's attention. Maybe the crimes are more personal."

"How?"

"What if the victims are all Fireflies?"

Bryce's frown deepened as he considered her theory. "We haven't confirmed that."

She glanced at Thompson's card. "Could you check with the prison and determine if Sarah Cameron and Dana Riley wrote Elijah? If they were both Fireflies, it would be our first link between the women."

His gaze shifted back to the chart on the wall. "I'll get a complete list of the Fireflies tomorrow."

"If Sarah's and Dana's names are on it, then you can track down the women and figure out who's missing."

"What's the motive for killing these women? Would Elijah order a hit on them? Pit one against the rest? Clean up loose ends?"

"I don't know. Elijah is brilliant. He's a master chess player who thinks a dozen moves ahead." She rubbed her fingers against her temples, reminding herself to take an aspirin soon. "Also search for social media accounts for these women."

"Done. Ann, is all this taking a toll on you?" Bryce asked.

"I can handle it." She slid her phone into her back pocket along with the business card.

"When's the last time you ate a real meal?" he asked.

She held up her cup. "I'm having coffee right now."

"That's it?"

"It's doing the trick."

"You have any food in this house?"

"As a matter of fact, I do. I stocked up yesterday, knowing my son, who never stops eating, will be home tomorrow. Would you like me to make you a sandwich?"

"You show me the supplies, and I'll make us both a meal."

"It's been a while since anyone cooked for me." Clarke had scrambled eggs for her when she was pregnant, and her mother relied on frozen food and takeout these days.

She led him to the kitchen, and all she had to do was point to the food in the pantry and refrigerator, and he ordered her to pour herself another cup of coffee and sit. He got to work, carefully setting out paper plates, bread slices, and all the cheeses and meats that went between them. He moved with an exact precision she found endearing.

"So neat and careful," she teased. "I don't imagine you've ever had to slap together a dozen sandwiches for a den of Cub Scouts?"

"I've fed as many hungry soldiers. And I'll bet you they eat more."

"You got me there."

He cut each sandwich on a sharp diagonal, indicating to her he liked, maybe craved, accuracy.

"You're a man of many talents," she said as he set the plate in front of her.

"I like to eat. I learned to cook."

"What about your brother? Is he a good cook as well?"

"Can make the best chow a dog would ever want. I wouldn't recommend you eat anything he makes."

She rose and from the refrigerator grabbed two cans of lemon-lime seltzer water. Normally, she drank out of a can, but considering the sandwich, she put ice into two paper cups and grabbed two pieces of paper towel off a thick roll. "Sorry, no real dishes yet. They're in one of these boxes or on order."

If he wondered why she had not taken perfectly good plates from her old home, he did not ask.

When he sat, she did as well and bit into her sandwich, discovering it had exactly the right ratio of ham to cheese, lettuce, and bread. Nothing fancy, but it reminded her that she needed food. She ate the entire sandwich before she crumpled her paper towel and tossed it on her plate.

He was watching her with a measure of satisfaction. And for the first time in a long time, she felt as if the world slowed a little.

She had spoken to Bryce and his patrolmen in Helena months ago, and of course he had been here with Nate, and she had been in the car with him yesterday. But each of those times had been filled with distractions. This was the first time it had been just the two of them. Her curiosity grew, and whatever shyness she might have had vanished as she cataloged the details that told part of his story. No wedding band—in fact, no rings. Crow's-feet etched at the corners of his eyes. A faint white scar along his jawline. The little finger on his left hand bent slightly, as if it had been broken. He was the kind of guy who found the path through the storm.

His interest in her was as keen, and she sensed he was cataloging her features and maybe searching for the marks left behind by her past. *Good luck with that one.* She had worked hard to make sure they were not visible.

"I hear the wheels in your mind grinding now," he said.

The rough timbre of his voice did not chase away her gaze. "They tend to do that."

"The case?"

She did not know how to read the cues the sexes transmitted between them. She had thought she knew in college, but it was clear she picked very imperfect men. She opted for honesty because it cut through the BS quickly. "Thinking about you."

"Me?"

"I'm attracted to you," she said carefully. This might be the moment where he told her she was off base. And if the attraction was mutual and he liked her, then she had to worry about what was wrong with him.

"I can see the smoke coming out of your ears," he said lightly. "Do you always overthink?"

"Always."

He arched a brow, intrigued and amused. "That so?"

"I've been off the market for a long time, so if I sound crazy or am out of line, tell me. We can pretend I never said anything—we can finish our drinks and get back to safer waters, like homicide."

"No reason for that."

"What does that mean?"

He came around the island and stood in front of her. She shifted on the stool so she faced him. Gently, he took her hand and pulled her up. The feel of his calloused skin against her palms awakened the nerves in her entire body.

"Can I kiss you?" he asked.

She moistened her lips, quickly trying to remember the last time she had kissed a man. Was it last year, two years ago?

"Stop overthinking," he said.

"Right." A smile tugged at the edges of her mouth. "Yes, you can kiss me."

He leaned forward and pressed his lips to hers. Desire singed her nerves like liquid fire. She leaned into the kiss, knowing the hunger that had been there for months was suddenly ravenous. Was she overdoing this? Did he feel this, too? As if he felt her thoughts, his hand came to her waist, and the touch silenced the questions. She raised her hand to his side.

"How's that?" he asked, his lips close to hers.

"Very nice." She wished now she had more than a mattress covered in rumpled blankets on her bedroom floor.

"Well, then how about we quit while we're ahead?" His hand did not move from her side.

When she had been with Elijah, it had been hurried and so hormone fueled it was almost over before it began. And with Clarke every kiss ended up with them in the bedroom. Both men had left her physically satisfied but emotionally empty. "What? You don't want to?"

"Oh, I surely want to, Dr. Bailey. And if you still have a mind to do more of this, I am your man." He kissed her on the lips again. "But I find things worth having take time."

"This isn't what I'm used to."

"That's what I figured. Which is exactly why we'll take our time." He kissed her again and stepped back with a look of regret in his eyes. "I'll see you tomorrow. We have that shop to visit."

Her body hummed with longing, disappointment, and a deeper sense that Bryce McCabe was a good man. "Great."

"Good. In the meantime, you can look at those financial records and let me know if you see any patterns. And I'll get that list from the warden."

"Perfect."

"By the way, I'm trying to reach Sarah Cameron's boyfriend. I want to talk to him about her and who she might have known."

"Let me guess. He's avoiding you."

"He is. But I suppose he's gun shy when it comes to the cops."

"Gun shy I can appreciate."

He winked. "Like riding a horse, Dr. Bailey. It's not that complicated."

That provoked the first real laugh she'd had in a long while. She walked him to the front door and watched as he settled his hat on his head. "When should I meet you at the Classy Cat? It opens at ten tomorrow."

"Ten it is." He strode to his truck, and when he was behind the wheel, he nodded toward her before he drove off.

Her phone buzzed with a text, and when she pulled it from her pocket, she saw it was from Gideon. All is well. Attached to the text was an image of Nate, Kyle, and Joan. The boys were sporting wide grins, and Joan looked pointedly toward the camera like a hostage trying to send a message to the world.

Ann studied Nate's smile and realized it telegraphed the youthful joy that had been missing the last year. He was going to be okay. So was she.

As she turned to go back inside, she glanced down to the card that had fluttered out when she had removed her phone. She picked it up and saw Paul Thompson's name, phone number, and the scrawled address of his motel.

Thompson was on a fishing expedition, too. And the bait he was using was her darkest secret.

CHAPTER SEVENTEEN

Missoula, Montana
Sunday, August 22
2:15 p.m.

Ann grabbed her purse and decided it was time to find Elijah. If he had leaked or suggested the truth to one of his groupies, she wanted to know about it. A quick address search, and she realized he was living blocks away. Paul Thompson might be the least of her problems. She drove the blocks separating their homes. She parked, walked up to the front door, and knocked.

Christ, he had to know the truth.

A full thirty seconds passed before the door opened. Elijah stood with a blue-tipped paintbrush in his hands and looking a little annoyed by the interruption. When he saw it was her, his expression turned curious.

"Ann, did you bring me a welcome basket?" he asked.

"I heard you'd moved in." Her heart pummeled against her ribs, slamming blood through her arteries.

"Would you like to come inside? Still in the midst of decorating. I could have hired someone, but I really don't like strangers in my home."

She ignored the small talk. "There's a reporter in town. His name is Paul Thompson."

"He's left me messages," Elijah said warily.

"He's digging into Clarke's and your pasts."

Elijah frowned. "I gathered as much. Why?"

"He's doing a podcast, he says. He wants the world to know your story."

He looked amused. "Who on the planet doesn't?"

"Apparently, the bare facts aren't enough. He wants a blow by blow."

"Why do you care, Ann? I've heard you've become pretty expert at dodging guys like him."

"This one is talking to your Fireflies."

"I'm sure they all have a story to tell. They crave fame. It's one of the unhealthy reasons why they were attached to me."

"When's the last time you were in contact with Sarah Cameron?" she asked.

"She was from Tennessee, as I remember."

A sense of vindication rushed her. His simple answer had validated her working theory about the victims. "So, she was a Firefly?"

He arched a brow. "That's why you're asking about her, right?"

"What about Dana Riley? Did she contact you lately?"

"Dana?" He seemed to riffle quickly through his memory. "Tall, light-brown hair. Looked a little like you, though not as smart."

Dana had also been a Firefly. "Have you communicated with her lately?"

"No. I haven't connected with any of my Fireflies since I was released from prison."

"None tried to track you down?"

His head cocked. "Why is that any of your business?"

"I'm looking for Dana," she lied.

"Why? Is she bothering you?" he asked carefully.

"No, I'm trying to find her." She had not come prepared with a better lie and realized she could quickly back herself into a corner. Elijah had always been perceptive, and ten years in prison had honed that radar.

He slowly shook his head as his eyes narrowed. He did not believe her, but for whatever reason, he played along. "The final letter I had from Dana was almost a year ago. She was one of my most prolific correspondents. I think one hundred and two letters from her, if I remember. She was funny, moderately smart, and a welcome distraction."

"Are there any other Fireflies in the area?"

"Why the sudden interest in the Fireflies? Who cares if Thompson talks to them? His story will soon be forgotten. Unless you're jealous."

She ignored the suggestion. "Did you ever talk to your Fireflies about me?"

"I might have mentioned you." A smile teased the edges of his lips. "I was pretty angry with you after the trial."

"Who else did you tell about me?"

"I'm not sure."

"You have a photographic memory."

"Then I guess I do remember. But I'm not going to tell all my secrets until you tell me yours."

She ran her fingers through her hair. "This was a mistake. I should not be talking to you."

As she turned to leave, he said, "There was a homicide near town on Tuesday. I hear the body was burned." He studied her face closely. "Is the victim Dana?"

"No, it wasn't Dana."

"There was also a homicide in Helena in July. I hear that body was also burned. Was that one Dana?"

"How do you know this?"

"Once you've been branded an arsonist, you make damn sure you have an alibi when there's a fire within a two-hundred-mile radius. And for the record, I have alibis for both dates. You can tell the cops. They're welcome to check." His eyes narrowed again. "I know the Montana victims weren't Sarah Cameron. Her death was widely reported in the Knoxville media in June."

"You knew about Sarah."

A slight roll of his shoulders hinted at his discomfort. "I don't know anything about her death, if that's what you're suggesting."

She had taken a risk coming here, but it had paid off. At least two victims were Fireflies. The warden's list of Fireflies would now be a critical predictor of future victims.

"I didn't kill those women, Ann," he said clearly. "And I can prove it."

"Who else would want Fireflies dead?"

"I don't know."

For the first time, she sensed he was off balance slightly. "Maybe you're cleaning up loose ends."

He stepped toward her, using the close proximity of his body to threaten. "Be careful. You're accusing me of murder."

"If you have alibis, then you have nothing to worry about."

A bitter smile twisted his lips. "I've been through the criminal justice system, and I know truth doesn't always matter."

"Again, who would kill these women?" she asked.

"I don't know."

"Then we're done here." She turned to leave.

"How's Nate?" Elijah asked in a clear, direct tone. "Is he back from his camping trip yet?"

She froze and scrambled to maintain her calm. She faced him, deciding not to question his sources. He had a talent for knowing things. "He's fine."

"He's not the real outdoor type, is he?"

"He loves spending time with his cousin and uncle."

"And Joan is along for the ride." Even, white teeth flashed. "Joan fly-fishing has to be a sight to behold."

She started walking toward her car.

"I'm glad Nate's been able to get away," he added as he followed her. "This town reared its ugly judgmental side after Clarke's death. Odd that people blame the victims. I suppose it's easier to find fault with them than to believe something bad like that could happen to us."

People had shied away from Nate and her because they were afraid. How many of them had looked at their own spouses and wondered whether they knew the real truth? But to utter any words of agreement created a bridge of understanding. And if anything she wanted to sever all connections between them.

"You've never apologized to me, you know," he said. "Of course, you didn't know the real truth behind the College Fire, but I lost ten years in prison in part because of the testimony you gave in court."

She reached the driver's-side door, knowing there was nothing she could say to counter that.

He approached the car, staring at her over the roof. "Do you know how much the world changes in ten years, Ann? You were pregnant with Nate when I went away. And now look at him."

She had thought she could control this but now realized her presence had stoked his deep-seated anger. "He's trying to get on with his life. He's happy."

"I didn't have a father when I was growing up, and it was hard. Is he struggling without his father?"

"We're managing."

"Oh, I know you're doing fine without Clarke, but a boy only has *one* father."

His tone poked at the secret tightly wound in her heart. She reached for the door handle.

In a voice only she could hear, Elijah said, "I know the truth."

She looked into his stark features. "You don't know anything."

"I do." Slowly, he came around the car until they stood less than a foot apart. "And soon I'm going to prove that Nate is *my* son."

She met his gaze. "He is my son. Not yours. Stay away from him."

Elijah's gray eyes lit with a white-hot flame. "I'm going to claim what is mine."

"No."

"Yes. In fact, I will use every damn cent the state paid me for its mistake to get partial custody of my son."

"He is not your son!" She spoke louder than she had expected and quickly lowered her voice. "His father was Clarke Mead."

"Look at the boy. Can anyone with a passing knowledge of genetics believe Clarke was his father?"

"Nate believes it. That's all that matters."

"He deserves the truth," Elijah said.

"Is that what you told your Fireflies? Did you tell them about Nate? Because one of them told Paul Thompson."

Elijah's fingers curled into fists. "Did he threaten you?"

"Why do you think I'm here? Of course he did. He thinks he has leverage to get an interview out of me." An icy chill flooded her veins. "Elijah, you have no idea how far I will go to protect my son."

He grabbed her by the arm, his fingers biting into her flesh. "I'm no different when it comes to the boy."

Ann snatched her arm away. "Stay the hell away from my son."

She opened the car door and slid behind the wheel. As he stood beside the car and watched her, she fumbled with her keys and started the engine with shaking hands. She now realized that she had confused his silence for apathy. He clearly had been thinking about Nate far more than she had realized. She had miscalculated badly.

Her head swirled with all the chaos Elijah could create in their lives. If a judge were to take up his petition for custody, it would alter Nate's life forever. Now more than ever, she needed to determine if Elijah or someone else was killing Fireflies. Once Elijah's followers were dead, what would there be to stop the killer from going after her or Nate?

She drove away, leaving him standing in the street. She was not sure how long she'd been driving when her phone rang. Maura's name appeared on the display.

Ann sat straighter and cleared her voice. "Maura. The house looks great."

"Thanks. I have to mop floors today, and then you can stick a 'For Sale' sign in the front yard."

"Terrific. I have your check. Can I meet you at the house first thing in the morning?"

"Sure. We can do a final inspection."

"I'm sure it's fine."

"I don't suppose you could pay me in cash?" Maura asked.

"Sure. But I'll have to stop by the bank. I might be able to get enough out of the ATM."

"No worries. And if it takes an extra day, I can wait. Cash is easier for me now."

"I'll call you when I have it." She wound her way toward the house.

"You sound upset. You okay?"

"I'm fine. Ready to get my life settled."

"Change isn't always fun."

"No, it is not."

"Try to enjoy the day," Maura said.

"Thanks."

At the next red light, Ann checked her text messages, and realized Bryce had obtained a list of the Fireflies.

Bryce: Riley and Cameron are on the list.

Ann: Assume the third victim is also on it.

Bryce: Searching for pictures of all 13.

Ann: I'll dig into the list as soon as I get home.

Bryce: Will be in touch.

She pulled into her driveway and sat looking at her new home. In the silence, she closed her eyes and tipped her face toward the sun. Like it or not, this case had forced a wedge under the lid of Pandora's box, and soon there would be no stopping the truth from escaping.

CHAPTER EIGHTEEN

Deer Lodge, Montana
Monday, August 23
7:15 a.m.

By Monday morning, Ann was on the road headed toward Deer Lodge to see Megan Madison, a Firefly on the list of thirteen women Bryce had sent her. Deer Lodge was less than an hour away, and she believed she could see Megan and then be back in Missoula to meet Bryce at the Classy Cat at ten.

When she pulled up in front of Megan Madison's middle-class home in Deer Lodge, she was surprised it all looked so normal. The yard was freshly cut, the flower beds mulched and dotted with the heart-shaped daisylike yellow leopard's-bane floating in a sea of green ground cover. The front door was painted a bright red, and a swirling *M* dangled from a hook on the front door. A green minivan was parked in the two-car driveway.

She had always pictured Elijah's Fireflies as women who lived on the outskirts of society. In her mind they were disaffected, lost souls who were so consumed by their devotion for him that they did not have the capacity to manage a normal life.

Her own confirmation bias had blinded her to the idea that these women could be, or at least could appear to be, highly functioning and productive. She parked at the neatly edged curb and walked toward the front door.

Everyone had a core identity that they rarely fully revealed to anyone, including family, friends, and lovers. People, once they stepped outside, put on masks designed to attract mates, cajole parents, raise children, or climb the corporate ladder. In everyday life, most people were chameleons and liked altering dress, speech, opinions, and preferences based on the audience.

Given that, Ann should not have been surprised by Sarah Cameron's success in business or Megan Madison's seemingly average life. Both blended in like the grasshopper did on a leaf, all the while hiding their secret obsessions with Elijah.

She had not called ahead to make an appointment, fearing if Megan recognized her from last year's news accounts, she would not speak to her. Adjusting her purse on her shoulder, she climbed the neatly swept stairs and rang the doorbell equipped with a camera. She stood to the side. Footsteps thudded in the house and paused by the front door before it opened slowly.

The woman staring back at her through the crack between the doorway and jamb was in her midforties. She was in good shape, kept her long blond hair loose around her shoulders, and wore knee-skimming shorts, a button-down shirt, and sneakers.

"Ms. Madison?" Ann asked as she met her gaze.

"That's right."

"I'm Ann Bailey."

A flicker of recognition turned leery, and the woman shifted her body to block the view into her home. "Ann," she said carefully.

"You've heard my name before?"

"You were in the news some last year."

Ann shook her head slowly. "Elijah told you about me, didn't he?"

Megan's face paled, and she dropped her voice. "I haven't written to Elijah in a long time. I told that to the reporter when he came by."

"Paul Thompson?"

"That's right." She glanced behind her. "Look, I don't want to talk about this with you or him."

"I don't want to pry into your life, but I'm trying to understand the Fireflies. Why was Elijah Weston so appealing?"

Megan's dim demeanor brightened like a bulb. "You know what he looks like."

"He's very attractive."

"He's more than that. He has an energy that is beyond the average person."

Ann noticed the wedding band on Megan's left ring finger. Did Elijah represent a clandestine escape from everyday life? "It had to be more than his looks."

Megan drew in a breath, like a schoolgirl who had seen a favorite teen idol onstage. Her demeanor shifted from middle aged to that of a teenager. "He was funny. And so smart. And he knew things about life that I'd never thought about. I could tell him what was going on with my day, and he would write back and give me advice. There were times when he was the only person I could talk to."

Ann glimpsed the girl living in the suburban wife's body. "Why did you stop writing?"

"My daughter found the letters. She was fourteen at the time. She called me crazy and threatened to tell my husband if I didn't stop. I didn't want him to know. I didn't need that kind of trouble. Ending our correspondence was the hardest thing I ever did."

"That must have been difficult. Like losing a trusted friend," she offered.

"It was."

"But you did stop."

"I wrote him one last letter and poured my heart out to him. I told him not to write me back, and he respected my wishes and did not. He was considerate that way."

"Did he ever ask you to do anything?"

"Like what?"

"There was another Firefly. Her name was Lana Long, and he asked her to spy for him. She was killed in a fire last year."

"I heard."

"Did you know Lana?"

"We didn't meet in person, but some of us were in a social media group."

"Really? The cops never found that."

"We were careful," she said. "It's not like we went by the name Elijah's Fireflies."

"What was the name of the site?"

"It doesn't matter anymore. The administrator pulled it down about six months ago."

"How many people were on it?"

"A dozen."

"How did you find each other?"

"Received an invitation," she said. "I didn't join for weeks because I was afraid, but my curiosity won out."

"When was this?"

"Eighteen months ago."

"Did you know where any of the Fireflies lived?"

"I had a vague idea about some. They were from everywhere. All over the country."

Inside the house, a telephone rang, and a young girl called out, *"Mom!"*

"Look, I've got to go."

"Can I give you my card? I could meet you somewhere for coffee, and we could talk more."

"No. I'm not doing that. I shouldn't have spoken to you at all."

"The police think two recent murders are connected to the Fireflies."

Megan paled as she shook her head. "I don't know anything about that."

"Just take my card."

"No. Now go away." She closed the door.

Ann was frustrated because Megan had shared a small portion of what she knew. She fished a business card from her purse and tucked it in the door. Maybe this conversation had stirred something in Megan, and she would want to talk later.

In her car, Ann backtracked to Missoula and pulled up in front of the Classy Cat at five minutes after ten and parked behind Bryce's vehicle. The sign on the shop door read **OPEN**.

She parked, got out of her car, and walked up as his driver's-side window lowered. "I meant to be here earlier, but I made a stop along the way."

"I was just about to call you. Thought you might have changed your mind." His mirrored sunglasses covered his eyes and whatever meaning they might convey.

However, the subtext under his tone was clear: Had she changed her mind about the case? Or him? "I haven't." He might change his once he realized the baggage she carried.

"Good. Get in."

She came around the front of the car and opened the passenger-side door, closing it quickly.

When she slid into the front passenger seat, he shifted toward her. The car's interior, which had felt perfectly adequate on Saturday, had shrunk. The soft scents of his soap and leather filled the cab.

This was another one of those awkward moments where most single women her age knew how to handle themselves.

"Those thoughts are churning again," he said.

"Am I that obvious?"

"Afraid so."

"Chalk it up to being out of practice." She smiled, feeling her muscles relax. How many times had she preached to Nate about the power of talking instead of bottling emotions?

"For both of us."

She shifted her gaze toward him. "You?"

He grinned, shaking his head. "Me."

"You ever been married?"

"Once in my early twenties. Hard being married to a guy who's deployed ten months out of the year. No kids, and no harm, no foul. Still friends. She's remarried and has a couple of kids."

She sensed a faint hint of sadness that she was not sure extended to his former wife or his childless state. "That's nice."

"Why were you late? That's not like you."

"I drove to Deer Lodge, and I spoke to Megan Madison."

"She's on the Firefly list."

"I stopped by her house."

"By yourself."

"I thought she might talk to me if I had the element of surprise."

"Domestic calls can be the most dangerous. I know cops who've died when they went to make a simple domestic call."

"She's a homemaker. She has a neat front lawn."

"They can wield a knife or a gun just as easy as anyone. In the future, don't do that."

She bristled at the order. "I used sound judgment, but you're right. I should have told you."

"When it comes to investigating this crime, you're in my backyard, and you need to play by my rules."

"Really?"

His jaw tensed and pulsed, irritation clearly rippling through his body. She thought back to the times Clarke had used his size to intimidate her. It was always subtle and for ridiculous things like which brand of gas grill they should purchase or whether Nate should play soccer or baseball. She had always stood up to him, but each time she'd sensed she was negotiating with a caged tiger.

As if reading her thoughts, Bryce tugged off his glasses. "I don't want you to get hurt."

"I have no intention of getting hurt."

"No one does," he said softly. "But I've seen it happen too many times."

Whereas Clarke's focus had always been on winning, Bryce's true concern rang clear. "I hear you. I do. Now would you like to hear what she told me?"

Shaking his head, he looked equally exasperated and curious. "Tell me."

"The Fireflies, at least some of them, shared a social media page. They talked to each other and swapped stories. They were their own little support group. The site was taken down about six months ago. It would be helpful if your IT guys could identify the site administrator."

"They can try."

"Terrific." She brushed her pant leg, considering whether she should tell him about her visit with Elijah. She decided to wait. "Ready to go inside?"

He regarded her for an extra beat, as if he sensed her unspoken words. "Yes."

Out of the vehicle, she hurried around the front of his car while he waited for her, and then together they entered the glass-paned front door. The Classy Cat was a tony shop fashioned after an Old West saloon. The shop was chock-full of all kinds of fancy Western wear, such as rhinestone belts, turquoise jewelry, and leather vests and skirts. Fashion had never been Ann's bailiwick, and whenever she had dressed up, she'd always felt a little self-conscious. As she ran her fingers over a soft, buttery leather vest, she wondered if her new single status required an edgier look.

Saloon doors separating the back office from the front swung open, and a woman dressed in a prairie dress, a silver concha belt, and boots appeared. Dark hair was swept back in a sleek ponytail.

Her gaze flickered to Bryce but then zeroed in on Ann, as if in a glance she had categorized them as a couple. "Yes, ma'am, what can I do for you?"

"I was looking for a pair of boots," Ann said quickly as she pulled her phone from her back pocket. "Dana Riley posted this pair in July, and I love them. I'm hoping you still have them in stock."

"Sure thing. May I?"

Ann handed her the phone, watching the recognition flicker on the woman's features as she nodded.

"That's a specialty pair. We didn't have too many of those. I do remember Dana. She was a live wire."

"You remember her?"

"Mid-July. It was a slow weekday, and when she showed up, I figured she was a tourist who was just looking. Then before I knew it, she bought herself a whole outfit, including the boots. Turned out to be a good day after all. I took pictures of her and posted them on my site."

On her phone, Ann searched the store and pulled up the July posts. She immediately spotted the boots. The woman had dipped her head and pulled her cowboy hat forward, successfully obscuring her face. It was dated three days after Dana was killed. "Did you post these the same day you took them?"

"Yes. Like I said, it was a slow day."

"Was she alone?" Ann asked.

"She commented she was with a guy, but she never said who. Why are you asking about Dana?" the woman asked.

Bryce approached and showed the woman his badge. "I'm Sergeant Bryce McCabe with Montana Highway Patrol. This is Dr. Ann Bailey. You are?"

The clerk looked a little confused. "Betsy Davis. Look, those boots had to have been bought by Dana. I asked for her ID, considering the purchase was so large. I've been burned before. And she produced a driver's license. She looked like her picture."

"Ms. Davis, Dana was murdered several days before that purchase was made, but her body was not found immediately. Without a body or missing-person report, there'd been no reason to red-flag the credit card account," Bryce said.

"I had no idea," Ms. Davis said.

"Are you sure she didn't say anything about the man she was with?" Ann asked.

"She said she was getting dressed for a date with him. Said they'd not seen each other in a while, and she was excited to be with him."

"And you never saw him?" Bryce asked.

"I didn't. He never came into the store."

"Did she mention if they were staying in town?" Bryce asked.

"She said they were moving back to California soon. Said they were meeting a friend there."

"Did she mention a specific location or a name?" Bryce kept his gaze trained on Betsy.

"No."

"Did she appear nervous or distressed?" Ann asked.

"No."

Bryce pulled up the Polaroid picture of Jane Doe. "Was this Dana Riley?"

Ms. Davis studied the picture. "Yes, that's her. Blond hair." She looked up at them both. "This isn't Dana?"

"No, ma'am," Bryce said.

"Did she kill Dana?"

"That's what we're trying to figure out," Bryce said as he pulled a card from his pocket and handed it to her. "If you think of anything that might be of help, would you call?"

She flicked the edge of the card with a manicured finger. "Sure, I will."

Neither Ann nor Bryce spoke until they were outside. Both were silent as they considered what Ms. Davis had said.

"Our third victim was posing as Dana Riley?" Ann asked. "The killer gave her Dana's credit card."

"Looks like it."

"If Jane Doe was a Firefly, it's not hard to assume who the man manipulating her is," she said.

"Elijah Weston."

***

Elijah arrived at Ann's former home and found Maura in the kitchen, singing to a song on a beat-up brown radio. She was wearing an apron dotted with small blue handprints and handwritten letters reading **Happy Mother's Day**. She had cinched the strands at her narrow waist, knotting it at the base of her back in a neat bow. The apron was another Ann remnant picked off the trash pile, and the handprints were Nate's.

"You look very domestic," he said.

She jolted at the sound of his voice and whirled around, wide eyed with hints of fear and then relief. "I didn't hear you come in."

He knew how to move quietly or announce his presence with heavy footfalls. Prison had called for both skills, and if he was anything, he was an adept student. "What are you doing here today?"

"Last day on the job. Ann comes by this afternoon to pay me, and then my work here is done."

The freshly scrubbed air smelled of a melody of cleaners. The dirt and grime were gone, but like all houses, the walls were infused with laughter, tears, shouting, and quiet conversations. He was glad Nate was not living here. The past could be a heavy weight to carry.

She peeled off her yellow rubber gloves and draped them carefully over the sink. "Don't you have volunteer work today?"

"Later," he said, moving toward her until only inches separated them.

"Why did you come by?"

"To see you," he lied.

She captured one of his buttons and gently twisted it between her fingers. "I'm finished here. This place can't get any cleaner. I have time to kill."

"Really?"

"The bedrooms are still staged."

He refused to fuck in the family bed and certainly not on Nate's old bed. He backed her up until she bumped into the counter. "What's wrong with here in the kitchen?"

"Nothing."

He traced a blue handprint. "Take the apron off."

She arched her breasts toward him as she reached behind her and undid the bow. She loosened the apron and bunched it in her hand, ready to drop it. He took it from her, neatly folded it, and placed it on the table behind them.

"You're very sentimental," she said curiously.

He hefted her up on the counter and slid his hands up her naked legs to the edges of her shorts. Her skin was smooth, soft, and nicely tanned.

She pulled the band from her hair, letting light-brown tresses fall around her shoulders. He gathered a lock of it in his hand. It smelled of flowers and sunshine. She reached for the snap of her pants, pushed open the folds, and wiggled out of them. He undid his top pants button, then the zipper.

He pressed into her hard, imagining she was Ann. Frustration twisted around lust, driving him to plunge deeper. She gripped his shoulders, gasping.

He wanted her to be Ann, and he wanted Clarke Mead's spirit, caged on the other side of life, to be watching and brimming with impotent fury. Soon, he'd take back everything the man had stolen from him.

CHAPTER NINETEEN

Missoula, Montana
Monday, August 23
12:15 p.m.

When Ann arrived home, there was a manila envelope leaning against her front door. It was not marked. She picked it up and studied it for a moment and then looked around as if she expected to see someone watching her.

Inside the house, she closed the door and let her purse slide from her shoulder. She opened the flap and pulled out two stapled sheets of paper. Scrawled on a sticky on the top page was a note from Paul Thompson. *"Thought you might like to see my notes on the Fireflies. Call me."*

Ann gripped the printout, walked into her office, and sat down. The thirteen names were in alphabetical order, as with the list Bryce had texted her. But this list also included the women's pictures. She flipped to the names she knew. Lana Long. Sarah Cameron. Megan Madison. Dana Riley. She scanned the remaining nine, searching for the Jane Doe in the Polaroid picture found at the crime scene. None of the pictures appeared to match images that had been taken from various DMV systems.

She did not think any of these women really looked like her, but they all shared similarities that mimicked her own features. Light-brown hair. Caucasian. Thirtyish.

It certainly was not illegal for Elijah to have a preference for a particular type of woman, but the pattern was unsettling. She had sometimes gone days, weeks, even months without thinking about Elijah. But it seemed he had been constantly preoccupied with her while he was in prison.

A truck pulled up in the driveway and honked. She pushed the list back in the envelope and put it in her desk. She hurried to the front door and was relieved and thrilled to see it was her brother, Joan, and the boys.

As Gideon rose slowly out of the driver's seat, the boys barreled out and both ran toward her, each carrying hand-carved pieces of wood that sort of resembled mini canoes.

"Mom!" Nate hugged her and glanced up at her with a beaming face that triggered a surge of emotions.

"Hey, big guy!" She ran her hand over his short hair, noting he smelled like fish and unwashed little boy.

Kyle held up his quasi boat. "Aunt Ann, look what we made. Dad showed us how to carve."

She took the roughly hewn chunk of wood and carefully inspected it. Maybe it was not a canoe but a dog. "It looks amazing. I had no idea we had such talented wood-carvers in the family."

Joan rose out of the passenger seat, looking far from the sophisticated Philadelphia detective she had been a year ago. Her clothes were splashed with dried mud, and her hair stuck up in the back. "Modern-day life is so badly underrated," she said. "Hot showers, refrigerators, toilets. There's no place like home."

"You have a good time?" Ann asked, smiling.

"It was great," Joan said. "Really. The boys had a blast, and I've never seen Gideon more in his element. It was a successful trip that I will adore in retrospect."

Gideon's face had tanned a shade deeper, and he moved with the relaxed confidence of a man who was at peace with himself. Ann was glad to see her brother happy, and if she was honest, she envied his place in the world.

"Looks like you survived a few days alone," he said.

"Turns out I was fairly busy. Working with Bryce McCabe on the Anaconda homicide."

"I tried to track the case," Joan said. "But no service in the backwoods."

"You both back on the job tomorrow morning?" Ann asked Gideon and Joan.

"My shift starts at eight tomorrow morning," Joan said. "Fingers crossed there are no death investigations before noon."

"I'm on the same schedule," Gideon said. "Get Kyle off to his first day of school, and then I'm back on duty."

"My Tuesday class is one to two p.m., so I'll pick up both boys from school," Ann said.

"Thanks," Gideon said.

"How did the house cleanout go?" Joan asked.

"So far so good." She considered whether to tell them about the list now or give them the night to settle in. Knowing her brother would be annoyed if she did not mention the list immediately, she said, "I got home and found an envelope waiting for me from Paul Thompson. It contained a list of Elijah's Fireflies."

Gideon cursed. "Who is this reporter?"

"He's doing an in-depth podcast, as if the world needed a blow by blow of the case."

"You haven't spoken to him, have you?" Joan asked.

"God no," Ann said. "But he's left several messages and stopped by the house twice."

"I'll talk to him," Gideon said.

"Thanks, but no," Ann insisted. "I'll deal with him."

"I want an update on the Anaconda case," Gideon said.

"Mom!" Nate shouted from down the hallway. "What's this on your wall?"

Ann muttered a curse as she explained to Gideon and Joan, "It's a timeline of the cases I'm working on with Bryce." She mentally reviewed the timeline as she hurried toward her office, hoping she had not pinned up any graphic crime scene photos. Thankfully, there were none. She ushered both boys out of the room. "It's a case I'm working on."

"A homicide?" Kyle asked.

"Yes. And that's all I'm saying."

"Are you working with Sergeant McCabe?" Nate asked.

"That is correct."

The boy frowned. "Will you be able to pick me up from school tomorrow?"

Ah, children and priorities. She smiled. "Yes. I said that I would. And Kyle is coming by here afterward, just like we planned. In the meantime, I bought ice cream bars and Popsicles. Which do you want first?"

"Ice cream bars," Nate said. "We ate burgers on the road."

"Yeah!" Kyle said.

"In the freezer, guys. Help yourself." As they thundered through the house, Ann prayed life would find a way to settle down and balance.

Kyle ran up to his father and Joan with his half-eaten ice cream bar in hand. She said goodbyes to the trio, leaving Nate and her alone in their home.

"You haven't unpacked much, Mom," Nate said.

"I know."

It still felt odd to be here with him and not at the ranch or even the house on Beech Street. But this was the new normal.

"Nate, let's grab your backpack and get those clothes cleaned," she said.

"I didn't wear everything I packed. Sergeant McCabe overpacked by twenty percent."

"I kind of remember you adding a few things before you left."

Nate shrugged as he bit into the ice-cream sandwich. "Maybe."

She dragged his pack to the small laundry room and dug out a pair of muddy shoes, which had leaked and smeared whatever clean clothes he'd had. She sorted it all, and soon the machine was kicking into gear.

In the next two hours, Nate showered, and she laid out tomorrow's clothes and school backpack and made his lunch. By 7:00 p.m., he was in bed asleep with *King Lear* on his chest.

She took the book from him, replaced the bookmark, and as she thumbed through the pages, she noticed the previous owner's bold handwriting scribbled on the inside front cover. It read *"Elijah Weston."*

The blood rushed from Ann's head as she stared at Elijah's precise script. Had he given this to Nate? And if he had, what made him think he had any rights? As she stared at her son, it took all her control not to wake him up and ask about the note.

She placed the book on the nightstand, shut off the light, and left his room. Quietly, she closed the door behind her. Her secret, no matter how much she wanted it to stay hidden, was going to come out, and the best she could hope for now was to try and control the message.

In her office, she pulled up one of Paul Thompson's podcasts, and putting in her earbuds as she listened to his smooth, deep voice, she scrounged through the papers on her desk for his card. He had dangled effective bait when he brought up Nate's paternity and then sweetened the trap with the list. And like it or not, she was going to bite.

***

I do not like to hurt people. But sometimes they make it impossible for me to be kind. I am not sure why some people insist on being cruel, but it is a sad fact of life.

Standing outside Ann's house, I reach for a stick of gum and pop it in my mouth. As I chew and fold the silver wrapper into the shape of a bird, I watch her move from room to room through the house as she closes all the shades, and then one by one shuts off the lights.

I imagine her lying in her bed, her mind abuzz with images of face-less, charred bodies. And that makes me smile.

CHAPTER TWENTY

Missoula, Montana
Tuesday, August 24
8:00 a.m.

Bryce's phone rang as he sat at his desk in his Helena office. "Sergeant McCabe."

"This is David Brown, Sarah Cameron's boyfriend. You've called me a few times. And sent a deputy by my house."

"I have a few questions for you."

"Cops have ruined my life. I don't trust you."

"You need to put your trust issues aside. I'm investigating two murders in Montana that we think are linked to Sarah's murder."

"I've never been to Montana."

"I didn't think you had," Bryce said. "I'm trying to figure out who might have been in contact with Sarah before she died."

"I told this all to the Knoxville detectives," Brown said.

"Run it past me again. Do you remember anyone who might have just showed up? Someone she'd not seen before."

"She was always meeting strangers," he said. "That's part of being a Realtor."

"She talk about anyone in particular?"

"Look," Brown said, lowering his voice. "Sarah and I had a big fight a few days before she died. I'm still pissed at her, but I also feel like shit knowing the way she died."

"What was the fight about?" Bryce asked.

"I caught her in bed with another guy."

"Who?"

A hush settled. "I'd never seen him before."

"You must have gotten a good look at him."

"Sure. Tall, lean. Shoulder-length brown hair."

"And you never caught a name?"

"Not at first. Sarah came back to me, begging to explain. She said he was a reporter, and she'd made a mistake."

"A reporter?"

"Does something on podcasts. He was doing a story on women like her."

Paul Thompson. "If I sent you a picture, could you identify him as the man?"

"Yeah, sure."

"Stand by for a text." He selected a picture of Thompson from his website and sent it to Brown.

Seconds passed. "That's him," Brown said.

"You're sure."

"Couldn't miss that winning smile." Bitterness layered over the words.

"Thanks, Mr. Brown."

"Did he kill Sarah?"

"I don't know."

"Let me know when you do," Brown said. "I owe it to her."

"Sure."

Bryce ended the call and immediately texted the information to Ann.

Bryce: Be careful.

Ann: Will do.

He hoped she had the sense to stay clear of Thompson until he could dig deeper.

***

Ann read Bryce's text and, though mindful of his warning, refused to be stopped by it. She entered the coffee shop. She spotted Paul Thompson sitting in a corner booth, and judging by his open laptop and array of papers, he had been here awhile. When the door opened, he looked up, his gaze expectant. He moved to rise, jostled the table, and his coffee sloshed on the pages. He appeared torn between mopping up the mess and greeting her, until the brown liquid migrated toward his computer.

"Dr. Bailey," he said as he lifted his laptop.

"Mr. Thompson." It was petty to enjoy his discomfort, but she did.

He quickly set the laptop on a chair and pulled napkins from the dispenser as coffee dripped over the side of the table. He tossed her a quick glance as he mopped. "Call me Paul. When you say Mr. Thompson, I think of my dad."

She pulled out a chair as he grabbed a fresh layer of napkins and sopped up the last of the liquid.

"Can I get you a coffee or tea?" he asked.

"No, thank you." She took a seat and did her best to look relaxed.

"Sure?" He gathered up the sopping mess of napkins and dumped them in the trash before he dried his hands and then threaded long fingers through his hair. "Thanks for suggesting this coffee shop. I never would have found the place if you had not mentioned it. It might be my new favorite hangout."

"Glad to be of service," she said.

He sat, and again his fingers combed through his hair. "You grew up here, right?"

He was trying to make conversation, trying to break the ice and win her over to his side. She imagined in his computer was a big fat dossier on her history. "I did. What about you?"

"Tennessee," he said.

"That was where you became interested in podcasts?"

"I was an English major and always liked storytelling. But try and pay the light bill with that. Then I got the idea for a podcast. As you might guess, there are lots of recording studios in Nashville, so all I had to do was find the right story."

"You've found several stories," she said. "I listened to the one about the missing girl in North Carolina. Very compelling."

"I thought so."

"Did your story help the police solve the case?"

He sat a little taller. "They've been inundated with fresh leads, but so far no arrests."

She imagined that most of those leads were dead ends. Everyone wanted to be famous, and attaching themselves to a successful podcast was a way to do it.

"I reviewed your list of the Fireflies. You've done a great deal of homework." She had cross-checked a sampling of the facts he'd listed by the thirteen names and discovered everything was correct.

"I'm a good investigator." His eyes darkened and shifted, as if he sensed they had moved beyond the pleasantries and were getting down to brass tacks.

"I can see that." She steered the conversation. "Why this case?"

"It's gripping," he said. "Elijah is the brilliant loner, outcast. The perfect archetype for a story. And now that Elijah is out of prison, people will be curious about his next move and the women who are attracted to him."

"That's all past tense," she said. "What do you think he wants now?"

Thompson sat back, regarding her for a beat, before he said, "To get revenge against the people who put him in jail."

Her heartbeat kicked against her ribs. "How can you be so sure?"

"He's already used one Firefly, Lana Long, to spy on your late husband last year. And there's an online group for the Fireflies. Lana did her share of talking to some of the others until she died," he said.

"You know about the online group?" she asked.

"I know how to dig."

"Why was the group taken down six months ago?" she asked.

He grinned. "I've been pretty generous with my information. Now it's your turn to talk."

"You said you were from Tennessee. You must have heard about Sarah Cameron's murder."

His eyes narrowed. "I did. Her death is part of the reason I'm determined to finish this podcast."

"Why?"

"I interviewed her. I liked her."

"*Liked* her? You slept with her."

He shrugged. "We were both adults. You *knew* Elijah in college."

Ann ignored him. "Do you have any idea about who could have hurt Sarah?"

"I have theories."

"Such as?"

"I've said too much. Now it's your turn. I want to interview you."

She drew in a careful breath, wondering whether he was recording this conversation. "When you and I first met, you mentioned my son."

"I shouldn't have done that," he said quickly. "I was trying to break through the ice and get your attention."

"You got my attention." She leaned in, lowering her voice. "If I agree to be interviewed, I want your word you will not involve my son."

He regarded her. "I will agree to that."

She was making a deal with the devil, but if she could protect Nate, she would do it. "Give me a couple of days. It's the beginning of the school year. Everything's crazy."

"Saturday."

She supposed he was trying to be generous, but she also sensed an underlying threat if she did not agree. "Text me the location."

"You won't regret this."

She already did.

***

Elijah pulled into the entrance to the trailer park south of town. His mother had lived here for at least twenty-five years, and he had lived here during his middle school years. As the car rumbled slowly past the long trailers, he noticed not much had changed. There were still some who kept their places up well enough, taking the time to install small fences, gardens, or porches.

As he rolled down the gravel road, the muscles in his body tightened, and he had the urge to turn the car around and leave. He had worked hard to put distance between himself and this life, but it seemed no amount of learning would erase the marks that had been left.

He parked by a collection of several broken chairs lying on the damp soil next to his mother's grayish-white trailer. Grabbing the box of her favorite brand of chocolates, he got out of the car and climbed the steps. Inside, the laughter of a television crowd boomed. You could set your clock by his mother. She never missed the morning lineup of game shows.

He knocked, taking a little pleasure in knowing she would hate any kind of interruption now. When she did not answer, he knocked harder, pounding until he heard a gruff, "All right, I'm coming. Hold your damn horses."

Footsteps shuffled toward the metal door, and it opened with a snap, releasing a cloud of whiskey-infused cigarette smoke.

Faded blue eyes narrowed, and the old woman stared at him as if just for a moment she did not recognize him. Then distrust turned to a cautious optimism. "Elijah."

"Mom. How are you?"

Her emaciated face was deeply lined, and her disheveled white hair made her look older than her fifty-two years. She did not rush to embrace him, taking time to survey his khakis and light-blue button-down shirt. "Not as well as you, from what I hear. Heard you hit pay dirt with the state."

He was not surprised she had mentioned the settlement right away. Or that she had not bothered to hug him. His mother, at her core, put her survival above all else.

"I brought you these," he said, shoving the box of gold-wrapped candy toward her.

She flicked her cigarette over the side of the rail and dug shorn fingernails into the box's thin plastic coating. She pulled off the top and inspected the box. In a monotone voice, she said, "They look fancy."

"I remember you liked this chocolate," he said.

"You remembered that? That's nice of you." She selected a center square, pulled off the foil, and bit into it. She grimaced, spit out the candy, and tossed it and the uneaten portion over the side rail. "I could use some cash."

His mother had been the youngest of seven children, and judging from academic awards he had found in a box under the stairs, she had been a brilliant student. But a few years before his birth, her bright path had begun to dim as her drinking increased. The madness took hold in her midtwenties, and by thirty she was a frequent resident of mental health facilities.

Elijah fished a couple hundred dollars from his pocket and handed it to her.

She nodded as she counted the money. "About covers the money I put in your canteen account when you were in prison."

It was ten times what she had given him. "That should make us square."

"You think this money evens us out? After all I done for you? All the secrets I keep? A reporter was willing to give me a hundred bucks to talk about you."

"Did you take the money?" he asked carefully.

"No."

"Did you figure I'd pay you more to be quiet?"

She shrugged. "Maybe I stayed quiet because you're my son."

"An accident of genetics."

She gripped his arm with a surprising strength. He paused, wishing it could be different with her. Wishing she cared. Wishing he cared. But whatever was going on in her head had long ago destroyed their chances at a normal relationship. The best he could do was send her money so that she kept quiet about him.

"I'll send you money as long as you don't talk about me. It's important people not know about my past."

She released her grip. "The cops don't know about it all, do they?"

"No, and I want to keep it that way."

She grinned. "That's my boy."

As he left, she turned back toward her game show and closed her door behind her with a hard bang. Behind the wheel of his car, he started the engine.

He glanced to the open envelope on the passenger seat and removed the letter from the DNA-testing company. There was no doubt, according to the paternity results, that Nate was his biological son. He had sensed it from the moment he had seen the boy with his mother, but now he had proof.

He backed out of the space and turned toward the park entrance. The stress stirring in his gut ebbed as he reached the main road, and he took the left back toward town.

Nate would never come here, never see that woman. He deserved better. And Elijah would see to it that the boy had the best. Until then, it was his duty to protect him, and the first order of business was to eliminate Paul Thompson.

CHAPTER TWENTY-ONE

Missoula, Montana
Tuesday, August 24
1:00 p.m.

Bryce was curious as he stood in the back of Ann's classroom and watched her hand out semester syllabi on bright yellow paper. She had texted him an hour ago and asked to see him.

He took a seat, the amphitheater half-full of at least a hundred students. All looked young as hell, but he guessed most were either senior or graduate level.

As she began to talk about what she hoped to cover in Forensic Perspectives, a woman to his right began to wave her hand wildly. "Dr. Bailey!"

Ann nodded to the woman. "No questions yet."

The woman was silent for only a moment before she flapped her hand again. "But I need to ask this very important question."

A second woman two rows in front of her twisted in her seat and said, "Can you shut up! The professor is talking."

The first woman leaned forward in her seat. "I can ask whatever question I want. This is a free country."

"And you are free to get the hell out of this classroom."

Bryce noted the first woman's eyes narrowed as she stood and curled her fingers into a fist. Her body language rippled with anger and tension, and whatever her issue, she was spoiling for a fight. He rose, and when he did, he caught Ann's gaze. She managed an imperceptible shake of her head, as if to ask him to stand down.

He held off, watching as the fight between the two women escalated into a shouting match. About half the students in the room had put down their phones and were watching. Behind Ann, the doors opened, and an armed security guard appeared as if on cue. The guard ordered both women to leave with him. The first woman resisted, but when he threatened to bring in the local police, she followed him and the other woman out of the room.

The room buzzed with nervous laughter, and Ann moved slowly behind her podium. She raised her hands, told everyone to calm down, and then asked if anyone could describe the two women.

"That first woman was crazy," a young woman with blue hair said.

"What was she wearing?" Ann asked.

She received a flurry of adjectives, none of which really hit the mark. When she asked for details about the second woman, she was bombarded with descriptions as varied and inaccurate as the first.

Ann listened, nodding as each student talked. She gave no hint whether she agreed with the students or not. "Turns out we have a real law enforcement officer here today," she said. "What do you think of our recap, Sergeant McCabe?"

Bryce felt the glare of the proverbial spotlight as the students turned in their seats. He was hard to miss, since his persona screamed *cop*. "Eyewitness testimony in a high-stress, unexpected situation is often unreliable. A few students got a couple of details right, but most were wrong."

"Can you describe the women?" Ann asked.

"The first female was approximately twenty to twenty-five years old. She was five feet five and weighed about one hundred and fifty pounds. Black hair, gray dress with white fringe. The second woman was about the same age, five eight, brunette, and she wore jeans and a blue T-shirt." Both women were dressed inconspicuously and would have been easily forgettable, as most criminals were.

Ann walked to the rear door, opened it, and the two women appeared. They stood on the stage, each on one side of Ann. They were just as he had described.

"They are paid actors," Ann said. "This was a setup."

Nervous laughter and murmurs rumbled over the crowd. Several pointed out they had been right about age and height—some teased others for being dead wrong.

"Sergeant McCabe is correct about eyewitness testimony. It is often wrong. Our perceptions are colored not only by stress and the brevity of the incident, but also by our own personal biases. It's human nature to mix up events with all the other distractions we have going on. My point is that we as forensic psychologists have to be better than the average witness. We have to note the fine details, because they will often give us greater insight than the subject's words. Stay on your toes, kids. This is day one, and you never know when I'll have another surprise for you."

"Are we going to get graded?" a young man joked.

Ann grinned. "Of course. Today's assignment is to find a quiet place, write up what you saw, and read chapter one of the textbook. See you on Thursday."

Bryce watched the students file out of the classroom. Several tossed him curious, even nervous, glances. When the aisle was clear, he made his way down the steps toward Ann. When he was a few feet from her, he smelled the faint scent of her soft perfume, and he realized the fragrance invigorated him.

"Nicely done, Dr. Bailey," he said. "Your actors had me fooled for a second."

"When I saw you stand, I knew it was going to be over before it started if I didn't stop you."

"All worked out in the end. You said you had something to tell me."

"I met with Paul Thompson this morning in a public coffee shop."

"After my text?"

She hesitated as if chewing on words and then met his gaze. "Yes."

"For a lady who appears cautious and reserved, you take a lot of risks."

"It was important to determine if he had more to say about the Fireflies."

Bryce would bet it was more than that. "And?"

"He admitted to sleeping with Sarah, just as Brown suggested. And he said the Fireflies communicate with each other."

"You already established they had the chat room. Which, by the way, my IT guy was able to find."

"And what did he discover?"

"Content was taken down. He's trying to locate the administrator." He leaned toward her a fraction and dropped his voice. "What aren't you telling me, Ann?"

"Mind if we take a walk, maybe sit in a car or go back to my house? I have more to tell you."

"Sure. We can go now."

She appeared relieved he did not argue or press for details as she gathered her bag. He followed her out of the building and then trailed her in his vehicle the few miles to her house.

She opened her front door. "I can make coffee."

"Sounds good." He removed his hat and set it on the table by the front door, next to Nate's worn copy of *King Lear*. He picked up the book and casually thumbed through the pages. This time he saw Elijah Weston's name on the inside front cover.

The boy had not ended up with one of Elijah's books by accident. "Did Nate finish reading this?"

"Twice."

"On a scale of one to ten, how smart is he?" He set the book down.

"Eleven."

"Seriously?"

"Yes."

"That comes with challenges."

"The goal is to keep him busy and his mind engaged."

"A full-time job." He suspected the small talk and coffee were delay tactics as she searched for the right words. "Unpacking still at a standstill?"

"I keep finding better things to do," she said.

Minutes later, she poured each of them a cup of coffee, and they sat at the kitchen island.

Bryce sipped. "I'm all ears."

She traced the brim of her cup. "When Thompson first made himself known to me, he alluded to something that threw me for a loop." She blew out a breath. "Back in college, I'd broken up with Clarke because I was convinced that we wanted different things in life. Elijah and I were tutors at the math center together. And one thing led to another, and we slept together." She looked up at him. "Then the house I shared with Joan caught fire."

"And Elijah was convicted of arson."

"Yes."

"Did Clarke know about your relationship with Elijah?"

"I didn't think so at the time, but now I will always wonder." She tried her coffee. "When I was in the emergency room after the fire, the doctors ran a pregnancy test as a precaution. That's when I found out I was pregnant with Nate. Clarke was with me. And he, of course, assumed the baby was his, as did I. It didn't take much to convince me to get married and stay in Missoula."

"When did you realize Elijah was the boy's biological father?"

She swallowed and did not seem surprised he had guessed. "A few years ago. Clarke was never stupid but never off-the-charts smart like Nate. Mannerisms, the way Nate smiled, even how much milk he puts on his cereal was all Elijah. I had a DNA test done, but I never told Clarke or Nate."

"Which brings us back to Paul Thompson. How could he know about your relationship with Elijah?"

"My very short relationship with Elijah wasn't really common knowledge. But if Elijah got ahold of a picture of Nate, he would have known," she said. "Elijah guesses the truth, tells a few Fireflies about me and Nate, and word spread among them."

"Even if he'd said nothing, it wouldn't be a stretch to make the connection, given the boy's likeness to Elijah."

"It's getting more and more obvious, and I'm sure more people are making the same assumption," she said. "I'm hoping if I talk to Thompson, he will back off his information about Nate."

"At the rate Nate is growing, everyone will see it."

"Nate will need to be told, but I was hoping for a few more years. And for all of Clarke's faults, he loved Nate."

"Is there any way I can talk you out of talking to Thompson?"

"I don't see how I have a choice."

"When are you to meet?"

"Saturday."

"What are you going to talk about?"

"Not your case, of course, or its connection to the Fireflies. I'll talk about Clarke and tell him what I know about Elijah."

A muscle pulsed in his jaw. "Maybe you can use the interview to our advantage. You're good at reading people and body language and coaxing facts that otherwise might have gone unsaid. Treat him as a suspect. Also be sure to tape the conversation."

"I'd planned to do all that. But I wanted to be up front with you. This past of mine is refusing to stay in the past."

A small smile. "They rarely do."

She stared at his lined face, deeply tanned by the Montana sun. She moved around the island and cupped his face with her hands. He stared up at her, and, carefully, she leaned forward and kissed him on the lips.

***

A charged jolt shot through Bryce's body as Ann kissed him. He rose and threaded his fingers into her hair and pulled her toward him. The kiss quickly deepened.

When he pulled back, she moistened her lips. "I want you."

"Same."

"I know you said something about moving slow, but . . ."

"Forget what I said," he growled as he kissed her again.

She took him by the hand and led him to her bedroom, where the double mattress and box spring still sat on the floor. The sheets were rumpled, and clothes from yesterday draped a cane rocking chair.

"Not exactly a palace," she said.

"It'll do."

He removed his weapon and set it on the floor by the bed and toed off his boots. A sense of urgency built in her as she shrugged off her blouse.

He was at her side, sliding his hand up over her flat belly to the curve of her breast. He squeezed her nipples gently, then pressed his fingertips to the hollow between her breasts. "Your heart is beating fast."

"Been a while."

He smiled and cupped her buttocks. "Just like riding a bike."

***

Bryce lay next to Ann, their naked bodies coiled together. He had learned on an Afghanistan mountainside to savor the good moments life tossed his way, because they came few and far between. When they showed, he locked out the outside world and zeroed in on what was directly in his line of sight. Sounded more Zen than he would ever admit to out loud, but the way he figured it, if he paused in the best places, he would have the reserves to power through the worst of the gunfire, the explosions, the screams, the blood.

And now his body was boneless, and he realized he might have touched perfection for a few brief moments. He understood hard work and duty, but Jesus, he had forgotten what bliss felt like.

Bryce's phone rang, and a curse growled in his throat. He felt Ann stir at his side, and he hugged her a little tighter. Just a few more seconds.

"It's not my phone," she said.

"Nope, fault's all mine."

She rose up on her elbow and kissed him on the lips. "It's for the best. I have to pick the boys up at school soon."

Bryce let the call go to voicemail, knowing he would not have a productive conversation with Gideon Bailey while lying naked in bed with Ann. "It's your brother."

"He never calls to chat." She checked her phone. "He didn't call me, so it can't be the boys."

Bryce kissed her. "The outside world is calling."

"Yes."

And just like that, the best of all moments ended.

CHAPTER TWENTY-TWO

Missoula, Montana
Tuesday, August 24
4:00 p.m.

Bryce pulled up in front of the small one-story house now surrounded by several cop cars, a forensic van, and yellow crime scene tape. Out of the vehicle, he tucked his jacket back so that the badge around his neck was visible and approached the young uniformed officer. He introduced himself, received the all clear to proceed, and then slid on gloves and booties before entering the house.

The smell was the first thing he noticed. It was the strong, sickly sweet smell of death that, despite the frigid temperature of the house, was thick enough to make a man's eyes water.

He paused in the entryway to study the main room, which was decorated in mauve and white and reminded him of the eighties. There were plenty of pictures on the walls of generations of families, and he quickly saw the same middle-aged woman appearing in all of them. He did not understand why he was here, but like Ann had said, Gideon did not ask for an assist just for the hell of it.

He found Gideon in the back bedroom, standing to the side as a forensic tech snapped pictures of a woman lying on her bed. Judging by the patchy discoloration on her face and arms, the slippage of her skin, and the bloating in her belly, she had been dead more than twenty-four hours.

Blood stained her gray flannel nightgown, blooming over most of her chest. She stared up at the ceiling, a look of stress and horror on her face.

"This is Edith Scott, age forty-eight," Gideon said. "She was found about two hours ago by a neighbor who had not seen her in a couple of days. Neighbor said Ms. Scott lives a very predictable life, and suddenly her newspapers were piling up on her porch. He had a spare key and let himself in."

"Where's the neighbor now?"

"Back at his house. I have a uniform sitting with him."

Bryce moved closer to the bed, noting the blood had soaked deep into the mattress. Ms. Scott's fingers were curled, and her mouth was agape in a silent scream.

"Why'd you call me?" Bryce asked.

"Ms. Scott works at the university, and she served on the jury that convicted Elijah of arson. According to her neighbor, she told everyone that would listen that he didn't belong here."

"Has Elijah approached her?"

"Neighbor didn't know, but Elijah is always cool and calm. He rarely shows his emotions."

Bryce's attention shifted back to the source of the blood. "How many times was she stabbed?"

"At least three, but the medical examiner will have to give the final count."

"The three murders I'm investigating all involve stabbing."

Gideon nodded slowly. "Thus the call. There's no arson or facial mutilation, but the knife wounds are very similar, from what Joan told me about the Helena victim."

Edith Scott did not fit the profile of the other three victims. Not only was she at least twenty years older, but she had been murdered in her home instead of at a scenic mountain overlook.

"I'd like to be present at the autopsy," Bryce said.

"I'm counting on it."

"Elijah Weston has had ten years to nurse a grudge," Bryce said.

"I've seen guys like Weston before. Careful not to get caught because he never comes straight at you. He'll catch you alone and take you out, and you'll be dead before you even know you're bleeding."

The sound of new voices and the rattle of a gurney had him turning to see Joan Mason. She nodded to Gideon and shifted her full attention to the body.

"I'd heard she might be the victim," Joan said, moving toward the bed, her face a mixture of sadness and clinical curiosity. "Do you have all the pictures you need of the body?"

Gideon looked to the technician, who nodded. "She's all yours now."

"Well then, gentlemen, unless you need to see anything else, everyone clear out so my assistant and I can take custody of the body."

"I'll call Dr. Christopher about the autopsy," Gideon said.

"I've already spoken to him. It'll be at nine in the morning," Joan said.

Bryce and Gideon left the room and walked through the house, looking for the smallest items that could tell them something about an individual. In the kitchen the white refrigerator was covered in magnets featuring pictures of Paris, Rome, and New York City, holding up appointment cards for various doctors. He opened the refrigerator and saw the dozen cans of ginger ale, bread, and yellow American cheese. The pantry was stocked with clear-broth soups. These bits of small data told him she had loved the idea of travel but may not have had the physical stamina to accomplish it.

"Was she ill?" Bryce asked.

"I don't know. Let me ask Joan if she's surveyed the medicine cabinet yet." Gideon disappeared down the hallway.

On the kitchen windowsill were several mason jars filled with water and the leafy stems of plants she was trying to root. Whatever had been going on with her, she'd planned to be around long enough to see the plants grow to maturity.

"There are some heavy-duty pain meds in the cabinet," Gideon said. "Prescribing doctor is an oncologist."

"Likely very ill." They would soon know what type of cancer and her prognosis.

There were personal photos, but judging by the settings and ages of the others in the pictures, they were coworkers. No images of young children, graduation photos, or even the vacation pictures the magnets suggested. There were a few books, a collection of celebrity magazines, and a small but serviceable television.

"What else can you tell me about Elijah Weston?" Bryce asked.

"As you must know, smart as hell. In the last year he's earned his master's in psychology and is now a PhD candidate. I wouldn't be surprised if he has his doctorate in a year."

"What's his endgame?"

"I heard yesterday that he's bought a house close to Ann's," Gideon said.

Bryce did not know how honest Ann had been with her brother about the boy. "And Nate."

Gideon's eyes narrowed with understanding. "I love that boy like he's my own, and he's been through a hell of a lot this last year. This past weekend was the first time I've heard him laugh out loud in months."

"I like the kid. He's an old soul but needs protecting." The boy had a devoted uncle, but Bryce knew in that moment he would also protect the boy.

Gideon rubbed his chin, eyeing Bryce less like a cop and more like a big brother. "What's your deal with Ann?"

"That's between us."

Gideon's stare lingered as if he'd gotten his answer. "Clarke Mead did a lot of damage. He hurt Ann and the boy."

"And Elijah, because I think he knew they were rivals for her," Bryce said pointedly, trying to determine what Gideon knew.

Gideon's eyes narrowed again. "She's told you?"

"About Nate? Yes."

"I don't want Elijah screwing up her life."

"How can you stop Elijah from claiming his paternal rights? He's not only smart, but he has a nice chunk of change to hire lawyers."

Gideon rubbed the back of his neck with his hand. "I'd like to prove that he had something to do with this. Hell, I'd like to link him to the recent murders. But I won't frame him."

"We have determined that two of the victims were Elijah's Fireflies."

"Really?"

"Dana Riley, who was killed near Helena, and Sarah Cameron from Knoxville, Tennessee."

"What about the body found near Missoula earlier this week?"

"I don't have an identity on Jane Doe yet, but Dr. Christopher is hoping a metal plate in her ankle will supply a name. We also have a list of the Fireflies, and we're trying to track them down."

"I've got a couple of uniforms canvassing the houses," Gideon said. "Hoping there are enough security cameras that might catch a glimpse of whoever killed Edith."

Bryce's mind kept tripping back to Ann. She had been the first hint of sunshine in what had been his otherwise dark and closed world. He was a master at putting one foot in front of the other and getting the job done. But he could never really claim any kind of true happiness. At the rate his life had been going, he could picture himself on the ranch with his brother, caring for broken and unwanted dogs. Not the worst of fates, but making love to Ann proved there could be more.

"As much as I'd like to confront Elijah," Gideon said, "I need to have more evidence. I'd bet the farm that he's got solid alibis for every murder. If I can't slide a tight noose of evidence around his neck, he'll slip free."

"He won't," Bryce said. "Been my experience that the smartest guys make the dumbest mistakes. See you at the autopsy."

***

I see the cops at Edith Scott's house. They don't see me because I am careful. *Hide in plain sight* is my motto. I knew it would not be long before Edith was found, but I was hoping it would take a day or two longer. Never underestimate the power of the nosy neighbor.

All my talk about not hurting people is true. I really did not hurt Edith. She went quick, and after getting a look at the pills in her bathroom, I did her a favor. Cancer is a shitty way to die. What I did was akin to ripping a Band-Aid off. Hurts for only a minute, and then it's over. Lights out, pain gone. Yeah, the knife is better than cancer. I did her a favor.

As I watch the cops, I know that Gideon Bailey and Bryce McCabe could be a problem. They both have potential to screw it all up.

I do not plan on being here forever. I just need a few more days, and then I can wrap up the last of my loose ends and blow this Popsicle stand for good.

My phone chimes with a text, and it scares the hell out of me. Like the universe is looking over my shoulder and whispering to me, *I see what you are doing.*

But the text is not from the universe. It's from someone I know. Maybe a new partner in crime. And it makes me smile.

CHAPTER TWENTY-THREE

Missoula, Montana
Tuesday, August 24
4:00 p.m.

Ann arrived at school to pick up the boys and on the way home took them out for pizza and ice cream. She had been eating out a lot lately, as if food would solve all Nate's and her worries. Thankfully, he was a growing boy and, like his cousin, was a bottomless pit with two hollow legs. She was not so lucky, and if this kept up, she would have to invest heavily in sweatpants.

After they dropped Kyle off, they headed home, and when they arrived, they discovered Maura's truck parked in the driveway.

"Is that the lady cleaning out the Beech Street house?" Nate asked.

"Yes."

His knotted brow signaled he still was not comfortable with letting the Beech Street house go.

"Head on inside," she said. "Get started on your homework."

"Okay."

Ann held the pizza box containing two leftover pieces and moved toward Maura's truck.

Maura rolled down the window. "Just wanted to thank you for the work. I also wondered if you'd be a reference for me."

"Of course. You did a good job of cleaning out the house."

"Thanks—a word from you will go a long way in this community."

"Would you like me to write a letter?" Ann asked.

"That would be great."

"I'll write it out now, and then you can take it with you."

"Terrific."

"Come inside. It should just take a minute."

"Sure." Maura followed her into the house.

Ann stepped around the boxes and hurried down to her office to get a yellow legal pad and a pen. As she came out, she found Maura surveying the unpacked containers.

"As you can see," Ann said, "I'm still getting moved in. It's taking a lot longer than I anticipated."

"I can help you get this house set up," Maura said. "Free of charge. As you have seen, I'm good at this kind of thing."

"That's not necessary. There's no reason why I can't find the time to get it done." She jotted a quick note proclaiming Maura a wonderful contractor and signed it.

Maura held up a thick book on forensic psychology. "I can have you unpacked and set up in a day."

The idea dangled like a carrot on a stick. But letting Maura into the Beech Street house versus the home Ann shared with Nate now was different. Ann folded her handwritten job reference and handed it to Maura. "No, but thank you."

"I get it. It's weird. This is your home. I know. But if you want to work side by side with me, we'll be done in half the time. I'm a hurricane when it comes to cleaning."

The idea of facing endless boxes and shelves to assemble felt like a weight on her shoulders. And the sooner she made this house a real home, the better it would be for Nate. "I'll be here for four hours tomorrow. And I'll pay you."

"Just name the time."

"Ten a.m." That would give Ann a little time to meet the Realtor at the Beech Street house and maybe straighten up some of the piles here.

Maura grinned broadly. "You'll be thanking yourself by the weekend."

"Okay." Ann raised the pizza box. "Are you hungry?"

"Kind of starving."

"There's a couple of slices left."

"Oh God no. You don't have to feed me."

"Take it. Please. If Nate and I eat any more, we'll pop. Take the pizza, and I'll see you tomorrow."

Maura accepted the pizza box. "Thank you, Ann. You won't be sorry."

***

Bryce received the phone records for Dana Riley and noted immediately that the last text she'd made was in mid-July, at least a week after her death.

He dialed the last number, landed in the voicemail of Jeff Reynolds. He left a detailed message that identified him and explained he had questions about Dana. Fifteen minutes later, Reynolds returned his call.

"Mr. Reynolds. Thank you for calling me back," Bryce said.

"Yeah, sure. I'm not sure why Montana Highway Patrol is calling me about Dana. Is she all right?"

"What's your relationship to Ms. Riley?" Bryce asked.

"We dated for three years."

"When is the last time you saw her?"

"Five or six months ago." He hesitated. "We broke up. She and I weren't getting along, so I decided to end it."

"Can I ask why you were having trouble?"

"It's kind of personal."

Bryce had hoped to converse a little longer before revealing his news, but he decided candor might shake loose information. He leaned forward at his desk, trying to imagine the other man's expression. "Mr. Reynolds, I'm sorry to inform you, but Dana is dead."

Reynolds went silent. In the background a door closed. "What? When?"

"Her body was found in July near Helena. We only just identified the remains."

"Remains? Jesus. What happened to her?" His tone crashed to a hoarse whisper.

"Her body was burned, making visual identification impossible. We were able to identify her with DNA. She had a prison record from Maryland."

"Yeah," Reynolds said more to himself. "She was arrested when she was about nineteen for theft. She went through a rough patch in her life, but when she got out of prison, she sobered up."

"Why did you break up?"

Reynolds cleared his throat. "We grew apart. I wanted to get married and start a family, and she wanted to go . . ."

"Go where?"

"To Montana. She had an obsession about the place."

"Why?"

"Look, I don't want to speak ill of the dead."

"I'm not here to judge her, but I need to figure out who killed her."

"How did she die?"

"For now, let's focus on why she wanted to come to Montana. That's a long way from Maryland."

"She had an obsession with a guy out there. He was in prison, if you can believe it."

"Elijah Weston?"

"Yeah, how did you know?"

"Mr. Weston had a solid following of women while he was in prison. He maintained an extensive correspondence with Ms. Riley."

"When I found out about it, I was pissed. But she swore that it was all over and she wasn't writing him anymore. I saw a picture of the guy. Good looking in a movie-star kind of way. Didn't look like he would set fires."

"He didn't, as it turns out. The charges were dropped against him. Many of the women who followed him lost interest once he was released from prison."

"Women like the bad boys." Reynolds's tone signaled bitterness. "Plain old working stiffs like me just aren't exciting enough."

"Did you hear from Dana at all after you two broke up?"

"She texted me a few times. She sent me pictures while she was driving west. When did you say she died?"

"Early July."

"That can't be right. We must have exchanged a dozen texts on the thirteenth. I remember because it was my birthday. She was actually really nice and seemed interested in me."

"What did she ask you?" Bryce asked.

"She wanted to know how I was doing. It was nice. Normal. I can send you screenshots."

"Do that. Did she say where she was?"

"Anaconda, I think. She said she was on her way to Missoula."

Dana had not sent those texts. The killer, who clearly had a sick sense of humor, had decided to engage in a conversation with Reynolds.

"Did she mention if she was traveling alone or with someone?" Bryce asked.

"I got the impression she was alone. After the thirteenth I never heard from her again." He sighed. "If Dana was dead, then who texted me?"

"That's what I'm trying to figure out," Bryce said.

"Was it whoever killed her?" Reynolds asked.

"I'm not sure."

"Where's Dana now?" he asked.

"She's with the medical examiner in Missoula."

"Sergeant McCabe, how did she die?"

"She was stabbed. And as I said, her body was burned and also mutilated, which is why it took us so long to identify her."

"I want her sent home." His voice faltered. "She doesn't belong out there. She was working out some kind of fantasy, but sooner or later real life takes over." He exhaled heavily, as if a weight were pressing against his chest. "I thought she'd return to me after she realized this was her home."

"I'm sorry for your loss."

He spoke to Reynolds a few more minutes. The man's voice cracked several times, and by the time they ended the call, he could barely speak.

Five minutes after they hung up, screenshots of Dana's July 13 texts to Reynolds appeared on his phone.

Dana: Hey, babe. Missing you.

Reynolds: Where are you?

Dana: Living the dream. But I'm lonely. Thinking about you.

Reynolds: Since when?

Dana: Always at night, when I'm lying in bed. Alone. Naked.

Reynolds: What do you do when you're naked?

Dana: What's the best nude memory you have of me?

Reynolds: You know.

Dana: I want you to say it.

Reynolds: In the red pickup.

Dana: Have you slept with anyone else?

Reynolds: No.

Dana: Good. Keep it that way.

Reynolds: Are you coming home?

Dana: What are you wearing?

Reynolds: Jeans. You?

The killer followed with a blushing emoji, and the conversation continued as he or she fed Reynolds enough vague sexual comments to keep him talking. This went on for an hour, and then the texts stopped. Why the hell had the killer played games with Dana's old boyfriend?

***

Elijah sat in the coffee shop at the corner table. As always, his back was to the wall, and he faced the door. In prison he had learned quickly to protect his back. He supposed this quirk would never leave him.

He often got out of his house or office simply to prove to himself that he could do whatever he wanted now. Freedom was a precious thing, and he intended to not only guard his but savor every moment of it going forward.

When the door opened, he looked up over his book and noted the entry of the tall, thin man. He was only a few years older than Elijah, but the guy had a youthful energy that hinted he had never been tested by life. A bad day for this guy was a delayed flight or a cold latte.

Elijah sipped his mug of black coffee. He dropped his gaze to his book, stealing a side glance here and there to track the man. No introductions were necessary. Since Ann had told him about Paul Thompson's visit, Elijah had done his own research.

He waited until Thompson was settled in a booth before he picked up his coffee and book and slid into the seat across from him.

Thompson looked up from his phone, his expression mirroring first outrage, then shock, and finally interest. "Mr. Weston."

Elijah knitted his fingers together and rested them on the table. "Mr. Thompson. I understand you've been talking to some of my friends."

"I have." He set his phone down but kept his hand close to the device, as if it would protect him from Elijah. "You've heard I'm doing a podcast."

"About me."

"That's right."

"Why?"

"You're fascinating. Yours is the classic tale of David and Goliath."

"Me being David?"

"The system was stacked against you, and you did come out on top," Thompson said.

"There are plenty of stories like that. How did mine catch your attention?" Elijah asked.

"My work has a following," Thompson said. "I receive tips on stories like yours all the time."

Elijah's eyes narrowed. "Who tipped you off about me?"

"That doesn't matter."

"It does to me."

"I can't reveal my sources."

"A classic response." Elijah sat back, sipping the coffee, disappointed it was no longer piping hot. "Have you spoken to Ann?"

"I have. She's promised to give me an interview on Saturday. You're welcome to join us."

"Did you threaten her?" Elijah asked softly, setting his cup down.

"I don't threaten."

"Maybe not technically, but I'll bet that you're good with words and can dance right up to the line of a threat." Elijah knew the technique well.

"I didn't say anything like that to her."

"Did you mention Nate?" Elijah asked carefully.

Thompson sat back, looking a little like a cornered animal.

Elijah smiled. "That, my friend, is a very dangerous card to play."

"What's that mean?" Thompson challenged.

Aware that Thompson could be taping this conversation, Elijah shrugged. "The boy is a minor."

"I've never been near the child," Thompson countered.

"Good. I would hate to see a child upset." He rose, sensing if he lingered, he might say something he would deeply regret.

"I want to interview you," Thompson said.

"No."

"What about Nate?"

Elijah stilled. It took all his self-control not to smash the coffee cup into the man's face.

"Don't you want to get ahead of this story and control it? I can help you do that," Thompson said.

Elijah gently tapped his fist on the table. "I don't need you to do that."

"I'm going to tell the story regardless. Did you know two of your Fireflies have been murdered? Are the names Dana Riley and Sarah Cameron familiar to you?"

Elijah refused to be sidetracked. "Leave Nate out of this." He carried his cup to the counter, handed it to the woman behind the register, and, smiling, thanked her.

Outside, he glanced at his hand and flexed the fingers into a fist. He had made hints about his relationship with Ann in a couple of his letters to the Fireflies. Nothing specific, but many were smart, and one look at the boy proved their genetic connection.

Nate would find out the truth eventually, but Elijah did not want him learning on a social media account or from a stranger. That news needed to come from his parents.

Ann did not want his protection, nor did she want him near Nate. But she was wrong on both counts. He would protect them both.

***

Bryce received the call from the medical examiner as he drove through the front entrance to his ranch. As he approached a known cell-signal dead zone on the property, he stopped the car before he answered. "Dr. Christopher. You're working late."

"No rest for the wicked," he joked.

Bryce laughed. "I hear you."

"I know the identity of the body found in Anaconda. The registration number on the ankle plate came through." Papers rustled in the background. "Her name is Nena Lassiter, and she's originally from San Diego, California."

He recognized the name from the list of Fireflies. "That's one hell of a job. Can you email me the details?"

"Sure."

"Thanks, Doc."

Bryce stared at the explosive oranges and yellows of the setting sun that skimmed the top of the mountain range in the distance. He had been looking for a reason to call Ann for hours. Not that he needed one. He was a grown man. Jesus. What the hell. He dialed.

She picked up on the second ring. "Bryce."

"Are you doing all right?"

"Yes, Nate is already asleep. Exhausted after school and a high-carbohydrate dinner."

He closed his eyes, trying to picture what she was wearing, if her hair was up or down, and the soft scent of her perfume. What they shared was new and fragile, and she was gun shy about commitment, so he kept the focus on work. "I just heard from Dr. Christopher. He's identified the Anaconda victim." He quickly detailed what he had learned.

Papers rustled in the background. "I'm looking at the pictures Thompson gave me. Nena's DMV picture looks a little like the woman in the Polaroid. She grew out her hair and dyed it blonder."

Making her look more like Ann. The idea that these women were mimicking Ann bothered him. "Ann, everything is really okay? No trouble from Thompson or Weston?"

"It's fine." No missing the forced positivity coating the words.

"Seriously?" He resented the hour-long drive separating them.

"Don't worry."

Christ, if she really needed him, he could race like a bat out of hell and still not get to her in time.

CHAPTER TWENTY-FOUR

Missoula, Montana
Wednesday, August 25
12:30 p.m.

Ann's class had wrapped up five minutes late, and she had been delayed another fifteen by a student with questions. Then came a text from Maura asking what had happened to their ten o'clock meeting at the house. Ann canceled Maura, citing work and promising to get back to her by the end of the day. Maura responded immediately, reminding her that an organized life is a good life, so they rescheduled for five.

After Ann made her way out of the building, she spotted Bryce standing by his vehicle. He walked toward her, his dark suit skimming his broad shoulders and flapping in the breeze enough to reveal his gun and badge clipped to his belt. His trademark cowboy hat shadowed his eyes. He carried a manila folder. She moistened her lips as she approached.

He opened the passenger-side door for her. "How was school this morning?"

"I did get a late start, and I might have exceeded the speed limit when I was driving to work, but school went great. Nice to be back."

"Don't be confessing to me," he said.

"Right. You're a sworn officer." She slid into the car.

"Who would like nothing better than to call it a day and take you to a motel room." He closed the door and got in the car.

Oh, that idea did tempt.

He handed her the manila folder, started the car, and turned on the air-conditioning. "I finally found Nena Lassiter's social media account, and it looked like she was working in a local bar. I spent the morning showing her mug shot to a half dozen local bars. I hit pay dirt at the fourth establishment. Nena had been in town about a month and was working as a waitress. Apparently, she was working her way across the country and had stopped in Montana to take in the sights. She'd established a history of missing work, so when she didn't show for work, no one went looking for her. They just assumed she had moved on to the next town."

Ann skimmed the woman's police record and studied her mug shot, featuring a thin, angled face, pale skin, dark eyes, and brown hair. "Only she didn't get far."

"Her phone is not sending a signal now," he said. "She appears to have one credit card, which was used multiple times this week. Mostly small gas stations and food places that don't have surveillance cameras."

"Did she get to know anyone while she was in town?" Ann asked.

"She hooked up with a guy by the name of Jerry Cantrell. He works at the local garage. He wasn't in yet this morning, but he should be at work by now."

"Can I join you?"

"Sure."

He glanced up at the academic building, as if daring prying eyes, before he leaned over and kissed her.

She savored his taste. “Hello.”

“Been wanting to do that for as long as I can remember,” he said.

“It hasn’t been that long.”

“Feels like a lifetime.”

“Maybe we can get away for a couple of hours of private time soon.” The heat simmering behind the words conjured memories of his body pressing against hers.

“Soon. Very soon.”

Drawing in a breath, he put the car in gear and drove to the auto repair shop on the north side of town. The two walked into the shop together. Bryce showed his badge to an older man behind the counter and asked for Cantrell. The whir of a pneumatic screwdriver blended with a Kid Rock song and drifted out from the garage when the old man opened the door.

Bryce stepped in front of Ann and brushed back his jacket. Her brother had made it clear that moments like this could be dicey. No telling what kind of trouble a cop’s arrival could trigger.

Inside the garage they found a short man with muscular arms covered in tattoos. He sported a white bandage at his right temple. He wiped grease from his hands as he eyed Bryce with suspicion and for Ann showed a flicker of appreciation. “I’m Cantrell. What can I do for you?”

Bryce showed his badge and identified himself and Ann. “We have a couple of questions about Nena Lassiter.”

Cantrell shook his head and dropped his gaze for a moment before asking, “What has she done?”

“Why do you say that?” Bryce asked.

“We hooked up three or four times while she was in town. And it was fun. Then she took off with a couple hundred bucks from my wallet. Did she rip off another guy?”

“Not that we are aware of,” Bryce said. “Did she talk about herself?”

Ann noted Bryce was avoiding a homicide notice, which likely would have put the man on guard. Once his defenses were in place, he would start filtering his responses.

"She was from California," Cantrell said. "She had dreams of seeing the country."

"What brought her to Missoula?" Bryce asked.

"Said she was here to catch up with a friend. They met once or twice, and then he dropped her."

"Did you catch the friend's name?" Ann asked.

"Thompson, I think," he said.

"Paul Thompson?" she asked.

"That's right. Don't tell me those two are on some kind of Bonnie-and-Clyde joyride."

"Nena is dead," Bryce said.

The news struck the smirk from Cantrell's face. "Shit. How?"

"Did you ever meet Paul Thompson?" Bryce asked.

"A couple of weeks ago. He and Nena met at her bar before it opened. When I got there, they ended whatever it was they were doing. He gathered up his papers and left."

"Did she say what they were talking about?" Bryce asked.

"No. And I didn't press. Our relationship wasn't based on conversation."

"Did Nena say anything else to you about Thompson?" Bryce asked.

"No."

"What about Elijah Weston?" Bryce asked.

"That crazy guy that got out of prison? Hell no. With Nena and me, it was just about the sex. We didn't talk much. And I sure didn't do anything illegal with her." He ran his hand over his head. "How did Nena die?"

"She was stabbed to death," Bryce said.

"She suffered a horrific death," Ann said. "If there is anything you can tell us . . ."

Cantrell rested his hands on his hips. "It sure as shit wasn't me," he said. "I don't hurt people."

"How did you hurt yourself?" Bryce asked.

"The day Nena took off, I damn near got killed by a hit-and-run driver. Ran me off the road outside of town, and my truck ended up in a ditch. I got a gash on my head that took ten stitches to fix." As proof, he peeled off his bandage and showed them the ragged healing scar along his hairline.

Ann sensed the weight of Bryce's stare on the man. "Did Nena mention anything that might have been a red flag to you?"

Cantrell shifted his gaze to her. "She liked that I'd been in prison. It was a turn-on for her. Said she'd been really into a guy in the joint once. They wrote letters. She asked me a couple of times what it was like being behind bars." He scratched the back of his neck. "Said she hoped to hook up with him one day soon." He paused. "Shit, she was talking about that Weston guy, wasn't she?"

"Maybe," Ann said.

"Everybody in town knows Weston's story." He leveled his gaze on Ann. "And your story, now that I think about it. You were at his trial, right?"

"Yes," she said.

Cantrell leaned a little closer to Ann. "In the right light, you look like Nena. Her hair was longer and blonder, but she looked like you."

Nervous energy coiled in her belly. How many of the Fireflies had altered their appearance to resemble her?

Bryce pulled up the Polaroid image of Nena on his phone. "Is this Nena?"

Cantrell studied the picture. "That's Nena."

Bryce handed Cantrell his card. "Call me if you think of anything else."

"Sure."

Outside, Ann rubbed her hands over her arms. Everywhere she turned Elijah's shadow lingered.

"Don't let him get to you," Bryce said.

"I haven't," Ann said.

"You're pale. You're tense."

"It's not like I see Elijah everywhere I turn. He's not physically following me, but he's always there. Do you think he could have killed those women?"

"I don't know."

"He's so clever."

"He's not going to get to you."

"I appreciate the sentiment, but no one can protect me twenty-four seven."

Bryce laid his hands on her shoulders. "That's not going to happen."

But lessons learned had taught her if someone wanted to kill you, there was no stopping them.

***

I sit outside Ann's house, knowing it is a matter of time before he shows. She is the center of his obsession, and sooner or later he will come sniffing around.

The others have been a warm-up for him and for me. The main event is Ann.

CHAPTER TWENTY-FIVE

Missoula, Montana
Wednesday, August 25
4:00 p.m.

Bryce parked in front of Elijah Weston's house. The one-story rancher had neatly cut grass, a large poplar tree in the front yard, and mulch bags piled high by the flower beds. It was also within walking distance of Ann's house.

He rose out of his car, settled his hat on his head, strode toward the front door, and rang the bell. Seconds later, footsteps echoed in the house, and the door opened to Elijah Weston. He was dressed in khakis and a blue T-shirt and wore dark-rimmed glasses. "Sergeant McCabe. This is a nice surprise."

"You're smarter than that. You knew I'd be coming by sooner or later."

"The police do like to rope me into their investigations. What's the latest case you are working on? Don't tell me another dead Firefly."

"That's right. Nena Lassiter."

Elijah seemed to search his memory. "Nena. From California."

"That's right."

"Wait just a moment—I have something for you." He vanished inside the house and returned quickly with a sheet of paper. "This is a copy of my calendar for the last three months. I'm assuming you'll need to confirm my alibi. I have several copies in case any of your cop friends want one."

Bryce took the paper and studied the computer printout. He keyed in on the dates in early June, July, and last Tuesday. Elijah had been attending back-to-back summer classes in June and July and last week had been volunteering at the university. Beside the dates he had written the names and phone numbers of several individuals.

"Call any of those names, and they can confirm I was either in class or working," he said.

"Do you always keep a detailed calendar like this?" Bryce asked.

"Since the day I was released from prison," Elijah said.

"You moved mighty close to Ann Bailey."

"There's no law against it," Elijah said.

"No law, just curious why you're so near her."

"Good school district. House promises to be a good flip when it's renovated. Is there anything else, Sergeant?" Elijah asked.

"Not for now."

"Don't forget my fingerprints and DNA are on file. My attorney couldn't get those expunged, so unless you have hard forensic data connecting me to any crime, we don't have much to say to each other."

"I'm sure we'll be in touch soon."

"Can't wait."

Bryce quelled the desire to grab Elijah by the collar and demand to know what the hell he was planning. Because as sure as he was living and breathing, he knew Elijah Weston had a bigger plan.

Instead, he turned and strode back to his vehicle, knowing in his bones there was another shoe to drop with this son of a bitch.

***

Bryce arrived at the medical examiner's office, slipped off his jacket, and shrugged on a surgical gown. Tugging on gloves, he moved through the double doors into the autopsy suite, where Gideon Bailey stood across the table from Dr. Christopher. Lying between them was the sheet-clad body of Edith Scott.

"Apologies for the delay," Bryce said. "Interviewing an associate of the last victim."

"How is the case going?" Gideon asked.

"All three victims have been identified," he said. "They were all one of Elijah's Fireflies. And the last victim was seen talking to Paul Thompson last week. Not hard to assume they were talking about Elijah Weston, who is the subject of Thompson's story."

Gideon's frown deepened, as it did whenever Elijah's name was mentioned. "Where's Thompson now?"

"I tried his cell. He didn't pick up. But it's time to figure out where he's staying in town."

"When you talk to him, I want to be present."

"I did stop by Elijah Weston's house," Bryce said. "You know he's living around the corner from Ann?"

"I knew it was close but not that close." Gideon cursed.

"How do you think Elijah would take to a reporter talking to the Fireflies?" Bryce asked.

"The media was all over him last year, but he didn't seem to care. Now he's emerging from his isolation and reinventing himself, so he might not be as patient about rehashing his past."

"There was a murder in town last year. The victim allegedly beat up Elijah shortly after his release."

"Yes. We never pulled any DNA or fingerprints from the scene. We never could officially close the case."

"And now Edith Scott is dead," Bryce said. "She served on the jury that convicted Elijah?"

"She was the foreman of the jury," Gideon said. "And when he came up for parole five years ago, she was part of the citizens committee who filed their objections to the parole board."

Bryce worked his fingers deeper into the gloves as he moved up to the table. Dr. Christopher pulled back the sheet to reveal the pale, drawn features of Edith Scott. The doctor adjusted the overhead microphone closer to his mouth.

"Today, we have the body of a forty-eight-year-old woman, Edith Scott, who suffered multiple knife wounds to the chest."

Bryce counted six knife wounds, each tightly grouped around her heart. There was nothing haphazard about the patterning, which was very similar to the other three victims. As tempted as he was to comment, he let the procedure play out.

Dr. Christopher began with an external examination that detailed basic characteristics of the woman's body, including an appendectomy scar, several old burns, and a heart-shaped tattoo on her right hip. She was underweight by about fifteen pounds, and her skin looked sallow.

The doctor lifted the eyelids and noted that the right pupil had been blown and the left eye was significantly bloodshot. "Interesting."

"How so?" Bryce asked.

"These are signs of suffocation." The doctor took swabs of the nasal passages. "I'll check to make sure there are no fabric fibers."

"Is there a way of telling if the other victims were suffocated?" Bryce asked.

"Not given the damage to the remains," Dr. Christopher said.

The doors to the room opened, and Joan Mason appeared, gowned up. She stood beside Gideon, but other than a slight softening of her features, most would never have guessed they were dating.

"You've been through the victim's house?" Dr. Christopher asked.

"Several times," Joan said. "I found no traces of illegal drugs, firearms, or anything to suggest that Ms. Scott might have had another life her coworkers weren't aware of. She was on heavy-duty pain medications and two drugs associated with nausea. Her refrigerator was stocked with soda, bread, and cheese. Not the best diet, but I'm guessing it was comfort food given the nausea."

"Alcohol?" Dr. Christopher asked.

"An unopened bottle of white in the pantry. I went through her mail and saw nothing that appeared troubling. No overdue bills, no threatening letters, no alarming correspondence from doctors. She had five books from the library that are due in two days. Also, no pictures of family or friends on the refrigerator. No pets. She had a quiet life."

Bryce had seen seemingly average people killed, but more often than not, they had engaged in some kind of risky behavior that no one had been aware of. That did not appear to be the case for Edith Scott. "Not the kind of behavior that makes an attack more likely," he said.

"No." Joan studied the body with a detached distance learned when she worked homicide back in Philadelphia. "I spoke to her neighbor as I was leaving." She checked her notepad. "A neighbor told me Ms. Scott was worried about Weston. She had been on the jury that convicted Weston of arson. Ms. Scott was mulling her legal options with her neighbor while they were at the mailboxes the other day."

"Unless he made a direct threat," Bryce said, "she had none."

"That was their conclusion," Joan said. She slid her notebook in her pocket and worked on a pair of clean gloves over the ones in place as she shifted closer to the instrument table.

Dr. Christopher focused on the body as Joan handed him the scalpel from the instrument table. He carefully pressed it against the skin and sliced a neat Y incision. Soon he had peeled the skin open, and

Joan handed him bolt cutters. He snapped the rib cage and, after careful inspection, set it on a tray Joan held out for him.

Congealed blood pooled in the interior cavity, which had to be suctioned out. Next Dr. Christopher inspected the heart. "Two direct cuts to the heart. This wound, here," he said, pointing, "severed the aorta. She would have bled out in a matter of minutes. The knife also cut into her lungs. Whoever did this was efficient and knew what they were doing." He searched the interior cavity.

"How do you compare the stab wounds to the other two victims?" Bryce said.

"Wound patterns almost identical," Dr. Christopher said.

"But Scott's murder deviates from the pattern," Gideon said.

"She also doesn't fit the profile of the victims we have identified," Bryce said. "We know three were Fireflies, and she certainly was not. Did you pull any hair or fiber samples from the body?"

"I didn't find skin scrapings under her nails at the scene," Joan said. "But I bagged her hands just in case."

"If she scratched her killer, then that could be a tremendous break," Bryce said.

"It'll take weeks on the DNA," Gideon said. "I've spoken to the lab, and they're backed up."

Dr. Christopher continued to examine each organ, and by the time he was finished, he confirmed the initial on-site conclusions were correct: Edith Scott had been stabbed to death in her own bed.

He also discovered several significant tumors in her liver. "Those pain and nausea meds Joan found line up with stage four liver cancer."

As Bryce and Gideon left the autopsy suite, Gideon's phone rang. "Detective Bailey." He listened, nodding, and his expression appeared to soften a fraction. "We'll be right there." He looked at Bryce. "My uniformed officer found several personal surveillance cameras. He's going through footage now."

"If he finds anything, alert me," Bryce said.

"Will do."

***

Ann picked the boys up from soccer and arrived at her house. They tumbled out of the car and hurried up the walk until they saw Maura sitting on her front porch. She was scrolling through her phone, smiling as she seemed to note a post or message, before she rose. Beside her were several box deliveries for Ann.

"Sorry I'm late," Ann said. "Crazy day."

"No worries," Maura said.

"Maura, you've met Nate, and this is my nephew, Kyle."

The boys greeted her, and when she offered her hand, they each shook it. Ann moved past them, unlocked the door, and allowed the boys to scramble inside. Shoes off, backpacks stowed, they ran toward the kitchen for snacks Ann had stocked.

"They're a hurricane," Ann said.

Maura grinned as her bag slid from her shoulder to the floor. "Where do you want me to start?"

"It would be nice to get the shelves up and these boxes of books unpacked. I've assembled a shelf, but the others are stacked in the corner."

"Assembly is also one of my talents. Get the boys situated, you get changed, and I'll start in."

"I'm not going to let you do this for free." She was relieved to think that this chaos might actually get fixed.

"You won't."

"Mom, can we order pizza?" Nate shouted.

"Again?" Ann asked.

"Yes!" Nate said.

"If it's the same pizza as last night's, I'll claim two slices as my fee," Maura said.

Ann would do better than that, but for the sake of no argument, she said, "Deal."

The next half hour—or was it an hour?—she changed, placed her order, got the boys set up in the kitchen to do homework, fed them, and cleaned up. It was the usual evening school-night chaos, and she was glad to have it back.

When she made her way to the living room, she dreaded the ongoing mess waiting for her. But when she entered, the four bookshelves had been assembled and lined the wall on either side of the small fireplace.

"Is that where you want the shelves?" Maura asked as she opened the first box of books.

"Yes, that's perfect. I can see the floor," Ann said. "It doesn't feel like an obstacle course anymore."

"Like I said, this is my thing." Maura held up a book on forensic psychology and behavior. "Thick reading."

"Hazard of the work."

Maura carefully placed it on the shelf. "Do you enjoy your work?"

"I do like teaching," Ann said.

"Have you ever worked with the cops? Seems they'd want your insight into cases."

"Not really." Ann carried a collection of books and handed them to Maura. "These go with that one."

"I read about that body they found near town last week," Maura said.

"Yes, it sounds horrible."

"That seems to me to be the kind of case a doctor like you would consult on," she said.

"Maybe."

“What would make someone do that to another person?” Maura asked.

“The human mind goes to some very strange places. It would be difficult to drill down on the motives.”

“Sick, if you ask me.” Maura aligned several more books, then rearranged a couple so that they lined up in descending order.

Putting names to the faces of the charred remains had been a stark reminder that what she had examined in the autopsy suite was not just evidence but the last vestiges of women. They had had hopes and dreams, made mistakes, enjoyed triumphs, made love, laughed, and cried. They had not deserved their grisly fates.

“Where’d you go?” Maura asked.

“Sorry. I do that from time to time. Absentminded professor.”

“Are you worried about him?” Maura asked.

“About who?”

“A killer like that on the streets. Jesus, you never know when he’ll strike.”

“I doubt we’re in danger.”

“How can you say that?”

“I just don’t see why we’d be a target.” She recalled the nights she had heard noises outside her house and found the small paper airplane left outside Nate’s window. She could not say for certain that she was not a target.

***

Bryce arrived back at his ranch and was greeted by the new female dog, Venus. She met him on the front porch, daring him to pass.

“I pay the light bill here, kid,” he said, meeting her gaze.

His tone was stern but intentionally nonthreatening. That would come next. As a gesture of goodwill, he extended his hand and waited patiently for her to sniff. She took her time, smelling his palm, his coat sleeve, and then his shoes.

"Dylan," he said. "Call your dog."

"Venus," his brother shouted as he opened the front door. "Come inside, girl."

The dog's ears perked, but she kept a close eye on Bryce.

"It's okay, girl." Dylan walked up to the dog, scratched her between the ears, and then fed her a small kibble treat.

"You've just rewarded her for keeping me out of my house," Bryce said.

Dylan handed him a kibble treat. "Make friends with her."

Bryce held out the treat for the dog. After a brief hesitation, she took it. "She's picky."

"Nothing wrong with a woman with discerning tastes."

"Maybe."

Dylan turned back toward the house, and the dog trotted after him. "Just made a big pot of chili."

"Terrific. I'm starving."

"Change and then you can give me a rundown on your case."

"Will do." It was nice to have company when he came through the front door.

As he grabbed a beer from the refrigerator, he wondered what it would be like to have Ann here. He had heard enough from Gideon to know they had grown up on a ranch, though he would wager the Bailey outfit was a hell of a lot more sophisticated than this ramshackle house and patch of dirt.

Ann reminded him of a purebred. Long and lean, beautiful. Each time he saw her, he searched for flaws but had yet to find one. Smart, a great mother, she was also recovering from the husband who had lied his way into their marriage.

Dylan came in the back door. "You're making the face again."

"Face?"

"The worried face."

"That's what I do."

Dylan dunked a wooden spoon in the big pot of chili, stirred, and then pulled a pan of corn bread from the oven.

"Damn, boy, you're going to make some lady a nice husband one day," Bryce teased.

He laughed. "Do you ever see either of us settling down?"

Bryce hesitated. Last year he would have laughed, said something along the lines of, "No way in hell." Now he wondered.

"That silence is very telling." Dylan dished out two bowls of chili and set them on the table.

"Not really. I shoot for the fences, and I miss more than I hit."

Dylan set the corn bread on a hot pad beside the chili. "You'll miss every time if you don't shoot."

Chairs dragged across the wooden floor, both sat, and neither spoke for several minutes as they ate. Bryce was surprised the chili and bread tasted so damned good.

Dylan sat back. "You're going for the woman with the complicated life?"

He thought about the quiet, studious Nate, who was on his way to becoming a carbon copy of Elijah Weston. "Yeah."

Dylan regarded him. "Complicated can be interesting."

Whoever was with Ann would one day have to contend with Elijah Weston, in one fashion or another. Still, Bryce had dealt with worse men, and the idea of waking up to Ann outweighed the challenges.

"Ask her and the boy out here. Kids love dogs," Dylan said.

"Maybe."

"When?"

"I don't know. But I might be spending more nights in Missoula."

"With her?"

"In a motel. I'm worried about her." He explained the particulars about the Firefly case and watched his brother's expression grow more serious. "If something goes down, I want to be close."

***

When Maura arrived at Elijah's house, she was filled with a girlish excitement she had not felt in years. He answered the door, stared at her with those sexy eyes that radiated a kind of deep-thinking vibe. Wordlessly he nodded for her to come inside.

She held up a bottle of wine. "Interested?"

"I don't drink."

"Not at all?"

"Never have touched the stuff." He took the bottle from her, set it on a small table by the door, and then reached for the top button of her blouse.

She watched as his nimble fingers unfastened one, two, and then all the buttons to her waist. He slid his hand into her open blouse and cupped her breast. Sensations rolled through her, and whatever ideas she had of teasing him about his teetotaling ways vanished in a rush of desire. What was it about this guy that set her on fire?

When he kissed the tops of her breasts, she hissed in a breath. "Bedroom."

He took her by the hand, and in his room they both quietly stripped off their clothes, and he tossed back the covers of the neatly made bed. She scrambled to the center, and he was on top of her and inside her in a blink.

Their lovemaking was fast, hot, and rougher than it had been before. He seemed possessed and driven, and she was glad she had finally been able to experience the intensity inside him.

Later, as they lay naked, he stared up at the ceiling, hand tucked under his head. "Were you able to do the errand I requested?"

She circled her fingers around his navel. "Yes."

He took her hand and guided it under the sheet. "Good girl."

She smiled, pushing back the sheet, took him in her hands, and paused with her lips only an inch from the tip of his penis. "No, bad girl. Very bad girl."

CHAPTER TWENTY-SIX

Missoula, Montana
Wednesday, August 25
9:00 p.m.

Elijah woke and slipped from the bed where Maura was sleeping. He pulled on his pants, grabbed his phone, and in the great room, he sat on the floor, legs crossed, and opened the app he had installed days ago. The app attached to a surveillance camera that should now be hidden in Ann's house. He put in his earbuds and turned up the volume.

On screen, he watched Nate lying on the couch, a book close to his face. There was a crumpled bag of chips on the coffee table and a half-empty cup of lemonade. The boy looked comfortable, lost in the words.

"Nate, time to wrap it up." Ann came around the corner and was drying her hands on a checkered dish towel. She picked up the bag of chips and carefully sealed the top. "Come on. You need to brush your teeth and wash your face."

Nate's gaze stayed locked on the page. "Mom, can I read five more minutes?"

"I've said yes to your last four five-minute requests. That puts us twenty minutes past bedtime."

"I can do math."

"Good. Then you can count the steps to your bedroom and the number of times you brush your teeth." She gently lifted his feet and set them on the ground.

Nate carefully placed his bookmark between the pages and closed the book. "I don't need that much sleep."

"You do."

"I'm ten."

"Still growing, pal." She coaxed him to standing and followed him down the hallway.

Elijah had only the one camera in position, so for the next few minutes, he could only listen to the distant banter of their conversation. He could not make out the precise words, but Nate still sounded annoyed, while Ann's tone remained steady. No screaming. No hitting. No threats. Just loving.

He drew in a breath. The boy loved his mother, and to take him away from her would be cruel. If she had given any hints that she was like his mother, he would have yanked the boy out of the house a year ago.

But he was not cruel. He did not want to hurt the boy.

From his pocket he fished out the paper detailing the DNA results. There was a 99.9 percent chance that the boy was his. He was a father. And he had rights.

But more than that, he understood Nate's mind. He understood that he would need someone like him one day to guide him and show him that when the dark thoughts began, there were ways to control and manage them. Whether Ann liked it or not, he needed to be in Nate's life.

Footsteps had him raising his gaze to see Maura wearing one of his shirts. "What are you doing?"

"Checking the camera," he said.

She yawned and smiled. "It's working?"

"Yes. But I wish you had time to put out the other two."

"It was too risky," she said. "Ann kept coming in the room, checking on me." She sat beside him on the floor. The lone fastened shirt button could not prevent the fabric from flopping open, revealing the curve of her full breasts. "I can go back. I made a point not to unpack all the boxes."

"How did you leave it with Ann?"

"We're the best buds." She leaned her head on his shoulder. "She appreciates the extra hand."

He shrugged, coaxing her head off. "I wish there was another camera."

"Like I said, I can go back."

He rose and crossed to the kitchen, retrieving a cold seltzer for himself.

She followed, her lips curling into a pout. "You're really mad at me."

"Disappointed is more like it."

A sly smile curled her lips as she unfastened the button nestled between her breasts. "I can make it up to you."

"There has to be more to us than sex."

"Why?" She slid off the shirt.

He found his irritation growing. "If you don't know the answer, then it's pointless for me to explain."

Color rose in her cheeks. "What can I do to fix it between us? I really like you, and I'll do anything."

He drank from the can, savoring the cool liquid in his throat. Draining it, he carefully set the can on the counter.

"Do you want more cameras in her house? I can make that happen."

"I want that and your help with Paul Thompson," he said.

Her expression stilled. "Him? Why?"

"I want access to his story notes."

"What makes you think he'll trust me?" she asked.

Elijah moved toward her and cupped her breast, twisting her nipple until she squirmed. "You have talents that I do not have. You're clever."

"You want me to sleep with him?" she asked.

"I want you to talk to him. Get the information any way you can."

Her brow knotted. "A.k.a. sex."

He tipped her chin up and stared deep into her eyes. He had assumed she was highly intelligent, but now he wondered if the insecurity that ran deep in her was going to undercut it all. He kissed her on the lips. "Is that a problem?"

"Am I now one of your Fireflies?" she challenged.

"Do you want to be?" There were those who needed a sense of belonging. They wanted someone else calling the shots so they could abdicate responsibility for their lives.

She ran her tongue over her lips. "And if I don't do this?"

"I only have people in my life that serve a purpose."

Her eyes narrowed. "What purpose does Ann serve?"

"That's none of your business." He tucked a curl behind her ear, noting her hair was blonder than it had been. "Did you change your hair?"

She curled a blond strand around her finger. "Do you like it?"

"I do."

"I thought you would prefer it if I looked more like her."

He understood the reference. "I do."

She slid her hands down his belly to the clasp of his jeans. "And?"

"Plant another camera and get the information from Thompson."

"And then we'll be fine?" she asked.

"Yes," he lied.

"I'll find him first thing in the morning."

"What's wrong with now?" he asked.

"Now? I thought maybe we could go for another round."

He shook his head, stepping back. "I have things to do, and I need to be alone."

She shoved out a breath. "Okay. I'll get what you want, but then you're going to owe me."

"We'll see about that."

***

With Nate sleeping soundly, Ann made herself a cup of tea and settled on the couch in the living room. Looking around the uncluttered space made her feel good. No more piles of boxes that required multiple searches when she wanted a pen or a paper clip.

She blew on the hot tea, savoring the sweet clover scents drifting to her nose. As she reached for the notes she had made on the case, her front doorbell rang. She walked to the door and glanced through the peephole to see Maura. Surprised, she opened the door. "Is everything all right?"

"I forgot my phone. I left it on the bookshelf. Impossible to live without it. Can I come in? I'll be quick."

"Sure." Ann stepped aside and watched as Maura walked directly to the bookshelf and then knelt as she reached by a book on the end. She hesitated only a moment and then rose, her phone in hand. "Here it is. Thank you so much!"

"Thank you for your help today, Maura. Have anyone call me for a reference."

"Let's not be strangers. I'd love to grab a drink with you sometime," Maura said.

"Sounds like a deal."

Maura held up the phone. "I've got to get going. I'm meeting a friend at a bar."

"Have a great time."

Maura's gaze broadened. "I always do."

***

Maura watched Paul Thompson leave his motel room, and she followed him when he drove to the Silver Maverick bar. She did not approach him but leaned against a wall in a darkened corner. The music pulsed and blended with the chatter of people as he sat at the bar. Elijah wanted her to use sex to get to Thompson, but he had not said she couldn't use a surrogate.

Maura looked around the room and spotted a woman with dark hair and a tightly fitting red dress. The woman had not the expectant gaze of a woman searching for a man but the hawkish glare of a sex worker hunting for a client.

Maura pushed off the wall and approached the woman. "What's your name?"

"Carla." The woman looked her over. "What do you want?"

Out of her pocket, she fished the two hundred Ann had given her earlier and a small vial of white powder. "There's a man at the bar. I want you to give him a good time and slip him this."

Carla arched a brow as she followed Maura's gaze to Thompson as he ordered a drink. "Why?"

"It's an easy two hundred. And he's an ex-boyfriend that deserves a little payback."

"What's in the vial? I don't want to kill anyone."

"Rohypnol. He'll sleep like a baby and wake up with a hangover in the morning."

"If he passes out before the sex?" Carla asked.

"Then it's less work for you. I'll be watching the room. When you leave his room, leave the door unlocked."

Carla took the money and the vial. "Okay."

Maura watched Carla signal the bartender for a drink, and as she reached for it, she brushed Thompson's shoulder. She grinned at him and leaned over to whisper something in his ear, as if sharing a secret.

For a moment Maura thought Carla had sold her out, but he laughed. She laughed. More drinks were ordered.

Fifteen minutes later, Thompson and Carla left. When he was out cold, Maura would copy his notes for Elijah.

"More than one way to skin a cat," she whispered.

***

I truly do not like to hurt people.

As I trace the outline of Nena Lassiter's face, I accept that pain is a necessary evil. It makes us stronger. It makes us better people. And it has been a part of the world since humans first walked the earth. Man discovered fire and inevitably got burned by it. Women have endured pain during childbirth. Athletes have pushed through pain to break records.

I do not like pain, but if great things are going to happen, then it is unavoidable. And as the saying goes, no pain, no gain.

"Don't worry, Ann," I whisper as I push open the door. "When our time comes, I promise to end it as quickly as I can."

CHAPTER TWENTY-SEVEN

Missoula, Montana
Thursday, August 26
6:00 a.m.

Showered, shaved, and dressed for work, Bryce received a text from Gideon, alerting him to check his email in-box. He filled a large cup of coffee and drank half before he refilled it and then moved through the silent house to his study. Flipping on the light, he slid behind his desk, and while his computer clawed its way through the slow internet connection, he drank his coffee. When he had decided to live at the ranch more often, he had accepted the high cost of the big satellite dish that enabled internet service. On a good day it provided enough connection for him to function.

He found Gideon's email and clicked. There were three attachments, each identified by the source's location.

The first was a doorbell camera located across the street from Edith Scott's house. It was easy to miss the hooded figure in the darkness at first. The individual moved quickly in the night's inky black, tested a front window, and then hurried around to the back of the house, out of the camera's range.

He opened the next file, which captured the figure prying open the sliding glass door and slipping into Scott's house. No lights came on, and there was only the flicker of movement in front of the kitchen window. And then nothing but stillness for almost a half hour.

"What are you waiting for?" he muttered. There had been no signs of struggle in the house, so the killer had surprised Edith. She had no defensive wounds. There were also no signs in the house that anything had been taken. So, what was the killer doing?

He imagined the man standing in the dark, lurking close to Edith while she slept. Was it a game? Did the killer enjoy the private knowledge that he was about to kill his next victim?

And then the patio door eased open and the figure moved outside, careful to close the door behind him, leaving everything as it had been found. The lack of disturbance had been part of the reason Edith had not been found for three days.

The final camera captured the grainy image of a car driving slowly through the neighborhood. The lights were off, and the vehicle rolled carefully around the corner and into obscurity.

The first two videos had not told him much. The killer was midsize, but beyond that he had no clue about race, age, or even sex. But the last video offered the needle in the haystack. The vehicle's license plate.

Bryce reached for his phone and texted.

Bryce: I know you saw this.

Gideon: The plates belong to a vehicle registered to Nena Lassiter. BOLO issued an hour ago.

Bryce: Any hits?

Gideon: Located the car fifteen minutes ago. See you on scene.

The Missoula address belonged to a motel on the outskirts of town. It was an hour's drive from the ranch, but if he pressed it, he could shave ten minutes off the time.

Fifty-five minutes later, Bryce pulled up in front of the motel right at 7:30 a.m. There were three cop cars parked by the blue four-door sedan now roped off by yellow crime scene tape.

Bryce parked and strode toward Gideon, who stood by his vehicle. "Have you opened it yet?"

Gideon shook his head. "Not yet. The forensic team is five minutes out. I don't want to overlook or inadvertently ruin a single bit of evidence."

"Have you had a look inside?" Bryce asked.

"I walked around the vehicle. There's trash inside, clothes on the floor, and a suitcase. Doesn't look like much."

"Oh, it's very important." Bryce fished gloves from his pocket, slid them on as he noted a **TOWING ENFORCED** sign. "How long has the car been in the lot?"

"According to the motel manager, it appeared sometime last night. The manager usually gives cars twenty-four hours before he tows. Said his lot is rarely full and ninety-five percent of the time the car is gone before he calls for the tow."

"What's the deal with this motel?" Bryce asked. "What kind of guests?"

"It's moderately priced and just a few miles from city center, so it attracts travelers on a budget. I've not had a call out here in a few years. A pimp and a sex worker fighting over drugs."

"Mind if I have a look inside the car?" Bryce asked.

"Be my guest."

Bryce crossed the lot and ducked under the yellow tape. He peered inside the driver's-side window, noting the purse on the floor, the scattered snack wrappers, and the discarded, wrinkled shirt on the front seat. In the back seat green garbage bags were filled with what looked like clothes, scattered fast-food wrappers, and several sets of shoes.

The forensic van appeared, and the two technicians immediately set up a worktable and over it a tent. The first tech, a tall, slim woman in her early thirties, slid on gloves and boots and reached for a camera. She methodically worked her way around the car, shooting the nondescript vehicle from all angles.

Bryce walked to the manager's office and up to the counter, where he found a stout man wearing a yellow collared shirt, blue slacks, and a name badge that read MIKE. His hair was long but combed back and tied at the base of his neck.

"Mike, I'm Sergeant Bryce McCabe with Montana Highway Patrol. I guess you know we're interested in that vehicle."

Mike looked past Bryce to the flash of the forensic tech's camera. "Yes, sir, and I've searched all the records of my residents, and no guest has registered that car."

"You told Detective Bailey the car has been here less than twenty-four hours."

"Now that I consider it, the car might have been here a little longer. I was off the last few nights, and I'm the one that calls in the tows."

"No one else has the authority?" Bryce asked.

"I used to let the night managers call, but a few got carried away. Our residents are supposed to register all cars, but if a family member or friend joins them after check-in, the car doesn't always get listed. Tow the wrong car, and you'll hear about it on Yelp for five years."

"How many rooms do you have on-site?" Bryce asked.

"Fifty," Mike said.

"And your occupancy rate?"

"We're at eighty percent. We have ten vacant rooms."

"Do you have a list of your current residents?" Bryce asked.

"I told Detective Bailey that I'll need a warrant before I hand out that information. He said he'd have it in the hour."

"Well, then I suppose I'll just have to go door to door. This early, I'll wake up a few folks, but that's the way it goes."

"Do you have to wake up guests?" Mike asked. "It's just an abandoned car. Christ, I'll pay the towing if you want to take it somewhere else."

"Can't do that," Bryce said. "That car is part of a crime scene now."

"Crime scene? I read the property reports for the last few days, and I can promise you there was no mention of any crime," Mike said.

"The crime happened across town, but that car was spotted near the original scene, and that connects it to this investigation," Bryce explained.

"I didn't know a scene could move."

"It certainly can move to multiple locations. Do you have surveillance cameras on this lot?"

"There's one in this office. It captures the front entrance to the lot, but not the back."

"I'll need that footage."

"As soon as you get me that warrant," he said.

Bryce tamped down his irritation. "You'll be the first man I come looking for when we have it." As he left the office, he strode directly toward the first room on the ground floor. He pounded on the door, stood to the side, and announced, "Police."

There was a rustle of the curtains by the large glass window, and then the door opened to a man wearing jeans and a T-shirt. His hair was tousled, his feet bare, and his shoulders slightly slouched.

Bryce identified himself and held up his badge. "Sorry to wake you. What is your name, sir?"

The man rubbed his eyes. "Mark Young. What's the deal?"

"Do you have a vehicle parked on this lot?" Bryce asked.

"It's that Ford Explorer right there," Mark said.

Bryce noted the Colorado plates. "Do you have your license and registration?"

"Ah, yeah, sure." Young dug a wallet from the back pocket of his jeans, removed his license and registration, and handed both to Bryce. "I've had the car about five years."

Bryce checked the details against the registration on the car, wrote down the man's name and phone number, and thanked him for his cooperation.

"What's going on?" Young asked.

"We have an unidentified car," Bryce said. "Just trying to make sure the owner isn't on-site."

Young looked past Bryce toward the car surrounded by cops, yellow tape, and two technicians shooting photographs. "Do you always do this for an unknown car? Is this some kind of terrorist thing?"

"Nothing like that." Bryce smiled. "The car is associated with a crime. Again, thank you."

He moved to the next door, and the process repeated several more times. Each motel guest was not happy to be awakened, but once they saw Bryce's stern expression and realized he was not going anywhere until they complied, they submitted.

A half hour later, Bryce knocked on his seventh door, room 107, and shouted, "Police."

A gravelly voice shouted back, "Just a minute!"

Bryce waited as curtains again fluttered by the window. The door opened to Paul Thompson.

Bryce had learned long ago not to be shocked by what he came across on the job. But seeing Thompson standing in the doorway, hair disheveled and shirt unevenly buttoned and looking nothing like his polished promo picture, took him by surprise. "Mr. Thompson." Flukes like this were rarely accidental. "May I see your license and registration?"

Thompson threaded his fingers through his hair. "What? Why? I haven't done anything wrong."

"License and registration." Bryce just might enjoy this.

Thompson cleared his throat. "What's going on? You don't have the right to show up and ask for that."

"I do. License and registration."

Thompson's next retort went unspoken when he met Bryce's gaze head-on. The reporter, like all boys on the playground, avoided the kid spoiling for a fight. "Just a minute."

As the reporter foraged in his pocket for his identification, Bryce studied the room, noting the double beds, the dresser with a television, and the entry into the bathroom. The bed closest to the door was covered with papers, and there was a laptop in the center. The bed farthest away was not only unmade, but each pillow bore impressions of a head.

"Are you in the room alone?" Bryce asked.

"Yes."

"Someone else was here last night."

"She's gone."

"Who was she?" Bryce asked.

"Carla. Just a woman from a bar." He produced his identification and rental car papers. "Here you go." He looked past Bryce to the parking lot and the collection of cops. "What's going on here?"

"That's what I'm trying to figure out." He noted the car had been rented ten days ago at the airport. "When did you arrive in Missoula?"

Thompson sniffed. "Ten days ago. Just like the rental agreement states."

"And you've been working on your podcast, correct?"

"You know that." He smoothed out his hair with his fingers, rebuttoned his shirt, and tucked it into his jeans. His attention shifted to the car surrounded by cops. "Whose car is that?"

Instead of answering, Bryce asked, "Do you have people who can vouch for your whereabouts for the last couple of weeks?"

"That's a broad time frame. Can you be more specific?"

"How about mid-August?"

"I'd have to check my calendar. Why do I need an alibi?"

As if Gideon had noticed Bryce was lingering at room 107, he approached. "Who's this?"

"Mr. Paul Thompson," Bryce said. "He's doing a story on Elijah Weston and the Fireflies."

Gideon's expression hardened. "Right, I've heard about him."

"I believe he's made contact with Dr. Ann Bailey," Bryce said.

"I've talked to a lot of people," Thompson said. "Is this some kind of shakedown? Did Dr. Bailey send you two to scare me off?"

"Mr. Thompson, we were investigating a crime, and as luck would have it, we've stumbled upon you," Gideon said.

"I haven't committed any crime." Thompson's tone hardened with defensiveness.

"Mr. Thompson, would you be willing to come to the station so we can ask you a few questions?" Bryce asked. "I'd really like to talk to you about your whereabouts for the last couple of months."

Thompson shook his head. "I'm not going anywhere with either of you until you tell me what's going on."

"We are asking for your cooperation," Gideon added. "Strictly voluntary, for now."

Thompson swiped his phone off the small table by the door and scrolled through the numbers in his contacts. "And if I don't come?"

"I'll arrest you and impound your work until I have a forensic expert review every piece of paper and digital file in your possession," Bryce said.

Gideon shook his head, slipping into the role of a concerned man. "Hell, that's going to take weeks, if not months, Bryce. Do you really want to go that route?"

"No, I don't," Bryce said. "I'd like to do this the easy way and simply have a conversation with Mr. Thompson. But either way, we're going to talk."

Gideon dropped his gaze and then looked back up at Thompson. "Just do it the easy way. None of us want the paperwork."

"I'm calling my attorney," Thompson said. "This is not right."

"Go ahead. Call your lawyer," Bryce said. "We'll be waiting right here. And don't close the door."

Thompson retreated to the back of his room, and the cops stepped away several feet, keeping an eye on him.

"What's the deal with Paul Thompson and Ann?" Gideon asked.

"He showed up at her front doorstep for an interview."

"Yes, Ann told me. She's seen a lot like him in the last year. Why is he such a big deal?"

Bryce lowered his voice. "Thompson suggested he might have information about Nate's paternity."

The lines in Gideon's face deepened into a frown as he glared at Paul Thompson pacing back and forth in his room, phone pressed to his ear.

"Nate's paternity?" Gideon glanced again toward room 107. "How the hell did Paul find out?"

"He said one of the Fireflies figured it out."

"The only one who knows besides me is Joan, and she'll take it to her grave. The source must be Elijah. He must have had some suspicion."

"It's getting harder to miss," Bryce said. "Weston must see himself in the boy."

"Shit." Gideon slid a hand in his pocket and rattled change. "But why tell one of his Fireflies? Unless he's using them for some reason."

"I don't know. But Nena Lassiter was a Firefly, and her car was seen at Edith Scott's house right after her estimated time of death. One of Nena's lovers also put her with Thompson. And now her car is parked in front of Paul Thompson's motel room."

"Why would Paul Thompson kill Edith?" Gideon asked. "And if he's that smart to pull off those murders, he's not sloppy enough to park Nena's car outside his motel room."

"That's why we need to have a long conversation with him," Bryce said.

Gideon rested his hands on his hips. "How do you want to play this? He'll be lawyered up before he steps out on the sidewalk."

"And I'll be on the phone to a judge looking for a warrant to search his room after you take him in for questioning."

"If I hold him, then I'll have to Mirandize him."

"If he goes willingly, you don't. Dangle some case details. Tell him about the dead Fireflies. Even if he's innocent, he won't be able to resist the new information."

"Basically, you need time to get into that room."

"Exactly."

Paul Thompson stepped out of his room, closed the door, and locked it behind him. He had washed his face, doused his hair in water, combed it flat, and put on a clean shirt. His backpack was slung over his shoulder.

"If you don't mind, Mr. Thompson, we'll be taking my car," Gideon said.

"Isn't Sergeant McCabe coming?" Thompson asked.

"Someone has to oversee the evidence collection in the vehicle," Bryce said.

"Whose car is it anyway?" Thompson asked.

"I'll share that with you once we get to the station," Gideon said. "Do you have your wallet and cell on you?"

"Yes."

"Good," Gideon said. "Might want to put the backpack back in your room."

"Why?"

"You won't be able to carry it into the station. You could leave it in my car, but it'll be safer here."

"What the hell is going on here?" The outrage that had heightened the color in Thompson's cheeks was washing out.

"Put the backpack away, and we'll chat," Gideon said. "I promise you that you'll want to hear what I have to say."

"You have to do better than that," Thompson said.

"I have information about the Fireflies that you'll find very interesting," Gideon said. "Most of what I have has not been released to the media."

Thompson's gaze shifted from Gideon to the car, which for the moment was not surrounded by cops. "I know that car."

"Do you?" Gideon asked.

"It belongs to Nena Lassiter."

"Yes, sir, it does," Gideon said. "How did you know that?"

"What's going on with her? Has she said something about me?" Thompson asked.

"This is one of many reasons why we need to talk," Gideon said.

Thompson muttered a curse. Finally, he returned to his room, set his backpack behind his bed, locked his door, and rejoined Gideon. When the two settled into the police car, Bryce was on the phone to a local judge and left him a voicemail requesting his warrant.

While he waited for a callback, he returned to the crime scene and watched as the crew continued photographing the vehicle.

The tech tried the door, discovered it was locked, and then obtained a long string from his van, which he worked between the door and jamb at the window's top corner. He tied a slipknot at the end and, using a pen, maneuvered the string around the weather stripping and down toward the door's vertical lock. He tightened the loop with a gentle twist and then tugged until the knob popped open.

Once the door opened, the technician released the trunk, and the crew immediately inspected the space. Bryce noted several suitcases, blankets, several gas cans, and rumpled junk food wrappers.

"Sergeant Bryce, have a look at this," the tech said as he held up what looked like a scrapbook.

On the title page of the handmade book was a picture of Nena and Elijah. His image appeared to have been generated from an online media report detailing his release from prison.

Each subsequent page was filled with similar versions of Nena and Elijah. In several of her pictures, she wore a wedding dress and was holding a handful of flowers. The edges of the pages were decorated with red ink drawn into the shape of flames.

The tech held up a purse, probed, and removed a wallet. He opened it and held up the California driver's license for Nena Lassiter. He handed off the find to an assistant and continued to search the space. He discovered two more wallets. One had belonged to Dana Riley and the other to Sarah Cameron.

Bryce studied Sarah's stoic features on the license. "Nena has Sarah's belongings," he said, more to himself. It made sense because links had already been established between the victims. And then to the technician: "Keep searching."

Minutes later, the tech held up a credit card receipt. "It belongs to Dana Riley."

Bryce now had a vehicle linked to four murders, and all the dead women appeared to be connected to Paul Thompson.

***

Elijah was waiting by the university classroom when the morning session started filing into the room, and he saw Ann bring Nate to the front of the building. She leaned over and kissed him, but he seemed to stiffen as he looked around. She did not force it and appeared to understand her boy was growing up and did not want to be mothered, but her smile was bittersweet.

Ann might be losing her boy, bit by bit, but at least she had had the last ten years. Cheated out of the time, he had not seen Nate take his first step, cut a tooth, or ride a school bus. Resentment clawed its way up his throat.

But he pushed the feelings back into the shadows and focused on the moment. When Ann walked away, he ducked into the classroom. Nate sat toward the front of the class, so Elijah chose a seat in the back, next to the door.

For the next hour, the teacher broke down several math problems, and when he asked for a volunteer, Nate raised his hand along with several other students. Each time the teacher chose someone other than Nate, Elijah sensed the old man did not want the kid showing up him or the other students.

When the class ended, Nate gathered up his books and made his way up the stairs. Elijah ducked out ahead of him and waited outside the room.

As the boy passed, Elijah said, "He should have called on you, Nate."

The boy turned and eyed Elijah. "You're not in this class."

"I wanted to speak to you."

"Why?"

As people filed past them, Elijah thought about the DNA results in his pocket that vindicated all the feelings he had had since he'd first seen a picture of Nate six years ago. One of his Fireflies had taken the image and included it in one of her letters to him. He had known from the moment he laid eyes on the towhead with gray eyes that they were father and son.

"Did you read *King Lear*?"

"A couple of times."

Prioritizing his own desires and dreams over the boy's would be as easy as it was wrong. Nate's feelings had to take precedence. The child would figure out their connection sooner or later, and when he did, Elijah wanted him to understand he was trying to do this right.

"I have another book for you," Elijah said. He dug the new paperback from his jacket pocket. "It's called *Huckleberry Finn*."

"By Mark Twain."

"That's right. It's a classic adventure story." He held out the book, realizing he feared the boy would refuse this symbol of peace.

But Nate took the book and thumbed through the stiff, unbroken pages. "Have you read it?"

"Yes. I love books that involve travel."

"Because you were in prison?"

The boy's candor held no malice, but rather exhibited a scientific curiosity that Elijah understood. "I liked them before prison. I read them as a kid. It was the only way I could see the world. But I reread them all in prison."

"What was it like?"

"Prison?"

"Yeah."

"Not great being told what to do all day long, and I had no friends or allies in prison. But I'm good at finding the best in a bad situation."

"I don't have many friends other than Kyle."

"You're lucky to have Kyle, then."

"Yeah."

"Remember, the world does turn, Nate."

His brow knotted. "What's that mean?"

"It means nothing stays the same. And if we play our cards right, it'll get better."

"When?"

Elijah smiled. "If I could predict that, I would be worth a lot more money."

The boy's phone buzzed with a text, and he glanced at the display. "That's my mom. I've got to go."

"Sure." He slid his hands into his pockets, wishing they had the kind of relationship that allowed him a hug.

"Thanks for the book," Nate said.

"Sure."

Nate started to walk away and then stopped. "Are you going to be in this class next week?"

"I could be."

"If you are, I'll tell you what I think of the book."

Elijah smiled. "Then I'll definitely be here. I can't wait to hear what you say."

"I can be picky."

"Good. That makes you a man of discerning tastes."

The boy tucked the book in his backpack, and Elijah stood in place, watching until he vanished around a corner. He had not said a tenth of what he had wanted to express to Nate, but discretion was the better part of valor. They had forged a start. And that was good enough.

***

Bryce was on the phone with the judge for nearly twenty minutes, arguing for a search warrant of Thompson's motel room. Not only did Bryce have a vehicle parked outside Thompson's motel room that contained evidence related to four murders, but he reiterated that the reporter had given Dr. Bailey a detailed list of the Fireflies. Finally, the judge had relented and given Bryce a warrant that allowed him to do a cursory search of the room.

When Bryce showed the warrant to the manager, Mike remained reluctant. He did not like the idea of invading a resident's privacy, because he'd hear about it on Yelp.

Still, he complied, and Bryce, along with a technician, entered Thompson's motel room at noon.

The room smelled of stale pizza, cigarette smoke, and faint hints of aftershave. At first, Bryce did not touch anything as he moved around the space, trying to get a handle on Paul Thompson's work. The papers strewn on the second bed were printed manuscript pages that appeared edited, presumably by Thompson's hand, in red ink. The pages at the top interview featured Sarah Cameron, and the ones after them introduced Dana Riley and Nena Lassiter.

He dug deeper into the stack and found interviews of people who knew Elijah back in college. There was a section with Elijah's mother, Lois Weston. Also in the mix were the original police reports from Elijah's case, a transcript from his trial, and a list of the jurors on his case. Thompson had spoken to five, including Edith Scott.

He picked up the Scott transcript.

Thompson: Thanks for seeing me today.

Scott: Sure.

Thompson: As I said on the phone, I'm doing a podcast about Elijah.

Scott: You're going to expose him, I hope. Send him back to prison.

Thompson: His conviction was overturned.

Scott: Don't be fooled. He's not innocent. It's a matter of time before he sets more fires. Or kills. I've seen the way he looks at me.

Thompson: You think he resents you for your guilty conviction?

Scott: I know he does.

Thompson: Are you worried for your safety?

Scott: I used to be, but not so much anymore.

Thompson: Why not?

Scott: Doesn't matter.

He picked up Thompson's backpack, and as tempted as he was to pull out the laptop, his warrant did not allow it. Right now, defying the warrant was not worth losing a case.

A knock on the motel room door pulled Bryce's attention toward it. The deputy, a stout man with salt-and-pepper hair and a full mustache, jabbed his thumb over his shoulder toward the parking lot. "The tech says you'll want to see this."

"Right." As he left the room, he said to the deputy, "Stay here and don't let anyone in but the forensic techs. Tell whoever has the camera to photograph everything in sight. I don't know how long we'll have access to the room, and I want something to refer back to."

"Yes, sir."

Bryce strode across the lot as the technician lifted a knife. "Where did you find that?"

"It was in the trunk wrapped in a hand towel. As you can see, there's dried blood on the handle and the blade."

Bryce inspected the blade, noting its pointed edge had broken at the tip and resembled the metal shard found in Nena Lassiter's sternum. This rough field examination would not be enough to prove this was the murder weapon. But once the evidence was processed off the knife, then the experts could compare the weapon to the wounds.

Why would Thompson kill the women he had interviewed? Why be so careless handling a victim's car stocked with evidence? Either Thompson was not that smart after all, or someone had set him up.

Either way, Bryce understood one truth: Thompson had interviewed four dead women as well scheduled an interview with Ann, and in his mind that put Ann in the crosshairs of a killer.

CHAPTER TWENTY-EIGHT

Missoula, Montana
Thursday, August 26
2:00 p.m.

Bryce drove to the police station and apprised Gideon of what he had found in the motel room and the abandoned car. Together, they went into the interview room where Thompson had been left with a cup of coffee and a pack of crackers.

Thompson rose the instant they entered. "I've been sitting here for hours. What the hell is going on?"

"I apologize for the delay," Gideon said. "We're trying to wrap our brains around what's going on here ourselves."

He motioned for Thompson to retake his seat and then sat across from him. Bryce pulled his chair out and sat at the end of the table, his chair angled so he faced Thompson.

"Let's start at the top," Bryce said, leaning back in his chair. "You produce podcasts featuring crimes, and you chose to profile Elijah Weston. Is that correct?"

"Yes."

"How long have you been creating productions like this?" Gideon asked.

"Five years. This is my tenth major project."

"You're well known?" Bryce asked.

"In the world of podcasts, I have a solid reputation."

"What drew you to Weston's case?" Bryce asked.

"What's not to love about the story?" he asked. "Ten years in prison, and he not only got his bachelor's degree, but he collected a group of thirteen women who were totally dedicated to him. He has kind of a Charles Manson vibe that makes me think he's not as innocent as anyone thinks."

"How many Fireflies have you interviewed?" Bryce asked.

"Four."

"They are?"

"Judy Monroe, Sarah Cameron, Dana Riley, and Nena Lassiter."

"Judy Monroe lives in Tennessee, correct?"

"Yes."

"When did you interview her?" Gideon asked.

"Late February or March. I'd need my notes to give the exact date. She told me about the Fireflies."

"Have you communicated with Ms. Monroe lately?" Bryce asked.

"Not for several weeks."

"When's the last time you communicated with Nena Lassiter?"

"A week ago, maybe. If you give me my phone, I can check texts. Why was Nena's car parked outside my motel? Was she looking for me? Is she some kind of stalker?"

"That's what we're trying to figure out," Gideon said.

Thompson arched a brow and leaned forward. "Her car is here, so I'd assume she's in town. Have you asked her?"

"We'll get to that," Bryce said. "What does Carla look like?"

"Dark-brown hair, blue eyes, cute. Nothing extraordinary. Normally, I wouldn't have bothered, but she was willing, and I figured what the hell. I woke up to Sergeant Bryce pounding on my door."

"What was the name of the bar where you met Carla?" Gideon asked.

"The Silver Maverick."

"Did you talk to anyone at the bar who might remember you?" Gideon asked.

"The bartender. I chatted her up a little bit."

"Would you be willing to give us a DNA sample so we can exclude yours from whatever DNA we find in the car?" Gideon asked.

"If it's Nena's car, then I was in it," he said, frowning. "She likes to drive, so we drove around in her car while I interviewed her. Look, I don't know what angle you two are playing, but I've done enough podcasts to know you don't give the cops shit without an attorney."

"Did you get ahold of your attorney?" Bryce asked.

"Yes. He doesn't do criminal work. He's a contract lawyer."

Bryce sighed, careful that he did not allow his personal distaste for the man to cloud his judgment. "I'm sure Detective Bailey can give you the names of local criminal defense attorneys to call."

"My guy is trying to find a local name," Thompson countered. "Look, I didn't do anything other than interview these women."

"Well, then we need to prove that," Bryce said.

"We're not trying to make this tough on you, Mr. Thompson," Gideon said easily. "But like you said, you've done enough of these podcasts to know we have to press in cases like this."

"What kind of case is it?" Thompson demanded.

"Lassiter's car was spotted near a murder scene several days ago and then found in your motel parking lot."

Thompson scooted to the edge of his chair. "A murder scene? Who the hell was killed? And where the hell is Nena?"

"Just to confirm, you did interview Edith Scott?" Gideon asked.

"About a week ago," Thompson said. "Are you telling me she's dead?"

"Yes, she is," Gideon said. "As are Dana Riley, Nena Lassiter, and Sarah Cameron."

"What the hell!" He held up both hands. "I haven't hurt anybody."

"When's the last time you saw Dana?" Bryce asked.

"I haven't seen Dana in six or seven weeks," he countered.

"Which is about the time she was killed," Bryce said carefully. "We only just identified her body."

Thompson ran his hands through his hair, the color fading from his face. "I don't know what the hell is going on, but I haven't hurt anyone."

"Like I said, a DNA swab can help us eliminate you," Bryce said.

"And like I said, I was in that car. I need to call my attorney again in Nashville."

"I'll get you a phone," Gideon said.

"Shit. How much is this going to cost me?" Thompson said.

Gideon shook his head. "When I got divorced, it cost me an arm and a leg. I can't imagine what this mess is going to run you."

"I've investigated enough cases to know cops screw up investigations all the time," Thompson said.

Neither spoke as they stared at him.

"They come into a case with an idea of who the killer is, and then they find evidence to support it. Confirmation bias. And it's easy to pin a case on an outsider like me."

"Call this Carla woman you hooked up with," Bryce said easily. "She might be able to clear up a couple of questions."

"I don't have her number!" Thompson shouted.

"All right, I'll get your phone so you can call your expensive lawyer," Gideon said. "Along with pencil and paper."

"I'll grab you another coffee and more crackers," Bryce offered. "It might be a long day."

They left, and when the door closed, Gideon looked at Bryce. "What do you think?"

"He's doing a good job of acting innocent," Bryce said.

"Isn't part of his job to be an actor?"

"I hear ya. And he's been around enough police stations and read enough files to know what to expect."

"Let's let him make a few calls, figure out what this is going to cost him, and then he might be open to sharing his files and the interviews he conducted for this podcast," Bryce said. "Considering the threat insinuated to Ann, he can stew all day."

"Did you find anything in his room?" Gideon asked.

"Lists of the Fireflies, which we already knew he had. The real gold will be the recordings on his computer, but the warrant does not cover it. It'll be a lot simpler if he opens it for us."

"Don't count on it," Gideon said.

"The car should have been towed to the forensic bay by now. Pulling it apart is priority number one. While Boy Wonder dials for attorneys, I'm going to watch the techs work on the car. You never know."

"Keep me posted."

"Back at you."

***

Elijah sat back and stared at the two cameras that captured Ann's living room. He replayed the morning footage, watching as Ann got the boy off to school. He had been pleased to see Nate shove the copy of *Huckleberry Finn* in his backpack.

His doorbell rang, surging annoyance through him, which only doubled when he glanced in the peephole and saw Maura standing on his porch. She had been fun and useful, but she was now growing irritating. He had not been clear about what he wanted, but the time had come for him to set her straight.

When he opened the door, her red lips widened into a grin, and she held up a brown paper bag. "I have burgers and news you're going to want to hear."

She kissed him on the lips and then slipped past him. "I was not sure what kind of burger you liked, so I got plain with all the condiments tossed in the bag. Also got two cheeseburgers. Can't go wrong either way."

Her words buzzed around his head like flies. What kept him quiet was her announcement of news. "Sounds great."

She moved into the kitchen with a familiarity that was unsettling. The more comfortable he allowed her to become, the harder it would be to extricate her. "I've tried several burger shops since I arrived in Missoula, and this one is my favorite."

"You never said why you came to Missoula," he said.

"Needed a change." She checked the cabinets and found two plates. "I pointed the car west, and here I am."

He wished he could read her thoughts. "What's the news?"

"I met with Paul Thompson last night."

"That was fast."

"I went by his motel, but he was leaving. I followed him, and he ended up in a bar. He's a good-looking man. I wanted to have sex with him, but I paid a girl to sleep with him."

"Really?"

"I'd have done it, but you and I have been seen together. Figured you wouldn't want anything connecting back to you."

He remained silent.

"Does it make you jealous that I said I wanted to sleep with him?"

"Maybe." It didn't, but she seemed to equate love with jealousy.

She unwrapped a burger. "I'd totally have hooked up with him."

He offered a frown, knowing that was what she expected.

"But it wouldn't have been like it is with us," she said quickly.

There was no *us*. "Did you learn anything?"

"Oh, I sure did." She was teasing this out as long as she could.

Like it or not, he had to play along. She served him a burger, and he took a bite, pretending he was not full and that he liked it.

"My girl, Carla, slipped Thompson Rohypnol, he passed out, and she left his motel room door slightly ajar." She dug a stack of papers from her purse. "I took pictures of Thompson's notes and printed them out."

Elijah's attention shifted to the printouts.

"His story might have started off with last year's fires, but his focus is all squarely on you now, baby. He's talked to four Fireflies."

"Why?"

"You're a mystery, darling. And many think you really are guilty of the College Fire."

That specter would follow him forever. But ghosts were the least of his concerns. "What's his angle?"

"He wants to turn you into the next big villain of the podcast world. He sees you as the master puppeteer of the Fireflies. A kind of a Charles Manson character."

He thought about Nate and how a story like that would affect him. "Is that what you think?"

She set her burger down and kissed him. "You did convince me to hide those cameras in Ann's house. And I paid a woman to have sex with Thompson."

Suddenly, he was disgusted with her. "You can't prove that."

Her smile dimmed slightly. "You asked me to do both."

"Your word against mine."

She managed a little-girl pout that looked ridiculous. "Why are you acting like this?"

"I'm not acting like anything. You're suggesting I'm some kind of evil mastermind."

"I didn't say that." She looked startled. "That's what Paul Thompson said in his notes."

"But you believe it."

"It's kind of true, don't you think?" she asked. "I read about that woman from last year. She was willing to do anything for you."

"She made her own choices, just like you made yours."

She frowned. "To please *you*."

Elijah wiped his hands on a paper towel. "It's time you leave."

"Why?"

"I have a study session."

"Is school that important?" she demanded.

"It's everything."

"What is it with men and their work? They pretend like it's their world, but it's just an excuse to hide from their true feelings."

"Maybe you've never been that important to any man," he said.

She scowled. "That's a shitty thing to say."

"Maybe. But you need to leave."

She frowned as if she would fight him, and then she grabbed her purse and stomped out of the house, slamming the door behind her. He locked it.

The truth was none of the Fireflies or the one-night stands could please him for very long. They were all disposable, and all were more trouble than they were worth in the end. And as much as he wanted to forget them and their smiling faces, they would not leave him alone.

CHAPTER TWENTY-NINE

Missoula, Montana
Thursday, August 26
4:00 p.m.

Ann arrived at the Beech Street house to find her Realtor and the prospective buyers standing in the driveway. They were early, but that did not ease her sense that she was somehow behind and needed to catch up.

She parked and, as she got out of the car, summoned a smile. "Am I late?"

"No," the Realtor said. "We're early. The buyers just flew in, and we came straight here from the airport."

Ann dug keys from her purse. "We just finished deep cleaning yesterday, so you'll find the place in top shape." As she shoved her key into the lock, her phone rang. Bryce's name appeared on her display.

"Excuse me," she said. "Go ahead and show yourselves around."

She turned from the group and walked several paces away. "What's up? I'm meeting with a Realtor now."

As if she had not spoken, he said, "We found Nena Lassiter's car and have discovered evidence that connects all the murders. The car's been towed to the forensic warehouse, which is where I am now. I think you should be here."

She looked back at the house and watched as the Realtor escorted the couple inside. "Have you found anything?"

"I'd like another set of eyes on the vehicle as we go through it."

She sensed he had found a great deal but was not willing to discuss it over the phone. "All right. I can be there in a half hour."

"You remember the address?"

"Yes." Ann worked her house key off her ring and approached the Realtor, who stood alone in the living room as the couple walked around. "I have an emergency. Can I give you this key and leave this to you?"

"I'm their agent, not yours."

"I know. My agent is supposed to set out the lockbox today. And I would not ask you otherwise, but I have to go."

The Realtor held out her hand. "What do you want me to do with the key when we're finished?"

"There's a planter out front. It's gray and white." The flowers she had planted in it had died over a year ago. "Just slip it under the pot, and I'll come back and get it."

"Sure." As Ann turned, the Realtor asked, "The couple mentioned they might like some of the furniture. How do you feel about all that?"

A smart person would have been a savvier negotiator. But in all honesty, she was donating every stick of furniture. "Make me an offer."

"For how much extra?" the Realtor asked.

The idea of dealing with whatever furniture did not sell suddenly felt like too much. "How about free of charge. I don't want any of it."

The Realtor was local and surely knew Ann's history with the house. Hell, everyone in town had heard something about her. "Understood, Dr. Bailey. I'll let you know. Come to think of it, I might have a second showing here today. Mind if I hang on to the key and then put it under the planter?"

"No problem. Thank you."

As Ann walked toward her car, she took what felt like her first deep breath in years. Maybe it was the air in the house or the memories, but each time she crossed that threshold, the air bottled in her lungs.

Twenty minutes later, she arrived at the forensic facility, parked, and made her way to the front desk. "Dr. Ann Bailey. I'm meeting Sergeant Bryce McCabe."

The receptionist nodded, checked her driver's license, and then gave her directions to the bay where the car was stored. Excitement tightened her nerves as she rode the elevator down two floors. Teaching was her first love, but there was a real thrill in working an active case. She understood now why Joan craved the work.

The elevator doors opened, and she stepped into the large garage warehouse area and saw across the room the blue four-door. All the doors were open, as were the vehicle's trunk and hood. All the contents had been spread out on tarps on the floor.

Bryce stepped around the car and moved toward her, his strides long and his shoulders back. A man of few words, he moved with an easy confidence. Ann's late husband had displayed all the same hallmarks, but underneath the pumped-up bravado was fear.

"Thanks for coming," Bryce said.

As the distance between them diminished, she inhaled his scent, realizing how it energized her. No aftershave but the faint hint of soap mingling with a masculine smell all his own.

"This is Nena's car?" she asked.

"Yes," he said. "It was found outside of Paul Thompson's motel room."

"Paul Thompson's motel room? That doesn't make sense. A car like this would have been hot evidence, and if the killer had any sense, he wouldn't have displayed it."

"Reverse psychology? Hiding in plain sight?" He handed her a pair of gloves.

As she worked the gloves onto her hands, she shook her head. "Maybe. The car is unremarkable. Perhaps Thompson, if he is the killer, assumed it would take us longer to identify Nena."

"Too smart or arrogant for his own good," Bryce said. "He's made it clear he thinks he's smarter than the cops."

"He's smarter than most, but to park the car outside his motel room is a terrible mistake."

"He's denying knowing anything about the vehicle," Bryce said. "Though he doesn't deny knowing the victims or being in this car with Nena."

"The podcast could be used to establish reasonable doubt. He's trying to undercut evidence before you find it."

"Maybe."

"The evidence will tell you more, of course, but I tend to believe him," she said.

"Assuming Thompson didn't park the car at the motel, who would?"

"Someone who's decided Thompson would be easy to frame," she said more to herself. "Someone who knew he was interviewing these women and who didn't appreciate Thompson's investigation."

"Like Elijah Weston?"

"He does think several steps ahead. But why kill the Fireflies?"

"Because they're talking to Thompson. He doesn't appreciate his past being reopened now that he's on a path to create a new future."

She thought about Nate and the troubling effect a story like this would have on him. "Show me what you've found."

"Let's start with the front seat and move our way backward," Bryce said.

"Sure."

He stopped at the edge of the blue tarp laid on the concrete by the open front door. It contained a variety of items you might find in anyone's car. A black leather purse and also a brown purse had their contents displayed around the bags. She noted the black purse was made of expensive leather and fashioned with a fine stitching. It contained a small bottle of Chanel perfume, a costly brand of lipstick, and a gold watch. The brown purse was more worn and appeared to be of lower quality. Its contents contained drugstore lipstick, tissues, and a bag of generic chocolate candy.

"Two purses representing two socioeconomic backgrounds," she said.

She moved to the back seat and again noticed a disparity in the discarded snack bags. One set favored dried fruit and nuts, whereas the other favored low-cost, high-sugar-content candies. There was also a collection of name-brand water bottles and soda cans. There had been at least two different women in this car.

Silent, she walked along the side of the car, her gaze skimming the blue paint coated in what looked like a thousand miles of dust and dirt. When she reached the trunk, she studied the collection of items laid out on a blue tarp. There were several items of clothing: designer jeans, the pair of blue cowboy boots that someone had purchased at the Classy Cat. To her right there were more clothes. These were lower end, likely from a box store, and they were speckled with dark-brown spots that looked like blood.

"These are the belongings of at least two, maybe three, different women."

"And we have four victims, including Edith Scott."

"Ms. Scott was the anomaly," Ann said. "The one-off that the killer murdered for very different reasons. She was not a Firefly. She was not devoted to Elijah—in fact, she openly hated him. Edith, like the Fireflies, was a potential threat to his new life."

"There's another way to spin this," Bryce said. "Do you think he might have used another Firefly to kill these women?"

"I don't know what Elijah is truly capable of," she said. That uncertainty sent her mind drifting to frightening places. "What would be the advantage to using or even killing these women?"

"Loose ends? Eliminate them all and whatever secrets they shared."

"I don't think so. When I spoke to Megan Madison, she was alive and well. She lives close enough to Missoula and Helena. Maybe she is more involved in all this. All groups, no matter how egalitarian, end up with members who carry more weight than others."

"Killing is Madison's way of winning Elijah's approval?" Bryce's voice was tight.

"Possibly."

"Both Thompson and Elijah knew all these women. They had the means to travel and track down each woman," Bryce said.

"I'd like to talk to Thompson," she said. "I'd like him to tell me what he knows, and then I can confront Elijah."

"That's my job, Ann."

"I might be able to get more out of each man. Elijah has a connection to me, and Thompson wants an exclusive interview with me. I'll use both their desires to my advantage."

"No, you're too close to the case, Ann. And until I know which of these two men might be behind the murders, I want you staying clear of them both."

"I can't do that, Bryce." Ann's fear for her son's safety grew by the minute. "These killings feel as if they're getting closer to me and my son. I can't hide from the danger, so I might as well run toward it."

***

An hour later, when Ann stepped inside the police conference room alone, it was just her and Paul Thompson. Thompson had lost the subtle smirk from their last meeting in the coffee shop. His shoulders rolled forward very slightly as he tapped an index finger on the table.

"Can I get you something to drink?" she asked. "There's a fresh pot of coffee. It's marginal at best, but I've tasted worse."

He shook his head slowly. "No, thanks. Bryce McCabe offered a cup as he was tightening the vise on my balls."

"That's a bit extreme." She chose the seat to his right and angled it directly toward him, knowing the positioning suggested they were on the same side.

"He was nice about it," Thompson said. "But there was no missing his meaning. I can fight murder charges, run up a shit ton of debt, or I can help."

"See this from Bryce's perspective," she said. "He has a murder to solve, and there are three other pending unsolved murders that are connected. Four dead women, Thompson."

He leaned toward her, his fist tightening. "I didn't kill those women."

"But you have the rare perspective of meeting and talking to them all. If you and I can work together, we might be able to see a pattern."

"The pattern is simple. It's Elijah Weston. These women were all fixated on him."

"What's your theory on the killer? Why would anyone want to single out the Fireflies?"

He shoved out a breath and sat back in his chair, reminding her of Nate when he was frustrated. "Like I said, Elijah Weston is cleaning up loose ends. I bet he parked that car in front of my motel room."

It would be easy to believe him and confirm her biases about Elijah. But it was the truth that mattered, not justifying personal fears. "What drew you to this story?"

Thompson looked around the room, searching up and down the four walls. "Are they listening?"

She leaned back in her chair. "Do you mean Gideon and Bryce?"

"Yeah. The dynamic duo."

She allowed a smile. "No. It's just you and me." She crossed her legs, taking extra care to look relaxed. "How did you hear about Elijah?"

"The troubles in Missoula actually made national news. You, if anybody, should know that. It was a popular topic in Nashville for a few weeks. My girlfriend and I talked about it a lot."

"We had our share of reporters." When a simple answer was full of extraneous information, she became suspicious that the response could be deceptive.

He cocked his head. "A bit of an understatement."

"Perhaps."

When she did not expand on her experiences, he shrugged. "Lucky for you the news cycle is fast and furious, and reporters move on to the next watering hole quickly."

"And yet here you are. I've briefly read over the cases you covered in your podcasts. They're all decades old."

"In some respects, it's easier if the cases are older. As time passes, reality feels more like fiction. Still titillating, but less dangerous. Distance and time make people more likely to talk. There's less fear of the guilty, because they're either too old, in jail for another crime, or dead."

"But the passage of time creates its own challenges. Police files get lost, witnesses die, and memories slip out of focus. This story is still fresh."

"It will appeal to my audience."

"So, you heard about this case strictly through the media?" Ann asked.

"Not exactly."

"What's that mean?"

"I did read about it. Thought it was interesting, but then I met a woman in Nashville. Her name is Judy Monroe. We started dating, and she confessed to me she was one of the Fireflies. The more she talked about writing Elijah in prison, the more curious I became about the story. Through the Freedom of Information Act, I obtained the list of the Fireflies from the prison."

"I've seen that list. The one you gave me was very detailed."

Pride flickered in his gaze. "Judy helped me. She had already set up a social media account. I made it my mission to find them and reach out to them all."

She recalled Judy's name and remembered her picture on Thompson's fact sheet had been blurred. "Were there Fireflies you approached who refused to talk to you?"

"Sure. There were about five or six, like Megan Madison, that didn't want to be interviewed. They were either embarrassed that they'd fallen for an incarcerated man, or, like I said, they lost interest in Elijah because he'd been released. Some women like knowing their man is in a box."

"Megan Madison doesn't seem the type to write a man behind bars."

"Her husband, Cooper, put her in the hospital about five years ago. She told me he joined AA and things are better now. But you're a shrink. You know when an abuser crosses that line it's easier to cross it again. Elijah must have been some kind of safe haven for her."

"That's very true."

"Did your husband ever hit you?" Thompson asked.

The sudden reversal of the script took her aback. As her defenses rose, she reminded herself she had to give a little to get more. "No. He never once hit me."

"What about your son?"

"Never. He adored Nate. He wanted to be a better father than his father had been to him." She was willing to give a bit of herself to keep him talking. "Clarke struggled to distance himself from the past, and he appeared to be winning."

"Appeared to be *winning*?"

She ignored the biting tone. "What is Judy Monroe like? What was her attraction to Elijah?"

"Judy has her share of control issues," he said.

"Tell me about her," Ann said.

"Fairly ordinary. She comes from a small town in West Virginia. Attractive. She's good with computers and math and for the most part is self-taught. For a short while she worked as my personal assistant."

"Did Judy ever come to Missoula to see Elijah?"

"She said she came out here a few times over the years. She seemed to know a lot about you and your son. She even had pictures of you and Nate. She's the one that figured Elijah might be your son's biological father."

Ann searched her memory for anyone over the years whom she had caught lingering too long or watching her while she was with Nate. Had there been someone at Nate's school, the university, or the grocery store? She could not remember any one person, but in the last couple of years, she had been distracted by her failing marriage, the separation, last year's fires, and the resulting media storm.

"Do you have copies of the pictures Judy took?" Ann asked.

"They're on my computer. Get my computer, and I'll show you."

"Sure." She rose, anxious to know what data this woman had collected about her son. "I'll be right back."

She closed the door behind her, and down the hallway she found Gideon in the break room with Bryce. Each held a cup of coffee. "I need Thompson's computer."

Gideon studied her closely. "Everything all right?"

"Not exactly," she said.

"Can we help?" Bryce asked.

"No. I'll have to see this one to the end," she said.

Bryce reached around the counter and handed Thompson's backpack to her. "I thought he might want this. Is he going into detox without it?"

"I'm sure that's part of it. I'll let you know." She turned to leave and stopped. "Can you fill up two cups with coffee for me?"

Bryce didn't question as he plucked two white disposable cups from a stack and carefully filled each.

"He told Bryce he didn't want any," Gideon said.

"He said Bryce had his balls in a vise when you asked."

Gideon chuckled. "Literally, not figuratively."

"Either way, he wasn't in the mood." She hoisted the backpack on her shoulder and took the cups from Bryce. Their gazes met for a moment, and as she stared into his intense eyes, calm washed over her. "Thanks."

"Anytime." He followed her down the hallway and reached for the door handle. However, instead of opening it, he said in a low voice, "When this is over, are you interested in taking a couple of days off with me?"

"That sounds really good. Though I'll still have reporters on my trail, psycho Elijah, and a genius son who's going to be more work as he grows older. When this is all said and done, if you decide to take a pass on that mini vacation, no harm, no foul."

Humor glinted in his gaze. "I'm not worried."

"That makes one of us." She paused outside the closed door and rolled her head from side to side.

"Be calm. Be cool. You'll get more if you don't rise to the bait."

"Thanks."

He opened the door, and she offered the cup to Thompson.

When the door closed, she said to the reporter, "Hopefully, your testicles don't feel as confined as they did."

That prompted a small smile he would never have allowed with Gideon or Bryce. "I'm not fooled. The cops have forensic evidence linking me to the murders. I could still get screwed."

"I asked the police to bring your backpack and laptop here so you would have access to it." She handed him his backpack, and she took her seat, sipping the coffee. Refuting his statement was pointless. He was right. So far, he was the only suspect with tangible evidence working against him.

He unzipped the backpack and removed the trim laptop. After typing in the passcode, he scrolled through the files until he found what he seemed to be looking for. He stared at the computer for a long moment, as if weighing the value of helping her. “How do I know you won’t screw me over?”

“I’ve just as much to lose at this point as you,” she said.

“No one is threatening you with prison.”

“My life and my son’s are endangered.”

He turned the computer around and showed her the image. “Point taken.”

Leaning forward, she studied the pictures. Her nerves tightened like a bowstring when she saw the image of Nate and her at the park. She remembered the day. It had been two years ago about this time of year, and Clarke had worked back-to-back shifts, and they hadn’t seen him in days. Nate was feeling lonely and restless, and they had gone out for ice cream.

They had sat on the park bench and stared up at the sky and searched for recognizable shapes with the cirrus clouds. Christ, she had even talked about how lucky he was to have a dad who loved him so much.

“I don’t remember anyone taking these.” But she had been distracted and worried about Nate. “Do you have a picture of her? The picture on your printout wasn’t clear.”

He chose another file, frowned, and then clicked on another and another. “The pictures I took of Judy aren’t here.” He fished his phone out and searched his images. “They’re gone from my phone as well.”

“That’s odd, isn’t it?” she asked.

“The files were here just a few days ago.” His tone had taken on an edge. “I’m not lying or playing games. They really are gone.”

"What do you think happened to them?" she asked.

"I know what you're thinking."

"What's that?" she asked.

"You think I've made Judy Monroe up."

"It is a plausible theory."

"I didn't make her up. She's real."

Instead of engaging him on this diversion, she took a different tack. "Have you left your computer unattended?"

"Almost never." He stilled. "Except when I left it in my hotel room."

"The device is password protected," she said. "And the police don't have a warrant allowing them access to your computer."

"They have good reason to frame me."

"And I have good reason to think the worst of you, but I'm trying very hard not to. Think beyond the obvious. Who else had access to your computer?"

"I went out drinking last night and hooked up with a woman. I've already told the cops her name was Carla, and I met her at the Silver Maverick."

"Do you think this woman did it?" Ann asked. "We've established the computer is password protected."

"No." He pinched the bridge of his nose. "She didn't strike me as that smart. But I did pass out for several hours."

"And Carla definitely wasn't Judy?"

"No. Of all the Fireflies I would have recognized Judy in bed." He shook his head. "Elijah has to be behind this. He has to have put Carla or Judy up to all this."

"Are the images of any other women missing?" she asked.

He searched, shook his head. "No. Those files are all intact."

"When did you and Judy break up?" she asked.

He tipped his head back. "I went to Knoxville in late May and met with Sarah."

"And you slept with her."

Thompson shoved out a breath. "Yeah, once."

"Could Judy have figured that out?"

"I broke up with her a few days after my return," he said carefully.

"How'd she take it?"

"Not well. She said all men should be on a leash."

"When's the last time you texted Judy?" she asked.

"It was a couple of days after we broke up." He scrolled through his text messages, then turned the phone around so she could read.

Judy: Wish you luck, lover.

Thompson: You too, babe.

Judy: You'll find I'm the best you'll never have again.

"I didn't respond." He looked up, and his stare was frantically intense.

"And you never heard from her again?"

"No." He rubbed his hand over the back of his neck. "I did not kill those women."

"Text Judy now and see if she responds."

He typed, Hey, babe. What're you doing?

The screen remained still, no bubbles, no hint that there was anyone on the other end.

"She always got back to me fast," he said.

"Logical to assume she's moved on and doesn't care about you anymore."

"Could Judy be working with Elijah? Unstable women are drawn to him."

"I don't know." Ann could not refute Thompson's claim. Elijah was outwardly calm and collected, but there was a darkness in him.

"You can have my notes, and you can read them all," Thompson said. "Maybe you can see something I've missed."

"I will."

"Hurry. Your brother is going to arrest me."

"You don't know that."

"I do. The charges won't stick, but there's enough evidence to hold me for a few days while they sort this out. And in the meantime, the real killer will be free."

***

I do not like to hurt people. I do not enjoy doing the things I have done. But there are times when I am backed into a corner. When messes need to be cleaned up. When lessons need to be taught.

CHAPTER THIRTY

Missoula, Montana
Thursday, August 26
6:00 p.m.

Ann carried Thompson's laptop out of the interview room and found both Bryce and Gideon waiting for her. "He's letting me print out his story notes, and then he wants his computer back."

"I have a printer in my office," Gideon said.

They walked to the small windowless office. Behind a desk with neatly arranged files stood a credenza outfitted with a printer. She opened the files, selected the printer, and hit "Print."

As they waited, she set the laptop on his desk, and her attention shifted to an image on his wall taken of the boys when they were about four years old. They had been fishing on the Yellowstone River. She remembered the picture well. Clarke had taken it.

"Joan and I can take Nate tonight," Gideon offered.

"Thanks, but I'm picking him up from practice in a little while. We're really trying to establish a new routine."

The printer spit out the last page. She verified she had what she needed and closed the laptop. After returning it to Thompson and making assurances she would read the notes tonight, she connected with Bryce in the hallway.

"Hopefully, there's something in his notes that will tell us about the killer," Ann said. "In the meantime, he also spoke to Judy Monroe, who was not only a Firefly but a former girlfriend. Find out what you can about her."

"Will do," Bryce said.

"Thanks." She liked the idea of having him close.

"I should also have more forensic data by tomorrow as well," Gideon said.

"Thompson did say he was in the car when he interviewed Nena," Ann said. "He said you might find his DNA."

"He told me," Bryce said. "It could be a preemptive reason he's planting so when it's found, his defense attorney can explain it to the jury."

"Maybe." Ann saw in Thompson a man as bewildered as the cops. But she had misjudged people before.

Ann left with Bryce, and neither spoke until he placed the files in the back seat of her car. "Until this is over, I'm sticking close."

"Why?"

"There are four dead women, and all of them spoke to Thompson. You just spoke to him, and now you have his notes. You'll be privy to whatever those women revealed to him. And Elijah is far from cleared in all this."

"Nothing I haven't told myself. When do you plan to talk to Thompson again?" Ann asked.

"As soon as you go through those notes. Then it's going to be a full-court press." He checked his watch. "Where are you headed next?"

"I have to get Nate. He's at soccer practice."

"Soccer. I haven't seen a soccer game in a very long time."

She cocked a brow. "Why do I think you've never seen a soccer game?"

"Been to my fair share of rodeos." Bryce kissed her gently on the lips. "But there's always a first time for soccer."

"That I would like to see." She leaned closer to him, wishing they had more time right now. "I've got to go."

"Stay safe, Ann."

"Always."

"I mean it," he said, all traces of humor vanishing from his face. "I don't want to find out that you're on this killer's list."

***

When Ann parked in front of her house, Nate was in the back seat staring out the window, lost in thought, as he often was. A sense of relief washed over her as she stared at the brick rancher that was slowly starting to feel familiar.

"Mom, can we order pizza?" Nate asked.

"I must have read your mind. Just placed an order on the app. Should be here in about ten minutes."

"Awesome."

As they got out of the car, her gaze swept the yard, the bushes by the house, and the yards of her neighbors. Nate raced ahead of her toward the front door and waited impatiently for her to unlock it.

She twisted her key in the lock and pushed open the door, and Nate hurried down the hallway toward his room. She was anxious to read through the Thompson interviews and maybe figure out how the reporter's visits to the Fireflies had triggered the killer.

She flipped on lights, moving through the freshly organized living room, feeling a sense that she and Nate were going to be okay. Life was not necessarily going to be easy, but they would be happy again.

She dropped the files on top of her desk and then changed into a loose-fitting T-shirt and yoga pants. When the doorbell rang, she grabbed her wallet and fished out a five-dollar bill for the tip. Her stomach rumbled, and she was anxious to eat and get to work.

She opened the door, finding the young delivery driver sporting an insulated red carrier. He was slim and had pulled back his thick dark hair in a ponytail that drew attention to his youthful face.

"Dr. Bailey?" he asked as he checked the name on the slip.

"That's right."

"Large thin crust, light on the cheese?"

"Correct."

He handed her the warm box, which smelled of tomato and oregano, and she gave him his tip. "Thanks."

"Thank you."

She closed the door, fastened the two locks, and called out, "Nate!"

The boy hurried out of his room. He had changed into shorts and a T-shirt and had washed his face. He was carrying a book as he settled on the barstool by the kitchen island.

She grabbed paper plates and several sheets of paper towels, then served them each a slice. "Eat up."

He bit into the pizza. "Remember when you used to cook all the time?"

That life seemed so long ago. "I do."

"I think I like the takeout better," he said.

"Sooner or later, I'll have to get my act together and cook for us again."

"No rush, Mom."

She chuckled, knowing it was hard to compete with pizza and burgers. "What are you reading?"

"*Huckleberry Finn*."

"That's a classic. What made you think of that one?"

"Elijah suggested it."

She stilled, her half-eaten pizza slice suspended in midair. "Elijah Weston."

"Yeah, from school. We both audit the same math class."

She set the pizza down, reached for her paper towel, and carefully wiped the grease from her fingertips as she checked her worry. "He gave you the copy of *King Lear*?"

"That's right."

"You told me you got the book at computer camp."

"He was there and suggested it."

She tightened her grip on the wadded paper towel. "Do you talk to him a lot?"

"Sometimes." He looked up at her over the edge of his book. "I know what Dad did to him."

"Did he tell you?"

"No. Everyone knows it."

She had tried to be honest with the boy about what was happening, but she had also sugarcoated what she could. Smart or not, he was a kid.

"He's cool, Mom," Nate said. "He doesn't treat me like a baby. And I've only seen him at school."

She cleared her throat while concentrating on appearing calm. "And what do you two talk about?"

"Books. He suggests books. He likes to read like I do."

"Really?"

Nate regarded her more closely. "You look sick, Mom."

"I'm not. Long day," she said, managing a smile. Her appetite gone, she cleared away her pizza plate and dumped it in the trash. "I want you to be careful around Elijah. We really don't know him that well."

"Because he was in prison? You know he was innocent."

"That's only part of it."

The boy shrugged. "He seems nice to me."

"You need to tell me when he reaches out to you, okay? No secrets."

"Okay. Maybe we can have him over for dinner sometime."

Ann cleared her throat, and instead of answering his query, she asked, "Are you still hungry?"

He studied the remaining slices. "No, I'm good."

"Okay. I'll wrap this up, and then I need to do some reading." The sooner she understood who was behind the murders, the sooner she might have a better idea of how Elijah fit into the crimes.

"Me too. This is a good book."

"Is it?"

"I like the idea of going on an adventure. Kind of felt like that when I went camping with Uncle Gideon."

"Uncle Gideon will always take you camping. But I don't want you going off with Elijah like that."

"You don't have to worry about Elijah, Mom."

"I worry about everyone when it comes to you."

He rolled his eyes. "I know."

The front bell rang, and she was annoyed by the distraction. She threaded her fingers through her hair as she hurried to the door. When she opened it and saw Bryce, she nearly stepped into his arms. "Hey, what brings you here so late?"

"I was about to drive back to the ranch, but thought I would check in."

"Come on in. Nate's at the kitchen table reading a book that Elijah Weston gave him."

"Really?" His tone was cautious.

"They seem to have struck up a friendship." She toned down the edge creeping up in her voice, knowing she had no right to lay this on Bryce. "I have extra pizza if you want it."

He glanced past her and then leaned forward and kissed her on the lips. His lips tasted of salt, and the stubble of his beard brushed her skin, sending an erotic shot to her loins. He drew back, squeezed her shoulder gently, and then, dropping his arm, followed her into the kitchen.

"Nate, have a look who stopped by. Sergeant McCabe."

Nate looked up. "You were right about the gear. I packed too much. But not as much as I would have. Thanks for the tip."

"Glad I could be of help," Bryce said easily. "Your mom says there's extra pizza."

The boy opened the pizza box top. "Mom and I don't like leftovers, so eat it all."

He picked up a slice and took a seat next to Nate. "I read that book once. But I was in the marines working on my college degree. Wish I'd gotten an earlier start like you."

"Did you ever take a boat down the Mississippi River while you were in the marines?" Nate asked.

"Not the Mississippi River. We did practice maneuvers on a few rivers."

"Did you like it?" Nate asked.

"I'd rather be on a horse than a boat. I'll take an open field over an ocean any day."

"I've never seen the ocean."

"Something to see." He took a bite.

"Mom's talked about driving west until we hit the Pacific," Nate said.

Ann had had a lot of fantasies about running away last winter. "Just haven't gotten around to it."

"We've been busy, Mom," Nate said. "You said next summer."

"We'll do it." Next summer felt like a lifetime away.

"You like dogs, Nate?" Bryce asked.

"Yeah," Nate said.

"Get your mom to bring you out to my ranch. My brother lives there, too, and he has four dogs. All retired military working dogs."

The boy's eyes brightened. "Can I bring Kyle?"

"Sure. You two can make a day of it," Bryce said.

"Can they do tricks?" Nate asked.

"I'm pretty sure they can," Bryce said. "You'll have to get Dylan to show you."

"Why does Dylan have so many dogs?" Nate asked.

"He takes the ones no one wants," Bryce said. "Their handlers couldn't keep them, and they're too much dog for most people. But they're friendly."

"What kind of dogs are they?"

"Three German shepherds and a Belgian Malinois."

Nate's phone rang, and Kyle's name appeared on the display. "Can I take this?"

"Go right ahead," Ann said.

"I'm going to tell Kyle about the dogs."

"Sounds good, Nate."

The boy scrambled off to his room and, to Ann's delight, acted like a kid without a care in the world.

"You're going to have a three-page report on the differences between the two dog breeds by morning," Ann said. "Be prepared for more questions."

"I don't mind." Bryce took her hand in his, rubbing his fingers against her smooth palms. "He's handling it all pretty well."

"I think so." She took the seat beside his, taking comfort in just having him close. "And yet I worry."

"Don't." He finished off the first slice.

"What have you found in Nena Lassiter's car so far?"

"The techs pulled hair strands and fingerprints from the front seat. The hair samples have been sent to the lab, and it'll take days at best. But Thompson's fingerprints were pulled from the dashboard. He was in the car."

"Did you find anything else? The pictures or facial skin? They would be the killer's most prized trophies—tangible fragments of the victims. The killer keeps them close and in a safe place."

"No to both. We're checking the cameras from the surrounding businesses near the motel. I'm hoping to get a glimpse of the driver. If it's Thompson, then the case against him gets really strong."

"He's not that stupid," she said. "Why would he park the car near his room? Why would he give me his files to read if he killed those women?"

"Saying that's true, who would want to set him up?" Bryce leaned back in his chair. "One of the Fireflies who didn't like him asking questions. Or someone who didn't appreciate him using Nate to get to you."

"Have you found anything that links Elijah to the car?"

"No prints. Maybe there'll be a hair sample. Again, the security cameras are going to tell more."

"Elijah is too careful to leave prints behind." She frowned. "Did you find anything attached to Judy Monroe?"

"I've placed calls to the Tennessee and West Virginia authorities. Should have pictures, maybe police records by morning."

"Can you contact the prison and see if they copied any of Judy's letters to Elijah?"

"I'll call as soon as I walk out of here."

"Good."

"Why don't you and the boys plan to come out to the ranch sooner rather than later? You could stay out there. There's room enough for you all, and those pups can distract anyone from anything. Hell, at the rate my brother is going, there might be another one in the brood by now. And no one will get to either of you at the ranch."

She smiled up at him, appreciating him for his kindness. "Nate has school and so do I. We can't run and hide now."

"A few days won't matter, Ann, but it might give me time to find this guy."

If it were just her, she would have refused, but she had Nate to consider. "Maybe tomorrow. We could drive out after school."

He leaned forward and kissed her. "And tonight?"

She savored the taste of him. "We'll be fine. Really. I'll lock all the doors and windows. And won't let in anyone I don't know."

"Even then, think twice about opening the door."

***

Elijah sat at his computer, watching the feed from Ann's living room. At first, he had been pleased to watch Nate talk to his mother about him and the book. He could see the tension straining her smile, but she had kept her cool. She was trying to keep the boy's world calm. But that was what Ann did. She kept cool.

They had mentioned Judy Monroe, and he thought back to the letters she had written him. She was highly intelligent, and he found her mind worked much like his. The pictures she had sent him were of a tall, athletically built woman with dark hair, gray eyes, and olive skin. Not his type, but she was clever enough to make him not care. Where was she now?

He hit "Rewind" and replayed the moment Bryce leaned in and kissed Ann. Her body melted into his. There was a familiarity between them. They had shared intimacy. Secrets.

He closed his eyes, trying to imagine what it had felt like when she'd kissed him. Her lips were soft. Her scent sweet. Her hair like silk.

He looked again at the frozen image of Ann and Bryce. The one thing those two did not share and would never share was Nate. Elijah and Ann had created the boy, and he was all theirs.

A man claimed what was his, and that was exactly what he intended to do.

***

It was 1:00 a.m. when Ann leaned back in her office chair and stretched the strain from her muscles. She had read through the transcripts of the interviews, and one theme had become clear. The women Thompson interviewed believed that by attaching themselves to Elijah Weston, they, too, would touch fame.

Writing to a man in prison also offered them a thrill that they had never experienced before. Elijah seemed to *know* and *understand* them like no one else. They said it was like reading their own real-life suspense novel that allowed them to safely savor the thrill of fear. Elijah's sharp good looks had also fueled sexual fantasies that the women had talked freely about to Thompson.

Danger. Sex. Fame. It was a heady cocktail that—for women who lived simple, ordinary lives—was impossible to resist.

When her doorbell rang, she glanced at her phone and realized it was after one. Rising, she moved to the window and looked outside.

Maura was standing on her porch. Her eyes were red, her shirt ripped, and her hair tousled as if she had been fighting.

Ann unlatched the door and opened it. "Are you okay?"

Maura blinked back tears. "Can I come in?"

"Sure." She stepped to the side. "Who did this to you?"

Maura shook her head and dropped her gaze as if she were gathering her thoughts. "I was stupid to trust him."

"Trust who?" Ann asked.

Tears welled in her eyes before she swiped them away. "Elijah."

Ann's blood chilled. She had always feared what Elijah was capable of doing. "What did he do to you?"

Again, Maura was silent, and for a moment she looked broken.

Ann reached toward her. "What did he do? Did he hit you?"

Maura took a step back, shaking her head. Her voice dropped to a raspy whisper. "He can't ever love me. His heart is taken."

Ann drew back, glancing toward her phone, readying to dial 911. Whatever was going on with Maura was wrong, and she needed more help than Ann could provide. "I don't understand."

Maura looked at her, the sadness gone from her gaze. In its place was a haunted, dark look. "He can't love me because I'm not you."

Ann took several steps back as she tightened the grip on her phone. "I don't understand."

Maura closed the distance. "Every time he fucked me, he whispered your name in my ear: *Ann, Ann, Ann.*"

"What are you talking about? You were with Elijah?"

"Several times. The Beech Street house was a favorite location. But he doesn't want me—he wants you!"

Ann took a step back from the anger tightening Maura's features and the wildness in her eyes. "I have nothing to do with Elijah."

Her eyes widened with a madwoman's intensity. "You're everything to him."

Ann realized she had been a fool to trust this woman. She had allowed her into her home and close to her son. "Who are you?"

"You haven't guessed?"

It did not matter who this woman was now. She was unbalanced. Ann, knowing she needed help, looked at her phone, ready to call 911.

Maura slapped the phone from her hand with such force, it hit the floor hard and slid out of reach. "You're not calling anyone. This is between you and me."

Ann spotted her phone on the floor a couple of feet away from her. "You need someone else to help you. Please, Maura, let me help you."

"You're the doctor, right? Don't you deal with troubled people all the time?" Maura asked.

"You're not troubled," Ann lied. "You just need a little help."

Maura chuckled. "Oh, I'm troubled. But in a good and productive way. After all is said and done, I'll be famous and have the man of my dreams."

Ann calculated the distance between her and Maura and then how fast she could snatch up her phone. Analyzing the risk versus reward, she lunged for her phone. As her fingers grazed the phone's smooth case, the snap of electricity crackled, and then she felt the jolt of high-wattage voltage shoot through her body. Every muscle in her body spasmed, and she fell to her knees, her body trembling. "Why?"

Maura knelt down. "I tried to be like you. But I just wasn't good enough. And then it occurred to me that no woman is going to be good enough while you're alive. There's no competing with you." She ran her fingertips along Ann's jawline. "But that's fine. I know how to make it so Elijah will not be able to resist me."

As Ann's body still spasmed, Maura hoisted her to her feet, supporting her weight as she staggered out the door toward the truck. She settled Ann in the front seat, and just as Ann was recovering her wits, Maura pressed a damp cloth against her face.

"Breathe in deeply, Ann," she said.

The sickly sweet, damp odor invaded her nostrils, and her head immediately swirled.

"I can't have you running off while I'm getting Nate."

"Leave us alone," Ann whispered. "Please."

"Oh, no, he's the bait that will prove to Elijah I'm the woman he needs."

PAUL THOMPSON'S CRIME FILES

Pemberton, West Virginia, is a small rural community an hour outside Martinsburg. A few folks in town commuted into Virginia and Maryland to work, but most of the two thousand residents lived and worked locally as farmers, as small-business owners, or in county government. This was an everyone-knows-your-name kind of town, where no one locked their doors and kids roamed free after school.

Judy and Donna Monroe, ages sixteen and fourteen, lived outside Pemberton in a small ramshackle home with peeling white paint and a yard filled with car parts their late father had collected. Their mother, Connie, worked twelve-hour shifts six days a week as a cashier at the go-kart park near Martinsburg. With Connie gone so often, the girls were on their own a lot. But that was the way it was in Pemberton. Kids looked out for each other while their parents put in long hours to put food on the table.

The Fourth of July was a big holiday for Pemberton, complete with a parade led by the town's lone fire truck, barbecue cooked by the fire department, and fireworks that lit the sky on fire. Folks took off from work or left early on the Fourth of July so that everyone in Pemberton could enjoy the party.

Connie always took off for the parade because she knew how much her girls loved this rare day of family time. But on July 4, 2005, Connie's boss had called her early, telling her she had to fill in for several employees who had called out sick. Connie had argued, been tempted not to go in, but when it came down to a choice between the parade and her job, she had no choice. She gave each of her girls a ten-dollar bill, kissed them on their heads, and told them to have fun.

That was the last time the three of them would be together again. Judy would later tell police that, during the course of the festivities, she had lost track of time and her younger sister. Donna had simply walked away. Judy, partying with a few local boys, did not sound the alarm until the fireworks exploded in the sky.

The town sheriff was called, but with night upon them, the search was futile. It resumed at sunrise, but despite hours and then days of searching by dozens of volunteers, Donna Monroe was never seen again.

The day Judy turned eighteen, she left West Virginia for a different kind of adventure.

CHAPTER THIRTY-ONE

Missoula, Montana
Friday, August 27
1:00 a.m.

Bryce read through all Paul Thompson's notes, and he was struck by how exhaustive and detailed the reporter was with his interviews. He categorized, analyzed, and drew conclusions better than many cops. Which was why it made no sense that Judy's interview and all notes pertaining to her were missing. Thompson was not the kind of guy to lose information.

Bryce decided to spend the night in a Missoula motel located near the center of town. He was determined to stay close to Ann and Nate until this case had more clear-cut answers. The evidence was conveniently pointing to Thompson, but like the missing file on Judy, it did not feel right. In all his years of law enforcement, a case this complicated had not closed this easily.

Standing from the motel desk, he packed up his files and slipped his sidearm back into its holster. He swung his coat around and slid into it, and then, grabbing the files, he left his room.

The drive to the Missoula jail took under twenty minutes. Though it was well after visiting hours, Bryce's badge got the attention of the night desk deputy, a reed-thin man with a thick black mustache and name badge reading TUCKER.

"I'll call up to his block," Deputy Tucker said.

"Appreciate it."

When the door buzzed, Bryce entered the transition area, where cops locked up weapons. The next set of doors opened, and he strode toward the only interview room. Ten minutes later Paul Thompson appeared, wearing an orange jumpsuit. His neatly combed hair now stuck up, and his face looked pale and drawn.

Bryce rose. "Have a seat. I've got a few questions."

"You can ask my attorney. He'll be here in the morning."

"I'm not trying to build a case against you," he said. "I've been through all your notes. They're careful and well done. You're not the kind of guy who misplaces an important interview."

"You're talking about Judy?"

"That's right. What can you tell me about her?"

Bloodshot eyes narrowed. "Why should I help you? You're the reason I'm here."

"Right now, I'm the only one standing between you and four counts of first-degree murder. Tell me about Judy. She's the one that first told you about the Fireflies." From one of the folders, Bryce pulled the Firefly list, which included pictures. He pointed to Judy's DMV photo. "This is Judy Monroe?"

"Yes. Though the picture doesn't do her justice."

"What do you mean?"

"Judy is prettier than that. After our first interview she went through a kind of makeover, and when she showed up for a second one, she'd dyed her hair blond and traded the glasses for contacts. She looks like a schoolteacher there, but she was hot."

"Hot." Bryce tapped his finger on the woman's face. "How long did you date?"

"About six months."

"How did you meet?"

"She cleaned out my house and then the office. She became a kind of personal organizer and assistant. It was a big help."

Ann had hired a woman to do the same for her. It made sense that people all over the country did this kind of work, but what were the chances one would place flyers near Ann's office now? "Have you heard the name Maura Ralston?"

"No, why?"

Bryce shook his head. "Never mind. What happened?"

"She started to resent my work on this podcast, especially when I left for Knoxville to talk to Sarah Cameron. When I returned to Nashville, we started fighting immediately. At that moment I could see the end in sight."

"But . . . ?"

Handcuffs on his wrists clinked when he rubbed his eyes. "The sex was great."

"Did she ever spend the night in your house? Did she have access to your computers?"

"She did. She was good with computers." He sighed.

Judy had not responded to Thompson's earlier text, but he wondered if the cell was still active and pinging. "What can you tell me about Judy?"

"She grew up hard in a small town in West Virginia. She had a sister who vanished from a Fourth of July party. Judy was about sixteen and her sister fourteen. She admitted she liked the attention she received when the cops were looking for her sister."

"Was the girl ever found?" Bryce asked.

"No."

"When did Judy get interested in Elijah?"

"She said from the moment she saw his picture on some internet site. She joked she liked that he was in prison, like he was on an enclosed display shelf. Of course, she said she realized how stupid it was to write an incarcerated man. Soon after that we were in bed."

They had been referring to this killer as *he* during the entire investigation. But a female killer made sense. Females were naturally leery of strange males, but those innate defenses dropped around another woman, especially if the women shared a mutual interest.

"When Sarah's body was identified, did you consider Judy might have killed her?"

"No. Like I said, I thought it was Sarah's boyfriend. I thought he found out Sarah and I had slept together." Thompson studied Bryce's face. "Do you think Judy did all this?"

"Do you think she's capable of killing Sarah, Dana, Nena, and Edith?"

"She's smart. Really clever. She has a love-hate relationship with technology. She knows it inside and out but doesn't trust it. Hates the idea of being tracked."

"What about her temperament?" Bryce asked.

"There is an element of crazy. That was the appeal initially."

"Did you notice anything else?"

"After we broke up, my social media accounts were hacked. It took me a solid week to get that untangled. And before I was supposed to leave for Montana, my tires were slashed. My car had to be towed the morning I left for Montana."

"Are Judy's fingerprints or DNA in any system?"

"She's in AFIS. She was arrested in North Carolina for repeated trespassing when she was about nineteen."

"Okay, Mr. Thompson, thank you. I'll look into this."

Thompson rose as he did. "Why would she do this to me?"

"You said it yourself—she liked the idea of a guy in a box. Look where you are."

"Shit, shit, shit."

Bryce called the deputy, and as Thompson was led back to his cell, he hurried to the transition area and retrieved his weapon. He thanked the deputy, and as he stepped outside and crossed the parking lot, he dialed Ann's number. It went to voicemail. He texted her. Call me.

As he sat in the jail parking lot and seconds ticked, the sense that something was wrong grew. Again, his mind went back to the professional organizers in Thompson's and Ann's lives. Being in someone's home was a very intimate experience, and there was no better way to find and exploit their vulnerabilities. He remembered Ann had found Maura via flyers posted around the university.

He dialed Gideon's number and, after the second ring, heard a groggy, "Bryce."

He recapped what he had learned from Thompson as he started the engine. At the very least, he could drive by Ann's house and make sure she was okay. "I'll be at Ann's house in twelve minutes." Distance driving had never bothered him, but these next five miles separating him from Ann felt like a million-mile journey.

"Do you think this woman called Maura killed the other women?" In the background, Joan's muffled voice asked what was happening.

"If this killer is Judy Monroe, she has an obsession with Paul Thompson and Elijah Weston. She murdered Fireflies who all most closely resembled Ann," Bryce said. "She's got Thompson locked behind bars, and if she wants to control Elijah, then her best bet is to get to Ann or Nate. He has a weakness for both."

"Do you think Weston is pulling the strings?" Gideon asked. "He reached a lot of women while he was behind bars, and now that he's out, there's no telling what kind of damage he could do."

"Go by Weston's," Bryce said. "I'll go to Ann's. I really hope that I'm overreacting, but the more I consider it, the more worried I am for Ann and Nate."

"I'm on my way," Gideon said.

***

Ann dreamed that she was drowning. As she looked up toward the sun beaming above the surface, she knew she had to reach it. But her leaden arms would not move, and she did not have the energy to kick her feet. It would be so easy to drift.

But she understood instinctively that if she did rest, she would die. Willing her limbs to move, she flutter kicked and waved her arms until, very slowly, her body began to rise. The sun grew brighter above the waves. And just like that, she broke through. She sucked in a breath, but instead of savoring fresh, cleansing air, her chest burned, and her head pounded.

She blinked and looked around the dimly lit room. It was the basement at the Beech Street house. And she was lying on the mattress Clarke had readied for her just over a year ago.

She jumped from that realization to the next. Someone was with her. Footsteps circled around her, and as she blinked, she struggled to clear her vision. "Who's there?"

"You know who it is."

Her mind tumbled backward to the moment it all had gone sideways. "Maura, where's Nate?"

"He's fine." The footsteps circled closer. "I got to know this place pretty well when I was cleaning it. Basements are so handy, don't you think?"

"What did you do to Nate?" Ann demanded.

"I gave him a little something to help him sleep. He'll be out for hours, and when he wakes, all this will be finished, and he, Elijah, and I will be headed to our new life."

"Where is my son?" Even as she whispered the words, her mind cleared, and her head spun slower.

"Sleeping in his old bedroom. I tucked him into bed like he was my little baby."

"You and Elijah." Of all the scenarios she had imagined, she had never placed Maura as Elijah's helpmate. "You two are working together?"

Maura crossed her fingers. "We're as thick as thieves. Two peas in a pod. Inseparable."

"Where is Elijah?"

"He'll be here soon. As soon as he figures out where we are."

"Why wouldn't he know?"

"It's a little game we play. Our version of hide-and-seek. We've been playing it for months."

"Months? How long have you been in town?" She willed her fingers to flex but discovered they barely moved. She kept trying, hoping to break through the drugs numbing her system.

"On and off for weeks."

"Have you been with Elijah the whole time?"

Maura smiled, but did not answer.

"How will Elijah know we are gone?" Ann said.

"He'll know."

The longer she could keep Maura talking, the more her brain cleared. She would not totally be right for hours, but if she could just summon enough function to get out of here, she could get help. "How?"

Maura squatted in front of her and laid her hands on Ann's shoulders. "He asked me to put cameras in your house, and I did."

The idea that Elijah had been watching her in the privacy of her own home made her stomach turn. "When?"

"When do you think?" Maura chuckled. "When I was cleaning."

"And Edith Scott? Did you or Elijah kill her?"

Maura leaned so close her warm breath brushed against Ann's ear. "I did. I couldn't have her stirring up trouble."

"And the other women?" She drew within herself, distancing herself from the fear. "You drove Nena's car to Paul Thompson's motel."

"When he interviewed Nena, she drove him around town. I knew his prints would be in the car. All I had to do was stock it with a little extra evidence."

"Does Thompson know you're working with Elijah?"

"I'm working on behalf of Elijah, *not* for him. I'm the one who's in control."

"You're good at controlling things—I can see that." Ann's mouth felt dry, and she blinked slowly several times to shake off the brain fog. "I understand why you would be drawn to a man who'd been in prison. But your name is not on the Firefly list."

"Maura Ralston isn't the first fake name I've used."

Ann struggled through the last bits of haze in her brain. Fragments from the case files, Paul Thompson's interviews, and forensic evidence melded into a clear picture. "The one interview missing from Thompson's file was Judy Monroe's. Her photo was also blurred."

A smile twitched the edges of her mouth. "That's a good guess."

"Judy," she said softly. "You deleted all records of you, didn't you?"

"I'm good with computers. And when Paul drinks bourbon and takes a sleeping pill, he sleeps really hard."

The subtle edge of anger hinted at her rage. "And the woman in the bar who met Thompson?"

"I hired her. I needed him distracted and out cold."

Treading lightly was critical. She remembered the injuries to Sarah Cameron. The killing wasn't well planned, and the facial mutilations were sloppy and fueled by rage. "When you found out he had slept with Sarah, you had to hurt her."

"He used me. He took my story and my body, then he betrayed me. Now he's not going anywhere, is he? And Sarah's pretty face is nothing but pulp." Her lips split into a wide grin. "I'll be sure to write Thompson when he's locked up for the rest of his life."

"Elijah is free. He's not as controllable anymore."

"He will be when I become you."

"If you become me, do you really think Elijah will love you?"

Maura nodded slowly. "I know he will."

Ann held her gaze. "He will let himself pretend for a while. But in the end, he'll use you and toss you aside."

Maura jerked back as if she had been slapped. From her pocket she removed a switchblade. A press of the button, and the blade popped open, gleaming bright and sharp. She pressed the tip to Ann's temple and drew it gently downward, drawing blood instantaneously.

***

When Elijah awoke at 1:30 a.m., he hit the bathroom, washed his hands, and went to the kitchen and made himself a bowl of Cheerios. Carefully, he poured just the right amount of milk on the cereal before heading over to his computer.

He rarely slept more than two hours at any stretch. As much as he sometimes wished he could shut down and let the world fall away, he never could steal more than the short bursts of downtime.

Elijah sat in front of his computer and clicked on the camera in Ann's house. He noticed the lights were still on and wondered why she was up so late. Normally, she was asleep by now.

As he studied the room, he noted the cell phone lying on the floor by the front door.

Setting his cereal aside, he backed up the tape until he reached the 1:00 a.m. time stamp. The doorbell rang and Ann opened it.

As he watched the next few minutes unfold, anger rolled over him, and for a moment he could not think clearly. It had been like that in the first days of prison. He had been so blinded by outrage he could not think, and he had gotten his ass beaten a couple of times before he wised up and learned to distance anger and arrow his thoughts toward the target.

He observed Maura carrying a sleeping Nate toward the door and then pausing in front of the camera. She winked as she rubbed her hand over the sleeping boy's head. She mouthed, "Find me."

Elijah froze the frame of her face and leaned closer to the screen. He replayed the tape and watched Ann's desperate struggle unfold in horrifying slow motion. He winced when Ann's body seized and dropped when the Taser touched her midsection.

He had miscalculated badly. He had thought Maura was like the others, needy and easily malleable. He'd assumed he was controlling her. But she was the one manipulating all of them.

His heart butted against his chest as he tried to slip into Maura's mind. He had studied psychopaths, lived among them, and likely was one, so he should be able to outthink her.

What had Maura wanted most from him? He had recognized the need in her, just as he had the other Fireflies. Once he'd established what they wanted, the rest had been easy. Maura had pretended she craved only sex, but he had sensed immediately her desires ran far deeper than the sensual. She had been intrigued by the media attention, what she perceived as the fame she associated with him. However, notoriety had not been her endgame. She not only wanted him—she wanted to control him.

He had spent the last six months getting his house in order. He'd thought he had anticipated all potential land mines, but he had ignored his initial distrust of her and miscalculated.

She might have taken this unexpected move, but she had a weakness for attention, which she craved like an addict desired a drug.

Once Elijah distanced himself from any unnecessary panic or fear, he felt certain that Nate would be fine for the immediate future. Maura was using him as bait.

Ann, however, was a different story. Maura saw her as a threat and a roadblock to her happiness. He calculated she had less than a couple of hours, if that, to live.

"If you think you know who you're playing with, Maura," he said, "you're dead wrong."

Elijah grabbed his keys and hurried to his car. He drove toward Ann's house but opted to park on the adjoining street. He settled a ball cap on his head and tugged on gloves before he moved along the sidewalk, keeping his head low. He rounded the corner and then raced toward her front door. It was unlocked.

He stepped inside, carefully closed the door behind him, and dug a flashlight from his pocket. He moved past the toppled table and Ann's discarded phone. He lifted the phone, saw two missed calls from Bryce McCabe, and then replaced it where he had found it.

If Maura had killed Ann, he did not want Gideon Bailey getting custody of his son. Elijah had established a bank account under a different name, so it would be easy enough for him to disappear with Nate.

Quickly, he walked toward Nate's bedroom. He moved to the boy's closet, grabbed the backpack, and then crossed to the dresser and began to fill it with all his clothes. He lifted the copy of *Huckleberry Finn* from the nightstand and noted the bookmark was nearly at the end. Pride swelled as he laid the book on top of the clothes and zipped the pack closed.

He moved down the hall to Ann's room. The bed was neatly made. At 1:00 a.m., when Maura had attacked, Ann would have been tired and her reaction time off. She would have been slow to realize Maura was lying and been easier to subdue.

He savored a selfish moment of pleasure, imagining a befuddled and then terrified Ann. She would have realized her mistakes when the Taser had sent electrical shock waves through her body.

However, when he pictured her begging for her son and terrified for his safety, his mood soured. He hoped for Maura's sake she had not hurt the boy.

He located the two cameras on the bookshelf and tucked them in the bag. No need to connect him to Maura. As he moved to the back door, blue and white lights flashed in the front window. The cops were here faster than he'd anticipated. Had a neighbor seen what had happened? Or had Sergeant McCabe sounded the alarm because Ann had not answered her phone? Regardless, he needed to leave.

Elijah clicked off his flashlight and hurried to the sliding glass door. Carefully, he slid it open. As he stepped outside, the front door opened, and Bryce called out.

He closed the door but stopped short of shutting it all the way, fearing the noise would give him away. He picked up the backpack, slung it over his shoulder, and rushed through the adjoining backyard toward his car.

As he reached the street, he looked back. The lights were on in the house, and he could see Bryce McCabe moving from room to room, searching for two people who were not there. Elijah slipped into the shadows.

CHAPTER THIRTY-TWO

Missoula, Montana
Friday, August 27
1:45 a.m.

The instant Bryce arrived at Ann's house, he hurried past her car and entered her unlocked front door. Immediately, he sensed something did not feel right. He reached for his weapon and called out her name. He stood in the silence and listened to what sounded like a door closing. Rushing to the back of the house, he tried the sliding door and discovered it, too, was not completely closed. Outside, he searched the backyard but saw no traces of movement.

Next came the search of the bedrooms. Nate's bed was unmade but empty, whereas Ann's remained untouched. "Damn it," he muttered. "Where are you, Ann?"

Police car lights flashed in front of the house, and he went outside to meet them. He ordered the other two officers to search the property as well as the yards and properties behind the house.

As they began their search, he called Gideon. "Ann and Nate aren't here. Do we know where Elijah Weston is?"

"He's not at his house," Gideon said.

Anger and worry tangled up in Bryce. "He has the resources to build himself a damn bunker or to hire a plane and take them anywhere he wants," Gideon said.

"Ann would have had her guard up if Elijah was standing on her doorstep in the middle of the night," Bryce said. "She's worried he'll take Nate away from her. If Judy Monroe is passing herself off as Maura Ralston, Ann would have opened her door to her."

"Elijah uses her to get close to Ann and land the striking blow," Gideon said. "She grabs Ann and Nate, and then he meets up with them."

"If Elijah used Maura slash Judy to take out the other women, he never would have positioned her near Nate," Gideon said.

"Perhaps it was a calculated risk. Ann dies, and he's left to raise Nate."

"If Ann is already dead, then Elijah would feel justified taking the boy."

CHAPTER THIRTY-THREE

Missoula, Montana
Friday, August 27
2:00 a.m.

Ann used her words every day to teach her students and now needed to find the right ones that did not stoke Maura's temper or challenge her.

"If you're going to become me, then you should let me teach you a few things," Ann said.

Maura dragged the blade along Ann's jawline with enough pressure to incite fear but not draw blood. "What could you teach me? You aren't that hard to mimic. You're like everyone else. It's easy to be anyone."

"But I am different to Nate and Elijah. They don't see me as the rest of the world does. And if you want to win them over and become me, you'll need to know a few things."

Maura pulled the blade from Ann's skin, holding the bloodied tip close. "What kind of things?"

"Nate is very smart," she said.

"Duh. I know that."

"He has to be kept busy not only physically, but intellectually. He's already auditing classes at the university."

"I know that. Do you think I've not been paying attention?" Anger and impatience hummed under the words.

"What are his favorite classes?" Ann asked.

"Does it matter? Learning is learning."

"He has favorites."

"Like?"

Ann glanced toward the knife but subdued the instinct to flinch. Control over the situation mattered. She needed to buy time.

"Tell me," Maura insisted as she again pressed the sharp edge into her skin.

"Pull the blade away," Ann said carefully.

"Why?" Maura demanded.

"It's hard to think. And if you want my help, I need to think."

The pressure eased a fraction. "He loves math. And . . ."

"And what?"

"Geology. Nate likes nothing better than to go rock hunting. His dad used to bring him rocks home after his travels."

Maura snorted. "Clarke was not his real dad."

"Nate loved Clarke as his father."

"But anyone can see that his real father is Elijah. Elijah loves that kid. He would do anything for him."

Maura's words emphasized the situation's stark reality. Even if Maura and Elijah were working together, if Ann died here today and Maura took Nate away with Elijah, it would be up to Elijah to protect the boy. She had never thought she would ever trust Elijah with her child, but she now had to.

"It's what Nate feels that matters. And Elijah understands this. Like me, he doesn't want to hurt Nate."

"This is stupid," Maura growled as she grabbed a handful of Ann's hair and pulled her head back. "You talk too much."

Ann's muscles were regaining mobility. Soon, she would have full use of her arms, and she could strike. What she needed was a distraction to grab Maura's attention. The element of surprise could capture critical seconds so she could overtake Maura. "Nate likes Cheerios for breakfast. Just a little milk. He's fussy when it's too wet or dry."

Maura dropped the knife blade another fraction. "What about Elijah? What does he like?"

"He's just as smart as Nate. And he once told me he had a similar quirk about his morning cereal."

"Like father like son," Maura said, smiling. "I can't believe you thought you could keep this secret."

The truth of Nate's paternity had terrified Ann. Now she realized it might save his life. "You're smart, too. You could not have made it this far if you weren't intelligent."

"No one really sees that, but I'm pretty damn brilliant." Maura raised a brow as if amused. "You know, I've killed five people. Not everyone can say that."

"Five." A heaviness snarled in Ann's chest as she thought about the victims. "I know about Sarah, Dana, Nena, and Edith. Who else?"

Maura shrugged. "That first one was back in West Virginia. I really didn't plan that one."

"What happened?"

"I felt all this rage. I was ignored, and she was getting all the attention. I got tired of it. So, I lured her away to the woods, and when she wasn't looking, I jabbed a knife in her back. See, if you can get the knife into the liver in the lower back, the person bleeds out. It's quick enough."

"Who was she?"

Maura sighed. "A girl in my town." She rolled her head from side to side. "But now she's gone. No more favorite girl in town."

"What happened between you two?" Ann maintained an even tone, as if she were sitting in her office counseling a student.

"It was a long time ago. We were kids." Her gaze turned distant.

"She was a friend? A sister?"

"Everyone in town loved her. I was no different. She was perfect."

"She disappointed you. Hurt you?"

"She broke my heart." The sadness was dismissed with a slight smile and a shrug. "But it is what it is."

"What happened after she died?" She slowly clenched her fingers into a tight fist.

"Everyone went to pieces. Posters were made with her picture. The police swarmed into town. Everyone was crying and holding vigils. I finally got tired of all the sorrow and left town and moved to Nashville."

Ann could feel her head clearing. "How did you meet Thompson?"

"Cleaning his house. I'm a good organizer, don't you think? I'm sure a shrink would say it's about control, but the truth is I like snooping in other people's lives. Amazing what you can learn about people when you're in their homes. Want to know what I learned about you?"

"Yes." How could she not have recognized the warning signs?

"You care about what the world thinks about you," she said. "You can't stand the idea that anyone sees you as less than perfect. What're people going to say when they learn you got knocked up by the town pariah and then passed him off as your husband's kid?" Maura shook her head. "I had a sister who thought she was perfect. She could have any man in town, and she loved to let me know it."

The assessment was uncomfortably correct. She cleared her throat. "Maybe you're right."

"I know I am." Triumph glittered in Maura's eyes.

As Ann absorbed Maura's words, she calculated what cost Nate might pay if she attacked Maura now. And then she balanced it against the cost the boy would pay if she did not.

In that split second she made her decision.

***

Elijah pushed up on the windows on the back of the Beech Street house and finally found one that was unlocked. He slipped inside the house without making a sound and stood in the dark, listening. Hearing only the hum of the air conditioner, he looked toward the basement door and saw the light. As he had expected, Maura had come here.

He moved quietly across the main floor and made his way to Nate's room. When he opened the door, he was surprised to see the boy lying on his bed. He was covered with a blanket, but he lay so still that Elijah thought he might be dead.

Fear knifed through him as he crossed the room and pressed his fingers to the boy's neck. He did not pray or believe in a higher power, but in this moment, he would have sold his soul to the devil to save the boy.

Finally, the boy's pulse thumped weakly against his fingertips. Faint, but it was there. He drew in a breath, wondering when the devil might claim his due.

Elijah smoothed his hand over the boy's head. "I won't let this stand," he whispered. "Nobody hurts you."

He lifted the boy in his arms, and when the child made a soft sound of protest, Elijah said, "It's okay. You're safe now."

The boy nestled closer to Elijah, and an overwhelming sense of contentment washed over him. He was his son's protector. And nothing had ever felt so right.

He carried Nate through the darkened house and unlocked the sliding door. Outside, he moved quickly to his car and laid the boy on the back seat.

The boy roused and opened his eyes. His look was curious, not afraid. "Where's Mom?"

Elijah knew Ann was in the basement with Maura. If Ann was not already dead and was clever enough, she would talk her way out of this, but chances were Maura would kill her.

A part of him was drawn to the idea of Ann dying. When she was dead, he would never have to wonder where she was, what she was doing, or who she was with. He would be free.

But as he looked at Nate, he realized he did not want to be free of Ann. God help him, but she had cursed him. "Damn," he muttered as he reached for his phone.

***

Bryce slowly drove past Ann's old house. He kept his lights off as he searched for signs of life. Seeing none, he parked and, drawing his weapon, hurried through the yard toward the garage. He peered through the window and saw Maura's truck. Gideon rolled up behind Bryce's vehicle and followed suit, rushing toward the garage.

"The house is dark," Gideon said. "I'd bet money Maura has them in the basement. There's only one entrance to the room, and Maura can do a lot of damage before either of us gets down the stairs."

"If we don't move, she's going to kill Ann," Bryce said. There were times when hesitating got good people killed, and he would not lose Ann today. "She has a better chance if we go in now."

Gideon drew his Glock.

***

Ann started when Maura's phone rang. Maura cringed, as if the interruption were the last thing she expected or wanted. She dug the phone out of her back pocket, and her harsh expression softened. "Elijah?"

"Maura."

Ann heard Elijah's calm, steady voice and had never been more grateful for it.

"I have Ann with me," Maura said. "And I have Nate."

"You don't have the boy," Elijah said. "I do."

"That's impossible. He's sleeping in his bed."

"Not anymore. If you don't believe me, go up and look."

A ripple of tension rolled through Ann's body. Elijah had Nate. Her son was safe. No matter what happened here now, Elijah would keep Nate safe.

Maura glanced toward Ann. "I go look and Ann gets away."

"That's a risk you'd take," Elijah said. "Or you can believe me."

"You have the kid." She closed her eyes a second. "Why do you care about Ann so much?"

"I do not," he said.

"Good. Because I'm going to kill her."

"Do whatever you want," he said.

Ann kept her gaze down, balled her fingers into fists, and readied to attack.

"You're lying," Maura said.

"I'm not." Elijah sounded bored. "I don't care about Ann or you."

That last comment caused Maura to flinch, and she averted her gaze. Ann realized these were her seconds to act before Maura regained her composure and took her frustration out on her.

And so, in one wobbly move, she rose and lunged.

Ann drove her shoulder into Maura's side. The strike caught Maura off guard, and she staggered back a step, trying to steady her balance. Ann shoved harder, tipping Maura off center and then backward.

They both hit hard. Maura took the brunt of the fall, the concrete floor knocking the breath from her lungs. Her cell phone flew across the floor, crashing into the wall. In the same moment, Ann's shoulder struck the floor. Pain ricocheted through her body.

Gritting her teeth and determined to get back to her son, Ann rose up on her knees as Maura stood, readjusted her grip on the knife, and raised it over her head. The blade glinted and sliced toward her.

Ann threw her body weight forward, and digging her fingers into Maura's wrist, she stopped the blade inches in front of her face. Blood pumped in her temples as she twisted Maura's hands and the sharp tip away from her.

Maura had been in this kind of life-and-death struggle before, and she adapted quickly. She drove her head forward, aiming to butt Ann in the face.

Ann jerked her head to the left, and the intended blow grazed the side of her face. She shoved Maura's wrist back so violently joints cracked.

"You bitch," Maura screamed.

"This is my life," Ann shouted as she manipulated Maura's shoulder into a painful angle. "You're not taking it!"

"Watch me!"

Maura shifted back suddenly, pulling Ann off balance. Ann's grip loosened, freeing Maura's hand just enough so she could bring the knife around and slash Ann's side.

CHAPTER THIRTY-FOUR

Missoula, Montana
Friday, August 27
2:30 a.m.

Gideon shoved the key in the front-door lock, twisted the door handle, and pushed open the door. Weapons drawn, both cops entered the house in time to hear a scream echoing from the basement.

They raced into the house, visually sweeping the darkened foyer and side hallway as they crossed the den toward the basement door.

Bryce heard the scuffle and struggle of bodies. He opened the door with such force it banged against the wall, and he raced down the steps with Gideon right on his heels.

When Bryce reached the concrete basement floor, he maneuvered his weapon toward the screams. His first image was of Ann lying on her back, blood staining her shirt as Maura straddled her body.

Rage and sadness collided as he pointed his weapon at Maura as she raised the knife, ready to strike Ann in the chest. The distance between them was too great to cover, given the speed of a knife blade. "Maura!"

She looked at him as she brought the knife down.

He didn't hesitate and shot her.

Maura's body recoiled slightly and then stilled, the knife motionless above Ann. Kicking her legs as she grabbed Maura's arm, Ann shoved the knife away.

Blood bloomed on Maura's shirt, and she toppled sideways. She lost her balance, and her body landed like deadweight. Maura rolled on her back, gasping. She stared up at the ducts in the basement ceiling and struggled to breathe. She still gripped the knife.

Gideon moved in and kept his weapon trained on Maura as Bryce holstered his weapon. Gideon hurried toward Maura and cuffed her wrists. Bryce shifted his focus to Ann as Gideon called for the rescue squad.

Ann's shirt was soaked in blood, and when he reached for the hem of her shirt, he feared the damage he would find. Moments like this passed at a painfully slow pace, and fears took a back seat as his brain assessed the damage.

Panic was engraved in Ann's expression as she struggled to right herself. Adrenaline still pumped through her body, but soon it would crash, and the pain would take over.

"Stay still," he said. "You're making the bleeding worse."

"I need to find Nate," she said. "Elijah told Maura he has Nate."

He pushed up her shirt, ran his hand through the blood, and felt the torn flesh. She winced and hissed in a breath, but she held steady as he examined her. "It's a long gash," he said roughly. "It's going to require stitches, but it doesn't look like it damaged anything vital."

She pressed her hand to her side. "I need to find my son."

"Are you sure Elijah called?" Bryce demanded.

"Yes, I heard his voice. He wouldn't lie about something like that."

"Where would he take the boy?" He pressed his hand over her blood-soaked fingers.

"Maybe to his house. Maybe they're already on the road." Tears glistened in her eyes. "I don't know where Nate is."

As Gideon pressed his fingertips to Maura's neck, he called for the paramedics and put a BOLO out on Elijah's vehicle.

"There's no pulse." He started CPR. "The ambulance is on the way, and the deputies are on scene."

Ann shoved Bryce's hands away. "I want to get up!" she insisted. "I have to find Nate!"

"Let the paramedics have a look at you first," Bryce said.

"I don't care about me," Ann shouted. "I want my son."

"You won't do Nate any good if you bleed out," Bryce said. "Be smart."

The thunder of footsteps across the first floor signaled the paramedics' arrival. The two hurried down the stairs, each carrying a small med kit.

One moved toward Maura and took over CPR from Gideon, and the other pressed clean gauze against Ann's side. He directed Bryce to hold the compress in place as he tore open fresh bandages.

"She said she killed a girl in her hometown and that she killed the Fireflies and framed Thompson," Ann said.

"We'll sort that out later," Bryce said.

"She's insane, Bryce."

"I know."

"We need to take you to the hospital," the paramedic said. "That wound is going to need stitches."

"It can wait," Ann said. "Patch me up. When I know Nate's safe, I'll go to the hospital."

The second paramedic checked Maura's pulse. "I'm not getting anything. She's gone."

Gideon's phone rang, and Ann shifted attention to him. "Nate?"

"There's no one at Elijah's house," Gideon said.

Tears welled in her eyes. "Where's my boy?"

"I sent a deputy to your house as well," her brother said. "Someone is inside."

***

The shot of painkiller had taken the edge off the gash in Ann's side, which for now was controlled by the compression bandage. The paramedic had cut off her bloody shirt, and she had changed into one of the extra shirts Bryce kept in his trunk.

Bryce settled Ann in the front seat of his car as Gideon came around.

"The deputies spotted Elijah at Ann's house. He's sitting on the front porch."

Ann tipped her head back. "Did they see Nate?"

"Not yet."

"Please, Bryce, take me to my son."

Bryce hooked her seat belt on and hurried to the driver's side. He started the engine and put the car in gear. Five minutes later he pulled up in front of her house behind the two deputies' vehicles.

Elijah sat on the front steps and was reading a book. He looked calm, as if it were perfectly normal to be reading in the middle of the night with cops surrounding him.

Ann reached for the door handle and pushed it open. She gripped her side and tried to stand.

"Hold on," Bryce said. "I'm coming around."

"It's Elijah."

"I see him."

By the time Bryce reached her door, she had struggled to her feet. The compression bandage pressed against her wound, but she could feel flesh opening and fresh blood warming her skin.

He grabbed her elbow, steadying her. "You're bleeding again."

She did not bother a glance down. "I want to see Nate."

Bryce walked in front of her, his hand on his weapon. "Elijah, where's Nate?"

Elijah carefully closed his book and rose. "He's inside sleeping."

"Is he all right?" Ann asked.

"He's fine. Drugged by Maura, but he should sleep it off and recover."

"You were at the Beech Street house?" she asked.

"Yes," Elijah said. "I took Nate out."

"And then you called Maura."

"Yes. A distraction seemed warranted." He nodded to the flecks of blood now darkening the side of the shirt she had borrowed from Bryce. "Did Maura do that to you?"

She glanced down. "It doesn't matter."

"Where's Maura?" Elijah asked.

"Dead." Ann moved past him into the house and directly to Nate's room as pain burned her midsection.

She found him lying in his bed, the blankets tucked up under his chin. She sat on the edge of the bed and touched his face. "Nate?"

Nate drew in a breath. "Mom?"

She closed her eyes. Tears spilled, but she wiped them away. "Hey, baby."

"I'm so sleepy."

"I know, honey." She brushed his bangs off his forehead, never more grateful to see anyone in her life. "You sleep, and we'll talk in the morning."

"Okay."

She stared at him for a moment and then rose carefully, moving with halting steps toward the door.

Bryce stood in the doorway. His grim face was backlit by the hallway light, making it impossible to read his expression. "Are you okay?"

"He's okay," Ann said. "So, I can do anything."

"Then you can go to the hospital," Bryce said.

"I want Nate to see a doctor," she said.

"We'll take you both."

Gideon parked and raced toward the house and Elijah as Ann stepped back outside. Her steps faltered. Bryce steadied her seconds before the paramedics parked in front of the house. She turned to Elijah as Gideon handcuffed him. Outrage sharpened her tone. "How much did you know?"

Elijah raised his eerily calm gaze to hers. "I slept with Maura, but I didn't know what she was planning."

Ann was the expert, and she had not seen through Maura's lies. "She wanted to become me and take Nate."

"If I had known," Elijah said, "it never would have gotten this far. And you know, if I hadn't called her, you wouldn't have had a chance. She would have killed you if I'd stormed the basement."

"Weston left you behind," Gideon growled.

Ann's heartbeat slowed as she thought about the choice Elijah had made. He had made a choice between Nate and her. And he had chosen the boy. She was not angry or resentful of the choice, because she would have done the same. "No one could have gotten in that basement and saved me from her until he called."

"He sure as hell could have tried," Gideon said.

"Maura would have killed me, thinking she was freeing Elijah from me. And he did get Nate to safety."

Elijah nodded. "Thank you, Ann."

"If you didn't know about Maura's plans, how did you know to call her?" Gideon asked.

"I'll let my attorney explain," Elijah said. "I learned a long time ago not to trust the cops."

Pain tightened around her midsection. "I'm taking Nate to the hospital," Ann said. "I want a doctor to check him out."

Elijah's expression softened a fraction. "They will find the boy is fine, but *you* are the one who needs to be checked by a doctor."

She wanted to deny the comment, but he was right. Standing was becoming more difficult. This time, when the paramedics rolled the stretcher up for her, she all but collapsed on it. When she lay back, pain speared through her, leaving her feeling helpless and angry that she had missed the warning signs with Maura. "I was such a fool."

Bryce took her hand. "You weren't. No one saw this coming."

She looked up at him through watery eyes. "I'm lucky to have you."

"Same."

When she thought about the insanity of her life, she wondered for the hundredth time why Bryce was not running away from her as fast as he could. "A smart man would run from me."

A half grin tipped the edges of his lips. "A smarter man knows when to stay and fight."

EPILOGUE

Missoula, Montana
Saturday, September 11
2:00 p.m.

"Nate, hurry up," Ann shouted. "We need to pick up Kyle and get out to Bryce's ranch."

"Coming!"

She eased her purse on her shoulder. It had taken fifty-one stitches to patch up the gash running along her side. Though they had been removed a few days ago, she still moved carefully.

She opened the front passenger door, and as she tossed her bag onto the passenger seat, she saw Elijah walking down the sidewalk.

He wore khakis, a long-sleeve dark-gray shirt, and wire-rimmed glasses that accentuated his gray eyes. He carried a book at his side. She had not seen him since Gideon had handcuffed him and she had been taken away by ambulance. She had heard his lawyer had him freed within twenty-four hours, and though he could have come to the hospital or her home, he had not. She was grateful he had given her the time and space to heal before this inevitable meeting.

"Elijah."

"Ann. You're looking well," he said.

"Still moving slowly but on the mend. Nate and I were just headed over to pick up Kyle."

"Those two are joined at the hip, aren't they?"

"They are." She tucked a curl behind her ear. "Thank you again for saving Nate. And me."

"You saved yourself."

"You helped me to do it." He stood staring at her, and she knew the next step had to be hers. "I need to tell Nate about you. I just haven't figured out how to do it yet."

"If he hasn't guessed, he will soon."

"I know. But I owe him honesty."

"I want to spend time with him," Elijah said. "I understand he's not going to call me Dad, but I'd like to be his friend."

Nate ran out the front door, slamming it behind him. He rushed up and grinned at Elijah. "What's up?"

Elijah held up a book. "I thought you might like to read this."

Nate glanced at the title. "*A Tale of Two Cities*."

"A little bit of a challenge, but you might like it," Elijah said.

"Cool, I'll read it later."

"Maybe one day we could get an ice cream and talk about it?" Elijah said.

"Mom, could I?" Nate asked.

Ann's knee-jerk response was to say no. Old habits were hard to break. She took a deep breath, unfurling the fist clamping around her heart. "Sure. That sounds fun. Maybe the three of us could have lunch sometime."

"That would be nice," Elijah said.

"Cool," Nate said. "Mom, we've got to get going. We're going to be late."

"Get in the car." When the door closed, and Nate was settled, she turned from the car toward Elijah. "I don't know how we're going to work this out."

"I used to think I knew, but I'm currently as clueless as you are. But I know I'll always put Nate first."

A bittersweet chuckle rumbled in her chest. "That never changes with kids."

She lowered herself into the driver's seat, and when she hooked her seat belt, he closed her door. She started the car and rolled down the window. "I'll call about next week."

"Looking forward to it."

She backed out of the driveway, and as she headed down the street, she could feel Elijah's stare. He had not been found guilty of any crime. But deep in her gut, she worried there was so much the world did not know about Elijah. God, she hoped she had made the right choice.

***

An hour later, dust kicked up around the tires of Ann's car as she drove herself, Nate, and Kyle onto the long driveway that fed into Bryce's ranch. It was a postcard-perfect fall day with cool air, an explosion of orange leaves on the horizon, and a blue sky dotted with white clouds. The mountains in the distance were already capped with the season's first snow, suggesting an early winter.

As the boys chatted excitedly in the back seat, she parked in front of the ranch house, then gingerly exited the vehicle. She was lucky in many respects. Her wound would heal, and Nate showed no aftereffects from Maura's narcotics and had been back to himself by the next day.

Bryce had invited Ann and the boys to the ranch and offered to drive into Missoula and pick them up, but she had been cleared to drive by her doctors and wanted to prove to herself she could get on with her life.

As the boys tumbled out of the car, the front door opened to Bryce, who stepped onto the porch with a young German shepherd puppy. Bryce was dressed in jeans, a flannel shirt, and boots, and if there was ever an image that could make a woman go weak in the knees, it was that one.

"Is that a puppy?" Nate shouted.

"I don't know. Could be a horse," Bryce said, smiling.

The boys ran across the yard as Bryce climbed down the stairs. "He's not a horse," Nate said.

"What's his name?" Kyle asked.

"His name is Thor, and he just got rejected from puppy training. Seems he's not tough enough."

"How old is he?" Nate asked.

"He's six months old," Bryce said.

"Why is his name Thor?" Kyle asked.

"Runs like lightning." Bryce handed each boy a red ball. "He loves to play fetch."

The dog licked Bryce's face before he set it down, and then Thor raced across the yard, barking. The boys chased after him, and the dog's excited barking mingled with the boys' laughter.

"Boys, if you go around the side of the house, you'll see my brother. He's working with the other dogs."

"What do the big dogs think about Thor?" Nate asked as the dog ran circles around him.

"They get annoyed by him, but they're tolerating him well enough."

The boys, with the dog running behind them, dashed around the side of the house.

Laughter bubbled in Ann's chest, and she realized she had not felt this normal in a very long time. "It's good to see them laugh."

"Good to see you smile," he said huskily.

Without hesitation, she closed the distance and kissed him on the lips. He leaned into her, gently wrapping his arm around her uninjured side. "How are those stitches doing?"

"Gone. Doc took them out a couple of days ago. It's one hell of a scar, but it beats the alternative."

He tipped his forehead toward hers. "I'll never forget you in that room, covered in blood with that crazy woman wielding a knife over your head."

"A lot of the details are blurred for me, which is just as well. It's not a moment I want to relive."

DNA and fingerprints had been pulled from Maura Ralston's body, and testing confirmed she was Judy Monroe. Bryce had traced Judy to a small town in West Virginia and confirmed that her younger sister had vanished during a Fourth of July party sixteen years ago. Not only had Judy's mother been devastated, but the townspeople had started locking their doors, demanding the kids always travel in pairs and never again trust strangers. Bryce had relayed Judy's confession to the town sheriff. It was cold comfort, but all agreed the closure would help with healing.

Judy had met Paul Thompson as he had said. He had hired her to organize his house, and in the process, they had become lovers, and she had told him about Elijah and the Fireflies. But when she had seen him with Sarah, she had unleashed her fury on him.

They tracked down several of Judy's other Nashville clients, and though some gave glowing reviews, others spoke of computer-security issues and missing personal items. One woman claimed she often felt as if someone had been in her home repeatedly after Judy had long gone.

A search of Maura's/Judy's truck unearthed the grisly discovery of the harvested skin neatly pinned to velvet boards. In another black box was a collection of Polaroid pictures, featuring not only the known victims but other women. It was impossible to identify them, but the case had been detailed in a ViCAP report in case another jurisdiction discovered old cases similar to these.

"I hear Paul Thompson has shifted his focus to finding Judy's sister," he said.

"He's going to tie it into the Firefly murders," she said. "He's promised to keep all mention of Nate out of it."

"And how does Elijah feel about it?"

"He's adamant that Nate not be included in the story and said that he'll be paying close attention." She rubbed her hand over his arm, savoring the feel of muscled biceps under the flannel. "He's not going away, and I've decided not to fight him about Nate. My kid will put the pieces together if he hasn't done it already, and I'd rather he hears the news from the both of us."

"You know how Nate's going to take it?" Bryce asked.

"I have no idea, but Elijah said he's willing to put Nate's interests first. For now, Elijah is going to be his friend. He and Nate share a love of chess, books, and math. None of us need the weight of this secret anymore."

He kissed her. "I'm proud of you."

"This is me being mature and levelheaded," she said, nervous laughter bubbling. "But at two o'clock in the morning, I wake up and spend the next few hours second-guessing and wondering if I've lost my mind. Are you sure you want to sign up for this?"

"I'm sure." He ran his calloused finger along her cheek. "In the very near future, if you should wake up and worry, roll over and tell me."

"You make it sound easy."

"Nothing worth having is easy. But if you want it bad enough, you'll find a way." He kissed her. "And I've a few ideas on how to distract you when you're worried in the middle of the night."

She smiled. "That's very kind of you."

He grinned. "Ma'am, I'm here to serve."

ABOUT THE AUTHOR

Photo © 2015 StudioFBJ

Mary Burton is the *New York Times* and *USA Today* bestselling author of thirty-five romance and suspense novels, including *Never Look Back*, *I See You*, *Hide and Seek*, and *Cut and Run*, as well as five novellas. She currently lives in Virginia with her husband and three miniature dachshunds. Visit her at www.maryburton.com.